RINGWORLD

Larry Niven

A Del Rey Book

BALLANTINE BOOKS • NEW YORK

A Del Rey Book
Published by Ballantine Books

ISBN 0-345-31675-4

Manufactured in the United States of America

First Edition: October 1970
Twenty-first Printing: December 1983

Cover painting by Don Davis

"If the hallmark of good SF is the ability to make fantastic concepts seem real, then *Ringworld* is a great novel. The star is the Ringworld itself, a gigantic wheel circling its sun. . . . What sort of civilization could build it? This question draws the protagonists (two humans and two aliens) there. The story is their exploration of Ringworld, slowly adding such details as geography, vegetation, or sociology to enlarge its scope and believability, as well as telling how all this affects each of the explorers, who are individually fascinating in their own right. *Ringworld* combines the hard science of 'old wave' SF with the emphasis on sociology and characterization of 'new wave' SF to produce one of the most imaginative novels in the field."

—*Locus*

FOUR TRAVELERS
COME TO THE RINGWORLD...

Louis Wu—human and old, old; bored with having lived too fully for far too many years. Seeking a challenge, and all too capable of handling it.

Nessus—a trembling coward, a puppeteer with a built-in survival pattern of nonviolence. Except that this particular puppeteer is insane.

Teela Brown—human; a wide-eyed youngster with no allegiances, no experiences, no abilities. And all the luck in the world.

Speaker-To-Animals—kzin; large, orange-furred, and carnivorous. And one of the most savage lifeforms known in the galaxy.

Why did these disparate individuals come together? How could they possibly function together?

And where, in the name of anything sane, were they headed?

Also by Larry Niven
Published by Ballantine Books:

TABLE OF CONTENTS

RINGWORLD

CHAPTER 1

Louis Wu

In the nighttime heart of Beirut, in one of a row of general-address transfer booths, Louis Wu flicked into reality.

His foot-length queue was as white and shiny as artificial snow. His skin and depilated scalp were chrome yellow; the irises of his eyes were gold; his robe was royal blue with a golden steroptic dragon superimposed. In the instant he appeared, he was smiling widely, showing pearly, perfect, perfectly standard teeth. Smiling and waving. But the smile was already fading, and in a moment it was gone, and the sag of his face was like a rubber mask melting. Louis Wu showed his age.

For a few moments, he watched Beirut stream past him: the people flickering into the booths from unknown places; the crowds flowing past him on foot, now that the slidewalks had been turned off for the night. Then the clocks began to strike twenty-three. Louis Wu straightened his shoulders and stepped out to join the world.

In Resht, where his party was still going full blast, it was already the morning after his birthday. Here in Beirut it was an hour earlier. In a balmy outdoor restaurant Louis bought rounds of raki and encouraged the singing of songs in Arabic and Interworld. He left before midnight for Budapest.

Had they realized yet that he had walked out on his own party? They would assume that a woman had gone with him, that he would be back in a couple of hours. But Louis Wu had gone alone, jumping ahead of the

1

midnight line, hotly pursued by the new day. Twenty-four hours was not long enough for a man's two hundredth birthday.

They could get along without him. Louis's friends could take care of themselves. In this respect, Louis's standards were inflexible.

In Budapest were wine and athletic dances, natives who tolerated him as a tourist with money, tourists who thought he was a wealthy native. He danced the dances and he drank the wines, and he left before midnight.

In Munich he walked.

The air was warm and clean; it cleared some of the fumes from his head. He walked the brightly lighted slidewalks, adding his own pace to their ten-miles-per-hour speed. It occurred to him then that every city in the world had slidewalks, and that they all moved at ten miles per hour.

The thought was intolerable. Not new; just intolerable. Louis Wu saw how thoroughly Munich resembled Cairo and Resht . . . and San Francisco and Topeka and London and Amsterdam. The stores along the slidewalks sold the same products in all the cities of the world. These citizens who passed him tonight looked all alike, dressed all alike. Not Americans or Germans or Egyptians, but mere flatlanders.

In three-and-a-half centuries the transfer booths had done *this* to the infinite variety of Earth. They covered the world in a net of instantaneous travel. The difference between Moskva and Sidney was a moment of time and a tenth-star coin. Inevitably the cities had blended over the centuries, until placenames were only relics of the past.

San Francisco and San Diego were the northern and southern ends of one sprawling coastal city. But how many people knew which end was which? Tanj few, these days.

Pessimistic thinking, for a man's two hundredth birthday.

But the blending of the cities was real. Louis had watched it happen. All the irrationalities of place and time and custom, blending into one big rationality of City, worldwide, like a dull gray paste. Did anyone today speak Deutsche, English, Français, Espanol? Everyone spoke Interworld. Style in body paints changed all at once, all over the world, in one monstrous surge.

Time for another sabbatical? Into the unknown, alone in a singleship, with his skin and eyes and hair their own color, a beard growing randomly over his face . . .

"Nuts," said Louis to himself. "I just got back from a sabbatical." Twenty years ago.

But it was wearing on toward midnight. Louis Wu found a transfer booth, inserted his credit card in the slot and dialed for Sevilla.

He emerged in a sunlit room.

"What the tanj?" he wondered, blinking. The transfer booth must have blown its zap. In Sevilla there should have been no sunlight. Louis Wu turned to dial again, then turned back and stared.

He was in a thoroughly anonymous hotel room: a setting prosaic enough to make its occupant doubly shocking.

Facing him from the middle of the room was something neither human nor humanoid. It stood on three legs, and it regarded Louis Wu from two directions, from two flat heads mounted on flexible, slender necks. Over most of its startling frame, the skin was white and glove-soft; but a thick, coarse brown mane ran from between the beast's necks, back along its spine, to cover the complex-looking hip joint of the hind leg. The two fore-legs were set wide apart, so that the beast's small, clawed hooves formed almost an equilateral triangle.

Louis guessed that the thing was an alien animal. In those flat heads there would be no room for brains. But he noticed the hump that rose between the bases of the necks, where the mane became a thick protective mop . . . and a memory floated up from eighteen decades behind him.

This was a puppeteer, a Pierson's puppeteer. Its brain and skull were under the hump. It was not an animal; it was at least as intelligent as a man. And its eyes, one to a head in deep bone sockets, stared fixedly at Louis Wu from two directions.

Louis tried the door. Locked.

He was locked *out,* not *in.* He could dial and vanish. But it never occurred to him. One does not meet a Pierson's puppeteer every day. The species had been gone from known space for longer than Louis Wu had been alive.

Louis said, "Can I help you?"

"You can," said the alien . . .

. . . in a voice to spark adolescent dreams. Had Louis visualized a woman to go with that voice, she would have been Cleopatra, Helen of Troy, Marilyn Monroe, and Lorelei Huntz rolled into one.

"Tanj!" The curse seemed more than usually appropriate. *There Ain't No Justice!* That such a voice should belong to a two-headed alien of indeterminate sex!

"Be not frightened," said the alien. "Know that you can escape if need be."

"In college there were pictures of things like you. You've been gone a long time . . . or so we thought."

"When my species fled known space, I was not among them," the puppeteer replied. "I remained in known space, for my species had need of me here."

"Where have you been hiding? And where on Earth are we?"

"That need not concern you. Are you Louis Wu MMGREWPLH?"

"You knew that? You were after me, in particular?"

"Yes. We found it possible to manipulate this world's network of transfer booths."

It could be done, Louis realized. It would take a fortune in bribe money, but it could be done. But—"Why?"

"That will take some explanation—"

"Aren't you going to let me out of here?"

The puppeteer considered. "I suppose I must. First you should know that I have protection. My armament would stop you should you attack me."

Louis Wu made a sound of disgust. "Why would I do that?"

The puppeteer made no answer.

"Now I remember. You're cowards. Your whole ethical system is based on cowardice."

"Inaccurate as it is, that judgment will serve us."

"Well, it could be worse," Louis conceded. Every sentient species had its quirks. Surely the puppeteer would be easier to deal with than the racially paranoid Trinocs, or the kzinti with their hair-trigger killer instincts, or the sessile Grogs with their . . . disturbing substitute for hands.

The sight of the puppeteer had jarred loose a whole atticful of dusty memories. Mixed with data on the puppeteers and their commercial empire, their interactions with humanity, their sudden and shocking disappearance —mixed with these were the taste of Louis's first tobacco cigarette, the feel of typewriter keys under clumsy, untrained fingers, lists of Interworld vocabulary to be memorized, the sound and taste of English, the uncertainties and embarrassments of extreme youth. He'd studied the puppeteers during a college history course, then forgotten about them for one hundred and eighty years. Incredible, that a man's mind could retain so much!

"I'll stay in here," he told the puppeteer, "if it makes you more comfortable."

"No. We must meet."

Muscles bunched and twitched beneath its creamy skin as the puppeteer nerved itself. Then the door to the transfer booth clicked open. Louis Wu stepped into the room.

The puppeteer backed away a few paces.

Louis dropped into a chair, more for the puppeteer's comfort than for his own. He would look more harmless sitting down. The chair was of standard make, a self-adjusting masseur chair, strictly for humans. Louis noticed a faint scent now, reminiscent both of a spice shelf and of a chemistry set, more pleasant than otherwise.

The alien rested on its folded hind leg. "You wonder why I brought you here. This will take some explanation. What do you know of my species?"

"It's been a long time since college. You had a commercial empire once, didn't you? What we like to call 'known space' was just a part of it. We *know* the Trinocs bought from you, and we didn't meet the Trinocs until twenty years ago."

"Yes, we dealt with the Trinocs. Largely through robots, as I recall."

"You had a business empire thousands of years old, at least, and scores of light years across, at least. And then you left, all of you. You left it all behind. Why?"

"Can this have been forgotten? We fled the explosion of the galactic core!"

"I know about that." Dimly, Louis even remembered that the chain reaction of novae in the hub of the galaxy had actually been discovered by aliens. "But why run now? The Core suns went nova ten thousand years ago. The light won't reach here for another twenty thousand years."

"Humans," said the puppeteer, "should not be allowed to run loose. You will surely harm yourselves. Do you not see the danger? Radiation along the wave front will make this entire region of the galaxy uninhabitable!"

"Twenty thousand years is a long time."

"Extermination in twenty thousand years is extermination nonetheless. My species fled in the direction of the Clouds of Magellan. But some of us remained, in case the puppeteer migration should meet danger. Now it has."

"Oh? What kind of danger?"

"I am not yet free to answer that question. But you may look at this." The puppeteer reached for something on a table.

And Louis, who had been wondering where the puppeteer kept its hands, saw that the puppeteer's mouths were its hands.

Good hands, too, he realized, as the puppeteer reached gingerly across to hand Louis a holo print. The puppeteer's loose, rubbery lips extended inches beyond its teeth. They were as dry as human fingers, and they were rimmed with little fingerlike knobs. Behind the square vegetarian teeth, Louis caught a glimpse of a flickering, forking tongue.

He took the holo print and looked into it.

At first it made no sense at all, but he kept looking, waiting for it to resolve. There was a small, intensely white disc that might have been a sun, G0 or K9 or K8, with a shallow chord sliced off along a straight black edge. But the blazing object could not have been a sun. Partially behind it, against a space-black background, was a strip of sky blue. The blue strip was perfectly straight, sharp-edged, solid, and artificial, and wider than the lighted disc.

"Looks like a star with a hoop around it," said Louis. "What is it?"

"You may keep it to study, if you wish. I can now tell you the reason I brought you here. I propose to form an exploration team of four members, including myself, and including you."

"To explore what?"

"I am not yet at liberty to tell you that."

"Oh, come now. I'd have to be off my head to jump as blind as that."

"Happy two hundredth birthday," said the puppeteer.

"Thanks," Louis said, bewildered.

"Why did you leave your own birthday party?"

"That's not your concern."

"But it is. Indulge me, Louis Wu. Why did you leave your own birthday party?"

"I just decided that twenty-four hours weren't enough for a two hundredth birthday. So I went ahead and lengthened it by moving ahead of the midnight line. As an alien you wouldn't understand—"

"You were elated, then, at how well things were going?"

"No, not exactly. No . . ."

Not elated, Louis remembered. Quite the contrary. Though the party had gone well enough.

He'd started it at one minute past midnight that morning. Why not. His friends were in every time band. There was no reason to waste a single minute of this day. There were sleep sets all over the house, for fast, deep cat naps. For those who hated to miss anything there were wake-up drugs, some with interesting side effects, others with none.

There were guests Louis hadn't seen in a hundred years, and others he met daily. Some had been Louis Wu's deadly enemies, long ago. There were women he had forgotten entirely, so that he was repeatedly amazed at how his taste had changed.

Predictably, too many hours of his birthday were spent performing introductions. The lists of names to be memorized beforehand! Too many friends had become strangers.

And a few minutes before midnight, Louis Wu had walked into a transfer booth, dialed, and disappeared.

"I was bored stiff," said Louis Wu. " 'Tell us about your last sabbatical, Louis.' 'But how can you stand to be that much alone, Louis? How clever of you to invite the Trinoc ambassador, Louis! Long time no see, Louis.' 'Hey, Louis, why does it take three Jinxians to paint a skyscraper?' "

"Why does it?"

"Why does what?"

"The Jinxians."

"Oh. It takes one to hold the paint sprayer, and two to shake the skyscraper up and down. I heard that one in kindergarten. All the dead wood of my life, all the old jokes, all in one huge house. I couldn't take it."

"You are a restless man, Louis Wu. Your sabbaticals —it was you who originated the custom, was it not?"

"I don't remember where it started. It caught on pretty well. Most of my friends do it now."

"But not as often as you. Every forty years or thereabouts, you tire of human companionship. Then you leave the worlds of men and strike for the edge of known space. You remain outside known space, all alone in a singleship, until your need for company reasserts itself. You returned from your last sabbatical, your fourth, twenty years ago.

"You are restless, Louis Wu. On each of the worlds of human space, you have lived enough years to be known as a native. Tonight you left your own birthday party. Are you becoming restless again?"

"That would be my problem, wouldn't it?"

"Yes. My problem is one of recruiting only. You would be a good choice as a member of my exploration team. You take risks, but you calculate them first. You are not afraid to be alone with yourself. You are cautious enough and clever enough to be still alive after two hundred years. Because you have not neglected your medical needs, your physique is that of a man of twenty. Lastly, and most important, you seem actually to enjoy the company of aliens."

"Sure." Louis knew a few xenophobes, and regarded them as dolts. Life got awfully boring with only humans to talk to.

"But you would not wish to jump blind. Louis Wu, is it not enough that I, a puppeteer, will be with you? What could you possibly fear that I would not fear first? The intelligent caution of my race is proverbial."

"So it is," said Louis. In point of fact, he was hooked. Xenophilia and restlessness and curiosity combined: wherever the puppeteer was going, Louis Wu was going too. But he wanted to hear more.

And his bargaining position was excellent. An alien would not live in such a room by choice. This ordinary-looking hotel room, this reassuringly normal room from the viewpoint of a man of Earth, must have been furnished especially for recruiting.

"You won't tell me what it is you intend to explore," said Louis. "Will you tell me where it is?"

"It is two hundred light years from here in the direction of the Lesser Cloud."

"But it would take us nearly two years to get there at hyperdrive speeds."

"No. We have a ship which will travel considerably faster than a conventional hyperdrive craft. It will cover a light year in five-fourths of a minute."

Louis opened his mouth, but nothing came out. One and a quarter minutes?

"This should not surprise you, Louis Wu. How else could we have sent an agent to the galactic core, to learn of the chain reaction of novae? You should have deduced the existence of such a ship. If my mission is successful, I plan to turn the ship over to my crew, with blueprints with which to build more.

"This ship, then, is your . . . fee, salary, what have you. You may observe its flight characteristics when we join the puppeteer migration. There you will learn what it is that we propose to explore."

Join the puppeteer migration . . . "Count me in," said Louis Wu. The chance to see an entire sentient species on the move! Huge ships carrying thousands or millions of puppeteers each, whole working ecologies . . .

"Good." The puppeteer stood up. "Our crew will number four. We go to choose our third member now." And he trotted into the transfer booth.

Louis slipped the cryptic holo into his pocket, and followed. In the booth he tried to read the number on the dial; for it would have told him where in the world he was. But the puppeteer dialed too fast, and they were gone.

Louis Wu followed the puppeteer out of the booth and into the dim, luxurious interior of a restaurant. He recognized the place by the black-and-gold decor and the space-wasteful configuration of horseshoe booths. Krushenko's, in New York.

Incredulous whispers followed in the path of the puppeteer. A human headwaiter, imperturbable as a robot, led them to a table. One of the chairs had been removed at that table and replaced by a big square pillow, which the alien placed between hip and hind hoof as it sat down.

"You were expected," Louis deduced.

"Yes. I called ahead. Krushenko's is accustomed to serving alien guests."

Now Louis noticed other alien diners: four kzinti at

the next table, and a kdatlyno halfway across the room. It figured, with the United Nations Building so close. Louis dialed for a tequila sour and took it as it arrived. "This was a good thought," he said. "I'm half starved."

"We did not come to eat. We came to recruit our third member."

"Oh? In a restaurant?"

The puppeteer raised its voice to answer, but what it said was not an answer. "You never met my kzin, Kchula-Rrit? I keep it as a pet."

Louis's tequila tried to go down the wrong way. At the table behind the puppeteer, four walls of orange fur were each and every one a kzin; and as the puppeteer spoke, they all turned with their needle teeth bared. It looked like a smile, but on a kzin that rictus is not a smile.

The-Rrit name belongs to the family of the Patriarch of Kzin. Louis, downing the rest of his drink, decided that it didn't matter. The insult would have been mortal regardless, and you could only be eaten once.

The nearest kzin stood up.

Rich orange fur, with black markings over the eyes, covered what might have been a very fat tabby cat eight feet tall. The fat was muscle, smooth and powerful and oddly arranged over an equally odd skeleton. On hands like black leather gloves, sharpened and polished claws slid out of their sheaths.

A quarter of a ton of sentient carnivore stooped over the puppeteer and said, "Tell me now, why do you think that you can insult the Patriarch of Kzin and live?"

The puppeteer answered immediately, and without a tremor in its voice. "It was I who, on a world which circles Beta Lyrae, kicked a kzin called Chuft-Captain in the belly with my hind hoof, breaking three struts of his endoskeletal structure. I have need of a kzin of courage."

"Continue," said the kzin of the black eyes. Despite limitations imposed by the structure of his mouth, the kzin's Interworld was excellent. But his voice showed no sign of the rage he must have felt. For all the emotion

shown by kzinti or puppeteer, Louis might have been
watching some time-dulled ritual.

But the meat set before the kzinti was blood-raw and
steaming; it had been flash-heated to body temperature
just before serving. And all of the kzinti were smiling.

"This human and I," said the puppeteer, "will explore
a place such as no kzin has ever dreamed. We will need a
kzin in our crew. Dare a kzin follow where a puppeteer
leads?"

"It has been said that puppeteers were plant-eaters,
that they would lead away from battle and not toward
it."

"You shall judge. Your fee, if you survive, will be the
plans for a new and valuable type of spacecraft, plus a
model of the ship itself. You may consider this fee to be
extreme hazard pay."

The puppeteer, Louis thought, was sparing no pains to
insult the kzinti. One *never* offers a kzin hazard pay. The
kzin is not supposed to have noticed the danger!

But the kzin's only remark was, "I accept."

The other three kzinti snarled at him.

The first kzin snarled back.

One kzin alone sounded like a catfight. Four kzinti in
heated argument sounded like a major feline war, with
atonics. Sonic deadeners went on automatically in the
restaurant, and the snarls became remote, but they went
on.

Louis ordered another drink. Considering what he
knew of kzinti history, these four must have remarkable
restraint. The puppeteer still lived.

The argument died away, and the four kzinti turned
back. He of the black eye-markings said, "What is your
name?"

"I take the human name of Nessus," said the puppeteer. "My true name is—" Orchestral music flowed for an
instant from the puppeteer's remarkable throats.

"Well and good, Nessus. You must understand that we
four constitute a kzinti embassy to Earth. This is Harch,
that is Ftanss, he with the yellow striping is Hroth. I,

being only an apprentice and a kzin of low family, bear no name. I am styled by my profession: Speaker-To-Animals."

Louis bridled.

"Our problem is that we are needed here. Delicate negotiations . . . but these are not your concern. It has been decided that I alone can be replaced. If your new kind of ship proves worth having, I will join you. Otherwise I must prove my courage another way."

"Satisfactory," said the puppeteer, and rose.

Louis remained seated. He asked, "What is the kzinti form of your title?"

"In the Hero's Tongue—" The kzin snarled on a rising note.

"Then why didn't you give that as your title? Was it a deliberate insult?"

"Yes," said Speaker-To-Animals. "I was angered."

Accustomed to his own standards of tact, Louis had expected the kzin to lie. Then Louis would have pretended to believe him, and the kzin would have been more polite in future . . . too late to back out now. Louis hesitated a fraction of a second before he said, "And what is the custom?"

"We must fight barehanded—as soon as you deliver the challenge. Or one of us must apologize."

Louis stood up. He was committing suicide; but he'd known tanj well what the custom was. "I challenge you," he said. "Tooth against tooth, claw against fingernail, since we cannot share a universe in peace."

Without lifting his head, the kzin who had been called Hroth spoke up. "I must apologize for my comrade, Speaker-To-Animals."

Louis said, "Huh?"

"This is my function," said the kzin with the yellow striping. "To be found in situations where one must apologize or fight is kzinti nature. We know what happens when we fight. Today our numbers are less than an eighth of what they were when kzin first met man. Our colony worlds are your colony worlds, our slave species are freed and taught human technology and human ethics. When we must apologize or fight, it is my function to apologize."

Louis sat down. It seemed that he would live. He said, "I wouldn't have your job for anything."

"Obviously not, if you would fight a kzin barehanded. But the Patriarch judges me useless for any other purpose. My intelligence is low, my health is bad, my coordination terrible. How else can I keep my name?"

Louis sipped at his drink and wished for someone to change the subject. He found the humble kzin embarrassing.

"Let us eat," said the one called Speaker-To-Animals. "Unless our mission is urgent, Nessus."

"Not at all. Our crew is not yet complete. My colleagues will call me when they have located a qualified fourth crewman. By all means let us eat."

Speaker-To-Animals said one thing more before he turned back to his table. "Louis Wu, I found your challenge verbose. In challenging a kzin, a simple scream of rage is sufficient. You scream and you leap."

"You scream and you leap," said Louis. "Great."

CHAPTER 2

And His Motley Crew

Louis Wu knew people who closed their eyes when they used a transfer booth. The jump in scenery gave them vertigo. To Louis this was nonsense; but then, some of his friends were *much* odder than that.

He kept his eyes open as he dialed. The watching aliens vanished. Someone called, "Hi! He's back!"

A mob formed around the door. Louis forced it open against them. "Finagle fool you all! Didn't *any* of you go home?" He spread his arms to engulf them, then pushed forward like a snowplow, forcing them back. "Clear the door, you boors! I've more guests coming."

"Great!" a voice shouted in his ear. Anonymous hands took his hand and forced the fingers around a drinking bulb. Louis hugged the seven or eight of his invited guests within the circle of his arms and smiled at his welcome.

Louis Wu. From a distance he was an oriental, with pale yellow skin and flowing white hair. His rich blue robe was carelessly draped, so that it should have hampered his movements; but it didn't.

Close up, it was all a fraud. His skin was not pale yellow-brown, but a smooth chrome yellow, the color of a comic-book Fu Manchu. His queue was too thick; it was not the white of age, but sheer clean white with a subliminal touch of blue, the color of dwarf star sunlight. As with all flatlanders, cosmetic dyes were the colors of Louis Wu.

A flatlander. You could tell at a glance. His features

15

were neither Caucasian nor Mongoloid nor Negroid, though there were traces of all three: a uniform blend which must have required centuries. In a gravitational pull of 9.98 meters/second, his stance was unconsciously natural. He gripped a drinking bulb and smiled around at his guests.

As it happened, he was smiling into a pair of reflective silver eyes an inch from his own.

One Teela Brown had somehow ended up nose to nose and breast to breast with him. Her skin was blue with a netting of silver threads; her coiffure was streaming bonfire flames; her eyes were convex mirrors. She was twenty years old. Louis had talked to her earlier. Her conversation was shallow, full of clichés and easy enthusiasms; but she was very pretty.

"I had to ask you," she said breathlessly. "How did you get a *Trinoc* to come?"

"Don't tell me *he's* still here."

"Oh, no. His air was running out and he had to go home."

"A little white lie," Louis informed her. "A Trinoc airmaker lasts for weeks. Well, if you really want to know, that particular Trinoc was once my guest and prisoner for a couple of weeks. His ship and crew got themselves killed at the edge of known space, and I had to ferry him to Margrave so they could set up an environment box for him."

The girl's eyes registered delighted wonder. Louis found it pleasantly strange that they were on a level with his own eyes; for Teela Brown's fragile beauty made her look smaller than she really was. Her eyes shifted over Louis's shoulder and widened even further. Louis grinned as he turned.

Nessus the puppeteer trotted out of the transfer booth.

Louis had thought of this as they were leaving Krushenko's. He had been trying to persuade Nessus to tell them something of their proposed destination. But the puppeteer was afraid of spy beams.

"Then come to my place," Louis had suggested.

"But your guests!"

"Not in my office. And my office is absolutely bug-proof. Besides, think of the hit you'll make at the party! Assuming everyone hasn't gone home by now."

The impact was all Louis could have desired. The tap-tap-tap of the puppeteer's hooves was suddenly the only sound in the room. Behind him, Speaker-To-Animals flickered into existence. The kzin considered the sea of human faces surrounding the booth. Then, slowly, he bared his teeth.

Someone poured half his drink into a potted palm. The grand gesture. From one of the branches a Gummidgy orchid-thing chattered angrily. People edged away from the transfer booth. There were comments: "You're okay. I see them too." "Sober pills? Let me look in my sporan." "Throws a hell of a party, doesn't he?" "Good old Louis." *"What* did you call that thing?"

They didn't know what to make of Nessus. Mostly they ignored the puppeteer; they were afraid to comment on him, afraid of sounding like fools. They reacted even more curiously to Speaker-To-Animals. Once mankind's most dangerous enemy, the kzin was being treated with awed deference, like some kind of hero.

"Follow me," Louis told the puppeteer. With luck the kzin would follow them both. "Excuse us," he bellowed, and pushed his way into the throng. In response to various excited and/or puzzled questions he merely grinned secretively.

Safely in his office, Louis barred the door and turned on the bugproofing set. "Okay. Who needs refreshment?"

"If you can heat some bourbon, I can drink it," said the kzin. "If you cannot heat it, I can still drink it."

"Nessus?"

"Any kind of vegetable juice will serve. Have you warm carrot juice?"

"Gah," said Louis; but he instructed the bar, which produced bulbs of warm carrot juice.

While Nessus rested on its folded hind leg, the kzin dropped heavily onto an inflated hassock. Under his weight it should have exploded like any lesser balloon. Man's second oldest enemy looked curious and ridiculous balanced on a hassock too small for him.

The Man–Kzin wars had been numerous and terrible. Had the kzinti won the first of these, mankind would have been a slave and a meat animal for the rest of eternity. But the kzinti had suffered in the wars which followed. They tended to attack before they were ready. They had little concept of patience, and no concept of mercy or of limited war. Each war had cost them a respectable chunk of population and the punitive confiscation of a couple of kzinti worlds.

For two hundred and fifty years the kzinti had not attacked human space. They had nothing to attack with. For two hundred and fifty years men had not attacked the kzinti worlds; and no kzin could understand it. Men confused them terribly.

They were rough and they were tough, and Nessus, an avowed coward, had insulted four fully-grown kzinti in a public restaurant.

"Tell me again," said Louis, "about a puppeteer's proverbial caution. I forget."

"Perhaps I was not strictly fair with you, Louis. My species judges me mad."

"Oh, *fine*." Louis sucked at the bulb an anonymous donor had handed him. It held vodka and droobleberry juice and shaved ice.

The kzin's tail lashed restlessly. "Why should we ride with an avowed maniac? You must be madder than most, to wish to ride with a kzin."

"You alarm yourselves too easily," said Nessus, in its soft, persuasive, unbearably sensual voice. "Men have never met a puppeteer who was not mad in the judgment of his own species. No alien has ever seen the puppeteer world, and no sane puppeteer would trust his very life to the fallible life-support system of a spacecraft, or the unknown and possibly deadly dangers of an alien world."

"A mad puppeteer, a full grown kzin, and me. Our fourth crew member had better be a psychiatrist."

"No, Louis, none of our candidates are psychiatrists."

"Well, *why not?*"

"I did not select at random." The puppeteer sucked at its bulb with one mouth and talked with the other. "First, there was myself. Our proposed voyage is intended to benefit my species; hence we must include a representative. Such a one should be mad enough to face an unknown world, yet sane enough to use his intellect to survive. I, as it happens, am just on the borderline.

"We had reason to include a kzin. Speaker-To-Animals, what I tell you now is secret. We have been observing your species for some considerable time. We knew of you even before you attacked humanity."

"Well that you did not show yourselves," rumbled the kzin.

"Doubtless. At first we deduced that the kzinti species was both useless and dangerous. Lines of research were initiated to determine whether your species could be exterminated in safety."

"I will tie your necks in a bow knot."

"You will commit no violence."

The kzin stood up.

"He's right," said Louis. "Sit down, Speaker. You don't stand to profit by murdering a puppeteer."

The kzin sat down. Again his hassock did not collapse.

"The project was cancelled," said Nessus. "We found that the Man–Kzin wars put sufficient restriction on kzinti expansion, made you less dangerous. We continued to watch.

"Six times over several centuries, you attacked the worlds of men. Six times you were defeated, having lost approximately two-thirds of your male population in each war. Need I comment on the level of intelligence displayed? No? In any case, you were never in real danger of extermination. Your nonsentient females were largely untouched by war, so that the next generation helped to replace the numbers lost. Still, you steadily lost an empire you had built up over thousands of years.

"It became apparent to us that the kzinti were evolving at a furious rate."

"Evolving?"

Nessus snarled a word in the Hero's Tongue. Louis jumped. He had not suspected that the puppeteer's throats could do *that*.

"Yes," said Speaker-To-Animals, "I thought that was what you said. But I do not understand the application."

"Evolution depends on the survival of the fittest. For several hundred kzin years, the fittest of your species were those members with the wit or the forebearance to avoid fighting human beings. The results are apparent. For nearly two hundred kzin years there has been peace between man and kzin."

"But there would be no point! We could not win a war!"

"That did not stop your ancestors."

Speaker-To-Animals gulped at his hot bourbon. His tail, naked and pink and ratlike, lashed in turmoil.

"Your species has been decimated," said the puppeteer. "All kzinti alive today are descended from those who avoided death in the Man–Kzin wars. Some among us speculate that the kzinti now have the intelligence or the empathy or the self-restraint necessary to deal with races alien to them."

"And so you risk your life to travel with a kzin."

"Yes," said Nessus, and shivered all over. "My motivation is strong. It has been implied that if I can demonstrate the worth of my courage, by using it to perform a valuable ·service for my species, I will be allowed to breed."

"Hardly a firm commitment," said Louis.

"Then there is other reason to take a kzin. We will face strange environments hiding unknown dangers. Who will protect me? Who would be better equipped than a kzin?"

"To protect a puppeteer?"

"Does that sound insane?"

"It does," said Speaker-To-Animals. "It also appeals to my sense of humor. What of this one, this Louis Wu?"

"For us there has been much profitable cooperation with men. Naturally we choose at least one human. Louis Gridley Wu is a proven survival type, in his casual, reckless way."

"Casual he is, and reckless. He challenged me to single combat."

"Would you have accepted, had not Hroth been present? Would you have harmed him?"

"To be sent home in disgrace, having caused a major interspecies incident? But that is not the point," the kzin insisted. "Is it?"

"Perhaps it is. Louis is alive. You are now aware that you cannot dominate him through fear. Do you believe in results?"

Louis maintained a discreet silence. If the puppeteer wanted to give him credit for cool intellection, that was fine with Louis Wu.

"You have spoken of your own motives," said Speaker. "Speak now of mine. What can it profit me to join your voyage?"

And they got down to business.

To the puppeteers, the quantum II hyperdrive shunt was a white elephant. It would move a ship a light year in one-and-a-quarter minutes, where conventional craft would cross that distance in three days. But conventional craft had room for cargo.

"We built the motor into a General Products Number Four hull, the biggest made by our company. When our scientists and engineers had finished their work, most of the interior was filled with the machinery of the hyperdrive shunt. Our trip outward will be cramped."

"An experimental vehicle," said the kzin. "How thoroughly has it been tested?"

"The vehicle has made one trip to the galactic core and back."

But that had been its only flight! The puppeteers could not test it themselves, nor could they find other races to do the work; for they were in the middle of a migration. The ship would carry practically no cargo, though it was over a mile in diameter. Furthermore, it could not slow down without dropping back into normal space.

"We do not need it," said Nessus. "But you do. We plan to turn the ship over to our crew, together with copies of the plans for making more. Doubtless you can improve the design yourselves."

"That will buy me a name," said the kzin. "A name. I must see your ship in action."

"During our trip outward."

"The Patriarch would give me a name for such a ship. I am sure he would. What name should I choose? Perhaps—" The kzin snarled on a rising note.

The puppeteer replied in the same language.

Louis shifted in irritation. He couldn't follow the Hero's Tongue. He considered leaving them to it, then had a better idea. He pulled the puppeteer's holo from his pocket, scaled it across the room into the kzin's furry lap.

The kzin held it delicately in his padded black fingers. "It appears to be a ringed star," he observed. "What is it?"

"It relates to our destination," said the puppeteer. "I cannot tell you more, not now."

"How cryptic. Well, when may we depart?"

"I estimate a matter of days. My agents are even now searching for a qualified fourth member for our exploration team."

"And so we wait upon their pleasure. Louis, shall we join your guests?"

Louis stood up, stretching. "Sure, let's give 'em a thrill. Speaker, before we go out there, I have a suggestion. Now, don't take this as an assault on your dignity. It's just an idea . . ."

The party had split into sections: tridee-watchers, bridge and poker tables, lovers in pairs and larger groups, tellers of tales, victims of ennui. Out on the lawn, under a hazy early-morning sun, was a mixed group of ennui victims and xenophiles; for the outdoor group included Nessus and Speaker-To-Animals. It also included Louis Wu, Teela Brown, and an overworked bartender.

The lawn was one of those tended according to the ancient British formula: seed and roll for five hundred years. Five hundred years had ended in a stock market crash, after which Louis Wu had had money and a certain venerable baronial family had not. The grass was green and glossy, obviously the real thing; nobody had ever tampered with its genes in search of dubious improvements. At the bottom of the rolling green slope was a tennis court where diminutive figures ran and jumped and swung their oversized fly swatters with great energy.

"Exercise is wonderful," said Louis. "I could sit and watch it all day."

Teela's laugh surprised him. He thought idly of the millions of jokes she had never heard, the old, old ones nobody ever told any more. Of the millions of jokes Louis knew by heart, 99 percent must be obsolete. Past and present mix badly.

The bartender floated next to Louis in tilted position. Louis's head was in Teela's lap, and his need to reach the keyboard without sitting up was responsible for the bartender's tilt. He tapped an order for two mochas, caught the bulbs as they dropped from the slot, and handed one to Teela.

"You look like a girl I knew once," he said. "Ever hear of a Paula Cherenkov?"

"The cartoonist? Boston-born?"

"Yah. Lives on We Made It, nowadays."

"My great-great grandmother. We visited her once."

"She gave me a severe case of whiplash of the heart, long ago. You could be her twin."

Teela's chuckle sent vibrations bouncing pleasantly along Louis's vertebrae. "I promise not to give you a case of whiplash of the heart if you'll tell me what it is."

Louis thought about that. The phrase was his own, created to describe to himself what had happened to him at that time. He hadn't used it often, but he'd never had to explain it. They always knew what he meant.

A calm, peaceful morning. If he went to sleep now he'd sleep for twelve hours. Fatigue poisons were giving him an exhaustion high. Teela's lap was a comfortable resting place for his head. Half of Louis's guests were women, and many of them had been his wives or lovers in other years. During the first phase of the party, he'd celebrated his birthday privately with three women, three who had been very important to him once, and vice versa.

Three? Four? No, three. And now it seemed that he was immune to whiplash of the heart. Two hundred years had left too much scar tissue on his personality. And now he rested his head idly and comfortably in the lap of a stranger who looked exactly like Paula Cherenkov.

"I fell in love with her," he said. "We'd known each other for years. We'd even dated. Then one night we got to talking, and wham. I was in love. I thought she loved me too.

"We didn't go to bed that night—together, I mean. I asked her to marry me. She turned me down. She was working on a career. She didn't have time to get married, she said. But we planned a trip to Amazon National Park, a sort of one week ersatz honeymoon.

"The next week was all highs and lows. First, the high. I had the tickets and the hotel reservations. Did you ever fall so hard for someone that you decided you weren't worthy of him?"

"No."

"I was young. I spent two days convincing myself I was worthy of Paula Cherenkov. I did it, too. Then she called and cancelled the trip. I don't even remember why. She had some good reason.

"I took her out to dinner a couple of times that week. Nothing happened. I tried to keep from pressuring her. Chances are she never guessed the pressure I was under. I was going up and down like a yo-yo. Then she lowered the boom. She liked me. We had fun together. We should be good friends.

"I wasn't her type," said Louis. "I thought we were in love. Maybe she thought so too, for about a week. She wasn't cruel. She just didn't know what was going on."

"But what was the whiplash?"

Louis looked up at Teela Brown. Silver eyes looked

blankly back, and Louis realized that she hadn't understood a word.

Louis had dealt with aliens. By instinct or by training, he had learned to sense when some concept was too foreign to be absorbed or communicated. Here was a similar, fundamental gap in translation.

What a monstrous gulf to separate Louis Wu and a twenty-year-old girl! Could he really have aged that drastically? And if so, was Louis Wu still human?

Teela, blank-eyed, waited for enlightenment.

"Tanj!" Louis cursed, and he rolled to his feet. Mud spots slid slowly down his robe and dripped off the hem.

Nessus the puppeteer was holding forth on the subject of ethics. He interrupted himself (quite literally, speaking with both mouths, to the delight of his admirers) to answer Louis's query. No, there had been no word from his agents.

Speaker-To-Animals, similarly surrounded, sprawled like a great orange hill across the grass. Two women were scratching at the fur behind his ears. The odd kzinti ears, that could expand like pink chinese parasols or fold flat against the head, were spread wide; and Louis could see the design tattooed on each surface.

"So," Louis called to him. "Was I not brilliant?"

"You were," the kzin rumbled without stirring.

Louis laughed inside himself. A kzin is a fearsome beast, yes? But who can fear a kzin who is having his ears scratched? It put Louis's guests at their ease, and it put the kzin at ease too. Anything above the level of a field mouse likes having its ears scratched.

"They have been taking turnabout," the kzin rumbled sleepily. "A male approaches the female scratching me and observes that he would enjoy the same attention. The two go off together. Another female moves in as a replacement. How interesting it must be, to belong to a race of two sentient sexes."

"Sometimes it makes things awfully complicated."

"Indeed?"

The girl at the kzin's left shoulder—space-black her skin was, embroidered with stars and galaxies, and her hair was the cold white stream of a comet's tail—looked up from her work. "Teela, take over," she said gaily. "I'm hungry."

Teela knelt obligingly beside the great orange head. Louis said, "Teela Brown, meet Speaker-To-Animals. May you both be—"

From nearby came a discordant blast of music.

"—very happy together. What was that? Oh, Nessus. What—?"

The music had come from the puppeteer's remarkable throats. Now Nessus nudged rudely between Louis and the girl. "You are Teela Jandrova Brown, ident number IKLUGGTYN?"

The girl was startled, but not frightened. "That's my name. I don't remember my ident number. What's the problem?"

"We have been combing Earth for you for nearly a week. Now I find you at a gathering I reached only by chance! I will have harsh words for my agents."

"Oh no," Louis said softly.

Teela stood up somewhat awkwardly. "I haven't been hiding, not from you and not from any other—extraterrestrial. Now, what's the problem?"

"Hold it!" Louis stepped between Nessus and the girl. "Nessus, Teela Brown obviously isn't an explorer. Pick someone else."

"But, Louis—"

"Just a moment." The kzin was sitting up. "Louis, let the herbivore choose his own team members."

"But look at her!"

"Look at yourself, Louis. Barely two meters long, slender even for a human. Are you an explorer? Is Nessus?"

"Just what the tanj is going *on?*" Teela demanded.

Urgently, Nessus said, "Louis, let us retire to your office. Teela Brown, we must make a proposal to you. You are under no obligation to accept, nor even to listen, but you may find our proposal interesting."

The argument continued in Louis's office. "She fits my qualifications," Nessus insisted. "We must consider her."

"She can't be the only one on Earth!"

"No, Louis. Not at all. But we have been unable to contact any of the others."

"Just what am I being considered for?"

The puppeteer started to tell her. It developed that Teela Brown had no interest in space, had never even been as far as the Moon, and had no intention of going beyond the borders of known space. The second quantum hyperdrive did not arouse her cupidity. When she started to look harassed and confused, Louis broke in again.

"Nessus, just what are the qualifications Teela fits so well?"

"My agents have been seeking the descendants of winners of the Birthright Lotteries."

"I quit. You're genuinely insane."

"No, Louis. My orders come from the Hindmost himself, from the one who leads us all. His sanity is not in question. May I explain?"

For human beings, birth control had long been an easy matter. Nowadays a tiny crystal was inserted under the skin of the patient's forearm. The crystal took a year to dissolve. During that year the patient would be unable to conceive a child. In earlier centuries clumsier methods had been used.

Earth's population had been stabilized, about the middle of the twenty-first century, at eighteen billion. The Fertility Board, a subsection of the United Nations, made and enforced the birth control laws. For more than half a thousand years those laws had remained the same: two children to a couple, subject to the judgment of the Fertility Board. The Board decided who might be a parent how many times. The Board might award extra children to one couple, deny any children at all to another, all on the basis of desirable or undesirable genes.

"Incredible," said the kzin.

"Why? Things were getting pretty tanj crowded, with eighteen billion people trapped in a primitive technology."

"If the Patriarchy tried to force such a law on kzinti, we would exterminate the Patriarchy for its insolence."

But men were not kzinti. For half a thousand years the laws had held good. Then, two hundred years ago, had come rumors of chicanery in the Fertility Board. The scandal had ultimately resulted in drastic changes in the birth control laws:

Every human being now had the right to be a parent once, regardless of the state of his genes. In addition, the Birthrights Second and Third could come automatically: for a high tested IQ, or for proven, useful psychic powers, such as Plateau eyes or absolute direction, or for survival genes, like telepathy or natural longevity or perfect teeth.

One could buy the birthrights at a million stars a shot. Why not? The knack for making money was a tested, proven survival factor. Besides, it cut down on bribery attempts.

One could fight for the Birthrights in the arena, if one had not yet used up his Birthright First. Winner to earn his Birthrights Second and Third; loser to lose his Birthright First and his life. It evened out.

"I have seen such battles on your entertainment shows," said Speaker. "I thought they were fighting for fun."

"Nope, they're serious," said Louis. Teela giggled.

"And the lotteries?"

"It comes out short," said Nessus. "Even with boosterspice to prevent aging in humans, more die on Earth than are born in any given year . . ."

And so each year the Fertility Board totaled up the year's deaths and emigrations, subtracted the year's births and immigrations, and put the resulting number of Birthrights into the New Year's Day lottery.

Anyone could enter. With luck you could have ten or twenty children—if that was luck. Even convicted criminals could not be excluded from the Birthright Lotteries.

"I've had four children myself," said Louis Wu. "One by lottery. You'd have met three of them if you'd come twelve hours earlier."

"It sounds very strange and complex. When the population of Kzin grows too great, we—"

"Attack the nearest human world."

"Not at all, Louis. We fight each other. The more crowded we grow, the more opportunity exists for one kzin to take offense at another. Our population problem adjusts itself. We have never been within an order of magnitude of your two times eight to the tenth humans on a single planet!"

"I think I begin to get it," said Teela Brown. "My parents were both lottery winners." She laughed somewhat nervously. "Otherwise I wouldn't even have been born. Come to think of it, my grandfather—"

"All of your ancestors for five generations were born by reason of winning lottery tickets."

"Really! I never knew that!"

"The records are quite clear," Nessus assured her.

"The question remains," said Louis Wu. "So what?"

"Those-who-rule in the puppeteer fleet have speculated that the people of Earth are breeding for luck."

"Huh!"

Teela Brown leaned forward in her chair, intensely curious. Doubtless she had never before seen a mad puppeteer.

"Think of the lotteries, Louis. Think of evolution. For seven hundred years your people bred by the numbers: two birthrights per person, two children per couple. Here and there one might win a third birthright, or be refused his first on adequate grounds: diabetic genes or the like. But most of humanity had two children.

"Then the law was changed. For the past two centuries, between ten and thirteen percent of each human generation has been born by right of a winning lottery ticket. What determines who will survive and breed? On Earth, luck.

"And Teela Brown is the daughter of six generations of winning gamblers . . ."

CHAPTER 3

Teela Brown

Teela was giggling helplessly.

"Come off it," said Louis Wu. "You can't breed for luck the way you breed for shaggy eyebrows!"

"Yet you breed for telepathy."

"That's not the same. Telepathy isn't a psychic power. The mechanisms in the right parietal lobe are well mapped. They just don't *work* for most people."

"Telepathy was once thought to be a form of psi. Now you claim that luck is not."

"Luck is luck." The situation would have been funny, as funny as Teela thought it was; but Louis realized what she did not. The puppeteer was serious. "The law of averages swings back and forth. The odds shift wrong and you're out of the game, like the dinosaurs. The dice fall your way and—"

"It is thought that some humans can direct the fall of a die."

"So I picked a bad metaphor. The point is—"

"Yes," the kzin rumbled. He had a voice to shake walls when he chose to use it. "The point is that we will accept whom Nessus chooses. You own the ship, Nessus. Where, then, is our fourth crewman?"

"Here in this room!"

"Now *just* a tanj *minute!*" Teela stood up. The silver netting flashed like real metal across her blue skin; her hair floated flaming in the draft from the air conditioner. "This whole thing is ridiculous. I'm not going anywhere. Why should I?"

"Pick someone else, Nessus. There must be millions of qualified candidates. Where's the hang-up?"

"Not millions, Louis. We have a few thousand names, and phone numbers or private transfer booth numbers for most of them. Each can claim five generations of ancestors born by virtue of winning lottery tickets."

"Well?"

Nessus began to pace the floor. "Many disqualify themselves by obvious bad luck. Of the rest, none seem to be available. When we call, they are out. When we call back, the phone computer gives us a bad connection. When we ask for any member of the Brandt family, every phone in South America rings. There have been complaints. It is very frustrating." Taptaptap, taptaptap.

Teela said, "You haven't even told me where you're going."

"I cannot name our destination, Teela. However, you may—"

"Finagle's red claws! You won't even tell us that?"

"You may examine the holo Louis Wu is carrying. That is the only information I can give you at this time."

Louis handed her the holo, the one that showed a baby-blue stripe crossing a black background behind a disc of blazing white. She took her time looking it over; and only Louis noticed how the angry blood flowed into her face.

When she spoke, she spit the words out one at a time, like the seeds of a tangerine. "This is the most ridiculous thing I ever heard of. You expect Louis and me to go charging out beyond known space with a kzin and a puppeteer for company, and all we know about where we're going is a length of blue ribbon and a light-spot! That's—ridiculous!"

"I take it, then, that you refuse to join us."

The girl's eyebrows went up.

"I must have a direct answer. Soon my agents may locate another candidate."

"Yes," said Teela Brown. "Yes, I do refuse."

"Remember, then, that by human law you must keep

secret the things you have been told here. You have been paid a consultant's fee."

"Who would I tell?" Teela laughed dramatically. "Who would believe me? Louis, are you really going on this ridiculous—"

"Yes." Louis was already thinking of other things, like a tactful way to get her out of the office. "But not right this minute. There's still a party going on. Look, do something for me, will you? Switch the musicmaster from tape four to tape five. Then tell anyone who asks that I'll be out in a minute."

When the door had closed behind her, Louis said, "Do me a favor. Do yourselves one, too. Let me be the judge of whether a human being is qualified for a jaunt into the unknown."

"You know what qualifications are paramount," said Nessus. "We do not yet have two candidates to choose from."

"You've got tens of thousands."

"Not really. Many disqualify themselves; others cannot be found. However, you may tell me where that human being fails to fit your own qualifications."

"She's too young."

"No candidate can qualify without being of Teela Brown's generation."

"Breeding for luck! No, never mind, I won't argue the point. I know humans crazier than that. A couple of 'em are still here at the party . . . Well, you saw for yourself that she's no xenophile."

"Nor is she a xenophobe. She does not fear either of us."

"She doesn't have the *spark*. She isn't—isn't—"

"She has no restlessness," said Nessus. "She is happy where she is. This is indeed a liability. There is nothing she wants. Yet how could we know this without asking?"

"Okay, pick your own candidates." Louis stalked from his office.

Behind him the puppeteer fluted, "Louis! Speaker! The signal! One of my agents has found another candidate!"

"He sure has," Louis said disgustedly. Across the living room, Teela Brown was glaring at another Pierson's puppeteer.

Louis woke slowly. He remembered donning a sleep headset and setting it for an hour of current. Presumably that had been an hour ago. After the set turned itself off the discomfort of having the thing on his head would have wakened him . . .

It wasn't on his head.

He sat up abruptly.

"I took it off you," said Teela Brown. "You needed the sleep."

"Oh boy. What time is it?"

"A little after seventeen."

"I've been a bad host. How goes the party?"

"Down to about twenty people. Don't worry, I told them what I was doing. They all thought it was a good idea."

"Okay." Louis rolled off the bed. "Thanks. Shall we join what's left of the party?"

"I'd like to talk to you first."

He sat down again. The muzziness of sleep was slowly leaving him. He asked, "What about?"

"You're really going on this crazy trip?"

"I really am."

"I don't see why."

"I'm ten times your age," said Louis Wu. "I don't have to work for a living. I don't have the patience to be a scientist. I did some writing once, but it turned out to be hard work, which was the last thing I expected. What's left? I play a lot."

She shook her head, and firelight shivered on the walls. "It doesn't sound like playing."

Louis shrugged. "Boredom is my worst enemy. It's killed a lot of my friends, but it won't get me. When I get bored, I go risk my life somewhere."

"Shouldn't you at least know what the risk is?"

"I'm getting well paid."

"You don't need the money."

"The human race needs what the puppeteers have got.

Look, Teela, you were told all about the second quantum
hyperdrive ship. It's the only ship in known space that
moves faster than three days to the light year. And it goes
almost four hundred times that fast!"

"Who *needs* to fly that fast?"

Louis wasn't in the mood to deliver a lecture on the
Core explosion. "Let's get back to the party."

"No, wait!"

"Okay."

Her hands were large, with long, slender fingers. They
glowed in reflected light as she brushed them nervously
through her burning hair. *"Tanj,* I'm messing this up.
Louis, are you in love with anyone right now?"

That surprised him. "I don't think so."

"Do I really look like Paula Cherenkov?"

In the semidarkness of the bedroom she looked like
the burning giraffe in the Dali painting. Her hair glowed
by its own light, a stream of orange and yellow flame
darkening to smoke. In that light the rest of Teela was
shadow touched by the flickering light of her hair. But
Louis's memory filled in the details: the long, perfect legs,
the conical breasts, the delicate beauty of her small face.
He had first seen her four days ago, on the arm of Tedron
Doheny, a spindly crashlander who had journeyed to
Earth for the party.

"I thought you were Paula herself," he said now. "She
lives on We Made It, which is where I met Ted Doheny.
When I saw you together I thought Ted and Paula had
come on the same ship.

"Close up, there were differences. You've got better
legs, but Paula's walk was more graceful. Paula's face
was—colder, I think. Maybe that's just memory."

From outside the door came bursts of computer music, wild and pure, strangely incomplete without the light
patterns to make it whole. Teela shifted restlessly, stirring the firelight shadows on the wall.

"What have you got in mind? Remember," said Louis,
"the puppeteers have thousands of candidates to choose
from. They could find our fourth crewman any day, any
minute. Then, off we go."

"That's all right," said Teela.

"You'll stay with me until then?"

Teela nodded her fiery head.

The puppeteer dropped in two days later.

Louis and Teela were out on the lawn, soaking up sunshine and playing a deadly serious game of fairy chess. Louis had spotted her a knight. Now he was regretting it. Teela alternated intellection with intuition; he could never tell which way she would jump. And she played for blood.

She was chewing gently at her underlip, considering her next move, when the servo slid up and bonged at them. Louis glanced up at the monitor screen, saw two one-eyed pythons looking out of the servo's chest. "Send him out here," he said comfortably.

Teela stood in one sudden, graceless motion. "You two may have secrets."

"Maybe. What have you got in mind?"

"Some reading to catch up on." She leveled a forefinger at him. "Don't touch that board!"

At the door she met the puppeteer coming out. She waved casually as they passed, and Nessus leapt six feet to the side. "I beg your pardon," he fluted. "You startled me."

Teela lifted an eyebrow and went inside.

The puppeteer stopped next to Louis and folded his legs under him. One head fixed on Louis; the other moved nervously, circling, covering all angles of vision. "Could the woman spy on us?"

Louis showed his surprise. "Sure. You know there's no defense against a spy beam, not in the open. So?"

"Anyone or anything could be watching us. Louis, let us go to your office."

"There ain't no justice." Louis was perfectly comfortable where he was. "Will you stop bobbing your head around, please? You act scared to death."

"I am frightened, though I know my death would matter little. How many meterorites fall to Earth in a year?"

"I wouldn't know."

"We are perilously close to the asteroid belt here. Yet it does not matter, for we have been unable to contact a fourth crew member."

"Too bad," said Louis. The puppeteer's behavior puzzled him. If Nessus had been human— But he wasn't. "You haven't given up, I trust."

"No, but our failures have been galling. For these past four days we have been seeking a Norman Haywood KJMMCWTAD, a perfect choice for our crew."

"And?"

"His health is perfect and vigorous. His age, twenty-four-and-a-third terrestrial years. Six generations of his ancestors were all born through winning lottery tickets. Best of all, he enjoys travel; he exhibits the restlessness we need.

"Naturally we tried to contact him in person. For three days my agent tracked him through a series of transfer booths, always a jump behind him, while Norman Haywood went skiing in Suisse, and surfing in Ceylon, to shops in New York, and to house parties in the Rockies and the Himalayas. Last night my agent caught up to him as he entered a passenger spacecraft bound for Jinx. The ship departed before my agent could conquer his natural fear of your jury-rigged ships."

"I've had days like that myself. Couldn't you send him a hyperwave message?"

"Louis, this voyage is supposed to be secret."

"Yah," said Louis. And he watched a python head circling, circling, searching out unseen enemies.

"We will succeed," said Nessus. "Thousands of potential crew members cannot hide forever. Can they, Louis? They do not even know we are seeking them!"

"You'll find someone. You're bound to."

"I pray that we do not! Louis, how can I do it? How can I ride with three aliens in an experimental ship designed for one pilot? It would be madness!"

"Nessus, what's really bugging you? This whole trip was your idea!"

"It was not. My orders came from those-who-lead, from two hundred light years away."

"Something's terrified you. I want to know what it is. What have you found out? Do you know what this trip is really all about? What's changed since you were ready to insult four kzinti in a public restaurant? Hey, easy, easy!"

The puppeteer had tucked his heads and necks between his forelegs and rolled into a ball.

"Come on," said Louis. "Come on out." He ran his hands gently along the backs of the puppeteer's necks—the parts that showed. The puppeteer shuddered. His skin was soft, like chamois skin, and pleasant to the touch.

"Come on out of there. Nothing's going to hurt you here. I protect my guests."

The puppeteer's wail came muffled from under his belly. "I was mad. Mad! Did I really insult four kzinti?"

"Come on out. You're safe here. *That's* better." A flat head peeped out of the warm shadow. "Now, you see? Nothing to be afraid of."

"Four kzinti? Not three?"

"My mistake. I miscounted. It was three."

"Forgive me, Louis." The puppeteer exposed his other head as far as the eye. "My manic phase has ended. I am in the depressive leg of my cycle."

"Can you do anything about it?" Louis thought of the consequences, if Nessus should hit the wrong leg of his cycle at a crucial time.

"I can wait for it to end. I can protect myself, to the extent possible. I can try not to let it affect my judgment."

"Poor Nessus. You're sure you haven't learned anything new?"

"Do I not know enough already to terrify any sane mind?" The puppeteer stood up somewhat shakily. "Why did I meet Teela Brown? I had thought she would have departed."

"I asked her to stay with me until we find your fourth crewmate."

"Why?"

Louis had wondered about that himself.

It had little to do with Paula Cherenkov. Louis had

changed too much since her time; and he was not a man to force one woman into the mold of another.

Sleeping plates were designed for two occupants, not one. But there had been other girls at the party . . . not as pretty as Teela. Could wise old Louis Wu still be snared by beauty alone?

But something more than beauty looked out of those flat silver eyes. Something highly complex.

"For purposes of fornication," said Louis Wu. He had remembered that he was talking to an alien, who would not understand such complexities. He realized that the puppeteer was still shivering, and added, "Let's go to my office. It's under the hill. No meteors."

After the puppeteer left, Louis went looking for Teela. He found her in the library, in front of a reading screen, clicking frames past at a speed high even for a speed-reader.

"Hi," she said. She froze a frame and turned. "How's our two-headed friend?"

"Scared witless. And I'm exhausted. I've been playing psychiatrist to a Pierson's puppeteer."

Teela brightened. "Tell me about a puppeteer's sex life."

"All I know is, he isn't allowed to breed. He broods on it. One may assume that he could breed if there weren't a law against it. Aside from that, he stayed off the subject completely. Sorry."

"Well, what did you talk about?"

Louis waved a hand. "Three hundred years of traumas. That's how long Nessus has been in human space. He hardly remembers the puppeteer planet. I get the feeling he's been scared for three hundred years." Louis dropped into a masseur chair. The strain of empathizing with an alien had exhausted his mind, used up his imagination.

"How about you? What are you reading?"

"The Core explosion." Teela waved at the reading screen.

There were stars in clusters and bunches and masses. You couldn't see black, there were so many stars. It might have been a dense star cluster, but it wasn't; it couldn't be. Telescopes wouldn't reach that far, nor would any normal spacecraft.

It was the galactic core, five thousand light years across, a tight sphere of stars at the axis of the galactic whirlpool. One man had reached that far, two hundred years ago, in an experimental puppeteer-built ship. The frame showed red and blue and green stars, all superimposed, the red stars biggest and brightest. In the center of the picture was a patch of blazing white the shape of a bloated comma. Within it were lines and blobs of shadow; but the shadow within the white patch was brighter than any star outside it.

"That's why you need the puppeteer ship," said Teela. "Isn't it?"

"Right."

"How did it happen?"

"The stars are too close together," said Louis. "An average of half a light year apart, all through the core of any galaxy. Near the center, they're packed even tighter. In a galactic core, stars are so close to each other that they can heat each other up. Being hotter, they burn faster. They age faster.

"All the stars of the core must have been just that much closer to going nova, ten thousand years ago.

"Then one star went nova. It let loose a lot of heat and a blast of gamma rays. The few stars around it got that much hotter. I gather the gamma rays also make for increased stellar activity. So a couple of neighboring stars blew up.

"That made three. The combined heat set off a few more. It was a chain reaction. Pretty soon there was no stopping it. That white patch is all supernovae. If you like, you can get the math of it a little further along in the tape."

"No thanks," she said—predictably. "I gather it's all over by now?"

"Yah. That's old light you're looking at, though it hasn't reached this part of the galaxy yet. The chain reaction must have ended ten thousand years ago."

"Then what is everyone excited about?"

"Radiation. Fast particles, all kinds." The masseur chair was beginning to relax him; he settled deeper into its formless bulk and let the standing wave patterns knead his muscles. "Look at it this way. Known space is a little bubble of stars thirty-three thousand light years out from the galactic axis. The novae began exploding more than ten thousand years ago. That means that the wave front from the combined explosion will get *here* in about twenty thousand years. Right?"

"Sure."

"And the subnuclear radiation from a million novae is traveling right behind the wave front."

". . . Oh."

"In twenty thousand years we'll have to evacuate every world you ever heard of, and probably a lot more."

"That's a long time. If we started now, we could do it with the ships we've got. Easily."

"You're not thinking. At three days to the light year, it would take one of our ships about *six hundred years* to reach the Clouds of Magellan."

"They could stop off to get more food and air . . . every year or so."

Louis laughed. "Try talking anyone into that. You know what I think? When the light of the Core explosion starts shining through the dust clouds between here and the galactic axis, that's when everyone in human space is suddenly going to get terrified. Then they'll have a century to get out.

"The puppeteers had the right idea. They sent a man to the Core as a publicity stunt, because they wanted financing for research. He sent back pictures like that one. Before he'd even landed, the puppeteers were gone; there wasn't a puppeteer on any human world. We won't do it that way. We'll wait and we'll wait, and when we finally decide to move we'll have to ship trillions of sentient beings completely out of the galaxy. We'll need the biggest, fastest ships we can build, and we'll need as many as we can get. We need the puppeteer drive *now*, so that we can start improving it *now*. The—"

"Okay. I'm going with you."

Louis, interrupted in midlecture, said, "Huh?"

"I'm going with you," said Teela Brown.

"You're out of your mind."

"Well, *you're* going, aren't you?"

Louis clamped his teeth on the explosion. When he did speak, he spoke more calmly than the situation deserved. "Yes, I'm going. But I've got reasons you don't, and I'm better at staying alive than you are, because I've been at it longer."

"But I'm luckier."

Louis snorted.

"And my reasons for going may not be as good as yours, but they're good enough!" Her voice was high and thin with anger.

"The tanj they are."

Teela tapped the face of the reading screen. A bloated comma of nova light flared beneath her fingernail. *"That's* not a good reason?"

"We'll get the puppeteer drive whether you come or not. You heard Nessus. There are thousands like you."

"And I'm one of them!"

"All *right,* you're one of them," Louis flared.

"What are you so tanj protective about? Did I *ask* for your protection?"

"I apologize. I don't know why I tried to dictate to you. You're a free adult."

"Thank you. I intend to join your crew." Teela had gone icily formal.

The hell of it was, she *was* a free adult. Not only could she not be coerced; an attempt to order her about would be bad manners and (more to the point) wouldn't work.

But she could be persuaded . . .

"Then think about this," said Louis Wu. "Nessus has gone to great lengths to protect the secrecy of this trip. Why? What's he got to hide?"

"That's his business, isn't it? Maybe there's something worth stealing, wherever we're going."

"So what? Where we're going is two hundred light years from here. *We're the only ones who can get there.*"

"The ship itself, then."

Whatever was unusual about Teela, she was no dummy. Louis himself hadn't thought of that. "Then think about our crew," he said. "Two humans, a puppeteer, and a kzin. None of us professional explorers."

"I see what you're doing, but honestly, Louis, I am going. I doubt you can stop me."

"Then you can at least know what you're getting into. Why the odd crew?"

"That's Nessus's problem."

"I'd say it's ours. Nessus gets his orders directly from those-who-lead—from the puppeteer headquarters. I think he figured out what those orders meant, just a few hours ago. Now he's terrified. Those . . . priests of survival have got four games going at once, not counting whatever it is we'll be exploring."

He saw that he had Teela's interest, and he pressed on. "First there's Nessus. If he's mad enough to land on an unknown world, can he possibly be sane enough to survive the experience? Those-who-lead have to know. After they reach the Clouds of Magellan they'll have to set up another commercial empire. The backbone of their commerce is the mad puppeteers.

"Then there's our furry friend. As ambassador to an alien race, he should be one of the most sophisticated kzinti around. Is he sophisticated enough to get along with the rest of us? Or will he kill us for elbow room and fresh meat?

"Third, there's you and your presumed luck, a blue-sky research project if I ever heard of one. Fourth is me, a presumably typical explorer type. Maybe I'm the control.

"You know what I think?" Louis was standing over the girl now, pounding his words home with an oratorical technique he'd mastered while losing an election for the UN in his middle seventies. He would honestly have denied trying to browbeat Teela Brown; but he wanted desperately to convince her. "The puppeteers couldn't care less about whatever planet we're being sent to. Why should they, when they're leaving the galaxy? They're testing our little team to destruction. Before we get ourselves killed, the puppeteers can find out a lot about how we interact."

"I don't think it's a planet," said Teela.

Louis exploded. "Tanj! What has *that* got to do with it?"

"Well, after *all*, Louis. If we're going to get killed exploring it, we might as well know what it *is*. I think it's a spacecraft."

"You do."

"A big one, a ring-shaped one with a ramscoop field to pick up interstellar hydrogen. I think it's built to funnel the hydrogen into the axis for fusion. You'd get thrust that way, and a sun too. You'd spin the ring for centrifugal force, and you'd roof the inner side with glass."

"Yah," said Louis, thinking of the odd picture in the holo he'd been given by the puppeteer. He'd spent too little time wondering about their destination. "Could be. Big and primitive and not very easy to steer. But why would those-who-lead be interested?"

"It could be a refugee ship. Core races would learn about stellar processes early, with the suns so close together. They might have predicted the explosion thousands of years ahead . . . when there were only two or three supernovas."

"Supernovae. Could be . . . and you've snaked me right off the subject. I've told you what kind of game I think the puppeteers are playing. I'm going anyway, for the fun of it. What makes you think *you* want to go?"

"The Core explosion."

"Altruism is great, but you couldn't possibly be worried about something that's supposed to happen in twenty thousand years. Try again."

"Dammit, if you can be a hero, so can I! And you're wrong about Nessus. He'd back out of a suicide mission. And—and why would the puppeteers want to know anything about us, or the kzinti either? What would they test us *for*? They're leaving the galaxy. They'll never have anything to do with us again."

No, Teela wasn't stupid. But— "You're wrong. The puppeteers have excellent reasons for wanting to know all about us."

Teela's look dared him to back it up.

"We don't know much about the puppeteer migration. We do know that every able-bodied, sane-minded puppeteer now alive is on the move. And we know that they're moving at just below lightspeed. The puppeteers are afraid of hyperspace.

"Now. Traveling at just below lightspeed, the puppeteer fleet should reach the Lesser Cloud of Magellan in about eighty-five thousand years. And what do they expect to find when they get there?"

He grinned at her and gave her the punch line. "Us, of course. Humans and kzinti, at least. Kdatlyno and pierin and dolphins, probably. They know we'll wait until the last minute and then run for it, and they know we'll use faster-then-light drives. By the time the puppeteers reach the Cloud, they'll have to deal with us . . . or with whatever kills us off; and by knowing us, they can predict the nature of the killer. Oh, they've got reason enough to study us."

"Okay."

"Still want to go?"

Teela nodded.

"Why?"

"I'll reserve that." Teela's composure was complete. And what could Louis do about it? Had she been under nineteen he would have called one of her parents. But at twenty she was a presumed adult. You had to draw the line somewhere.

As an adult she had freedom of choice; she was entitled to expect good manners from Louis Wu; certain areas of her privacy were sacrosanct. Louis could only persuade; and at that he had failed.

So that Teela didn't have to do what she did next. She suddenly took his hands and, smiling, pleading, said, "Take me with you, Louis. I'm luck, really I am. If Nessus didn't choose right you could wind up sleeping alone. You'd hate that, I know you would."

She had him in a box. He couldn't keep her off Nessus's ship, not when she could go directly to the puppeteer.

"All right," he said. "We'll call him."

And he *would* hate sleeping alone.

CHAPTER 4

Speaker-To-Animals

"I want to join the expedition," Teela said into the phonescreen.

The puppeteer howled on a long-drawn E-flat note.

"I beg your pardon?"

"Excuse me," said the puppeteer. "Report to Outback Field, Australia, tomorrow at 0800. Bring personal possessions not to exceed fifty pounds Earth weight. Louis, you will do the same. Ahh—" The puppeteer raised his heads and howled.

Anxiously Louis demanded, "Are you sick?"

"No. I foresee my own death. Louis, I could wish that you had been less persuasive. Farewell. We meet at Outback Field."

The screen went dark.

"See?" Teela crowed. "See what you get for being so persuasive?"

"Me and my silver tongue. Well, I did my oratorical best. Don't blame me if you die horribly."

That night, freely falling in darkness, Louis heard her say, "I love you. I'm going with you because I love you."

"Love you too," he said with sleepy good manners. Then it percolated through, and he said, "That's what you were reserving?"

"Mm hmm."

"You're following me two hundred light years because you can't bear to let me go?"

"Yawp."

46

"Sleeproom half-light," said Louis. Dim blue light filled the room.

They floated a foot apart between the sleeping plates. In preparation for space they had cleaned off the skin dyes and hair treatments of flatland style. The hair in Louis's queue was now straight and black; his scalp was gray with stubble. Yellow-brown skin tones, brown eyes with no perceptible slant, changed his image considerably.

The changes in Teela were equally drastic. Her hair was dark and wavy now, tied back from her face. Her skin was nordic-pale. Her oval face was dominated by big brown eyes and a small, serious mouth; her nose was almost unnoticeable. In the sleeping field she floated like oil on water, utterly relaxed.

"But you've never even been as far as the Moon."

She nodded.

"And I'm not the world's greatest lover. You told me that yourself."

She nodded again. There was no reticence in Teela Brown. In two days and nights she had not lied, nor shaded the truth, nor so much as dodged a question. Louis would have known. She had told him of her first two loves: the one who had lost interest in her after half a year, the other, a cousin, who had been offered a chance to emigrate to Mount Lookitthat. Louis had told her little of his own experience, and she had seemed to accept his reticence. But she had none. And she asked the damndest questions.

"Then why me?" he asked.

"I don't know," she confessed. "Could it be the charisma? You're a hero, you know."

He was the only living man to have made first contact with an alien species. Would he ever live down the Trinoc episode?

He made one more try. "Look, I *know* the world's greatest lover. Friend of mine. It's his hobby. He writes *books* about it. He's got doctorates in physiology and psychology. For the past hundred and thirty years he's been—"

Teela had her hands over her ears. "Don't," she said. "Don't."

"I just don't want you to get killed somewhere. You're too young."

She wore the puzzled look, *that* puzzled look, the one that meant he'd used proper Interworld words in a nonsense sequence. *Whiplash of the heart? Killed somewhere?* Louis sighed within himself. "Sleeproom nodes merge," he said, and something happened to the sleeper field. The two regions of stable equilibrium, the anomalies which kept Louis and Teela from falling out of the field, moved together and merged into one. Louis and Teela followed, sliding "downhill" until they bumped and clung.

"I really was sleepy, Louis. But never mind . . ."

"Think about privacy before you drift away to dreamland. Spacecraft tend to be cramped."

"You mean we couldn't make love? Tanj, Louis, I don't care if they watch. They're *aliens.*"

"I care."

She gave him *that* puzzled look. "Suppose they weren't aliens. *Then* would you object?"

"Yes, unless we knew them very well. Does that make me out of date?"

"A little."

"Remember that friend I mentioned? The world's greatest lover? Well, he had a colleague," said Louis, "and she taught me some things he was teaching her. You need gravity for this," he added. "Sleeproom field off." Weight returned.

"You're trying to change the subject," said Teela.

"Yes. I give up."

"Okay, but just keep one thing in mind. One thing. Your puppeteer friend might have wanted four species instead of three. You could just as easily be holding a Trinoc instead of me."

"Horrible thought. Now, we do this in three stages, starting with straddle position . . ."

"What's straddle position?"

"I'll show you . . ."

By morning Louis was glad enough that they would be

traveling together. When his doubts returned it was too late. It had already been too late for some considerable time.

The Outsiders were traders in information. They bought high and they sold high, but what they bought once they sold again and again, for their trading ground was the entire galactic whorl. In the banks of human space their credit was virtually unlimited.

Presumably they had evolved on some cold, light moon of a gas giant; some world very like Nereid, Neptune's larger moon. Now they lived in the gaps between the stars, in city-sized ships whose sophistication varied enormously, from photon sails to engines theoretically impossible to human science. Where a planetary system held potential customers, and where such a system included a suitable world, the Outsiders would lease space for trade centers, rest and recreation areas, supply dumps. Half a thousand years ago they had leased Nereid.

"And that must be their major trade area," said Louis Wu. "Down there." He pointed with one hand, keeping the other on the controls of the transport ship.

Nereid was an icy, craggy plain beneath bright starlight. The sun was a fat white point giving off as much light as a full Moon; and that light illuminated a maze of low walls. There were hemispherical buildings, and a cluster of small thruster-driven ground-to-orbit ships with passenger sections open to space; but more than half the plain was covered with those low walls.

Speaker-To-Animals, hovering hugely behind Louis, said, "I would know the purpose of the maze. Defense?"

"Basking areas," said Louis. "The Outsiders live on thermoelectricity. They lie with their heads in sunlight and their tails in shadow, and the temperature difference between the two sets up a current. The walls are to make more shadow-borderlines."

Nessus had calmed down during the ten-hour flight. He trotted about the lifesystem of the transport ship, inspecting this and that, poking a head and eye into corners, tossing comments and answers to questions over his shoul-

der. His pressure suit, a baggy balloon with padding over
the hump that concealed his brain, looked light and comfortable; the air and food regenerator packages were im-
probably small.

He had given them a strange moment just before takeoff.
Music had played suddenly through the cabin, complex
and lovely, rich in minor tones, like the sad call of a sex-
maddened computer. Nessus whistled. With his twin
mouths, rich in nerves and muscles appropriate to mouths
which were also hands, the puppeteer was a walking or-
chestra.

He had insisted that Louis fly the craft, and his confidence in Louis's ability was such that he had not
strapped down. Louis suspected special, secret gadgets to
protect the passengers of the puppeteer-built ship.

Speaker had come aboard with a twenty-pound luggage
case which, when opened, had held little more than a collapsed microwave oven for heating meat. That, and a
haunch of raw something-or-other, of kzinti rather than
terrestrial origin. For some reason Louis had expected the
kzin's pressure suit to look like bulky medieval armor. It
didn't. It was a multiple balloon, transparent, with a mon-
strously heavy backpack and a fishbowl helmet packed
with esoteric-looking tongue controls. Though it held no
identifiable weapons, the backpack had a look of battle
gear, and Nessus had insisted that he store it.

The kzin had spent most of the voyage napping.

And now they all stood looking over Louis's shoulder.

"I'll drop us next to the Outsider ship," said Louis.

"No. Take us east. We have been using an isolated area
to park the *Long Shot*."

"What for? Would the Outsiders spy on you?"

"No. The *Long Shot* uses fusion drives instead of
thrusters. The heat of takeoffs and landings would disturb
the Outsiders."

"Why *Long Shot?*"

"It was so named by Beowulf Shaeffer, the only sentient
being ever to fly that ship. He took the only extant holographs of the Core explosion. Is not *Long Shot* a gambler's
term?"

"Maybe he didn't expect to come back. I'd better tell you: I've never flown anything with a fusion drive. My ship rides on reactionless thrusters, just like this one."

"You must learn," said Nessus.

"Wait," said Speaker-To-Animals. "I myself have had experience with fusion-driven spacecraft. Therefore I will pilot the *Long Shot*."

"Impossible. The pilot's crash couch is designed to fit a human frame. The control panels follow human custom."

The kzin made angry noises deep in his throat.

"There, Louis. Ahead of us."

The *Long Shot* was a transparent bubble over a thousand feet in diameter. As Louis guided their craft to circle the behemoth, he could find no cubic inch of her that was not packed with the green-and-bronze machinery of hyperspace shunt motors. Her hull was a General Products #4 hull, easily recognized by one familiar with spacecraft, so big that it was commonly used only to ship entire prefab colonies. But she didn't look like a spacecraft. She was the tremendous counterpart of some primitive orbital satellite, built by a race whose limited resources and limited technology required that every smallest bit of space be used.

"And where do we sit?" Louis inquired. "On top?"

"The cabin is underneath. Land beneath the curve of the hull."

Louis brought his ship down on dark ice, then slid her carefully forward, under the bulging belly of the *Long Shot*.

There were lights in the lifesystem; they gleamed through the *Long Shot's* hull. Louis saw two tiny rooms, the lower just big enough to hold a crash couch and a mass indicator and a horseshoe-shaped bank of instruments, the upper room no larger. He felt the kzin move up behind him.

"Interesting," said the kzin. "I presume that Louis is intended to ride in the lower compartment, and we three in the upper."

"Yes. The fitting of three crash couches into so small

a space gave us considerable difficulty. Each is equipped with a stasis field for maximum safety. Since we will ride in stasis, it matters little that there is no room to move about."

The kzin snorted, and Louis felt him leave his shoulder. He let the ship settle a last few inches, then snapped off a succession of switches.

"I have a point to make," he said. "Teela and I are collecting the same fee between us that Speaker-To-Animals is collecting alone."

"Do you wish additional pay? I will consider your suggestions."

"I want something you don't need any more," Louis told the puppeteer. "Something your race left behind them." He'd picked a good moment for bargaining. He didn't expect it to work, but it was certainly worth a try. "I want the location of the puppeteer planet."

Nessus's heads swung out from his shoulders, then turned back to face each other. For a moment Nessus held his own stare before asking, "Why?"

"Once upon a time the location of the puppeteer world was the most valuable secret in known space. Your own kind would have paid a fortune in blackmail to keep that secret," said Louis. "That was what made it valuable. Fortune hunters searched every G and K star in sight looking for the puppeteer world. Even now, Teela and I could sell the information to any news network for good money."

"But if that world is outside known space?"

"Ah-h-h," said Louis. "My history teacher used to wonder about that. The information would still be worth money."

"Before we depart for our ultimate destination," the puppeteer said carefully, "you will know the coordinates of the puppeteer world. I think you will find the information more surprising than useful." Again, for a heartbeat, the puppeteer peered into his own eyes.

He broke the pose. "I direct your attention to four conical projections—"

"Yah." Louis had already noticed the open-mouthed

cones, pointing outward and downward around the double cabin. "Are those the fusion motors?"

"Yes. You will find that the ship behaves very like a ship driven by reactionless thrusters, except that there is no internal gravity. Our designers had little room to spare. Concerning the operation of the quantum II hyperdrive, there is a thing I must warn you about—"

"I have a variable-sword," said Speaker-To-Animals. "I urge calm."

It took a moment for the words to register. Then Louis turned, slowly, making no sudden gestures.

The kzin stood against a curved wall. In one clawed fist he held something like an oversized jumprope handle. Ten feet from the handle, held expertly at the level of the kzin's eyes, was a small, glowing red ball. The wire which joined ball to handle was too thin to be visible, but Louis didn't doubt it was there. Protected and made rigid by a Slaver stasis field, the wire would cut through most metals, including—if Louis should choose to hide behind it—the back of Louis's crash couch. And the kzin had chosen a position such that he could strike anywhere in the cabin.

At the kzin's feet Louis saw the unidentified haunch of alien meat. It had been ripped open, and, of course, it had been hollow.

"I would have preferred a more merciful weapon," said Speaker-To-Animals. "A stunner would have been ideal. I could not procure one in time. Louis, take your hands off the controls and put them on the back of your couch."

Louis did. He had thought of playing with the cabin gravity; but the kzin would have cut him in two if he'd tried it.

"Now, if you will all remain calm, I will tell you what will happen next."

"Tell us why," Louis suggested. He was estimating chances. The red bulb was an indicator to tell Speaker where his invisibly thin wire blade ended. But if Louis could grab that end of the blade, and keep from losing his fingers in the process—

No. The bulb was too small.

"My motive should be obvious," said Speaker. The

black markings around his eyes had taken on the look of a
bandit's mask in a cartoon. The kzin was neither tense nor
relaxed. And he stood where he was almost impossible to
attack.

"I intend to give my world control of the *Long Shot*.
With the *Long Shot* as a model we will build more such
ships. Such ships would give us a killing superiority in
the next Man–Kzin war, provided that men do not also
have designs for *Long Shot*. Satisfactory?"

Louis made his voice sarcastic. "You couldn't be afraid
of where we're going."

"No." The insult slid right past him. How would a kzin
recognize sarcasm? "You will all disrobe now, so that I
may know that you are unarmed. When you have done so
I will request the puppeteer to don his pressure suit. We
two will board the *Long Shot*. Louis and Teela will stay
behind, but I will take your clothing and your luggage
and your pressure suits. I will disable this ship. Doubtless
the Outsiders, curious as to why you have not returned to
Earth, will come to help you long before your lifesystem
fails. Do you all understand?"

Louis Wu, relaxed and ready to take advantage of any
slip the kzin might make . . . Louis Wu glanced at Teela
Brown from the corner of his eye and saw a horrible thing.
Teela was bracing herself to jump the kzin.

Speaker would cut her in two.

Louis would have to move first.

"Don't be foolish, Louis. Stand up slowly and move
against the wall. You shall be the first toooo . . ."

Speaker let the word trail off in a kind of croon.

Louis halted his leap, caught by a thing he didn't understand.

Speaker-To-Animals threw back his big orange head
and mewed: an almost supersonic squeal. He threw his
arms wide, as if to embrace the universe. The wire blade
of his variable-sword cut through a water tank without
slowing noticeably; water began dripping out on all four
sides of the tank. Speaker didn't notice. His eyes didn't
see, his ears didn't hear.

"Take his weapon," said Nessus.

Louis moved. He approached cautiously, ready to duck if the variable-sword should move his way. The kzin was waving it gently, like a baton. Louis took the handle from the kzin's unresisting fist. He touched the proper stud, and the red ball retracted until it touched the handle.

"Keep it," said Nessus. He clamped his jaws on Speaker's arm and led the kzin to a crash couch. The kzin made no resistance. He was no longer making sounds; he stared into infinity, and his great furry face showed only a vast calm.

"What happened? What did you do?"

Speaker-To-Animals, totally relaxed, stared at infinity and purred.

"Watch," said Nessus. He moved carefully back from the kzin's crash couch. He held his flat heads high and rigid, not so much pointed as aimed, and at no time did his eyes leave the kzin.

The kzin's eyes focused suddenly. They flicked from Louis, to Teela, to Nessus. Speaker-To-Animals made plaintive snarling sounds, sat upright, and switched to Interworld.

"That was very, very nice. I wish—"

He stopped, started over. "Whatever you did," he told the puppeteer, "do not do it again."

"I judged you to be a sophisticate," said Nessus. "My judgment was accurate. Only a sophisticate would fear a tasp."

Teela said, "Ah."

Louis said, "Tasp?"

The puppeteer addressed himself to Speaker-To-Animals. "You understand that I will use the tasp every time you force me to. I will use it if you make me uneasy. If you attempt violence too often, or if you startle me too often, you will soon become dependent on the tasp. Since the tasp is a surgically implanted part of me, you would have to kill me to possess it. And you would still be ignobly bound by the tasp itself."

"Very astute," said Speaker. "Brilliantly unorthodox tactics. I will trouble you no more."

"Tanj! Will *somebody* tell me what a tasp is?"

Louis's ignorance seemed to surprise everybody. It was Teela who answered. "It jolts the pleasure center of the brain."

"From a distance?" Louis hadn't known that that was even theoretically possible.

"Sure. It does for you just what a touch of current does for a wirehead; but you don't need to drop a wire into your brain. Usually a tasp is just small enough to aim with one hand."

"Have you ever been hit by a tasp? None of my business, of course."

Teela grinned derision for his delicacy. "Yes, I know what it feels like. A moment of—well, there's no describing it. But you don't use a tasp on yourself. You use it on someone who isn't expecting it. That's where the fun comes in. Police are always picking up taspers in the parks."

"Your tasps," said Nessus, "induce less than a second of current. Mine induces 'prox ten seconds."

The effect on Speaker-To-Animals must have been formidable. But Louis saw other implications. "Oh, wow. That's beautiful. That's lovely! Who but a puppeteer would go around with a weapon that does good to the enemy?"

"Who but a prideful sophisticate would fear too much pleasure? The puppeter is quite right," said Speaker-To-Animals. "I would not risk the tasp again. Too many jolts from the puppeteer's tasp would leave me his willing slave. I, a kzin, slaved to an herbivore!"

"Let us board the *Long Shot,*" Nessus said grandly. "We have wasted enough time on trivialities."

Louis was first aboard the *Long Shot.*

He was not surprised to find his feet trying to dance on Nereid's rock surface. Louis knew how to move in low gravity. But his hindbrain stupidly expected gravity to change as he entered the *Long Shot's* airlock. Braced for the change, he stumbled and almost fell when it didn't come.

"I *know* they had induced gravity then," he grumbled as he moved into the cabin. ". . . Oh."

The cabin was primitive. There were hard right angles everywhere, suitable for bumping knees and elbows. Everything was bulkier than necessary. Dials were badly placed . . .

But, more than primitive, the cabin was *small*. There had been induced gravity when the *Long Shot* was built; but, even in a ship a mile wide, there had been no room for the machinery. There was barely room for a pilot.

Instrument board and mass indicator, a kitchen slot, a crash couch, and a space behind the couch where a man might wedge himself with his head bent to the low ceiling.

Louis braced himself in that space and opened the kzin's variable-sword to three feet.

Speaker-To-Animals came aboard, moving in self-conscious slow motion. He climbed past Louis without slowing, up into the overhead compartment.

The overhead compartment had been a recreation room for the ship's single pilot. Exercise machinery and a reading screen had been ripped out, and three new crash couches installed. Speaker climbed into one of these.

Now Louis followed him up the rungs, one-handed. Keeping the variable-sword unostentatiously in sight, he closed the cover on the kzin's crash couch and flipped a knife switch.

The crash couch became a mirror-surface egg. Inside, no time would pass until Louis turned off the stasis field. If the ship should happen to ram an antimatter asteroid, even the General Products hull would be ionized vapor; but the kzin's crash couch would not lose its mirror finish.

Louis relaxed. It had all been like a kind of ritualistic dance; but its purpose was real enough. The kzin had good reason to steal the ship. The tasp had not altered that. Speaker must not be given an opportunity.

Louis returned to the pilot's cabin. He used the ship-to-suit circuit. "Come on in."

Something over a hundred hours later, Louis Wu was outside the solar system.

CHAPTER 5

Rosette

There are singularities in the mathematics of hyperspace. One such singularity surrounds every sufficiently large mass in the Einsteinian universe. Outside of these singularities, ships can travel faster than light. Inside, they disappear if they try it.

Now the *Long Shot,* some eight light-hours from Sol, was beyond Sol's local singularity.

And Louis Wu was in free fall.

There was tension in his gonads and discomfort in his diaphragm, and his stomach thought he wanted to belch. These sensations would pass. There was a paradoxical urge to fly . . .

He had flown many times in free fall, in the huge transparent bubble of the Outbound Hotel, which circled Earth's Moon. Here, he would smash something vital if he so much as flapped his arms.

He had chosen to accelerate outward under two gravities. For something like five days he had worked and eaten and slept in the pilot's crash couch. Despite the excellent facilities of the couch, he was dirty and unkempt; despite fifty hours of sleep, he was exhausted.

Louis felt his future foreshadowed. For him, the keynote of the expedition would be discomfort.

The sky of deep space looked not much different from the lunar night sky. In the solar system the planets add little to a naked-eye view. One remarkably bright star glared in the galactic south; and that star was Sol.

Louis used flywheel controls. The *Long Shot* rotated, and stars went by beneath his feet.

Twenty-seven, three hundred and twelve, one thousand even—Nessus had given him these coordinates just before Louis closed the crash couch on him. They were the location of the puppeteer migration. And now Louis realized that this was not in the direction of either of the Clouds of Magellan. The puppeteer had lied to him.

But, Louis thought, it *was* about two hundred light years away. And it was along the galactic axis. Perhaps the puppeteers had chosen to move out of the galaxy along the shortest direction, then travel above the plane of the galaxy to reach the Lesser Cloud. Thus they would avoid interstellar debris: suns, dust clouds, hydrogen concentrations . . .

It didn't particularly matter. Louis's hands, like a pianist's about to begin a concert, hovered over the instrument panel.

Descended.

The *Long Shot* vanished.

Louis kept his eyes away from the transparent floor. He had already stopped wondering why there were no covers for all that window space. The sight of the Blind Spot had driven good men mad; but there were those who could take it. The *Long Shot's* pilot must have been such a man.

He looked instead at the mass pointer: a transparent sphere above the instrument panel, with a number of blue lines radiating from its center. This one was oversized, despite limitations on cabin space. Louis settled back and watched the lines.

They changed visibly. Louis could fix his eye on a line and watch it sweep slowly across the curvature of the sphere. It was unusual and unnerving. At normal hyperdrive speeds the lines would remain fixed for hours.

Louis flew with his left hand on the panic switch.

The kitchen slot to his right fed him odd-tasting coffee and, later, a handmeal that came apart in his hands, into separate strata of meat and cheese and bread and some kind of leaf. The autokitchen must be hundreds of years overdue for reprogramming. Radial lines in the mass indicator grew large, and swept upward like the second hand on a watch, and shrank to nothing. A fuzzy blue line at the bottom of the sphere grew long, and longer . . . Louis pulled the panic switch.

An unfamiliar red giant glared beneath his feet.

"Too fast," Louis snarled. "Too tanj fast!" In any normal ship you only had to check the mass indicator every six hours or so. On the *Long Shot* you hardly dared blink!

Louis let his eyes drop to the bright, fuzzy red disc and its starry background.

"Tanj! I'm already out of known space!"

He wheeled the ship to see the stars. A foreign sky streamed beneath him. "They're mine, all mine!" Louis chortled, rubbing his hands together. On sabbaticals Louis Wu was his own entertainment.

The red star returned to view, and Louis let it swing another ninety degrees. He'd let his ship get too close to the star, and now he'd have to circle around it.

He was then an hour and a half on his way.

He was three hours on his way when he dropped out again.

The foreign stars didn't bother him. City lights drowned the starlight over most of the Earth; and Louis Wu had been raised a flatlander. He had not seen a star until he was twenty-six. He checked to be sure he was in clear space, he closed covers on instrument panels, and then, finally, he stretched.

"Wow. My eyes feel like boiled onions."

Releasing himself from the crash web, he floated, flexing his left hand. For three hours he had flown with that hand closed on the hyperdrive switch. From elbow to fingertips it felt like a single cramp.

Under the ceiling were rungs for isometric exercises. Louis used them. The kinks left his muscles, but he was still tired.

Mmmm. Wake Teela? It would be nice to talk to her now. Lovely idea there. Next time I go on sabbatical *I'll* take a woman in stasis. Get the best of both worlds. But he looked and felt like something washed from a flooded grave-yard. Unfit for polite company. Oh, well.

He should not have let her board the *Long Shot.*

Not for his own sake! He was glad enough that she had stayed over, those two days. It had been like the story of Louis Wu and Paula Cherenkov, rewritten for a happy ending. Perhaps it had been better.

Yet there was something shallow about Teela. It wasn't only her age. Louis's friends were of all ages, and some of the youngest were very deep indeed. Certainly they suffered most. As if hurting were part of the learning process. Which it probably was.

No, there was a lack of empathy in Teela, a lack of the ability to feel someone else's pain . . .

Yet she could sense another's pleasure, and respond to pleasure, and create pleasure. She was a marvelous lover: painfully beautiful, almost new to the art, sensuous as a cat, and startlingly uninhibited . . .

None of which would qualify her as an explorer.

Teela's life had been happy and dull. Twice she had fallen in love, and twice she had been first to tire of the affair. She had never been in a bad stress situation, never been really hurt. When the time came, when Teela found her first genuine emergency, she would probably panic.

"But I picked her as a lover," said Louis to himself. "Damn Nessus!" If Teela had ever been found in a stress situation, Nessus would have rejected her as unlucky!

It had been a mistake to bring her. She would be a liability. He would spend too much of his time protecting her when he should be protecting himself.

What kinds of stress situations might they face? The puppeteers were good businessmen. They did not overpay. The *Long Shot* was a fee of unheard-of value. Louis had the chilly suspicion that they would earn it.

"Sufficient unto the day," Louis said to himself.

And he returned to his crash couch and slept for an hour under the sleep headset. Waking, he swung the ship into line and dropped back into the Blind Spot.

Five-and-a-half hours from Sol he dropped out again.

The puppeteer's coordinates defined a small rectangular section of the sky as seen from Sol, plus a radial distance in that direction. At that distance, those coordinates defined a cube half a light year on a side. Somewhere in that volume, presumably, was a fleet of ships. Also in that volume, unless instruments had fouled him up, were Louis Wu and the *Long Shot*.

Somewhere far behind him was a bubble of stars some seventy light years in diameter. Known space was small and very far away.

No point in searching for the fleet. Louis wouldn't know what to look for. He went to wake Nessus.

Anchored by his teeth to an exercise rung, Nessus peered over Louis's shoulder. "I need certain stars for reference. Center that green-white giant and throw it on the scope screen . . . "

The pilot's cabin was crowded. Louis hunched over the instrument panel, protecting buttons from the puppeteer's careless hooves.

"Spectroanalysis . . . yes. Now the blue-and-yellow double at two o'clock . . .

"I have my bearings. Swing to 348, 72."

"What exactly am I looking for, Nessus? A cluster of fusion flames? No, you'd be using thrusters."

"You must use the scope. When you see it, you will know."

On the scope screen was a sprinkling of anonymous stars. Louis ran the magnification up until . . . "Five dots in a regular pentagon. Right?"

"That is our destination."

"Good. Let me check the distance. —Tanj! That's wrong, Nessus. They're too far away."

No comment.

"Well, they couldn't be ships, even if the distance

meter isn't working. The puppeteer fleet must be moving at just under lightspeed. We'd see the motion."

Five dull stars in a regular pentagon. They were a fifth of a light year distant, and quite invisible to the naked eye. At present scope magnification they would have to be full sized planets. In the scope screen one was faintly less blue, faintly dimmer than the others.

A Kemplerer rosette. How very odd.

Take three or more equal masses. Set them at the points of an equilateral polygon and give them equal angular velocities about their center of mass.

Then the figure has stable equilibrium. The orbits of the masses may be circular or elliptical. Another mass may occupy the center of mass of the figure; or the center of mass may be empty. It doesn't matter. The figure is stable, like a pair of Trojan points.

The difficulty is that there are several easy ways in which a mass can be captured by a Trojan point. (Consider the Trojan asteroids in Jupiter's orbit.) But there is no easy way for five masses to fall accidentally into a Kemplerer rosette.

"That's wild," Louis murmured. "Unique. Nobody's ever found a Kemplerer rosette . . . " He let it trail off.

Here between the stars, what could be lighting those objects?

"Oh, no you don't," said Louis Wu. "You'll never make me believe it. What kind of an idiot do you take me for?"

"What is it that you will not believe?"

"You know tanj well what I won't believe!"

"As you please. That is our destination, Louis. If you will take us within range, a ship will be sent to match our velocity."

The rendezvous ship was a #3 hull, a cylinder with rounded ends and a flattened belly, painted shocking pink, and windowless. There were no engine apertures. The engines must be reactionless: thrusters of the human type, or something more advanced.

On Nessus's orders Louis had let the other ship do

the maneuvering. The *Long Shot*, on fusion drives alone, would have required months to match velocities with the puppeteer "fleet". The puppeteer ship had done it in less than an hour, blinking into existence alongside the *Long Shot* with her access tube already reaching like a glass snake toward the *Long Shot's* airlock.

Disembarking would be a problem. There wasn't room to release all the crew from stasis at once. More important, this would be Speaker's last chance to take control of the ship.

"Do you think he will obey my tasp, Louis?"

"No. I think he'll risk one more shot at stealing the ship. Tell you what we'd better do . . ."

They disconnected the instrument panel from the *Long Shot's* fusion motors. It was nothing that the kzin couldn't fix, given a little time and a touch of the mechanical intuition possessed by any toolmaker. But he would not have the time . . .

Louis watched the puppeteer move through the tube. Nessus was carrying Speaker's pressure suit. His eyes were tightly closed; which was a pity, because the view was magnificent.

"Free fall," said Teela when he opened her crash couch. "I don't feel so good. Better guide me, Louis. What's happening? Are we there?"

Louis told her a few details while he guided her to the airlock. She listened, but Louis guessed she was concentrating on the pit of her stomach. She looked acutely uncomfortable. "There'll be gravity on the other ship," he told her.

Her eyes found the tiny rosette where Louis pointed. It was a naked-eye object now, a pentagon of five white stars. She turned with astounded questions in her eyes. The motion spun her semicircular canals; and Louis saw her expression change in the moment before she bolted into the airlock.

Kemplerer rosettes were one thing. Free-fall sickness was something else again. Louis watched her recede against the unfamiliar stars.

As the couch cover opened, Louis said, "Don't do anything startling. I'm armed."

The kzin's orange face did not change expression. "Have we arrived?"

"Yah. I've disconnected the fusion drive. You'd never reconnect it in time. We're in the sights of a pair of big ruby lasers."

"Suppose I were to escape in hyperdrive? No, my mistake. We must be within a singularity."

"You're in for a shock. We're in five singularities."

"Five? Really? But you lied about the lasers, Louis. Be ashamed."

At any rate, the kzin left his couch peaceably enough. Louis followed with the variable-sword at the ready. In the airlock the kzin stopped, suddenly caught by the sight of an expanding pentagon of stars.

He could hardly have had a better view.

The *Long Shot,* edging close in hyperdrive, had stopped half a light-hour ahead of the puppeteer "fleet": something less than the average distance between Earth and Jupiter. But the "fleet" was moving at terrible speed, falling just behind its own light, so that the light which reached the *Long Shot* came from much further away. When the *Long Shot* stopped the rosette had been too small to see. It had been barely visible when Teela left the lock. Now it was impressively large, and growing at enormous speed.

Five pale blue dots in a pentagon, spreading across the sky, growing, spreading . . .

For a flashing instant there were five worlds around the *Long Shot.* Then they were gone, not fading but gone, their receding light reddened to invisibility. And Speaker-To-Animals held the variable-sword.

"Finagle's eyes!" Louis exploded. "Don't you have any curiosity at all?"

The kzin considered. "I have curiosity, but my pride is much stronger." He retracted the wire blade and handed the variable-sword back to Louis. "A threat is a challenge. Shall we go?"

The puppeteer ship was a robot. Beyond the airlock the lifesystem was all one big room. Four crash couches, as varied in design as their intended occupants, faced each other in a circle around a refreshment console.

There were no windows.

There was gravity, to Louis's relief. But it was not quite Earth's gravity; nor was the air quite Earth's air. The pressure was a touch too high. There were smells, not unpleasant but odd. Louis smelled ozone, hydrocarbons, puppeteer—dozens of puppeteers—and other smells he never expected to identify.

There were no corners. The curved wall merged into floor and ceiling; the couches and the refreshment console all looked half melted. In the puppeteer world there would be nothing hard or sharp, nothing that could draw blood or raise a bruise.

Nessus sprawled bonelessly in his couch. He looked ridiculously, ludicrously comfortable.

"He won't talk," Teela laughed.

"Of course not," said the puppeteer. "I would only have had to start over when you arrived. Doubtless you have been wondering about—"

"Flying worlds," the kzin interrupted.

"And Kemplerer rosettes," said Louis. A barely audible hum told him that the ship was moving. He and Speaker stowed their luggage and joined the others in the couches. Teela handed Louis a red, fruity drink in a squeezebulb.

"How much time have we got?" he asked the puppeteer.

"An hour until we land. Then you will be briefed on our final destination."

"That should be long enough. Okay, speak to us. Why flying worlds? Somehow it doesn't seem safe to throw habitable worlds about with such gay abandon."

"Oh, but it is, Louis!" The puppeteer was terribly earnest. "Much safer than this craft, for instance; and this craft is very safe compared to most human-designed craft. We have had much practice in the moving of worlds."

"Practice! How did that happen?"

"To explain this, I must speak of heat . . . and of population control. You will not be embarrassed or offended?"

They signified negative. Louis had the grace not to laugh; Teela laughed.

"What you must know is that population control is very difficult for us. There are only two ways for one of us to avoid becoming a parent. One is major surgery. The other is total abstinence from sexual congress."

Teela was shocked. "But that's *terrible!*"

"It is a handicap. Do not misunderstand me. Surgery is not a substitute for abstinence; it is to enforce abstinence. Today such surgery can be reversed; in the past it was impossible. Few of my species will willingly undergo such surgery."

Louis whistled. "I should think so. So your population control depends on will power?"

"Yes. Abstinence has unpleasant side effects, with us as with most species. The result has traditionally been overpopulation. Half a million years ago we were half a trillion in human numbering. In kzinti numbering—"

"My mathematics is good," said the kzin. "But these problems do not seem to relate to the unusual nature of your fleet." He was not complaining, merely commenting. From the refreshment console Speaker had procured a double-handed flagon of kzinti design and half a gallon's capacity.

"But it does relate, Speaker. Half a trillion civilized beings produce a good deal of heat as a byproduct of their civilization."

"Were you civilized so long ago?"

"Certainly. What barbarian culture would support so large a population? We had long since run out of farming land, and had been forced to terraform two worlds of our system for agriculture. For this it was necessary to move them closer to our sun. You understand?"

"Your first experience in moving worlds. You used robot ships, of course."

"Of course . . . After that, food was not a problem.

Living space was not a problem. We built high even then, and we like each other's company."

"Herd instinct, I'll bet. Is that why this ship smells like a herd of puppeteers?"

"Yes, Louis. It is reassuring to us to smell the presence of our own kind. Our sole and only problem, at the time of which I speak, was heat."

"Heat?"

"Heat is produced as a waste product of civilization."

"I fail to understand," said Speaker-To-Animals.

Louis, who as a flatlander understood perfectly, forebore to comment. (Earth was far more crowded than Kzin.)

"An example. You would wish a light source at night, would you not, Speaker? Without a light source you must sleep, whether or not you have better things to do."

"This is elementary."

"Assume that your light source is perfect, that is, it gives off radiation only in the spectra visible to kzinti. Nonetheless, all light which does not escape through the window, will be absorbed by walls and furniture. It will become randomized heat.

"Another example. Earth produces too little natural fresh water for its eighteen billions. Salt water must be distilled through fusion. This produces heat. But our world, so much more crowded, would die in a day without the distilling plants.

"A third example. Transportation involving changes in velocity always produces heat. Spacecraft filled with grain from the agricultural worlds produce heat on reentry and distribute it through our atmosphere. They produce more heat on takeoff."

"But cooling systems—"

"Most kinds of cooling systems only pump heat around, and produce more heat for power."

"U-u-urr. I begin to understand. The more puppeteers, the more heat is produced."

Do you understand, then, that the heat of our civilization was making our world uninhabitable?"

Smog, thought Louis Wu. *Internal combustion engines.*

Fission bombs and fusion rockets in the atmosphere. Industrial garbage in the lakes and oceans. It's often enough that we've half killed ourselves in our own waste products. Without the Fertility Board, would the Earth be dying now in its own waste heat?

"Incredible," said Speaker-To-Animals. "Why didn't you leave?"

"Who would trust his life to the many deaths of space? Only such a one as me. Should we settle worlds with our insane?"

"Send cargos of frozen fertilized ova. Run the ships with crews of the insane."

"Discussions of sex make me uncomfortable. Our biology is not adapted to such methods, but doubtless we could evolve something analogous . . . but to what purpose? Our population would be the same, and our world would still have been dying of its own waste heat!"

Irrelevantly, Teela said, "I wish we could see out."

The puppeteer was astounded. "Are you sure? Are you not subject to the fear of falling?"

"On a puppeteer ship?"

"Ye-es. In any case, our watching cannot increase the danger. Very well." Nessus spoke musically in his own tongue, and the ship vanished.

They could see themselves and each other; they could see four crash couches resting on emptiness, and the refreshment console in the middle. All else was black space. But five worlds glowed in white splendor behind Teela's dark hair.

They were of equal size: perhaps twice the angular diameter of the full Moon as seen from Earth. They formed a pentagram. Four of the worlds were circled by strings of tiny, glaring lights: orbital suns giving off artificial yellow-white sunlight. These four were alike in brightness and appearance: misty blue spheres, their continental outlines invisible at this distance. But the fifth . . .

The fifth world had no orbital lights. It glowed by its own light, in patches the shapes of continents and the colors of sunlight. Between the patches was a black that matched the black of surrounding space; and this black, too, was filled with stars. The black of space seemed to encroach on continents of sunlight.

"I've never seen anything so beautiful," said Teela, with tears in her voice. And Louis, who had seen many things, was inclined to agree.

"Incredible," said Speaker-To-Animals. "I hardly dared believe it. You took your worlds with you."

"Puppeteers don't trust spacecraft," Louis said absently. There was a touch of cold in the thought that he might have missed this; that the puppeteer might have chosen someone in his place. He might have died without seeing the puppeteer rosette . . .

"But how?"

"I had explained," said Nessus, "that our civilization was dying in its own waste heat. Total conversion of energy had rid us of all waste products of civilization, save that one. We had no choice but to move our world outward from its primary."

"Was that not dangerous?"

"Very. There was much madness that year. For that reason it is famous in our history. But we had purchased a reactionless, inertialess drive from the Outsiders. You may guess their price. We are still paying in installments. We had moved two agricultural worlds; we had experimented with other, useless worlds of our system, using the Outsider drive.

"In any case, we did it. We moved our world.

"In later millenia our numbers reached a full trillion. The dearth of natural sunlight had made it necessary to light our streets during the day, producing more heat. Our sun was misbehaving.

"In short, we found that a sun was a liability rather than an asset. We moved our world to a tenth of a light-year's distance, keeping the primary only as an anchor. We needed the farming worlds, and it would have been dangerous to let our world wander randomly through space. Otherwise we would not have needed a sun at all."

"So," said Louis Wu. "That's why nobody ever found the puppeteer world."

"That was part of the reason."

"We searched every yellow dwarf sun in known space, and a number outside it. Wait a minute, Nessus. Somebody would have found the farming planets. In a Kemplerer rosette."

"Louis, they were searching the wrong suns."

"What? You're obviously from a yellow dwarf."

"We evolved under a yellow dwarf star somewhat like Procyon. You may know that in half a million years Procyon will expand into the red giant stage."

"Finagle's heavy hand! Did your sun blow up into a red giant?"

"Yes. Shortly after we finished moving our world, our sun began the process of expansion. Your fathers were still using the upper thigh bone of an antelope to crack skulls. When you began to wonder where our world was, you were searching the wrong orbits about the wrong suns.

"We had brought suitable worlds from nearby systems, increasing our agricultural worlds to four, and setting them in a Kemplerer rosette. It was necessary to move them all simultaneously when the sun began to expand, and to supply them with sources of ultraviolet to compensate for the reddened radiation. You will understand that when the time came to abandon galaxy, two hundred years ago, we were well prepared. We had had practice in moving worlds."

The rosette of worlds had been expanding for some time. Now the puppeteer world glowed beneath their feet, rising, rising to engulf them. Scattered stars in the black seas had expanded, to become scores of small islands. The continents burned like sunfire.

Long ago, Louis Wu had stood at the void edge of Mount Lookitthat. The Long Fall River, on that world, ends in the tallest waterfall in known space. Louis's eyes had followed it down as far as they could penetrate the void mist. The featureless white of the void itself had grasped at his mind, and Louis Wu, half hypnotized, had sworn to live forever. How else could he see all there was to see?

Now he reaffirmed that decision. And the puppeteer world rose about him.

"I am daunted," said Speaker-To-Animals. His naked pink tail lashed in agitation, though his furry face and burry voice carried no emotion. "Your lack of courage had deserved our contempt, Nessus, but our contempt has blinded us. Truly you are dangerous. Had you feared us enough, you would have ended our line. Your power is terrible. We could not have stopped you."

"Surely a kzin cannot fear an herbivore."

Nessus had not spoken mockingly; but Speaker reacted with rage. "What sapient being would not fear such power?"

"You distress me. Fear is the brother of hate. One would expect a kzin to attack what he fears."

The conversation was getting sticky. With the *Long Shot* millions of miles in their wake, and known space hundreds of light years away, they were all very much within the power of the puppeteers. If the puppeteers found reason to fear them—

Change the subject, fast! Louis opened his mouth—

"Hey," said Teela. "You people keep talking about Kemplerer rosettes. What's a Kemplerer rosette?"

And both aliens started to answer, while Louis wondered why he had thought Teela shallow.

CHAPTER 6

Christmas Ribbon

"The joke's on me," said Louis Wu. "Now I know where to find the puppeteer world. Very nice, Nessus. You kept your promise."

"I told you that you would find the information more surprising than useful."

"A good joke," said the kzin. "Your sense of humor surprises me, Nessus."

Below, a tiny eel-shaped island surrounded by a black sea. The island rose like a fire salamander, and Louis thought he could pick out tall, slender buildings. Obviously aliens would not be trusted on the mainland.

"We do not joke," said Nessus. "My species has no sense of humor."

"Strange. I would have thought that humor was an aspect of intelligence."

"No. Humor is associated with an interrupted defense mechanism."

"All the same—"

"Speaker, no sapient being ever interrupts a defense mechanism."

As the ship dropped the lights resolved: sun-panels along street levels, windows in buildings, light sources in parklike areas. In a last instant Louis glimpsed buildings slender as rapier blades, miles tall. Then the city flashed up to engulf them, and they were down.

Down in a parkland of colorful alien plants.

Nobody moved.

Puppeteers were the second most harmless-looking sentients in known space. They were too shy, too small, too weird to seem dangerous. They were merely funny.

But suddenly Nessus was a member of his species; and his species was mightier than men had dreamed. The mad puppeteer sat quite still, his necks bobbing to observe his chosen underlings. There was nothing funny about Nessus. His race moved worlds, five at a time.

So that Teela's giggle was a shocking sound.

"I was just thinking," she explained. "The only way to keep from having too many little puppeteers is no sex at all. Right, Nessus?"

"Yes."

She giggled again. "No wonder puppeteers don't have a sense of humor."

Through a park that was too regular, too symmetrical, too well tamed, they followed a floating blue light.

The air was thick with the spicy-chemical smell of puppeteer. That smell was everywhere. It had been strong and artificial in the one-room life support system of the transfer ship. It had not diminished when the airlock opened. A trillion puppeteers had flavored the air of this world, and for all of eternity it would smell of puppeteer.

Nessus danced; his small clawed hooves seemed barely to touch the resilient surface of the walk. The kzin glided, catlike, his naked pink tail whipping rhythmically back and forth. The sound of the puppeteer's walk was a tap dance in three-four time. From the kzin came not the slightest whisper of motion.

Teela's walk was almost as silent. Her walk always looked clumsy; but it wasn't. She never stumbled, never bumped anything. Louis, then, was the least graceful of the four.

But why should Louis Wu be graceful? An altered ape, whom evolution had never entirely adapted to walking on flat ground. For millions of years his fathers had walked on all fours where they had to, had used the trees where they could.

The Pleiocene had ended that, with millions of years of drought. The forests had left Louis Wu's ancestors behind, high and dry and starving. In desperation they had eaten meat. They had done better after learning the secret of the antelope's thighbone, whose double-knobbed shoulder joint had left its mark in so many fossil skulls.

Now, on feet still equipped with vestigial fingers, Louis Wu and Teela Brown walked with aliens.

Aliens? They were all aliens here, even mad, exiled Nessus, with his brown and unkempt mane and his restless, searching heads. Speaker, too, was uneasy. His eyes, within their black spectacle markings, searched the alien vegetation for things with poison stings or razor teeth. Instinct, probably. Puppeteers would not permit dangerous beasts in their parks.

They came upon a dome that glowed like a huge, half-buried pearl. There the floating light split in two.

"I must leave you," said Nessus. And Louis saw that the puppeteer was terrified.

"I go to confront those-who-lead." He spoke low and urgently. "Speaker, tell me quickly. Should I not return, would you seek me out to slay me for the insult I delivered in Krushenko's Restaurant?"

"Is there risk that you will not return?"

"Some risk. Those-who-lead may dislike what I must tell them. I ask again, would you hunt me down?"

"Here on an alien world, amid beings of such awesome power and such lack of faith in a kzin's peaceful intent?" The kzin's tail lashed once, emphatically. "No. But neither would I continue with the expedition."

"That will be sufficient." Nessus trotted off, trembling visibly, following the guidelight.

"What's he scared of?" Teela complained. "He's done everything they told him to. Why would they be angry with him?"

"I think he's up to something," said Louis. "Something devious. But what?"

The blue light moved on. They followed it into an irridescent hemisphere . . .

Now the dome had vanished. From a triangle of couches, two humans and a kzin looked out into a tame jungle of brilliant alien plants, watching the approach of a strange puppeteer. Either the dome itself was invisible from inside, or the park scene was a projection.

The air smelled of many puppeteers.

The strange puppeteer pushed its way through a last fringe of hanging scarlet tendrils. (Louis remembered when he had thought of Nessus as "it". When had Nessus graduated to "him"? But Speaker, a familiar alien, had been "him" from the beginning.) The puppeteer stopped there, just short of the presumed boundaries of the pearly dome. Its mane was silver where Nessus's was brown, and was neatly coiffeured in complex ringlets; but its voice was Nessus's thrilling contralto.

"I must apologize for not being present to greet you. You may address me as Chiron."

A projection, then. Louis and Teela murmured polite demurrers. Speaker-To-Animals bared his teeth.

"The one you call Nessus knows all that you are about to learn. His presence was required elsewhere. However, he mentioned your reactions on learning of our engineering skills."

Louis winced. The puppeteer continued. "This may be fortunate. You will understand the better when you learn of our own reactions to a more ambitious work of engineering."

Half the dome went black.

Annoyingly, it was the side of the dome opposite to the projected puppeteer. Louis found a control to turn his couch; but he reflected that he would have needed two swiveled heads with independently operating eyes to watch both halves of the dome at once. The darkened side showed starry space forming a backdrop for a small, blazing disc.

A ringed disc. The scene was a blow-up of the holo in Louis Wu's pocket.

The light source was small and brilliant white, very like a view of Sol as seen from the general neighborhood of Jupiter. The ring was huge in diameter, wide enough to stretch half-across the darkened side of the dome; but it was narrow, not much thicker than the light source at its axis. The near side was black and, where it cut across the light, sharp-edged. Its further side was a pale blue ribbon across space.

If Louis was growing used to miracles, he was not yet so blasé as to make idiotic-sounding guesses. Instead he said, "It looks like a star with a ring around it. What is it?"

Chiron's reply came as no surprise.

"It is a star with a ring around it," said the puppeteer. "A ring of solid matter. An artifact."

Teela Brown clapped her hands and burst into giggles. She strangled the giggles after a few moments and managed to look wonderfully solemn; but her eyes glowed. Louis understood perfectly. He felt a touch of the same joy. The ringed sun was his/her private toy: a new thing in a mundane universe.

(Take Christmas ribbon, pale blue and an inch wide, the kind you use to wrap presents. Set a lighted candle on a bare floor. Take fifty feet of ribbon, and string it in a circle with the candle at the center, balancing the ribbon on edge so that the inner side catches the candle-light.)

But the kzin's tail was lashing back and forth, back and forth.

(After all, that wasn't a candle in the middle. That was a sun!)

"By now you know," said Chiron, "that we have been moving north along the galactic axis for the past two hundred and four of your Earth years. In kzin years—"

"Two hundred and seventeen."

"Yes. During that time we have naturally observed the space ahead of us for signs of danger and the unexpected. We had known that the star EC-1752 was ringed with an uncharacteristically dense and narrow band of dark matter. It was assumed that the ring was dust or rock. Yet it was surprisingly regular.

"Some ninety days ago our fleet of worlds reached a position such that the ring occluded the star itself. We saw that the ring was sharply bounded. Further investigation revealed that the ring is not gas nor dust, nor even asteroidal rock, but a solid band of considerable tensile strength. Naturally we were terrified."

Speaker-To-Animals asked, "How were you able to deduce its tensile strength?"

"Spectroanalysis and frequency shifts gave us a relative difference in velocities. The ring is clearly rotating about its primary at 770 miles per second, a velocity high enough to compensate for the pull of gravity from the primary, and to provide an additional centripetal acceleration of 9.94 meters per second. Consider the tensile strength needed to prevent the structure from disintegrating under such a pull!"

"Gravity," said Louis.

"Apparently."

"Gravity. A touch less than Earth's. There's somebody living there, on the inner surface. Hooo," said Louis Wu, for the full impact was beginning to hit him, and the little hairs were rising along his spinal column. He heard the swish, swish of the kzin's tail cutting air.

It was not the first time men had met their superiors. Thus far men had been lucky . . .

Abruptly Louis stood up and walked toward the dome wall. It didn't work. The ring and the star receded before him until he touched a smooth surface. But he saw something he hadn't noticed before.

The ring was checkered. There were regular rectangular shadows along its blue back.

"Can you give us a better picture?"

"We can expand it," said the contralto voice. The G2 star jerked forward, then shot blazing off to the right, so that Louis was looking down on the lighted inner surface of the ring. Blurred as it was, Louis could only guess that the brighter, whiter areas might be cloud, that regions of faintly deeper blue might be land where lighter blue was sea.

But the shadowed areas were quite visible. The ring seemed to be laid out in rectangles: a long strip of glowing baby blue followed by a shorter strip of deep, navy blue, followed by another long strip of light blue. Dots and dashes.

"Something's causing those shadows," he said. "Something in orbit?"

"Yes, just that. Twenty rectangular shapes orbit in a Kemplerer rosette much nearer the primary. We do not know their purpose."

"You wouldn't. It's been too long since you had a sun. These orbiting rectangles must be there to separate night from day. Otherwise it would always be high noon on the ring."

"You will understand now why we called for your help. Your alien insights were bound to be of value."

"Uh huh. How big is the ring? Have you studied it much? Have you sent probes?"

"We have studied the ring as best we could without slowing our velocity and without otherwise attracting notice to ourselves. We have sent no probes, of course. Since they would have to be remotely controlled by hyperwave, such probes might be traced back to us."

"You can't track a hyperwave signal. It's theoretically impossible."

"Perhaps those who built the ring have evolved different theories."

"Mmm."

"But we have studied the ring with other instruments." As Chiron spoke, the scene on the dome wall changed to blacks and whites and grays. Outlines shifted and wavered. "We have taken photographs and holographs in all electromagnetic frequencies. If you are interested—"

"They don't show much detail."

"No. The light is too much bent by gravitational fields and solar wind and intervening dust and gasses. Our telescopes cannot find further detail."

"So you haven't really learned much."

"I would say that we have learned a good deal. One puzzling point. The ring apparently stops on the close order of 40 percent of neutrinos."

Teela merely looked bewildered; but Speaker made a startled sound, and Louis whistled, very low.

That eliminated *everything*.

Normal matter, even the terrifically compressed matter

in the heart of a star, would stop almost no neutrinos. Any neutrino stood a fifty-fifty chance of getting through several light years' thickness of lead.

An object in a Slaver stasis field reflected *all* neutrinos. So did a General Products hull.

But nothing known would stop 40 percent of neutrinos, and let the rest through.

"Something new, then," said Louis. "Chiron, how big is this ring? How massive is it?"

"The ring masses two times ten to the thirtieth power in grams, measures .95 times ten to the eighth power miles in radius, and something less than ten to the sixth power miles across."

Louis was not comfortable thinking in abstract powers of ten. He tried to translate the numbers into pictures.

He had been right to think of inch-wide Christmas ribbon, balanced on edge and strung in a loop. The ring was more than ninety million miles in radius—about six hundred million miles long, he estimated—but less than a million miles across, edge to edge. It massed a little more than the planet Jupiter . . .

"Somehow that doesn't seem massive enough," he said. "Something that big should weigh as much as a good sized sun."

The kzin agreed. "One has the ludicrous picture of billions of beings trying to live on a construct no thicker than bookfilm."

"Your intuition is wrong," said the puppeteer with silver curls. "Consider the dimensions. If the ring were a ribbon of hullmetal, for example, it would be approximately fifty feet thick."

Fifty feet? That was hard to believe.

But Teela's eyes had been turned to the ceiling, and her lips had been moving silently but rapidly. "He's right," she said. "The math works out. But what's it *for*? Why would anyone build such a thing?"

"Room."

"Room?"

"Room to live," Louis amplified. "That's what it's all about. Six hundred trillion square miles of surface area is three million times the surface area of the Earth. It'd be like having three million worlds all mapped flat and joined edge to edge. Three million worlds within aircar distance. That'd solve *any* population problem.

"And what a problem they must have had! You don't go into a project like that one just for kicks."

"A point," said the kzin. "Chiron, have you searched neighboring stars for other, similar rings?"

"Yes, we—"

"And found none. As I thought. If the race that built the ring had known of faster-than-light travel, they would have settled other stars. They would not have needed the ring. Therefore there is only one ring."

"Yes."

"I am reassured. We are superior to the ringmakers in at least one respect." The kzin stood suddenly. "Are we to explore the habitable surface of the ring?"

"A physical landing might prove to be overambitious."

"Nonsense. We must inspect the vehicle you have prepared for us. Is its landing gear sufficiently versatile? When may we depart?"

Chiron whistled, a startled burst of discord. "You must be mad. Consider the power of those who built this ring! They make my own civilization seem savages!"

"Or cowards."

"Very well. You may go to inspect your craft when the one you call Nessus returns. For the time previous to that event, there are more data regarding the ring."

"You try my patience," said Speaker. But he sat down.

You liar, thought Louis. *You fake it well, and I'm proud of you.* His own stomach was queasy as he returned to his couch. A baby blue ribbon stretched across the stars; and man had met superior beings—again.

The kzinti had been first.

When men first used fusion drives to cross the gaps between the stars, the kzinti were already using the gravity polarizer to power their interstellar warships. It made their ships faster and more maneuverable than human ships.

Man's resistance to the kzinti fleet would have been nominal, had it not been for the Kzinti Lesson: *A reaction drive is a weapon devastating in direct proportion to its efficiency as a drive.*

Their first foray into human space had been a terrific shock to the kzinti. Human society had been peaceful for centuries, for so long that they had virtually forgotten war. But human interstellar ships used fusion-powered photon drives, launched by a combination of photon sail and asteroid-based laser cannon.

So the kzinti telepaths continued to report that the human worlds had no weapons at all . . . while giant laser cannon chopped at the kzinti ships, and smaller mobile cannon darted in and out on the light pressure of their own beams . . .

Slowed by unexpected human resistance and by the barrier of lightspeed, the war had run for decades instead of years. But the kzinti would have won eventually.

Except that an Outsider ship had stumbled across the small human colony on We Made It. They had sold the mayor the secret of the Outsider hyperdrive shunt, on credit. We Made It had not known of the kzinti war; but they learned of it fast enough when they had built a few faster-than-light ships.

Against hyperdrive the kzinti hadn't a prayer.

Later the puppeteers had come to set up trading posts in human space . . .

Man had been very lucky. Three times he had met races technologically superior to him. The kzinti would have crushed him without the Outsider hyperdrive. The Outsiders, again, were clearly his superiors; but they wanted nothing that man could give them, except supply bases and information, and these they could buy. In any case the Outsiders, fragile beings of Helium II metabolism, were too vulnerable to heat and gravity to make good warriors. And the puppeteers, powerful beyond dreams, were too cowardly.

Who had built the Ringworld? And . . . were they warriors?

Months later, Louis was to see Speaker's lie as his personal turning point. He might have backed out then—on Teela's behalf, of course. The Ringworld was terrifying enough as an abstraction in numbers. To think of approaching it in a spacecraft, of *landing* on it . . .

But Louis had seen the kzin in terror of the puppeteers' flying worlds. Speaker's lie was a magnificent act of courage. Could Louis show himself a coward now?

He sat down and turned to face the glowing projection; and as his eyes brushed Teela he silently cursed her for an idiot. Her face was alive with wonder and delight. She was as eager as the kzin pretended to be. Was she too stupid to be afraid?

There was an atmosphere on the ring's inner side. Spectroanalysis showed the air to be as thick as Earth's, and of approximately the same composition: definitely breathable to man and kzin and puppeteer. What kept it from blowing away was a thing to be guessed at. They would have to go and look.

In the system of the G2 sun there was nothing at all but the ring itself. No planets, no asteroids, no comets.

"They cleaned it out," said Louis. "They didn't want anything to hit the ring."

"Naturally," said the puppeteer with silver curls. "If something did strike the ring, it would strike at a minimum of 770 miles per second, the speed of rotation of the ring itself. No matter how strong the material of the ring, there would always be the danger of an object missing the outer surface and crossing the sun to strike the unprotected, inhabited inner surface."

The sun itself was a yellow dwarf somewhat cooler than Sol and a touch smaller. "We will need heat suits on the ring," said the kzin—rubbing it in, Louis thought.

"No," said Chiron. "The temperature of the inner surface is quite tolerable, to all of our species."

"How would you know that?"

"The frequency of the infrared radiation emitted by the outer surface—"

"You see me exposed as a fool."

"Not at all. We have been studying the ring since its discovery, while you have had a few eights of minutes.

The infrared frequency indicates an average temperature of 290 degrees Absolute, which of course applies to the inner as well as the outer surface of the ring. For you this will be some ten degrees warmer than optimum, Speaker-To-Animals. For Louis and Teela it is optimum.

"Do not let our attention to details mislead or frighten you," Chiron added. "We would not permit a landing unless the ring engineers themselves insisted. We merely wish you to be ready for any eventuality."

"You don't have any detail of surface formations?"

"Unfortunately, no. The resolving power of our instruments is insufficient."

"We can do some guessing," said Teela. "The thirty hour day-night cycle, for instance. Their original world must have turned that fast. Do you suppose that's their original system?"

"We assume that it is, since they apparently did not have hyperdrive," said Chiron. "But presumably they could have moved their world to another system, using our own techniques."

"And should have," the kzin rumbled, "rather than destroy their own system in the course of building their ring. I think we will find their own system somewhere nearby, as denuded of worlds as this one. They would have used terraforming techniques to settle all of the worlds of their own system, before adapting this more desperate expedient."

Teela said, "Desperate?"

"Then, when they had finished building their ring around the sun, they would have been forced to move all their worlds into this system to transfer their populations."

"Maybe not," said Louis. "They might have used big STL ships to settle their ring if it was close enough to their own system."

"Why desperate?"

They looked at her.

"I would have thought they built the ring for—for—" Teela floundered. "Because they wanted to."

"For kicks? For scenery? Finagle's fist! Teela, think of

the resources they'd have had to divert. Remember, they must have had a hell of a population problem. By the time they needed the ring for living room, they probably couldn't afford to build it. They built it anyway, because they needed it."

"Mmm," said Teela, looking puzzled.

"Nessus returns," said Chiron. Without another word the puppeteer turned and trotted away into the park.

CHAPTER 7

Stepping Discs

"That was rude," said Teela.

"Chiron doesn't want to meet Nessus. Didn't I tell you? They think Nessus is crazy."

"They're all crazy."

"Well, they don't think so, but that doesn't make you wrong. Still want to go?"

Teela's answer was the same uncomprehending look she'd given him when he tried to explain *whiplash of the heart*. "You still want to go," Louis confirmed sadly.

"Sure. Who wouldn't? What are the puppeteers afraid of?"

"I understand that," said Speaker-To-Animals. "The puppeteers are cowards. But I fail to see why they insist on knowing more than they do. Louis, they have already passed the ringed sun, traveling at nearly lightspeed. Those who built the ring assuredly did not have faster-than-light travel. Thus they can be no danger to the puppeteers, now or ever. I fail to understand our role in this matter."

"It figures."

"Must I take that as an insult?"

"No, of course not. It's just that we keep running up against population problems. Why should you understand?"

"Quite so. Explain, if you please."

Louis had been scanning the tame jungle for a glimpse of Nessus. "Nessus could probably tell this better. Too bad. Okay, imagine a trillion puppeteers on this world. Can you do it?"

"I can smell them individually. The very concept makes me itch."

"Now imagine them on the Ringworld. Better, yes?"

"Uurr. Yes. With more than eight-to-the-seventh-power times as much room . . . But still I fail to understand. Do you suppose the puppeteers plan conquest? But how would they transfer themselves to the ring afterward? They do not trust spacecraft."

"I don't know. They don't make war, either. That's not the point. The point is, is the Ringworld safe to live on?"

"Uurr."

"You see? Maybe they're thinking of building their own Ringworlds. Maybe they expect to find an empty one, out there in the Clouds of Magellan. Not an unreasonable hope, by the way. But it doesn't matter. They have to know if it's safe before they do *anything*."

"Here comes Nessus." Teela stood up and moved to the invisible wall. "He looks drunk. Do puppeteers get drunk?"

Nessus wasn't trotting. He came tippy-toe, circling a four-foot chrome-yellow feather with exaggerated wariness, moving one foot at a time, while his flat heads darted this way and that. He had almost reached the lecture dome when something like a large black butterfly settled on his rump. Nessus screamed like a woman, leapt forward as if clearing a high fence. He landed rolling. When he stopped rolling he remained curled into a ball, with his back arched and his legs folded and his heads and necks tucked between his forelegs.

Louis was running. "Depressive cycle," he shouted over his shoulder. By luck and memory he found the entrance in the invisible dome. He darted out into the park.

All the flowers smelled like puppeteer. (If all the life of the puppeteer world had the same chemical basis, how could Nessus take nourishment from warm carrot juice?) Louis followed a right-angle zigzag of manicured dusty orange hedge and came upon the puppeteer.

He knelt beside him. "It's Louis," he said. "You're safe." He reached gently into the tangled mop over the puppeteer's skull and scratched gently. The puppeteer jerked at the touch, then settled down.

This was a bad one. No need to make the puppeteer face the world just yet. Louis asked, "Was that thing dangerous? The one that landed on you."

"That? No." The contralto voice was muffled, but beautifully pure, and without inflection. "It was only a . . . flower-sniffer."

"How did it go with those-who-lead?"

Nessus winced. "I won."

"Fine. What did you win?"

"My right to breed, and a set of mates."

"Is that what has you so scared?" It wasn't unlikely, Louis thought. Nessus could be the counterpart to a male black widow spider, doomed by love. Then again, he might be a nervous virgin . . . of either sex, or of any sex . . .

The puppeteer said, "I might have failed, Louis. I faced them down. I bluffed them."

"Go on." Louis was aware that Teela and Speaker-To-Animals had joined them. He continued scratching gently in Nessus's mane. Nessus had not moved.

The muffled, inflectionless contralto voice said, "Those-who-lead offered me the legal right to reproduce my kind if I survive the voyage we must make. But this was not enough. To become a parent I need mates. Who will willingly mate with a straggly-maned maniac?

"It was necessary to bluff. Find me a mate, I told them, or I will withdraw from the voyage. If I withdraw, so will the kzin, I said. They were enraged."

"I can believe that. You must have been in the manic state."

"I worked myself up to it. I threatened them with ruin to their plans, and they capitulated. Some selfless volunteer, I said, must agree to mate with me if I return from the ring."

"Beautiful. Nice going. Did you get volunteers?"

"One of our sexes is . . . property. Nonsentient; stupid. I needed only one volunteer. Those-who-lead——"

Teela broke in. "Why don't you just say *leaders?*"

"I had tried to translate into your terms," said the puppeteer. "A more accurate translation of the term would be, *those-who-lead-from-behind.* There is a selected chairman or speaker-for-all or . . . the accurate translation of his title is *Hindmost.*

"It was the Hindmost who accepted me as his mate. He said that he would not ask another to so sacrifice his self-respect."

Louis whistled. "That's something. Go ahead and cringe, you deserve it. Better to be scared now, now that it's all over."

Nessus stirred, relaxing somewhat.

"That pronoun," said Louis. "It bugs me. Either I should be calling you *she,* or I should be calling the Hindmost *she.*"

"This is indelicate of you, Louis. One does not discuss sex with an alien race." A head emerged from between Nessus's legs and focused, disapproving. "You and Teela would not mate in my sight, would you?"

"Oddly enough, the subject did come up once, and Teela said——"

"I am offended," the puppeteer stated.

"Why?" asked Teela. The puppeteer's exposed head dived for cover. "Oh, come out of there! I won't hurt you."

"Truly?"

"Truly. I mean honest. I think you're cute."

The puppeteer unrolled completely. "Did I hear you call me cute?"

"Yah." She looked up at the orange wall of Speaker-To-Animals and, "You too," she said generously.

"I do not mean to give offense," said the kzin. "But do not ever say that again. Ever."

Teela looked puzzled.

There was a dusty orange hedge, ten feet tall and perfectly straight, equipped with cobalt blue tentacles that hung limp. From the look of them, the hedge had once been carnivorous. It was the border to the park; and Nessus led his little group toward it.

Louis was expecting a gap in the hedge. He was unprepared when Nessus walked straight into it. The hedge parted for the puppeteer and closed after him.

They followed.

They walked out from under a sky-blue sky; but when the hedge had closed after them, the sky was black and white. Against the black sky of perpetual night, drifting clouds blazed white in the light cast upon their underbellies by miles of city. For the city was there, looming over them.

At first glance it differed from Earthly cities only in degree. The buildings were thicker, blockier, more uniform; and they were higher, terribly high, so that the sky was all lighted windows and lighted balconies with straight hairline cracks of darkness marking the zenith. Here were the right angles denied to puppeteer furniture; here on the buildings, where a right angle was far too big to bash a careless knee.

But why had the city not loomed similarly over the park? On Earth there were few buildings more than a mile high. Here, none were less. Louis guessed at light-bending fields around the park's borders. He never got around to asking. It was the least of the miracles of the puppeteer world.

"Our vehicle is at the other end of the island," said Nessus. "We can be there in a minute or less, using the stepping discs. I will show you."

"You feel all right now?"

"Yes, Teela. As Louis says, the worst is over." The puppeteer pranced lightly ahead of them. "The Hindmost is my love. I need only return from the Ringworld."

The path was soft. To the eye it was concrete set with iridescent particles, but to the feet it was damp, spongy soil. Presently, after walking a very long block, they came to an intersection. "We must go this way," said Nessus, nodding ahead of him. "Do not step on the first disc. Follow me."

At the center of the intersection was a large blue rectangle. Four blue discs surrounded the rectangle, one at the mouth of each walk. "You may step on the rectangle if you wish," said Nessus, "but not on inappropriate discs. Follow me." He circled the nearest disc, crossed the intersection, trotted onto the disc on the opposite side, and vanished.

For a stunned moment nobody moved. Then Teela yelled like a banshee and ran at the disc. And was gone.

Speaker-To-Animals snarled and leapt. No tiger could have aimed as accurately. Then Louis was alone.

"By the Mist Demons," he said wonderingly. "They've got open transfer booths."

And he walked forward.

He was standing on a square at the center of the next intersection, between Nessus and Speaker. "Your mate ran ahead," said Nessus. "I hope she will wait for us."

The puppeteer walked off the rectangle in the direction he was facing. Three paces brought him to a disc. And he was gone.

"What a layout!" Louis said admiringly. He was alone, for the kzin had already followed Nessus. "You just walk. That's all. Three paces takes you a block. It's like magic. And you can make the blocks as long as you like!" He strode forward.

He wore seven league boots. He ran lightly on his toes, and the scene jumped every three paces. The circular signs on the corners of buildings must be address codes, so that once a pedestrian reached his destination he would know it. Then he would circle the discs to get to the middle of the block.

Along the street were shop windows Louis would have liked to explore. Or were they something else entirely? But the others were blocks ahead. Louis could see them flickering at the end of that canyon of buildings. He increased his pace.

At the end of a footstep the aliens were before him, blocking his path.

"I feared you would miss the turn," said Nessus. And he led off to the left.

"Wait—" But the kzin had vanished too. Where the blazes was Teela?

She must have gone ahead. Louis turned left and walked—

Seven league boots. The city went by like a dream. Louis ran with visions of sugarplums dancing in his head. Freeway paths through the cities, the discs marked in a different color, ten blocks apart. Long-distance discs a hundred miles apart, each marking the center of a city, the receiver squares a full block across. Paths to cross oceans: one step to an island! Islands for stepping stones!

Open transfer booths. The puppeteers were fearfully advanced. The disc was only a yard across, and you didn't have to be entirely on it before it would operate. One footstep and you were stepping off the next receiver square. It beat the tanj out of slidewalks!

As he ran, Louis's mind conjured up a phantom puppeteer hundreds of miles tall, picking his way delicately along a chain of islands; stepping with care lest he miss an island and get his ankles wet. Now the phantom puppeteer grew larger, and his stepping stones were worlds ... the puppeteers were fearfully advanced ...

He was out of stepping discs, at the shore of a calm black sea. Beyond the edge of the world, four fat full moons rose in a vertical line against the stars. Halfway to the horizon was a smaller island, brilliantly lighted. The aliens were waiting for him.

"Where's Teela?"

"I do not know," said Nessus.

"Mist Demons! Nessus, how do we find her?"

"She must find us. There is no need to worry, Louis When—"

"She's lost on a strange world! Anything could happen!"

"Not on this world, Louis. There is no world as safe as ours. When Teela reaches the edge of this island, she will find that the stepping discs to the next islands will not work for her. She will follow the discs around the shoreline until she finds one that does work."

"Do you think it's a lost computer we're talking about? Teela's a twenty-year-old girl!"

Teela popped into place beside him. "Hi. I got a little lost. What's all the excitement?"

Speaker-To-Animals mocked him with a dagger-toothed grin. Louis, avoiding Teela's puzzled/questioning eyes, felt heat rising in his cheeks. But Nessus said only, "Follow me."

They followed the puppeteer where stepping discs formed a line along the shore. Presently there was a dirty brown pentagram. They stepped onto it . . .

They stood on bare rock, brilliantly lit by sun tubes. An island of rock the size of a private spaceport. In its center stood one tall building and a single spacecraft.

"Behold our vehicle," said Nessus.

Teela and Speaker showed disappointment; for the kzin's ears disappeared into their flaps, while Teela looked wistfully back toward the island they had just left, toward a wall of light formed by miles-high buildings standing shoulder to shoulder against interstellar night. But Louis looked, and he felt the relief loosening overtight muscles. He had had enough of miracles. The stepping discs, the tremendous city, the four tributary worlds hanging, pumpkin-colored, above the horizon . . . all were daunting. The ship was not. It was a General Products #2 hull fitted into a triangular wing, the wing studded with thruster units and fusion motors. Familiar hardware, all of it, and no questions asked.

The kzin proved him wrong. "This seems an odd design from the viewpoint of a puppeteer engineer. Nessus, would you not feel safer if the ship were entirely within the hull?"

"I would not. This ship represents a major innovation in design. Come, I will show you." Nessus trotted toward the ship.

The kzin had raised a good point.

General Products, the puppeteer-owned trading company, had sold many diversified wares in known space; but its fortunes had been founded on the General Products

hull. There had been four varieties, from a globe the size
of a basketball to another globe more than a thousand
feet in diameter: the #4 hull, the hull of the *Long Shot*.
The #3 hull, a round-ended cylinder with a flattened
belly, made a good multicrewed passenger ship. Such a
ship had landed them on the puppeteer world a few hours
ago. The #2 hull was a wasp-waisted cylinder, narrow
and needle-tapered at both ends. Ordinarily it was just
roomy enough for one pilot.

The General Products hull was transparent to visible
light. To all other forms of electromagnetic energy, and
to matter in any form, it was impervious. The company's
reputation backed that guarantee, and the guarantee had
held for hundreds of years and for millions of ships. A
General Products hull was the ultimate in safety.

The vehicle before them was based on a General Products #2 hull.

But . . . as far as Louis could see, only the life-support
system and the hyperdrive shunt were within the hull.
Everything else—a pair of flat thruster units aimed downward, two small fusion motors facing forward, larger
fusion motors on the wing's trailing edges, and a pair of
tremendous pods on the wingtips—pods which must con-
tain detection and communications equipment, since
Louis could find no such equipment anywhere else—all
this was on the great delta wing!

Half the ship was on the wing, exposed to any danger
that could worry a puppeteer. Why not use a #3 hull and
put everything inside?

The puppeteer had led them beneath the delta wing,
to the tapered stern of the hull section. "Our purpose was
to make as few breaks in the hull as possible," said
Nessus. "You see?"

Through the glasslike hull Louis saw a conduit as thick
as his thigh leading through the hull into the wing section.
Things looked complex at that point, until Louis tumbled
to the fact that the conduit was designed to slide back into
the hull in one section. Then he picked out the motor that
did it all, and the metal door that would seal off the
opening.

"An ordinary ship," said the puppeteer, "requires many breaks in its hull: for sensors which do not use visible light, for reaction motors if such are used, for apertures leading to fuel tanks. Here we have only two breaks, the conduit and the airlock. One passes passengers and the other passes information. Both can be closed off.

"Our engineers have coated the hull's inner surface with a transparent conductor. When the airlock is closed and the aperture for the wiring conduit is sealed, the interior is an unbroken conducting surface."

"Stasis field," Louis guessed.

"Exactly. If danger threatens, the entire life-support system goes into Slaver-type stasis for a period of several seconds. No time passes in stasis; hence nothing can harm the passengers. We are not so foolish as to trust to the hull alone. Lasers using visible light can penetrate a General Products hull, killing passengers and leaving the ship unharmed. Antimatter can disintegrate a General Products hull entirely."

"I didn't know that."

"It is not widely advertised."

Louis moved back under the delta wing to where Speaker-To-Animals was inspecting the motors. "Why so many motors?"

The kzin snorted. "Surely a human cannot have forgotten the Kzinti Lesson."

"Oh." Naturally any puppeteer who had studied kzinti or human history would know the Kzinti Lesson. A reaction drive is a weapon, powerful in direct ratio to its efficiency. Here were thrusters for peaceful use, and fusion drives for weapons capability.

"Now I know how you learned to handle fusion-drive craft."

"Naturally I have been trained in war, Louis."

"Just in case of another Man–Kzin war."

"Must I demonstrate my skill as a warrior, Louis?"

"You shall," the puppeteer interrupted. "Our engineers intended that this ship be flown by a kzin. Would you care to inspect the controls, Speaker?"

"Shortly. I will also need performance data, test flight

records, and so forth. Is the hyperdrive shunt of standard type?"

"Yes. There have been no test flights."

Typical, Louis thought as they walked toward the airlock. They just built the thing and left it here to wait for us. They had to. No puppeteer was willing to test-fly it.

Where was Teela?

He was about to call out when she reappeared on the pentagramic receiver plate. She had been playing with the stepping-discs again, ignoring the ship entirely. She followed them aboard, still looking wistfully back toward the puppeteer city beyond the black water.

Louis waited for her at the inner airlock door. He was ready to blast her for her carelessness. You'd think that after getting lost once she might learn a little caution!

The door opened. Teela was radiant. "Oh, Louis, I'm *so* glad I came! That city—it's such *fun!*" She grasped his hands and squeezed, beaming inarticulately. Her smile was like sunlight.

He couldn't do it. "It's been fun," he said, and kissed her hard. He moved toward the control room with his arm around Teela's slim waist, his thumb tracing the rim of her hip.

He was sure now. Teela Brown had never been hurt; had never learned caution; did not understand fear. Her first pain would come as a horrifying surprise. It might destroy her entirely.

She'd be hurt over Louis Wu's dead body.

The gods do not protect fools. Fools are protected by more capable fools.

A General Products #2 hull is twenty feet wide and three hundred feet long, tapering to points fore and aft.

Most of the ship was outside the hull, on the thin, oversized wing. The lifesystem was roomy enough to include three living-bedrooms, a long, narrow lounge, a control cabin, and a bank of lockers, plus kitchen, autodocs, reclaimers, batteries, etc. The control panel was fitted out according to kzinti custom, and was labeled in kzinti. Louis felt he could fly the ship in an emergency, but it would have taken a big emergency to make him try it.

The lockers held an ominous plethora of exploration gear. There was nothing Louis could have pointed to, saying, "That's a weapon." But there were things which could be used as weapons. There were also four fly-cycles, four flying backpacks (lift belt plus catalytic ram-jet), food testers, phials of dietary additives, medkits, air sensors and filters. Someone was sure as tanj convinced that this ship would be landing somewhere.

Well, why not? A species as powerful as the Ring-worlders, and as sealed in by their presumed lack of hyperdrive craft, might invite them to land. Perhaps this was what the puppeteers were expecting.

There was nothing aboard that Nessus could not point to and say, "That is not a weapon. That we took aboard for such-and-such a purpose."

There were three species aboard; four, if one thought of male and female human as of different species, which was something a kzin or a puppeteer might well do. (Suppose Nessus and the Hindmost were of the same sex? Why shouldn't it take two males and a nonsentient female to produce a baby?) Then the presumed Ringworlders could see at a glance that many kinds of sentient life could deal amicably with each other.

Yet too many of these items—the flashlight-lasers, the dueling stunners—could be used as weapons.

They took off on reactionless thrusters, to avoid damaging the island. Half an hour later they had left the feeble gravity wells of the puppeteer rosette. It occurred to Louis then that aside from Nessus, whom they had brought with them, and aside from the projected image of the puppeteer Chiron, they had seen not a single puppeteer on the puppeteer world.

After they had entered hyperdrive, Louis spent an hour-and-a-half inspecting every item in the lockers. Better safe than surprised, he told himself. But the weaponry and the other equipment left a bitter aftertaste, a fore-boding.

Too many weapons, and not one weapon that could

not be used for something else. Flashlight-lasers. Fusion reaction motors. When they held a christening ceremony on the first day in hyperdrive, Louis suggested that the ship be called *Lying Bastard*. For their own reasons, Teela and Speaker agreed. For his own reason, Nessus did not object.

They were in hyperdrive for a week, covering a little more than two light years. When they dropped back into Einsteinian space they were within the system of the ringed G2 star; and the foreboding was still with Louis Wu.

Someone was sure as tanj convinced that they would land on the Ringworld.

CHAPTER 8

Ringworld

The puppeteer worlds had been moving at nearly light-speed along galactic north. Speaker had circled in hyper-space to galactic south of the G2 sun, with the result that the *Liar,* as it fell out of the Blind Spot, was already driving straight into the Ringworld system at high velocity.

The G2 star was a blazing white point. Louis, returning from other stars, had seen Sol looking very like this from the edge of the solar system. But this star wore a barely visible halo. Louis would remember this, his first sight of the Ringworld. From the edge of the system, the Ringworld was a naked-eye object.

Speaker ran the big fusion motors up to full power. He tilted the flat thruster discs out of the plane of the wing, lining their axes along ship's aft, and added their thrust to the rockets. The *Liar* backed into the system blazing like twin suns, decelerating at nearly two hundred gravities.

Teela didn't know that, because Louis didn't tell her. He didn't want to worry her. If the cabin gravity were interrupted for an instant—they'd all be flattened like bugs beneath a heel.

But the cabin gravity worked with unobtrusive perfection. Throughout the lifesystem there was only the gentle pull of the puppeteer world, and the steady, muted tremor of the fusion motors. For the rumble of the drives forced its way through the only available opening, through a wiring conduit no thicker than a man's thigh; and once inside, it was everywhere.

Even in hyperdrive, Speaker preferred to fly in a transparent ship. He liked a good field of view, and the Blind Spot didn't seem to affect his mind. The ship was still transparent, except for private cabins, and the resulting view took getting used to.

The lounge and the control cabin, wall and floor and ceiling, all of which curved into one another, were not so much transparent as invisible. In the apparent emptiness were blocks of solidity: Speaker in the control couch, the horseshoe-shaped bank of green and orange dials which surrounded him, the neon-glowing borders of doorways, the cluster of couches around the lounge table, the block of opaque cabins aft; and, of course, the flat triangle of the wing. Beyond and around these were the stars. The universe seemed very close . . . and somewhat static; for the ringed star was directly aft, hidden behind the cabins, and they could not watch it grow.

The air smelled of ozone and puppeteers.

Nessus, who should have been cowering in terror with the rumble of two hundred gravities in his ears, seemed perfectly comfortable sitting with the others around the lounge table.

"They will not have hyperwave," he was saying. "The mathematics of the system guarantees it. Hyperwave is a generalization of hyperdrive mathematics, and they cannot have hyperdrive."

"But they might have discovered hyperwave by accident."

"No, Teela. We can try the hyperwave bands, since there is nothing else to try while we are decelerating, but—"

"More tanj waiting!" Teela stood up suddenly and half-ran from the lounge.

Louis answered the puppeteer's questioning look with an angry shrug.

Teela was in a foul mood. The week in hyperdrive had bored her stiff, and the prospect of another day-and-a-half of deceleration, of continued inaction, had her ready to climb walls. But what did she expect from Louis? Could he change the laws of physics?

"We must wait," Speaker agreed. He spoke from the control cabin, and he may have missed the emotional overtones of Teela's last words. "The hyperwave zaps are clear of signals. I will guarantee that the Ringworld engineers are not trying to speak to us by any known form of hyperwave."

The subject of communications had become general. Until they could reach the Ringworld engineers, their presence in this inhabited system smacked of banditry. Thus far there had been no sign that their presence had been detected.

"My receivers are open," said Speaker. "If they attempt to communicate in electromagnetic frequencies, we will know it."

"Not if they try the obvious," Louis retorted.

"True. Many species have used the cold hydrogen line to search for other minds circling other stars."

"Like the kdatlyno. They cleverly found you."

"And we cleverly enslaved them."

Interstellar radio is noisy with the sound of the stars. But the twenty-one centimeter band is conveniently silent, swept clean for use by endless cubic light years of cold interstellar hydrogen. It was the line any species would pick to communicate with an alien race. Unfortunately the nova-hot hydrogen in the *Liar's* exhaust was making that band useless.

"Remember," said Nessus, "that our projected freely falling orbit must not cross the ring itself."

"You have said so too many times, Nessus. My memory is excellent."

"We must not appear a danger to the inhabitants of the ring. I trust you will not forget."

"You are a puppeteer. You trust nothing," said Speaker.

"Cool it," Louis said wearily. The bickering was an annoyance he didn't need. He went to his cabin to sleep.

Hours passed. The *Liar* fell toward the ringed star, slowing, preceded by twin spears of nova light and nova heat.

Speaker found no sign of coherent light impinging on the ship. Either the Ringworlders hadn't noticed the *Liar* yet, or they didn't have com lasers.

During the week in hyperspace, Speaker had shared hours of leisure with the humans. Louis and Teela had developed a taste for the kzin's cabin: for the slightly higher gravity and the holoscapes of orange-yellow jungle and ancient alien fortress, for the sharp and changing smells of an alien world. Their own cabin was unimaginatively decorated, with cityscapes and with farming seas half-covered with genetically tailored seaweeds. The kzin liked their cabin better than they did.

They had even tried sharing a meal in the kzin's cabin. But the kzin ate like a starved wolf, and he complained that the man's-food smelled like burnt garbage, and that was that.

Now Teela and Speaker talked in low tones at one end of the lounge table. Louis listened to the silence and the distant thunder of the fusion drives.

He was used to depending for his life on a cabin gravity system. His own yacht would do thirty gee. But his own yacht used thrusters, and thrusters were silent.

"Nessus," he said into the drone of suns burning.

"Yes, Louis?"

"What do you know about the Blind Spot that we don't?"

"I do not understand the question."

"Hyperspace terrifies you. This—this backing through space on a pillar of fire—doesn't. Your species built the *Long Shot;* they must know something about hyperspace that we don't."

"Perhaps so. Perhaps we do know something."

"What? Unless it's one of your precious secrets."

Speaker and Teela were listening now. Speaker's ears, which, folded, could vanish into depressions in his fur, were spread like translucent pink parasols.

"We know that we have no undying part," said Nessus.

"I will not speak for your race. I have not the right. My species has no immortal part. Our scientists have proved this. We are afraid to die, for we know that death is permanent."

"And?"

"Ships disappear in the Blind Spot. No puppeteer would go too near a singularity in hyperdrive; yet still they disappeared, in the days when our ships carried pilots. I trust the engineers who built the *Liar*. Hence I trust the cabin gravity. It will not fail us. But even the engineers fear the Blind Spot."

There was a ship's night, during which Louis slept poorly and dreamed spectacularly, and a ship's day, during which Teela and Louis found each other impossible to live with. She was not frightened. Louis suspected he would never see her frightened. She was merely bored stiff.

That evening, in the space of half an hour, the ringed star came out from behind the sternward block of living-sleeping cabins. The star was small and white, a shade less intense than Sol, and it nestled in a shallow pencil-line of arc blue.

They stood looking over Speaker's shoulder as Speaker activated the scope screen. He found the arc-blue line of the Ringworld's inner surface, touched the expansion button—

One question answered itself amost immediately.

"Something at the edge," said Louis.

"Keep the scope centered on the rim," Nessus ordered.

The rim of the ring expanded in their view. It was a wall, rising inward toward the star. They could see its black, space-exposed outer side silhouetted against the sunlit blue landscape. A low rim wall, but low only in comparison to the ring itself.

"If the ring is a million miles across," Louis estimated, "The rim wall must be at least a thousand miles high. Well, now we know. That's what holds the air in."

"Would it work?"

"It should. The ring's spinning for about a gravity. A

little air might leak over the edges over the thousands of years, but they could replace it. To build the ring at all, they must have had cheap transmutation—a few tenth-stars per kiloton—not to mention a dozen other impossibilities."

"I wonder what it looks like from the inside."

Speaker heard, and he touched a control point, and the view slid. The magnification was not yet great enough to pick up details. Bright blue and brighter white slid across the scope screen, and the blurred straight edge of a navy blue shadow . . .

The further rim slid into view. Here the rim wall was tilted outward.

Nessus, standing in the doorway with his heads poised above Speaker's shoulders, ordered, "Give us what magnification you can."

The view expanded.

"Mountains," said Teela. "How lovely." For the rim wall was irregular, sculptured like eroded rock, and was the color of the Moon. "Mountains a thousand miles high."

"I can expand the view no further. For greater detail we must approach closer."

"Let us first attempt to contact them," said the puppeteer. "Are we at rest?"

Speaker consulted the ship's brain. "We are approaching the primary at perhaps thirty miles per second. Is that slow enough?"

"Yes. Begin transmissions."

No laser light was falling on the *Liar*.

Testing for electromagnetic radiation was more difficult. Radio, infrared, ultraviolet, X-rays—the whole spectrum had to be investigated, from the room-temperature heat given off by the dark side of the Ringworld, up to light quanta energetic enough to split into matter-antimatter pairs. The twenty-one centimeter band was empty; and so were its easy multiples and divisors, which might have been used merely because the hydrogen absorption band *was* so obvious. Beyond that point Speaker-To-Animals was playing blind man's bluff with his receivers.

The great pods of communications equipment on the *Liar*'s wing had opened. The *Liar* was sending radio messages on the hydrogen absorption frequency and others, bathing successive portions of the ring's inner surface with laser light of ten different frequencies, and sending Interworld-Morse in alternate blasts of the fusion motors.

"Our autopilot would eventually translate any possible message, " said Nessus. "We must assume that their ground-based computers are at least as capable."

Speaker's reply was venomous. "Can your leucotomized computers translate total silence?"

"Concentrate your sendings at the rim. If they have spaceports, the spaceports must be at the rim. To land a spacecraft anywhere else would be horribly dangerous."

In the Hero's Tongue Speaker-To-Animals snarled something horribly insulting. Effectively it ended the conversation; but Nessus stayed where he had been for hours now, with his heads poised alertly above the kzin's shoulders.

The Ringworld waited beyond the hull, a checkered blue ribbon trailing across the sky.

"You tried to tell me about Dyson spheres," said Teela.

"And you told me to go pick lice out of my hair." Louis had found a description of Dyson spheres in the ship's library. Excited by the idea, he had made the mistake of interrupting Teela's game of solitaire to tell her about it.

"Tell me now," she coaxed.

"Go pick lice out of your hair."

She waited.

"You win," said Louis. For the past hour he had been staring broodingly out at the ring. He was as bored as she was.

"I tried to tell you that the Ringworld is a compromise, an engineering compromise between a Dyson sphere and a normal planet.

"Dyson was one of the ancient natural philosophers, pre-Belt, almost pre-atomic. He pointed out that a civilization is limited by the energy available to it. The way for the human race to use all the energy within its reach, he said, is to build a spherical shell around the sun and trap every ray of sunlight.

"Now if you'll quit giggling for just a minute, you'll see the idea. The Earth traps only about half a billionth of the sun's output. If we could use *all* that energy . . .

"Well, it wasn't crazy then. There wasn't even a theoretical basis for faster-than-light travel. We never did invent hyperdrive, if you'll recall. We'd never have discovered it by accident, either, because we'd never have thought to do our experiments out beyond the singularity.

"Suppose an Outsider ship hadn't stumbled across a United Nations ramrobot? Suppose the Fertility Laws hadn't worked out? With a trillion human beings standing on each other's shoulders, and the ramships the fastest thing around, how long could we get along on fusion power? We'd use up all the hydrogen in Earth's oceans in a hundred years.

"But there's more to a Dyson sphere than collecting solar power.

"Say you make the sphere one astronomical unit in radius. You've got to clear out the solar system anyway, so you use all the solar planets in the construction. That gives you a shell of, say, chrome steel a few yards thick. Now you put gravity generators all over the shell. You'd have a surface area a billion times as big as the Earth's surface. A trillion people could wander all their lives without ever meeting one another."

Teela finally got a full sentence in edgewise. "You're using the gravity generators to hold everything down?"

"Yah, against the inside. We cover the inside with soil—"

"What if one of the gravity generators broke down?"

"Picky, picky, picky. Well . . . you'd get a billion people drifting up into the sun. All the air swarming up after them. A tornado big enough to swallow the Earth. Not a prayer of getting a repair crew in, not through that kind of a storm . . ."

"I don't like it," Teela said decisively.

"Let's not be hasty. There may be ways to make a gravity generator foolproof."

"Not that. You couldn't see the stars."

Louis hadn't thought of that aspect. "Never mind. The point about Dyson spheres is that any sentient, industrial race is eventually going to need one. Technological civilizations tend to use more and more power as time goes on. The ring is a compromise between a normal planet and a Dyson sphere. With the ring you get only a fraction of the available room, and you block only a fraction of the available sunlight; but you can see the stars, and you don't have to worry about gravity generators."

From the control room Speaker-to-Animals snarled something complicated, a sound powerful enough to curse the very air of the cabin. Teela giggled.

"If the puppeteers have been thinking along the same lines as Dyson," Louis continued, "they might very well expect to find the Clouds of Magellan riddled with Ringworlds, edge to edge."

"And that's why we were called in."

"I'd hate to bet on a puppeteer's thoughts. But if I had to, that's the way I'd bet."

"No wonder you've been spending all your time in the library."

"Infuriating!" screamed the kzin. "Insulting! They deliberately ignore us! They pointedly turn their backs to invite attack!"

"Improbable," said Nessus. "If you cannot find radio transmissions, then they do not use radio. Even if they were routinely using radio lasers, we would detect some leakage."

"They do not use lasers, they do not use radio, they do not use hyperwave. What are they using for communication? Telepathy? Written messages? Big mirrors?"

"Parrots," Louis suggested. He got up to join them at the door to the control room. "Huge parrots, specially bred for their oversized lungs. They're too big to fly. They just sit on hilltops and scream at each other."

Speaker turned to look Louis in the eye. "For four hours I have tried to contact the Ringworld. For four hours the inhabitants have ignored me. Their contempt has been absolute. Not a word have they vouchsafed me.

My muscles are trembling for lack of exercise, my fur is matted, my eyes refuse to focus, my sthondat-begotten *room* is too small, my microwave heater heats all meat to the same temperature, and it is the wrong temperature, and I cannot get it fixed. Were it not for your help and your suggestions, Louis, I would despair."

"Can they have lost their civilization?" Nessus mused. "It would be silly of them, considering."

"Perhaps they are dead," Speaker said viciously. "That too would be silly. Not to contact us has been silly. Let us land and find out."

Nessus whistled in panic. "Land on a world which may have killed its indigenous species? Are you mad?"

"How else can we learn?"

"Of course!" Teela chimed in. "We didn't come all this way just to fly in circles!"

"I forbid it. Speaker, continue your attempts to contact the Ringworld."

"I have ended such attempts."

"Repeat them."

"I will not."

In stepped Louis Wu, volunteer diplomat. "Cool it, furry buddy. Nessus, he's right. The Ringworlders don't have anything to say to us. Otherwise we'd know it by now."

"But what can we do other than keep trying?"

"Go on about our business. Give the Ringworlders time to make up their minds about us."

Reluctantly the puppeteer agreed.

They drifted toward the Ringworld.

Speaker had aimed the *Liar* to pass outside the Ringworld's edge: a concession to Nessus. The puppeteer feared that hypothetical Ringworlders would take it as a threat if the ship's course should intersect the ring itself. He also claimed that fusion drives of the *Liar's* power had the look of weapons; and so the *Liar* moved on thrusters alone.

To the eye there was no way of judging scale. Over the hours the ring shifted position. Too slowly. With cabin gravity to compensate for from zero to thirty gee of thrust, the inner ear could not sense motion. Time passed in a vacuum, and Louis, for the first time since leaving Earth, was ready to gnaw his fingernails.

Finally the ring was edge-on to the *Liar*. Speaker used the thrusters, braking the ship into a circular orbit around the sun: and then he sent them drifting in toward the rim.

Now there was motion.

The rim of the Ringworld grew from a dim line occluding a few stars, to a black wall. A wall a thousand miles high, featureless, though any features would have been blurred by speed. Half a thousand miles away, blocking ninety degrees of sky, the wall sped past at a hellish 770 miles per second. Its edges converged to vanishing points, to points at infinity at either end of the universe; and from each point at infinity, a narrow line of baby blue shot straight upward.

To look into the vanishing point was to step into another universe, a universe of true straight lines, right angles, and other geometric abstractions. Louis stared hypnotized into the vanishing point. Which point was it, the source or the sink? Did the black wall emerge or vanish in that meeting place?

. . . from out of the point at infinity, something came at them.

It was a ledge, growing like another abstraction along the base of the rim wall. First the ledge appeared; then, mounted on the ledge, a row of upright rings. Straight at the *Liar* they came, straight at the bridge of Louis's nose. Louis shut his eyes and threw his arms up to protect his head. He heard a whimper of fear.

Death should have come in that instant. When it didn't, he opened his eyes. The rings were going by in a steady stream; and he realized that they were no more than fifty miles across.

Nessus was curled in a ball. Teela, her palms pressed flat against the transparent hull, was staring avidly outward. Speaker was fearless and attentive at the control board. Perhaps he was better than Louis at judging distance.

Or perhaps he was faking it. The whimper could have come from Speaker.

Nessus uncurled. He looked out at the rings, which were smaller now, converging. "Speaker, you must match velocities with the Ringworld. Hold us in position by thrusting at one gravity. We must inspect this."

Centrifugal force is an illusion, a manifestation of the law of inertia. Reality is centripetal force, a force applied at right angles to the velocity vector of a mass. The mass resists, tends to move in its accustomed straight line.

By reason of its velocity and the law of inertia, the Ringworld tended to fly apart. Its rigid structure would not allow that. The Ringworld applied its own centrifugal force to itself. The *Liar,* matching speed at 770 miles per second, had to match that centripetal force.

Speaker matched it. The *Liar* hovered next to the rim wall, balanced on .992 gee of thrust, while her crew inspected the spaceport.

The spaceport was a narrow ledge, so narrow as to be a dimensionless line until Speaker moved the ship inward. Then it was wide, wide enough to dwarf a pair of tremendous spacecraft. The craft were flat-nosed cylinders, both of the same design: an unfamiliar design, yet clearly the design of a fusion-ramship. These ships were intended to fuel themselves, picking up interstellar hydrogen in scoops of electromagnetic force. One had been cannibalized for parts, so that it stood with its guts open to vacuum and its intimate structure exposed to alien eyes.

Windows showed around the upper rim of the intact ship, allowing those eyes to gauge that ship's size. In the random starlight, the glitter of windows was precisely like crystal candy sprinkled on a cake. Thousands of windows. That ship was *big.*

And it was dark. The entire spaceport was dark. Perhaps the beings who used it did not need light in the "visible" frequencies. But to Louis Wu, the spaceport looked abandoned.

"I don't understand the rings," said Teela.

"Electromagnetic cannon," Louis answered absently. "For takeoffs."

"No," said Nessus.

"Oh?"

"The cannon must have been intended for landing the ships. One can even surmise the method used. The ship must go into orbit alongside the rim wall. It will not attempt to match the ring's velocity, but will position itself twenty-five miles from the base of the rim wall. As the ring rotates, the coils of the electromagnetic cannon will scoop up the ship and accelerate it to match the velocity of the ring. I compliment the ring engineers. The ship need never come close enough to the ring to be dangerous."

"You could also use the ring for takeoff."

"No. Observe the facility to our left . . ."

"I'll be tanjed," said Louis Wu.

The "facility" was little more than a trap door big enough to hold one of the ramships.

It figured. 770 miles per second was ramscoop speed. The ring's launching facility was merely a structure for tumbling the ship off into the void. The pilot would immediately accelerate away on ramscoop-fusion power.

"The spaceport facility seems to be abandoned," said Speaker.

"Is there power in use?"

"My instruments sense none. There are no anomolous hot spots, no large-scale electromagnetic activities. As for the sensors which operate the linear accelerator, they may use less power than we can sense."

"Your suggestion?"

"The facilities may still be in operational condition. We can test this by proceeding to the mouth of the linear accelerator and entering."

Nessus curled himself into a ball.

"Wouldn't work," said Louis. "There could be a key signal to start the thing, and we don't know it. It might react only to a metal hull. If we tried to go through the cannon at the speed of the Ringworld, we'd hit one of the coils and blow everything to bits."

"I have flown ships under similar conditions during simulated war maneuvers."

"How long ago?"

"Perhaps too long. Never mind. Your suggestion?"

"The underside," said Louis. The puppeteer uncurled at once.

They hovered beneath the Ringworld floor, matching velocities, thrusting outward at 9.94 meters per second. "Spotlights," said Nessus.

The spots reached across half a thousand miles; but if their light touched the back of the ring, it did not return. The spots were for landings.

"Do you still trust your engineers, Nessus?"

"They should have anticipated this contingency."

"But I did. I can light the Ringworld, if I may use the fusion drives," said the kzin.

"Do so."

Speaker used all four: the pair facing forward, and the larger motors facing back. But on the forward pair, the pair intended for emergency braking and possibly for weapons, Speaker choked the nozzle wide open. Hydrogen flowed though the tube too fast, emerged half-burnt. Fusion-tube temperature dropped until the exhaust, usually hotter than the core of a nova, was as cool as the surface of a yellow dwarf star. Light thrust forward in twin spears to fall across the black underside of the Ringworld.

First: the underside was not flat. It dipped and rose; there were bulges and indentations.

"I thought it would be smooth," said Teela.

"Sculptured," said Louis. "I'll make you a bet. Wherever we see a bulge, there's a sea on the sunlit side. Where we see a dent, there's a mountain."

But the formations were tiny, unnoticeable until Speaker drew the ship close. The *Lying Bastard* drifted in from the Ringworld's edge, half a thousand miles beneath her underbelly. Sculptured bulges and sculptured indentations, they drifted by, irregular, somehow pleasing ...

For many centuries excusion boats had drifted in like manner across the surface of Earth's Moon. The effect here was much the same: airless pits and peaks, sharp-edged blacks and whites, exposed on the Moon's dark side by the powerful spotlights carried by all such boats.

Yet there was a difference. At any height above the Moon, you could always see the lunar horizon, sharp and toothy against black space, and gently curved.

There were no teeth in the Ringworld's horizon, and no curves. It was a straight line, a geometer's line, unimaginably distant; barely visible as black-against-black. How could Speaker stand it? Louis wondered. Hour after hour, driving the *Liar* across and beneath the belly of this . . . artifact.

Louis shuddered. Gradually he was learning the size, the scale of the Ringworld. It was unpleasant, like all learning processes.

He drew his eyes away from that terrible horizon, back to the illuminated area below/above them.

Nessus said, "All the seas seem to be of the same order of magnitude."

"I've seen a few ponds," Teela contradicted him. "And —look, there's a river. It has to be a river. But I haven't seen any *big* oceans."

Seas there were in plenty, Louis saw—if he was right, and those flat bulges were seas. Though they were not all the same size, they seemed evenly distributed, so that no region was without water. And—"Flat. All the seas have flattened bottoms."

"Yes," said Nessus.

"That proves it. All the seas are shallow. The Ringworlders aren't sea-dwellers. They use only the top of an ocean. Like us."

"But all the seas have squiggly shapes," said Teela. "And the edges are always ragged. You know what that means?"

"Bays. All the bays anyone can use."

"Though your Ringworlders are land-dwellers, they do not fear boats," said Nessus. "Else they would not need the bays. Louis, these people will resemble humans in outlook. Kzinti hate water, and my species fears to drown."

You can learn a lot about a world, Louis thought, by looking at its underside. Someday he would write a monograph on the subject . . .

Teela said, "It must be nice to carve your world to order."

"Don't you like your world, playmate?"

"You know what I mean."

"Power?" Louis liked surprises; he was indifferent to power. He was not creative; he did not make things; he preferred to find them.

He saw something ahead of them. A deeper bulge . . . and a projecting fin, black in the light of the throttled drives, hundreds of thousands of square miles in area.

If the others were seas, this was an ocean, the king of all oceans. It went by them endlessly; and its underbelly was not flat. It looked like a topographical map of the Pacific Ocean: valleys and ridges, shallows and depths and peaks tall enough to be islands.

"They wanted to keep their sea life," Teela guessed. "They needed one deep ocean. The fin must be to keep the depths cool. A radiator."

An ocean not deep enough, but easily broad enough, to swallow the Earth.

"Enough of this," the kzin said suddenly. "Now we must see the inner surface."

"First there are measurements to take. Is the ring truly circular? A minor deviation would spill the air into space."

"We know that there is air, Nessus. The distribution of water on the inner surface will tell us how the ring deviates from circularity."

Nessus surrendered. "Very well. As soon as we reach the further rim."

There were meteor wormholes. Not many, but they were there. Louis thought with amusement that the Ring-worlders had been remiss in cleaning out their solar system. But no, these must have come from outside, from between the stars. One conical crater floated by in the fusion light, and Louis saw a glint of light at the bottom. Something shiny, reflecting.

It must be a glimpse of the ring floor. The ring floor, a substance dense enough to stop 40 percent of neutrinos, and presumably very rigid. Above/inward from the ring floor, soil and seas and cities, and above these, air. Below/outward from the ring floor, a spongy material, like foam plastic perhaps, to take the brunt of a meteoroid impact. Most meteoroids would vaporise within the thick foamed material; but a few would get through, to leave conical holes with shiny bottoms . . .

Far down the length of the Ringworld, almost beyond its infinitely gentle curve, Louis's eyes found a dimple. That must have been a big one, he thought. Big enough to show by starlight, that far away.

He did not call attention to the meteoroid dimple. His eyes and mind were not yet used to the proportions of the Ringworld.

CHAPTER 9

Shadow Squares

Blazing, the G2 sun dawned beyond the straight black rim of the ring. It was uncomfortably bright until Speaker touched a polarizer; and then Louis could look at the disc, and he found an edge of shadow cutting its arc. Shadow square.

"We must be careful," Nessus warned. "If we were to match velocities with the ring and hover above the inner surface, we would surely be attacked."

Speaker's answer came in a slurred rumble. The kzin must be tiring after so many hours behind the horseshoe of controls. "By what weapon would we be attacked? We have shown that the Ringworld engineers do not have so much as a working radio station."

"We cannot guess at the nature of their communications. Telepathy, perhaps, or resonant vibrations in the ring floor, or electrical impulses in metal wires. Similarly, we know nothing of their weaponry. Hovering over their surface, we would be a serious threat. They would use what weapons they have."

Louis nodded his agreement. He was not naturally cautious, and the Ringworld held him by the curiosity bump; but the puppeteer was right.

Hovering over the surface, the *Liar* would be a potential meteor. A big one. Moving at merely orbital speed, such a mass was a hellish danger; for one touch of atmosphere would send it shrieking down at several hundred miles per second. Moving at faster than orbital speed, holding a curved path with the drives, the ship would

116

be a lesser but a surer threat; for if the drive were to fail, "centrifugal force" would hurl the ship outward/down at populated lands. The Ringworlders would not take meteors lightly. Not when a single puncture in the ring floor would drain all the world's breathing-air and spew it at the stars.

Speaker turned from the control board. It put him eye to eye with the puppeteer's flat heads. "Your orders, then."

"First you must slow the ship to orbital speed."

"Then?"

"Accelerate toward the sun. We can inspect the ring's habitable surface to some extent as it diminishes below us. Our major target shall be the shadow squares."

"Such caution is unnecessary and humiliating. We have no slightest interest in the shadow squares."

Tanj! Louis thought. Tired and hungry as he was, would he now be called on to play peacemaker for the aliens? It had been too long since any of them had eaten or slept. If Louis was tired, the kzin must be exhausted, spoiling for a fight.

The puppeteer was saying, "We have a definite interest in the shadow squares. Their area intercepts more sunlight than does the Ringworld itself. They would make ideal thermoelectric generators for the Ringworld's power supply."

The kzin snarled something venomous in the Hero's Tongue. His reply in Interworld seemed ludicrously mild. "You are unreasonable. We surely have no interest in the source of the Ringworld's power. Let us land, find a native, and *ask* him about his power sources."

"I refuse to consider landing."

"Do you question my skill at the controls?"

"Do you question my decisions as leader?"

"Since you broach the subject—"

"I still carry the tasp, Speaker. My word governs the disposal of the *Long Shot* and the second quantum hyperdrive, and I am still Hindmost aboard this ship. You will bear in mind—"

"Stop," said Louis.

They looked at him.

"Your arguments are premature," said Louis. "Why not turn our telescopes on the shadow squares? That way you'll both have more facts to shout at each other. It's more fun that way."

Nessus faced himself, eye to eye. The kzin sheathed his claws.

"On a more pragmatic level," said Louis, "we're all bushed. Tired. Hungry. Who wants to fight on an empty stomach? I'm going to catch an hour under a sleep set. I suggest you do the same."

Teela was shocked. "You don't want to watch? We'll be seeing the inner side!"

"You watch. Tell me what happens." He left.

He woke groggy and ravenous. Hunger pulled him from between sleeping plates, then kept him in the cabin long enough to dial a handmeal. Eating one-handed, he strolled out into the lounge.

"What's happening?"

Teela answered, rather coldly, across the top of a reading screen. "You missed everything. Slaver ships, Mist Demons, space dragons, cannibal starseeds, all attacking at once. Speaker had to fend them off with his bare hands. You'd have loved it."

"Nessus?"

The puppeteer answered from the control room. "Speaker and I have agreed to move on to the shadow squares. Speaker is alseep. We will be in clear space soon."

"Anything new?"

"Yes, considerable. Let me show you."

The puppeteer did things to the scope screen controls. He must have studied kzinti symbology, somewhere.

The view in the scope screen was like Earth seen from a great height. Mountains, lakes, valleys, rivers, large bare spots that might be desert.

"Desert?"

"So it would seem, Louis. Speaker took temperature and humidity spectra. Evidence accumulates that the Ringworld has reverted to savagery, at least in part. Why else would there be deserts?

"We found another deep salt ocean on the opposite side of the ring, as big as the one on this side. Spectra confirmed the salt. Clearly the engineers found it necessary to balance such tremendous masses of water."

Louis bit into his handmeal.

"Your suggestion was a good one," Nessus remarked. "You may be our most skilled diplomat, despite Speaker's training and mine. It was after we turned the scope on the shadow squares that Speaker agreed to a closer look."

"Oh? Why?"

"We found a peculiarity. The shadow squares are moving at a speed comfortably greater than orbital velocity."

Louis stopped chewing.

"That is not impossible," the puppeteer added. "The shadow squares may hold matching stable elliptical orbits. They need not maintain a constant distance from the primary."

Louis swallowed mightily to clear the way for speech. "That's crazy. The length of the day would vary!"

Teela said, "We thought it might be to separate summer from winter, by making the nights shorter and then longer. But that doesn't make sense either."

"No, it doesn't. The shadow squares make their circuit in less than a month. Who needs a three-week year?"

"You see the problem," said Nessus. "The abnormality was too small to detect from our own system. What causes it? Does gravity increase anomalously near the primary, requiring a higher orbital speed? In any case, the shadow objects merit a closer look."

Passing time was marked by the sharp black edge of a shadow square passing across the sun.

Presently the kzin left his room, exchanged civilities with the humans in the lounge, and replaced Nessus in the control room.

Shortly thereafter he emerged. There was no sound to indicate trouble; but Louis suddenly saw that the puppeteer was backing away from a murderous kzinti glare. Speaker was ready to kill.

"Okay," Louis said resignedly. "What's the trouble?"

"This leaf-eater," the kzin began, and strangled on his anger. He started over. "Our schizophrenic leader-from-behind has had us in a minimum-fuel orbit since I went to rest. At this rate it will take us four months to reach the belt of shadow squares." And Speaker began to curse in the Hero's Tongue.

"You put us in that orbit yourself," the puppeteer said mildly.

The kzin's voice rose in volume. "It was my intention to leave the Ringworld slowly, so that we might have a long look at the inner surface. We might then accelerate directly toward the shadow squares, arriving within hours instead of months!"

"There is no need to bellow, Speaker. If we accelerate toward the shadow squares, our projected orbit will intersect the Ringworld. I wish to avoid that."

"He can aim for the sun," said Teela.

They all turned to look at her.

"If the Ringworlders are afraid that we'll hit them," Teela explained patiently, "then they're probably projecting our course. If our projected course hits the sun, then we're not dangerous. See?"

"That would work," said Speaker.

The puppeteer shuddered. "You are the pilot. Do as you like, but do not forget—"

"I do not intend to fly us through the sun. In due time I will match our course to the shadow squares." And the kzin stomped back into the control room. It is not easy for a kzin to stomp.

Presently the ship turned parallel to the ring. There was little sense of anything happening; the kzin, following orders, was using thrusters only. Speaker killed the ship's orbital velocity, so that the ship was falling toward the sun; and then he swung the nose inward and began to increase velocity.

The Ringworld was a broad blue band marked with ripples and clots of blazing white cloud. It was receding visibly now. Speaker was in a hurry.

Louis dialed two bulbs of mocha and handed one to Teela.

He could understand the kzin's anger. The Ringworld terrified him. He was convinced he would have to land . . . and desperate to get it over with before he lost his nerve.

Presently Speaker returned to the lounge. "We will reach the shadow square orbit in fourteen hours. Nessus, we warriors of the Patriarchy are taught patience from childhood, but you leaf-eaters have the patience of a corpse."

"We're moving," said Louis, and half rose. For the ship's nose was swinging aside from the sun.

Nessus screamed and leapt the length of the lounge. He was in the air when the *Liar* lit up like the interior of a flashbulb. The ship lurched—

Discontinuity.

—The ship lurched despite the cabin gravity. Louis snatched at the back of a chair and caught it; Teela fell with incredible accuracy into her own crash couch; the puppeteer was folded into a ball as he struck a wall. All in an intense violet glare. The darkness lasted only an instant, to be replaced by glowing light the color of a UV tube.

It was coming from outside, from all around the hull. Speaker must have finished aiming the *Liar* and turned it over to the autopilot. And then, thought Louis, the autopilot must have reviewed Speaker's course, decided that the sun was a meteoroid large enough to be dangerous, and taken steps to avoid it.

The cabin gravity was back to normal. Louis picked himself off the floor. He was unhurt. So, apparently, was Teela. She was standing along the wall, peering sternward through the violet light.

"Half my instrument board is dead," Speaker announced.

"So are half your instruments," said Teela. "The wing's gone."

"Excuse me?"

"The wing's gone."

So it was. So was everything that had been attached to the wing: thrusters, fusion plants, communication equipment pods, landing gear. The hull had been polished clean. Nothing was left of the *Liar* save what had been protected by the General Products hull.

"We have been fired upon," said Speaker. "We are still being fired upon, probably by X-ray lasers. This ship is now in a state of war. Accordingly I take command."

Nessus was not arguing. He was still curled in a ball. Louis knelt beside him and probed with his hands.

"Finagle knows I'm no doctor for aliens. I can't see that he's been hurt."

"He is merely frightened. He attempts to hide in his own belly. You and Teela will strap him down and leave him."

Louis was not surprised to find himself obeying orders. He was badly shaken. A moment ago this had been a spacecraft. Now it was little more than a glass needle falling toward the sun.

They lifted the puppeteer into the crash couch, his own, and tied him down with the crash web.

"We face no peaceful culture," said the kzin. "An X-ray laser is invariably a weapon of war. Were it not for our invulnerable hull we would be dead."

Louis said, "The Slaver stasis field must have gone on too. No telling how long we were in stasis."

"A few seconds," Teela corrected him. "That violet light has to be the fog of metal from our wing, fluorescing."

"Excited by the laser. Right. It's dissipating, I think."
True enough, the glow was already less intense.

"Unfortunate that our automatics are so single-mindedly defensive. Trust a puppeteer to know nothing of attack weapons!" said Speaker. "Even our fusion motors were on the wing. And still the enemy fire on us! But they will learn what it means to attack a kzin."

"You're going to chase them down?"

Speaker did not recognize sarcasm. "I am."

"With what?" Louis exploded. "You know what they left us? A hyperdrive and a lifesystem, that's what they left us! We haven't got so much as a pair of attitude jets. You've got delusions of grandeur if you think we can fight a war in *this!*"

"So the enemy believes! Little do they know—"

"What enemy?"

"—that in challenging a kzin—"

"Automatics, you dolt! An enemy would have started shooting the moment we came in range!"

"I too have wondered at their unusual strategy."

"Automatics! X-ray lasers for blasting meteors. Programmed to shoot down anything that might hit the ring. The moment our projected freely falling orbit intercepted the ring, pow! Lasers."

"That . . . is possible." The kzin began closing panels over dead portions of the control board. "But I hope you are wrong."

"Sure. It'd help if you had someone to blame, wouldn't it?"

"It would help if our course did not intercept the ring." The kzin had closed off half the board. He continued to close panels as he talked. "Our velocity is high. It will take us out of the system, beyond the local discontinuity, to where we can use the hyperdrive to return to the puppeteer fleet. But first we must miss the ring."

Louis hadn't thought that far ahead. "You had to be in a hurry, didn't you?" he said bitterly.

"At least we will miss the sun. The automatics will not have fired until our projected course circled the sun."

"The lasers are still on," Teela reported. "I can see stars through the glow, but the glow is still there. That means we're still aimed at the ring surface, doesn't it?"

"It does if the lasers are automatic."

"If we hit the ring, will we be killed?"

"Ask Nessus. His race built the *Liar.* See if you can get him to unroll."

The kzin snorted in disgust. By now he had closed off most of the control board. Only a pitiful few lights still glowed to show that part of the *Liar* lived on.

Teela Brown bent over the puppeteer, who was still curled into a ball behind the fragile netting of his crash web. Contrary to Louis's prediction, she had shown not the least sign of panic since the beginning of the laser attack. Now she slid her hands along the bases of the puppeteer's necks, scratching gently, as she had seen Louis do once before.

"You're being a silly coward," she rebuked the frightened puppeteer. "Come on and show your heads. Come on, look at me. You'll miss all the excitement!"

Twelve hours later, Nessus was still effectively in catatonia.

"When I try to coax him out, he only curls up tighter!" Teela was near tears. They had retired to their room for dinner, but Teela couldn't eat anything. "I'm doing it wrong, Louis. I know it."

"You keep stressing excitement. Nessus isn't after excitement," Louis pointed out. "Forget it. He isn't hurting himself or us. When he's needed he'll uncurl, if only to protect himself. Meanwhile let him hide in his own belly."

Teela paced awkwardly, half-stumbling; she still hadn't completely adjusted to the difference between ship's gravity and Earth's gravity. She started to speak, changed her mind, changed it again, and blurted, "Are you scared?"

"Yah."

"I thought so," she nodded, and resumed pacing. Presently she asked, "Why isn't Speaker scared?"

For the kzin had been nothing but active since the attack: cataloguing weaponry, doing primitive trig calculations to plot their course, occasionally delivering concise, reasonable orders in a manner to command instant obedience.

"I think Speaker's terrified. Remember how he acted

when he saw the puppeteer worlds? He's terrified, but he won't let Nessus know it."

She shook her head. "I don't understand. I don't! Why is everyone frightened but me?"

Love and pity tore at Louis's insides with a pain so old, so nearly forgotten that it was almost new. *I'm new here, and everyone knows but me!* "Nessus was half right," he tried to explain. "You've never been hurt at all, have you? You're too lucky to be hurt. We're afraid of being hurt, but you don't understand, because it's never happened to you."

"That's crazy. I've never broken a *bone* or anything— but *that's* not a psi power!"

"No. Luck isn't psi. Luck is statistics, and you're a mathematical fluke. Out of forty-three billion human beings in known space, it would have been surprising if Nessus hadn't found someone like you. Don't you see what he did?

"He took the group of people who were descendants of winners of the Birthright Lotteries. He says there were thousands, but it's a good bet that if he hadn't found what he was after in those thousands, he would have started looking through the larger group of people with one or more ancestors born through the Lotteries. That gives him tens of millions of choices . . ."

"What *was* he after?"

"You. He took his several thousand people and started eliminating the unlucky ones. Here a man broke his finger when he was thirteen. This girl had personality problems. That one had acne. This man gets in fights and loses. That one won a fight, but lost the lawsuit. This guy flew model rockets until he burnt a thumbnail off. This girl loses constantly at roulette . . . You see? You're the girl who's always won. The toast never falls on the buttered side."

Teela was looking thoughtful. "It's a probability thing, then. But, Louis, I don't always win at roulette."

"But you never lost enough to hurt you."

"N-no."

"That's what Nessus looked for."

"You're saying I'm some kind of freak."

"No, tanj it! I'm saying you're *not*. Nessus kept elimi-nating candidates who were unlucky, until he wound up with you. He thinks he's found some basic principle. All he's really found is the far end of a normal curve.

"Probability theory says you exist. It also says that the next time you flip a coin, your chances of losing are just as good as mine: fifty-fifty, because Lady Luck has no memory at all."

Teela dropped into a chair. "A fine good luck charm I turned out to be. Poor Nessus. I failed him."

"Serves him right."

The corners of her mouth twitched. "We could check it out."

"What?"

"Dial a piece of toast. Start flipping it."

The shadow square was blacker than black, of the ex-pensively achieved, definitive black used in high school blackbody experiments. One corner notched an acute an-gle into the blue broken line of the Ringworld. With that notch as a mark, a brain and eye could sketch in the rest of it, a narrow oblong of space-blackness, suspiciously void of stars. Already it cut off a good chunk of sky; and it was growing.

Louis wore bulbous goggles of a material that developed black spots under the impact of too much vertically im-pinging light. Polarization in the hull was no longer enough. Speaker, who was in the control room controlling whatever was left to control, also wore a pair. They had found two separate lenses, each on a short strap, and managed to force them on Nessus.

To Louis's goggled eyes, the sun, twelve million miles distant, was a blurred rim of flame around a wide, solid black disc. Everything was hot to the touch. The breath-ing-air plant was a howling wind.

Teela opened her cabin door and hastily shut it again. Presently she reappeared wearing goggles. She joined Louis at the lounge table.

The shadow square was a looming absence. It was as if a wet cloth had swept across a blackboard, erasing a swath of chalk-mark stars.

The howl of the air plant made speech impossible.

How would it dump the heat, out here where the sun was a looming furnace? It couldn't, Louis decided. It must be storing the heat. Somewhere in the breathing-air circuit was a point as hot as a star, growing hotter by the second.

One more thing to worry about.

The black oblong continued to swell.

It was the size that made it seem to approach so slowly. The shadow square was as broad as the sun, nearly a million miles across, and much longer: two-and-a-half million miles long. Almost suddenly, it became tremendous. Its edge slid across the sun, and there was darkness.

The shadow square covered half the universe. Its borders were indefinite, black-on-black, terrible to see.

Part of the ship glowed white behind the block of cabins. The air plant was radiating waste heat while it had the chance. Louis shrugged and turned back to watch the shadow square.

The scream of breathing-air stopped. It left a ringing in the ears.

"Well," Teela said awkwardly.

Speaker came out of the control room. "A pity the scope screen is no longer connected to anything. There are so many questions it could answer."

"Like what?" Louis half-shouted.

"Why are the shadow squares moving at more than orbital velocity? Are they indeed power generators for the ring engineers? What holds them face-down to the sun? All the questions the leaf-eater asked could be answered, if we had a working scope screen."

"Are we going to hit the sun?"

"Of course not. I told you that, Louis. We will be behind the shadow square for half an hour. Then, an hour later, we will pass between the next shadow square and the sun. If the cabin becomes too hot we can always activate the stasis field."

The ringing silence closed in. The shadow square was a featureless field of black, without boundaries. A human eye can draw no data from pure black.

Presently the sun came out. Again the cabin was filled with the howl of the air plant.

Louis searched the sky ahead until he found another shadow square. He was watching its approach when the lightning struck again.

It looked like lightning. It came like lightning, without warning. There was a moment of terrible light, white with a violet tinge. The ship lurched—

Discontinuity.

—lurched, and the light was gone. Louis reached under his goggles with two forefingers to rub dazzled eyes.

"What was that?" Teela exclaimed.

Louis's vision cleared slowly. He saw that Nessus had exposed a goggled head; that Speaker was at work in one of the lockers; that Teela was staring at him. No, at something behind him. He turned.

The sun was a wide black disc, smaller than it had been, outlined in yellow-white flame. It had shrunk considerably during the moment in stasis. The "moment" must have lasted hours. The scream of the air plant had faded to an irritating whine.

Something else burned out there.

It was a looping thread of black, very narrow, outlined in violet-white. There seemed to be no endpoints. One end faded into the black patch that hid the sun. The other diminished ahead of the *Liar,* until it was too small to see.

The thread was writhing like an injured earthworm.

"We seem to have hit something," Nessus said calmly. It was as if he had never been away. "Speaker, you must go outside to investigate. Please don your suit."

"We are in a state of war," the kzin answered. "I command."

"Excellent. What will you do now?"

The kzin had sense enough to remain silent. He had

nearly finished donning the multiple balloon and heavy backpack which served him as a pressure suit. Obviously he intended to go out for a look.

He went out on one of the flycycles: a dumbbell-shaped thruster-powered vehicle with an armchair seat in the constriction.

They watched him maneuver alongside the writhing thread of black. It had cooled considerably; for the fringe of brightness around the goggle-induced black had dimmed from violet-white through white-white to orange-white. They watched Speaker's dark bulk leave the flycycle and move about near the heated, writhing wire.

They could hear him breathing. Once they heard a startled snarling sound. But he never said a word into the suit phone. He was out there a full half-hour, while the heated thing darkened to near-invisibility.

Presently he returned to the *Liar*. When he entered the lounge, he had their complete and respectful attention.

"It was no thicker than thread," said the kzin. "You will notice that I hold half a grippy."

He held up the ruined tool for them to see. The grippy had been cut cleanly along a plane surface, and the cut surface polished to mirror brightness.

"When I was close enough to see how thin the thread was, I swung the grippy at it. The thread cut cleanly through the steel. I felt only the slightest of tugs."

Louis said, "A variable-sword would do that."

"But a variable-sword blade is a metal wire enclosed in a Slaver stasis field. It cannot bend. This—thread was in constant motion, as you saw."

"Something new, then." Something that cut like a variable-sword. Light, thin, strong, beyond human skill. Something that stayed solid at temperatures where a natural substance would become a plasma. "Something really new. But what was it doing in our way?"

"Consider. We were passing between shadow squares when we hit something unidentified. Subsequently we

found a seemingly infinite length of thread, at a temperature comparable to the interior of a hot star. Obviously we
hit the thread. It retained the heat of impact. I surmise
that it was strung between the shadow squares."

"Probably was. But why?"

"We can only speculate. Consider," said Speaker-To-
Animals. "The Ringworld engineers used the shadow
squares to provide intervals of night. To fulfill their purpose, the rectangles must occlude sunlight. They would
fail if they drifted edge-on to the sun.

"The Ringworld engineers used their strange thread to
join the rectangles together in a chain. They spun the
chain at faster than orbital speed in order to put tension
on the threads. The threads are taut, the rectangles are
held flat to the ring."

It made an odd picture. Twenty shadow squares in a
Maypole dance, their edges joined by threads cut to
lengths of five million miles . . . "We need that thread,"
said Louis. "There's no limit to what we could do with it."

"I had no way to bring it aboard. Or to cut a length
of it, for that matter."

The puppeteer interposed. "Our course may have been
changed by the collision. Is there any way to determine
if we will miss the Ringworld?"

Nobody could think of one.

"We may miss the ring, yet the collision may have
taken too much of our momentum. We may fall forever
in an elliptical orbit," lamented the puppeteer. "Teela,
your luck has played us false."

She shrugged. "I never told you I was a good luck
charm."

"It was the Hindmost who so misinformed me. Were
he here now, I would have rude words for my arrogant
fiancé."

Dinner that night became a ritual. The crew of the Liar
took a last supper in the lounge. Teela Brown was hurting-
ly beautiful across the table, in a flowing, floating black-
and-tangerine garment that couldn't have weighed as much
as an ounce.

Behind her shoulder, the Ringworld was slowly swelling. Occasionally Teela turned to watch it. They all did. But where Louis had to guess at the feelings of the aliens, in Teela he saw only eagerness. She felt it, as he did: they would not miss the Ringworld.

In his lovemaking that night there was a ferocity that startled, then delighted her. "So that's what fear does to you! I'll have to remember."

He could not smile back. "I keep thinking that this could be the last time." With anyone, he added, to himself.

"Oh, Louis. We're in a General Products hull!"

"Suppose the stasis field doesn't go on? The hull might survive the impact, but we'd be jelly."

"For Finagle's sake, stop worrying!" She ran her fingernails across his back, reaching around from both sides. He pulled her close, so that she couldn't see his face . . .

When she was deeply asleep, floating like a lovely dream between the sleeping plates, Louis left her. Exhausted, satiated, he lolled in a hot bathtub with a bulb of cold bourbon balanced on the rim.

There had been pleasures to sample one more time.

Baby blue with white streaks, navy blue with no details, the Ringworld spread across the sky. At first only the cloud cover showed detail: storms, parallel streamers, woolly fleece, all diminutive. Growing. Then, outlines of seas . . . the Ringworld was approximately half water . . .

Nessus was in his couch, strapped down, curled protectively around himself. Speaker and Teela and Louis Wu, strapped down and watching.

"Better watch this," Louis advised the puppeteer. "Topography could be important later."

Nessus obliged: one flat python head emerged to watch the impending landscape.

Oceans, bent lightning-forks of river, a string of mountains.

No sign of life below. You'd have to be less than a thousand miles up to see signs of civilization. The Ringworld went past, snatching detail away almost before it could be recognized. Detail wasn't going to matter; it was being pulled from beneath them. They would strike unknown, unseen territory.

Estimated intrinsic velocity of ship: two hundred miles per second. Easily enough to carry them safely out of the system, had not the Ringworld intervened.

The land rose up and sidewise, 770 miles per second sidewise. Slantwise, a salamander-shaped sea came at them, growing, underneath, gone. Suddenly the landscape blazed violet!

Discontinuity.

CHAPTER 10

The Ring Floor

An instant of light, violet-white, flashbulb-bright. A hundred miles of atmosphere, compressed in an instant to a star-hot cone of plasma, slapped the *Liar* hard across the nose. Louis blinked.

Louis blinked, and they were down.

He heard Teela's frustrated complaint: "Tanj! We missed it all!"

And the puppeteer's answer: "To witness titanic events is always dangerous, usually painful, and often fatal. Be grateful for the Slaver stasis field, if not for your undependable luck."

Louis heard these things and ignored them. He was horribly dizzy. His eyes tried to find a level . . .

The sudden transition, from terrible fall to stable ground, would have been dizzying enough without the *Liar's* attitude to make it worse. The *Liar* was thirty-five degrees short of being exactly upside down. With her cabin gravity still working perfectly, she wore the landscape like a tilted hat.

The sky was a high-noon sky from Earth's temperate zone. The landscape was puzzling: shiny-flat and translucent, with distant reddish-brown ridges. One would have to go outside to see it properly.

Louis released his crash web and stood up.

His balance was precarious; for his eyes and his inner ear disagreed on the direction of *down*. He took it slowly. Easy. No hurry. The emergency was over.

He turned, and Teela was in the airlock. She was not

wearing a pressure suit. The inner door was just closing.

He bellowed, "Teela, you silly leucoto, come out of there!"

Too late. She couldn't possibly have heard him through the closed hermetic seal. Louis sprang to the lockers.

The air samplers on the *Liar's* wing had been vaporized with the rest of the *Liar's* external sensors. He would have to go out in a pressure suit and use the chest sensors to find out if the Ringworld's air could be breathed safely.

Unless Teela collapsed and died before he could get out. Then he would know.

The outer door was opening.

Automatically the internal gravity went off in the airlock. Teela Brown dropped headfirst through the open door, clutched frantically for a door jamb, had it for just long enough to change her angle of fall. She landed on her tail instead of her skull.

Louis climbed into his pressure suit, zipped up the chest, donned the helmet and closed the clamps. Outside and overhead, Teela was on her feet, rubbing herself where she had landed. She hadn't stopped breathing, thank Finagle for his forebearance.

Louis entered the lock. No point in checking his suit's air. He'd only be in the suit long enough for the instruments to tell him if he could breath outside air.

He remembered the tilt of the ship in time to grab at the jamb as the airlock opened. As the cabin gravity went off, Louis swung around, hung by his hands for an instant, and dropped.

His feet shot out from under him the moment they touched ground. He landed hard on his gluteus maximi.

The flat, grayish, translucent material beneath the ship was terribly slippery. Louis tried once to stand, then gave it up. Sitting, he examined the dials on his chest.

His helmet spoke to him in Speaker's burry voice. "Louis."

"Yah."

"Is the air breathable?"

"Yah. Thin, though. Say a mile above sea level, Earth standard."

"Shall we come out?"

"Sure, but bring a line into the lock and tie it to something. Otherwise we'll never get back up. Watch out when you get down. The surface is almost frictionless."

Teela was having no trouble with the slippery surface. She stood awkwardly, with her arms folded, waiting for Louis to quit fooling around and take off his helmet.

He did. "I have something to tell you," he said. And he spoke rudely to her.

He spoke of the uncertainties in spectroanalysis of an atmosphere from two light years away. He spoke of subtle poisons, metal compounds, and strange dusts, organic wastes and catalysts, which can poison an otherwise breathable atmosphere, and which can only be detected from an actual air sample. He spoke of criminal carelessness and culpable stupidity; he spoke of the unwisdom in volunteering one's services as a guinea pig. He said it all before the aliens could leave the airlock.

Speaker came down hand over hand, landed on his feet and moved a few steps away, cat-careful, balanced like a dancer. Nessus came down gripping the rope with alternate sets of teeth. He landed in tripod position.

If either of them noticed that Teela was upset, they gave no sign. They stood below the tilted hull of the *Liar*, looking about them.

. They were in an enormous, shallow gully. Its floor was translucent gray and perfectly flat and smooth, like a vast glass tabletop. Its borders, a hundred yards from the ship in either direction, were gentle slopes of black lava. The lava seemed to ripple and flow before Louis's eyes. It must be still hot, he decided, from the impact of the *Liar's* landing.

The shallow lava walls stretched away behind the ship, away and away, perfectly straight, until they dwindled to a vanishing point.

Louis tried to stand up. Of the four of them, he was the only one having trouble with his balance. He reached his feet, then stood precariously balanced, unable to move.

Speaker-To-Animals unsheathed his flashlight-laser and

fired at a point near his feet. They watched the point of green light . . . in silence. There was no crackle of solid material exploding into vapor. No steam or smoke formed where the beam struck. When Speaker released the trigger button, the light was gone instantly; the spot was not glowing, nor was it marked in any way.

Speaker delivered the verdict. "We are in a furrow plowed by our own landing. The ring foundation material must have ultimately stopped our fall. Nessus, what can you tell us about it?"

"This is something new," the puppeteer answered. "It seems to retain no heat. Yet it is not a variant on the General Products hull, nor on the Slaver stasis field."

"We'll need protection to climb the walls," said Louis. He wasn't particularly interested in the ring foundation material. Not then. "You'd better stay here, all of you, while I climb up."

After all, he was the only one wearing a heat-insulated pressure suit.

"I'll come along," said Teela. Moving without effort, she came up under his arm. He leaned heavily on her, stumbling but not falling, as they moved toward the black lava slope.

The lava was good footing, though steep. "Thanks," he said, and he started up. A moment later he realized that Teela was following him. He said nothing. The faster she learned to look before she leapt, the longer she'd live.

They were a dozen yards up the slope when Teela yelled and began dancing. Kicking high, she turned and pelted downslope. She slid like an ice skater when she hit the ring floor. Sliding, gliding, she turned with her hands on her hips and glared upward, baffled and injured and angry.

It could have been worse, Louis told himself. She could have slipped and fallen and burned her bare hands —and he'd still have been right. He continued to climb, repressing ugly pangs of guilt.

The bank of lava was approximately forty feet high. At the top it gave way to clean white sand.

They had landed in a desert. Searching the near dis-

tance with his eyes, Louis could find no sign of vegeta-
tion-green or water-blue. That was a piece of luck. The
Liar could as easily have plowed through a city.

Or through several cities! The *Liar* had plowed quite a
furrow . . .

It stretched long miles across the white sand. In the
distance, beyond where that gouge ended, another began.
The ship had bounced, not once, but many times. The
gouge of the *Liar's* landing went on and on, narrowing
to no more than a dotted line, a trace . . . Louis let his
eyes follow that trace, and he found himself looking into
infinity.

The Ringworld had no horizon. There was no line
where the land curved away from the sky. Rather, earth
and sky seemed to merge in a region where details the
size of continents would have been mere points, where
all colors blended gradually into the blue of sky. The
vanishing point held his eyes fixed. When he blinked, as
he finally did, it was with deliberate effort.

Like the void mist of Mount Lookitthat, seen decades
ago and light-centuries away . . . like the undistorted
deeps of space, as seen by a Belt miner in a singleship
. . . the Ringworld's horizon could grip the eye and the
mind of a man before he was aware of the danger.

Louis turned to face into the gully. He shouted, "The
world is flat!"

They looked up at him.

"We ripped quite a line coming down. I can't see that
there's anything living around here, so we were lucky.
Where we hit, the earth splashed; I can see a scattering
of small craters, secondary meteorites, back along the way
we came."

He turned. "In the other direction . . . "and he stopped.

"Louis?"

"That's the biggest tanj mountain I ever saw in my
life."

"Louis!"

He had spoken too softly. "A mountain!" he bellowed.
"Wait'll you see it! The Ringworld engineers must have
wanted to put one big mountain in the world, one moun-

tain too big to use. Too big to grow coffee on, or trees, too big even for skiing. It's magnificent!"

It was magnificent. One mountain, roughly conical, all alone, forming no part of a chain. It had the look of a volcano, a mock-volcano, for beneath the Ringworld there was no magma to form volcanos. Its base was lost in mist. Its higher slopes showed clear through what must be thinning air, and its peak had a shiny look of snow: dirty snow, not bright enough to be clean snow. Perhaps permafrost.

There was a crystal clarity to the edges of the peak. Could it thrust clear out of the atmosphere? A real mountain that size would collapse of its own weight; but this mountain would be a mere shell of ring foundation material.

"I'm going to like the Ringworld engineers," said Louis Wu to himself. On a world built to ordered specification, there was no logical reason for such a mountain to exist. Yet every world should have at least one unclimbable mountain.

Beneath the curve of the hull, they waited for him. Their questions boiled down to one. "Did you see any sign of civilization?"

"No."

They made him describe everything he'd seen. They established directions. *Spinward* was back along the meteoric furrow dug by the *Liar's* landing. *Antispinward* was the opposite direction, toward the mountain. *Port* and *starboard* were to the left and right of a man facing spinward.

"Could you see any of the rim walls to port or starboard?"

"No. I don't understand why. They should have been there."

"Unfortunate," said Nessus.

"Impossible. You can see for thousands of miles up there."

"Not impossible. Unfortunate."

ĩain: "Could you see nothing beyond the desert?"

"No. A long way to port, I saw a trace of blue. Might have been ocean. Might have been just distance."

"No buildings?"

"Nothing."

"Contrails in the sky? Straight lines that might have been freeways?"

"Nothing."

"Did you see any sign of civilization?"

"If I had, I'd tell you. For all I know, the whole ten trillion of 'em moved to a real Dyson sphere last month."

"Louis, we must find civilization."

"*I* know that."

It was too obvious. They had to get off the Ringworld; and they weren't going to move the *Liar* by themselves. True barbarians would not be help enough, no matter how numerous or how friendly.

"There is one bright aspect to all this," said Louis Wu. "We don't have to repair the ship. If we can just get the *Liar* off the ring, the ring's rotation will fling it, and us, out of the star's gravity well. Out to where we can use the hyperdrive."

"But first we must find help."

"Or force help," said Speaker.

"But why do you all just stand here talking?" Teela burst out. She had been waiting silent in the circle, letting the others thrash it out. "We've got to get out of here, don't we? Why not get the flycycles out of the ship? Let's get moving! *Then* talk!"

"I am reluctant to leave the ship," the puppeteer stated.

"Reluctant! Are you expecting help? Is anyone the least bit interested in us? Did anyone answer our radio calls? Louis says we're in the middle of a desert. How long are we going to sit here?"

She could not realize that Nessus had to work up his courage. And, thought Louis, she had no patience at all.

"Of course we will leave," said the puppeteer. "I merely stated my reluctance. But we must decide where we will go. Else we will not know what to take and what to leave behind."

"We head for the nearest rim wall!"

"She's right," said Louis. "If there's civilization any-where, it'll be at the rim wall. But we don't know where it is. I should have been able to see it from up there."

"No," said the puppeteer.

"You weren't there, tanjit! You could see forever up there! Thousands of miles without a break! Wait a min-ute."

"The Ringworld is nearly a million UN miles across."

"I was just about to realize that," said Louis Wu. "Scale. It keeps fouling me up. I just can't visualize any-thing this big!"

"It will come to you," the puppeteer reassured him.

"I wonder. Maybe my brain isn't big enough to hold it. I keep remembering how narrow the ring looked from deep space. Like a thread of blue ribbon. Blue ribbon," Louis repeated, and shivered.

If each rim wall were a thousand miles high, then how far away would it need to be before Louis Wu couldn't see it at all?

Assume that Louis Wu can see through a thousand miles of dust-laden, water-vapor-laden, somewhat terres-trial air. If such air gave way to effective vacuum at forty miles . . .

Then the nearest rim wall must be at least twenty-five thousand miles away.

If you flew that far on Earth, you would have re-turned to your starting point. But the nearest rim wall might be much further than that.

"We cannot drag the *Liar* behind our skycycles," Speaker was saying. "Were we attacked, we would have to cut the ship loose. Better to leave it here, near a promi-nent landmark."

"Who said anything about dragging the ship?"

"A good warrior thinks of everything. We may end by dragging the ship in any case, if we cannot find help at the rim."

"We will find help," said Nessus.

"probably right," said Louis. "The spaceports are m. If the whole ring went back to the stone age, and civilization started to spread again, it would start with returning ramships. It would have to."

"You speculate wildly," said Speaker.

"Maybe."

"But I agree with you. I might add that if the ring has lost all of its great secrets, we might still find machinery at the spaceport. Working machinery, machinery which can be repaired."

But which rim was closer?

"Teela's right," Louis said suddenly. "Let's get to work. At night we'll be able to see further."

Hours of hard labor followed. They moved machinery, sorted it out, lowered heavy items by wire from the ship's airlock. The sudden shifts of gravity posed problems, but none of the equipment was particularly fragile.

Sometime during those hours, Louis caught Teela in the ship while the aliens were outside. "You've been looking like someone poisoned your favorite orchid-thing. Care to talk about it?"

She shook her head, avoiding his eyes. Her lips, he saw, were perfect for pouting. She was one of those rare, lucky women whom crying does not make ugly.

"Then I'll talk. When you went out the lock without a pressure suit, I dressed you down good. Fifteen minutes later you tried to climb a slope of congealing lava wearing nothing but ship-slippers."

"You *wanted* me to burn my feet!"

"That's right. Don't look so surprised. We need you. We don't want you killed. I want you to learn to be careful. You never learned before, so you'll have to learn now. You'll remember your sore feet longer than you remember my lectures."

"Need me! That's a laugh. You know why Nessus brought me here. I'm a good luck charm that failed."

"I'll grant you blew that one. As a good luck charm, you're fired. Come on, smile. We need you. We need you to keep me happy, so I don't rape Nessus. We need you to do all the heavy work while we lie about in the sun. We need you to make intelligent suggestions."

She forced a smile. It broke apart and she was crying. She buried her face in his shoulder and sobbed against him, wrackingly, her fingernails digging hard into his back.

It was not exactly the first time a woman had cried on Louis Wu; but Teela probably had more reason than most. Louis held her, rubbing his fingers along the muscles of her back in a half-automatic attempt at a massage, and waited it out.

She talked into the material of his pressure suit. "How was I to know the rock would burn me!"

"Remember the Finagle Laws. The perversity of the universe tends toward a maximum. The universe is hostile."

"But it *hurt!*"

"The rock turned on you. It attacked you. Listen," he pleaded. "You've got to learn to think paranoid. Think like Nessus."

"I *can't*. I don't know how he thinks. I don't understand him at all." She raised her tear-stained face. "I don't understand *you*."

"Yah." He ran his thumbs hard along the edges of her shoulder blades, then down her vertebrae. "Listen," he said presently. "Suppose I said the universe is my enemy. Would you think I was nuts?"

She nodded vigorously, angrily.

"The universe is against me," said Louis Wu. "The universe hates me. The universe makes no provision for a two-hundred-year-old man.

"What is it that shapes a species? Evolution, isn't it? Evolution gives Speaker his night vision and his balance. Evolution gives Nessus the reflex that turns his back on danger. Evolution turns a man's sex off at fifty or sixty. Then evolution quits.

"Because evolution is through with any organism once that organism is too old to breed. You follow me?"

"Sure. You're too old to breed," she mocked him bitterly.

"Right. A few centuries ago some biological engineers carved up the genes of a ragweed and produced boosterspice. As a direct result, I am two hundred years old and still healthy. But not because the universe loves me.

"The universe hates me," said Louis Wu. "It's tried to kill me many times. I wish I could show you the scars. It'll keep trying, too."

"Because you're too old to breed."

"Finagle in hysterics, woman! You're the one who doesn't know how to take care of herself! We're in unknown territory; we don't know the rules, and we don't know what we might meet. If you try to walk on hot lava, you could get more than sore feet next time. Stay alert. You understand me?"

"No," said Teela. "No."

Later, after she had washed her face, they carried the fourth flycycle into the airlock. For half an hour the aliens had left them alone. Had they decided to avoid two humans dealing with strictly human problems? Maybe. Maybe.

Between high walls of black lava stretched an infinite strip of ring foundation material as flat as a polished tabletop. In the foreground, a tremendous glass cathode tube lay on its side. Beneath the curving flank of the transparent cylinder, a cluster of machinery and four odd figures looking slightly lost.

"How about water?" Louis was asking. "I couldn't see any lakes. Do we have to haul our own water?"

"No." Nessus opened the aft section of his own flycycle to show them the water tank and the cooler-extractor which would condense water from the air.

The flycycles were miracles of compact design. Aside from their highly individualistic saddles, they were built all alike: a pair of four foot spheres joined by the constriction that held the saddle. Half the rear section was luggage space, and there was harness for stringing additional gear. Four flat feet, extended now for landing, would recess against the two spheres during flight.

The puppeteer's flycycle had a reclining saddle, a bellybed with three grooves for his three legs. Nessus would lie immobile on his belly, controlling the vehicle with his mouths.

The 'cycles intended for Louis and Teela held padded
contour chairs with neck rests and power controls for attitude. Like Nessus's and Speaker's, these saddles rested
in the constriction in the 'cycle's dumbbell shape, and
were split to accommodate leg supports. Speaker's saddle
was much larger and broader, and without a neck rest.
There was rigging for tools on both sides of his saddle.
For weapons?

"We must carry anything that could conceivably be
used as a weapon," Speaker was saying, as he prowled
restlessly among the scattered machinery.

"We brought no weapons," Nessus answered. "Because
we wished to show ourselves as peaceful, we brought no
weapons at all."

"Then what are these?" Speaker had already assem-
bled a somewhat sparse collection of lightweight artifacts.

"All tools," said Nessus. He pointed. "These are flashlight-lasers with variable beams. At night one can see
great distances with these, for one can narrow the beam
indefinitely by turning this ring. Indeed, one must be
careful not to burn holes in nearby objects or persons, for
the beam can be made perfectly parallel and extremely
intense.

"These dueling pistols are for settling arguments between ourselves. They fire a ten-second charge. One must
be careful not to touch this safety button, because—"

"Because then it fires an hour's charge. That's a Jinxian
model, isn't it?"

"Yes, Louis. And this item is a modified digging tool.
Perhaps you know of the digging tool found in a Slaver
stasis box—"

He meant the Slaver disintegrator, Louis decided. The
disintegrator was indeed a digging tool. Where its narrow beam fell, the charge on the electron was temporarily
suppressed. Solid matter, rendered suddenly and violently
positive, tended to tear itself into a fog of monatomic
dust.

"It is worthless as a weapon," the kzin rumbled. "We
have studied it. It works too slowly to be used against an
enemy."

"Exactly. A harmless toy. This item—" The item held in the puppeteer's mouth looked like a double-barreled shotgun, except that the handle had a characteristic puppeteer-built look, like quicksilver caught in the act of flowing from one shape to another.

"This item is exactly like the Slaver disintegrator digging tool, except that one beam suppresses the positive charge on the proton. One should be careful not to use both beams at once, as the beams are parallel and separate."

"I understand," said the kzin. "If the twin beams were allowed to fall next to each other, there would be a current flow."

"Exactly."

"Do you believe these makeshifts will be adequate? There is no guessing what we shall meet."

"That's not quite true," said Louis Wu. "This isn't a planet, after all. If there was an animal the Ringworlders didn't like, chances are they left it home. We won't meet any tigers. Or mosquitoes."

"Suppose the Ringworlders liked tigers?" Teela wondered.

It was a valid point, despite its facetious sound. What did they know of Ringworld physiology? Only that they came from a water world using approximately G2 starlight. On that basis they might look like humans, puppeteers, kzinti, grogs, dolphins, killer whales, or sperm whales; but they probably wouldn't.

"We will fear the Ringworlders more than their pets," Speaker predicted. "We must take all possible weapons. I recommend that I be placed in charge of this expedition until such time as we may leave the Ring."

"I have the tasp."

"I have not forgotten that, Nessus. You may think of the tasp as an absolute veto power. I suggest that you show reluctance to use it. Think, all of you!" The kzin loomed over them, five hundred pounds of teeth and claws and orange fur. "We are all supposed to be sentient. Think of our situation! We have been attacked. Our ship is half destroyed. We must travel an unknown distance across unknown territory. The powers of the Ringworlders were once enormous. Are they still enormous, or do they now use nothing more complex than a spear made from a sharpened bone?

"They might equally well have transmutation, total-conversion beams, anything that may have been required to build this—" the kzin looked around him, at the glassy floor and the black lava walls; and perhaps he shuddered. "—this incredible artifact."

"I have the tasp," said Nessus. "The expedition is mine."

"Are you pleased with its success? I mean no insult, I intend no challenge. You must place me in command. Of the four of us, I alone have had training in war."

"Let's wait," Teela suggested. "We may not find anything to fight."

"Agreed," said Louis. He didn't fancy being led by a kzin.

"Very well. But we must take the weapons."

They began to load the flycycles.

There was other equipment besides weaponry. Camping equipment, food testing and food rebuilding kits, phials of dietary additives, lightweight air filters . . .

There were communicator discs designed to be worn on a human or kzinti wrist or a puppeteer neck. They were bulky and not particularly comfortable.

"Why these?" Louis asked. For the puppeteer had already shown them the intercom system built into the flycycles.

"They were originally intended to communicate with the *Liar's* autopilot, so that we might summon the ship when necessary."

"Then why do we need them now?"

"As translators, Louis. Should we run into sentient beings, as seems likely, we will need the autopilot to translate for us."

"Oh."

They were finished. Equipment still rested beneath the *Liar's* hull, but it was useless stuff: free-fall equipment for deep space, the pressure suits, some replacement parts for machinery vaporized by the Ringworld defense system. They had loaded even the air filters, more because they were no more bulky than handkerchiefs, than because they were likely to be needed.

Louis was bone tired. He mounted his flycycle and looked about him, wondering if he had forgotten anything. He saw Teela staring straight upward, and even through the mist of exhaustion he saw that she was horrified.

"There ain't no justice," she swore. *"It's still noon!"*

"Don't panic. The—"

"Louis! We've been working for a good six hours, I know we have! How could it be still noon?"

"Don't worry about it. The sun doesn't set, remember?"

"Doesn't set?" her hysteria ended as suddenly as it had begun. "Oh. Of course it doesn't set."

"We'll have to get used to it. Look again; isn't that the edge of a shadow square against the sun?"

Something had certainly nipped a chord out of the sun's disc. The sun diminished as they watched.

"We had best take flight," said Speaker. "When darkness falls we should be aloft."

CHAPTER 11

The Arch of Heaven

Four flycycles rose in a diamond cluster through waning daylight. The exposed ring flooring dropped away.

Nessus had shown them how to use the slave circuits. Now each of the other 'cycles was programmed to imitate whatever Louis's did. Louis was steering for them all. In a contoured seat like a masseur couch without the masseur attachments, he guided his 'cycle with pedals and a joystick.

Four transparent miniature heads hovered like hallucinations above his dashboard. These included a lovely raven-haired siren, a ferocious quasi-tiger with eyes that were too aware, and a pair of silly-looking one-eyed pythons. The intercom hookup was working perfectly, with results comparable to delirium tremens.

As the flycycles rose above the black lava slopes, Louis watched the others for their expressions.

Teela reacted first. Her eyes scanned the middle distance, and rose, and found infinity where they had always before found limits. They went big and round, and Teela's face lit like sunlight breaking through storm clouds. "Oh, *Louis!*"

"What an extraordinarily large mountain!" Speaker said.

Nessus said nothing. His heads bobbed and circled nervously.

Darkness fell quickly. A black shadow swept suddenly across the giant mountain. In seconds it was gone. The sun was only a golden sliver now, cut by blackness. And something took shape in the darkening sky.

An enormous arch.

Its outline grew rapidly clear. As the land and sky grew dark, the true glory of the Ringworld sky emerged against the night.

The Ringworld arched over itself in stripes of baby blue swirled with white cloud, in narrower stripes of near-black. At its base the arch was very broad. It narrowed swiftly as it rose. Near the zenith it was no more than a broken line of glowing blue-white. At the zenith itself the arch was cut by the otherwise invisible ring of shadow squares.

The skycycles rose quickly, but in silence. The sonic fold was a most effective insulator. Louis heard no windsong from outside. He was all the more startled when his private bubble of space was violated by a scream of orchestral music.

It sounded as though a steam organ had exploded.

The sound was painfully loud. Louis slapped his hands over his ears. Stunned, he did not at once realize what was happening. Then he flicked the intercom control, and Nessus's image went like a ghost at dawn. The scream (a church choir being burnt alive?) diminished considerably. He could still hear it keening at second hand (a gutshot stereo set?) through Speaker's and Teela's intercom.

"Why did he do that?" Teela exclaimed in astonishment.

"Terrified. It'll take him awhile to get used to it."

"Used to what?"

"I take command," Speaker-To-Animals boomed. "The herbivore is incapable to make decisions. I declare this mission to be of military nature, and I take command."

For a moment Louis considered the only alternative: claiming the leader's place for himself. But who wanted to fight a kzin? In any case, the kzin would probably make a better leader.

By now the flycycles were half a mile up. Sky and

land were mostly black; but on the black land were blacker shadows, giving form if not color to the map; and the sky was sprinkled with stars, and mastered by that ego-smashing arch.

Oddly, Louis found himself thinking of Dante's *Divine Comedy*. Dante's universe had been a complex artifact, with the souls of men and angels shown as precisely machined parts of the vast structure. The Ringworld was obtrusively an artifact, a *made* thing. You couldn't forget it, not for an instant; for the handle rose overhead, huge and blue and checkered, from beyond the edge of infinity.

Small wonder Nessus had been unable to face it. He was too afraid—and too realistic. Perhaps he saw the beauty; perhaps not. Certainly he saw that they were marooned on an artificial structure bigger in area than all the worlds of the former puppeteer empire.

"I believe I can see the rim walls," said Speaker.

Louis tore his eyes away from the arching sky. He looked to "port" and "starboard" and his heart sank.

To the left (they were facing back along the gouge of the *Liar's* landing, so that *left* was *port*), the edge of the rim wall was a barely visible line, blue-black on blue-black. Louis could not guess its height. Its base was not even hinted. Only the top edge showed; and when he stared at it it disappeared. That line was about where the horizon might have been; so that it might as easily have been the base as the top of something.

To right and starboard, the other rim wall was virtually identical. The same height, the same picture, the same tendency of the line to fade away beneath a steady stare.

Apparently the *Liar* had smashed down very close to the median line of the ring. The rim walls seemed equally distant . . . which put them nearly half a million miles away.

Louis cleared his throat. "Speaker, what do you think?"

"To me the port wall seems fractionally higher."

"Okay." Louis turned left. The other 'cycles followed, still on slave circuits.

Louis activated the intercom for a look at Nessus. The puppeteer was hugging his saddle with all three legs; his heads were tucked between his body and the saddle. He was flying blind.

Teela said, "Speaker, are you sure?"

"Of course," the kzin answered. "The portside rim wall is visibly larger."

Louis smiled to himself. He had never had war training, but he knew something of war. He'd been caught on the ground during a revolution on Wunderland, and had fought as a guerilla for three months before he could get to a ship.

One mark of a good officer, he remembered, was the ability to make quick decisions. If they happened to be right, so much the better . . .

They flew to port over black land. The Ring glowed far brighter than moonlight, but moonlight does little to light a landscape from the air. The meteor gully, the rip the *Liar* had torn across the Ringworld's surface, was a silver thread behind them. Eventually it faded into the dark.

The skycycles accelerated steadily and in silence. At a little below the speed of sound, a rushing sound penetrated the sonic fold. It reached a peak at sonic speed, then cut off sharply. The sonic fold found a new shape, and again there was silence.

Shortly thereafter the 'cycles reached cruising speed. Louis relaxed within the 'cycle seat. He estimated that he would be spending more than a month in that seat, and he might as well get used to it.

Presently (because he was the only one flying, and it would not do to fall asleep) he began testing his 'cycle.

The rest facilities were simple, comfortable, and easy to use. But undignified.

He tried pushing his hand into the sonic fold. The fold was a force field, a network of force vectors intended to guide air currents around the space occupied by the fly-cycle. It was not intended to behave like a glass wall. To Louis's hand it felt like a hard wind, a wind that pushed straight toward him from every direction. He was in a protected bubble of moving wind.

The sonic fold seemed idiot-proof.

He tested that by pulling a facial tissue from a slot and dropping it. The tissue fluttered underneath the 'cycle, and there it rested on the air, vibrating madly. Louis was willing to believe that if he fell out of his seat, which would not be easy, he would be caught by the sonic fold and would be able to climb back up again.

It figured. Puppeteers . . .

The water tube gave him distilled water. The food slot gave him flat reddish-brown bricks. Six times he dialed a brick, took a bite, and dropped the brick into the intake hopper. Each brick tasted different, and they all tasted good.

At least he would not get bored with eating. Not soon, anyway.

But if they could not find plants and water to shovel into the intake hopper, the food slot would eventually stop delivering bricks.

He dialed a seventh brick and ate it.

Unnerving, to think how far they were from help. Earth was two hundred light years away; the puppeteer fleet, two light years distant, was receding at nearly lightspeed; and even the half-vaporized *Liar* had been invisible from the beginning of the flight. Now the meteoric gouge had faded from sight. How easy would it be to lose the ship entirely?

Tanj near impossible, Louis decided. To antispinward was the largest mountain men had ever seen. There couldn't be many such supervolcanos on the Ringworld. To find the *Liar,* one would aim for the mountain, then troll spinward for a linear gouge several thousand miles long.

. . . But the arch of the Ringworld blazed overhead: three million times the surface area of the Earth. There was room to get quite thoroughly lost on the Ringworld.

Nessus was beginning to stir. First one head, then the other emerged from beneath the puppeteer's torso. The puppeteer tongued switches, then spoke.

"Louis, may we have privacy?"

The transparent images of Speaker and Teela appeared to be dozing. Louis switched them out of the intercom circuit. "Go ahead."

"What has been happening?"

"Couldn't you hear?"

"My ears are in my heads. My hearing was blocked."

"How are you feeling now?"

"Perhaps I will return to catatonia. I feel very lost, Louis."

"Me too. Well, we've come twenty-two hundred miles in the last three hours. We'd have done better with transfer booths, or even stepping discs."

"Our engineers were unable to arrange stepping discs." The puppeteer's heads glanced at each other, eye to eye. A moment only they held the position; but Louis had seen that gesture before.

Now, tentatively, he tagged it as puppeteer's laughter. Would a mad puppeteer develop a sense of humor?

He continued speaking. "We're moving to port. Speaker decided that the portside rim wall was closer. I think we could have flipped a coin for it and got better accuracy. But Speaker's the boss. He took over when you went catatonic."

"That is unfortunate. Speaker's flycycle is beyond range of my tasp. I must—"

"Hold it a second. Why not leave him in command?"

"But, but, but—"

"Think about it," Louis urged. "You can always veto him with the tasp. If you don't put him in charge, he'll take over anyway, every time you relax. We need an undisputed leader."

"I suppose it cannot hurt," the puppeteer fluted. "My leadership will not materially improve our chances."

"That's the spirit. Call Speaker and tell him he's the Hindmost."

Louis hooked himself into Speaker's intercom to hear the exchange. If he was expecting fireworks he was disappointed. The kzin and the puppeteer spoke a few hiss-

ing, spitting phrases in the Hero's Tongue. Then the kzin
cut himself out of the circuit.

"I must apologize," said Nessus. "My stupidity has
brought disaster on us."

"Don't worry about it," Louis consoled him. "You're
just in the depressive leg of your cycle."

"I am a sentient being, and I can face facts. I was
terribly wrong about Teela Brown."

"True enough, but that wasn't your fault."

"It was indeed my fault, Louis Wu. I should have realized why I was having trouble finding candidates other
than Teela Brown."

"Huh?"

"They were too lucky."

Louis whistled tunelessly through his teeth. The puppeteer had evolved a brand new theory.

"Specifically," said Nessus, "They were too lucky to
become involved in such a dangerous project as ours. The
Birthright Lotteries have indeed produced psychic, hered-
itary luck. Yet that luck was not available to me. When
I tried to contact the Lottery Families, I found only
Teela Brown."

"Listen—"

"I was unable to contact others because they were too
lucky. I was able to contact Teela Brown, to involve her
in this ill-fated expedition, because she did not inherit
the gene. Louis, I apologize."

"Oh, go to sleep."

"I must apologize to Teela too."

"No. That's my fault. I could have stopped her."

"Could you?"

"I don't know. I honestly don't. Go to sleep."

"I cannot."

"Then you fly. *I'll* go to sleep."

And so it was. But before Louis dropped off, he was
surprised to realize how smoothly the flycycle was riding.
The puppeteer was an excellent pilot.

Louis woke at first light.

He was not used to sleeping under gravity. Never in

his life had he spent a night in sitting position. When he yawned and tried to stretch, muscles seemed to crack and crumble under the strain. Groaning, he rubbed sticky eyes and looked about him.

The shadows were funny; the light was funny. Louis looked up and found a white sliver of noonday sun. *Stupid,* he told himself as he waited for the tears to stop. His reflexes were faster than his brain.

To his left all was darkness, deepening with distance. The missing horizon was a blackness born of night and chaos, beneath a navy sky in which outlines of the Ringworld arch glowed faintly.

To the right, to spinward, was full day.

Dawn was *different* on the Ringworld.

The desert was coming to an end. Its weaving border, clear and sharp, curved away to right and left. Behind the 'cycles was desert, yellow-white and bright and barren. The big mountain still blocked an impressive chunk of sky. Ahead, rivers and lakes showed in diminishing perspective, separated by patches of green-brown.

The 'cycles had maintained their positions, widely separated in a diamond pattern. At this distance they seemed silver bugs, all alike. Louis was in the lead. His memory told him that Speaker had the spinward position; Nessus was to antispinward, and Teela brought up the rear.

To spinward of the mountain was a hanging thread of dust, like the trail left by a ground-effect jeep crossing a desert, but larger. It had to be larger, though it was only a thread at this distance . . .

"Are you awake, Louis?"

"Morning, Nessus. Have you been flying all this time?"

"Some hours ago I turned that chore over to Speaker. You will notice that we have already traveled seven thousand-odd miles."

"Yah." But it was only a figure, a tiny fraction of the distance they would have to travel. A lifetime of using the transfer booth network had ruined Louis's sense of distance.

"Look behind us," he said. "See that dust trail? Any idea what it might be?"

"Of course. It must be the vaporized rock from our meteoric landing, recondensed in the atmosphere. It has not had time to settle out of so large a volume."

"Oh. I was thinking of dust storms . . . Tanj forever, look how far we slid!" For the dust trail was at least a couple of thousand miles long, if it was as far away as the ship.

Sky and earth were two flat plates, infinitely wide, pressed together; and men were microbes crawling between the plates . . .

"Our air pressure has increased."

Louis pulled his eyes away from the vanishing point. "What did you say?"

"Look at your pressure gauge. We must have been at least two miles above our present level when we landed."

Louis dialed a ration brick for breakfast. "Is the air pressure important?"

"We must observe all things in an unfamiliar environment. One never knows what detail might be crucial. For instance, the mountain which we chose as a landmark bulks large behind us. It must be even larger than we thought. Again, what of that silver-shining point ahead of us?"

"Where?"

"Almost at the hypothetical horizon line, Louis. Directly ahead."

It was like searching out a single detail in a map seen edge-on. Louis found it anyway: a bright mirror-gleam, just large enough to be more than a point.

"Reflected sunlight. What could it be? A glass city?"

"Improbable."

Louis laughed. "You're too polite. It's as *big* as a glass city, though. Or an acre of mirrors. Maybe it's a big telescope, reflector type."

"Then it has probably been abandoned."

"How so?"

"We know that this civilization has returned to savagery. Why else would they allow vast regions to return to desert?"

Once Louis had believed that argument. Now . . . "You may be oversimplifying. The Ringworld's bigger than we realized. I think there's room here for savagery and civilization and anything in between."

"Civilization tends to spread, Louis."

"Yah."

They'd find out about the bright point, anyway. It was directly in their path.

There wasn't any coffee spigot.

Louis was swallowing the last of his breakfast brick when he noticed two green lights glowing on his dashboard. They puzzled him until he remembered switching Teela and Speaker out of the intercom last night. He switched them back in.

"Good morning," said Speaker. "Did you see the dawn, Louis? It was artistically stimulating."

"I saw it. Morning, Teela."

Teela didn't answer.

Louis looked more closely. Teela was fascinated, rapt, like one who has reached Nirvana.

"Nessus, have you been using your tasp on my woman?"

"No, Louis. Why should I?"

"How long has she been like this?"

"Like what?" Speaker demanded. "She has not been communicative recently, if that is what you mean."

"I mean her expression, tanjit!"

Teela's image, poised on his dashboard, looked at infinity through the bulk of Louis's head. She was quietly, thoroughly happy.

"She seems relaxed," said the kzin, "and in no discomfort. The finer nuances of human expression—"

"Never mind that. Land us, will you? She's got Plateau trance."

"I do not understand."

"Just land us."

They fell from a mile up. Louis endured a queasy period of free fall before Speaker gave them thrust again. He watched Teela's image for her reaction, but he saw none. She was serene and undisturbed. The corners of her mouth turned very slightly up.

Louis fumed as they dropped. He knew something about hypnosis: bits and oddments of information such as a man will collect over two hundred years of watching tridee. If only he could remember . . .

Greens and browns resolved into field and forest and a silver thread of stream. It was lush, wild country below them, the kind of country flatlanders expect to find on a colony world, more's the pity.

"Try to put us in a valley," Louis told Speaker. "I'd like to get her out of sight of the horizon."

"Very well. I suggest that you and Nessus cut yourselves out of autopilot and follow me down on manual. I will land Teela myself."

The diamond of flycycles broke up and re-formed. Speaker moved port-and-spinward, toward the stream Louis had spotted earlier. The others followed.

They were still dropping as they crossed the stream. Speaker turned spinward to follow its course. By now he was virtually crawling through the air, moving just above the treetops. He searched for a stretch of bank not blocked by trees.

"The plants seem very Earthlike," said Louis. The aliens made noises of agreement.

They rounded a curve of stream.

The natives were in the middle of a broad section of stream. They were working a fishing net. As the line of 'cycles came into view the natives looked up. For a long moment they did nothing more than let go of the net, while they stared upward with their mouths open.

Louis, Speaker, and Nessus all reacted in the same way. They took off straight upward. The natives dwindled to points; the stream to a winding silver thread. The lush, wild forest blurred into green-browns.

"Put yourselves on autopilot," Speaker ordered, in an

unmistakable tone of command. "I will land us else-where."

He must have *learned* that tone of command—strictly for use in dealing with humans. The duties of an ambassador, Louis mused, were various indeed.

Teela had apparently noticed nothing at all.

Louis said, "Well?"

"They were men," said Nessus.

"They were, weren't they? I thought I might be hallucinating. How would men get here?"

But nobody tried to answer.

CHAPTER 12

Fist-of-God

They had landed in a pocket of wild country surrounded by low hills. With the hills hiding the mock-horizon, and the glow of the Arch drowned by daylight, it might have been a scene on any human world. The grass was not precisely grass, but it was green, and it made a carpet over places that should have been covered by grass. There were soil and rocks, and bushes which grew green foliage and which were gnarled in almost the right ways.

The vegetation, as Louis had remarked, was eerily Earth-like. There were bushes where one would expect bushes, bare spots where one would expect bare spots. According to instruments in the scooters, the plants were earthly even at the molecular level. As Louis and Speaker were related by some remote viral ancestor, so the trees of this world could claim both as brother.

There was a plant that would have made a nice hedge/fence. It looked like wood; but it grew up at forty-five degrees, sprouted a crown of leaves, dropped back at the same angle, sprouted a cluster of roots, rose again at forty-five degrees . . . Louis had seen something like it on Gummidgy; but this row of triangles was glossy-green and bark-brown, the colors of Earth life. Louis called it *elbow root*.

Nessus moved about within the little pocket of forest, collecting plants and insects for testing in the compact laboratory of his scooter. He wore his vacuum suit, a transparent balloon with three boots and two glove/

160

mouthpieces. Nothing of the Ringworld could attack him without piercing that barrier: not a predator, not an insect, not a grain of pollen nor a fungus spore nor a virus molecule.

Teela Brown sat astride her flycycle with her larger-than-delicate hands resting lightly on the controls. The corners of her mouth curved slightly upward. She was poised against a flycycle's acceleration, relaxed yet alert, setting off the lines and curves of her body as if she were posing for a figure study. Her green eyes looked through Louis Wu, and through a barrier of low hills, to see infinity at the Ringworld's abstract horizon.

"I do not understand," said Speaker. "Exactly what is the trouble? She is not asleep, yet she is curiously unresponsive."

"Highway hypnosis," said Louis Wu. "She'll come out of it by herself."

"Then she is in no danger?"

"Not now. I was afraid she might fall off her 'cycle, or do something crazy with the controls. She's safe enough on the ground."

"But why does she take so little interest in us?"

Louis tried to explain.

In the asteroid belt of Sol, men spend half their lives guiding singleships among the rocks. They take their positions from the stars. For hours at a time a Belt miner will watch the stars: the bright quick arcs which are fusion-driven singleships, the slow, drifting lights which are nearby asteroids, and the fixed points which are stars and galaxies.

A man can lose his soul among the white stars. Much later, he may realize that his body has acted for him, guiding his ship while his mind traveled in realms he cannot remember. They call it *the far look*. It is dangerous. A man's soul does not always return.

On the great flat plateau on Mount Lookitthat, a man may stand at the void edge and look down on infinity. The mountain is only forty miles tall; but a human eye, tracing the mountain's fluted side, finds infinity on the solid mist that hides the mountain's base.

The void mist is white and featureless and uniform. It stretches without change from the mountain's fluted flank to the world's horizon. The emptiness can snatch at a man's mind and hold it, so that he stands frozen and rapt at the edge of eternity until someone comes to lead him away. They call it *Plateau trance.*

Then there is the Ringworld horizon . . .

"But it's all self-hypnosis," said Louis. He looked into the girl's eyes. She stirred restlessly. "I could probably bring her out of it, but why risk it? Let her sleep."

"I do not understand hypnosis," said Speaker-To-Animals. "I know of it, but I do not understand it."

Louis nodded. "I'm not surprised. Kzinti wouldn't make good hypnotic subjects. Neither would puppeteers, for that matter." For Nessus had given over his collecting of samples of alien life and quietly joined them.

"We can study what we cannot understand," said the puppeteer. "We know that there is something in a man that does not want to make decisions. A part of him wants someone else to tell him what to do. A good hypnotic subject is a trusting person with a good ability to concentrate. His act of surrender to the hypnotist is the beginning of his hypnosis."

"But what is hypnosis?"

"An induced state of monomania."

"But why would a subject go into monomania?"

Nessus apparently had no answer.

Louis said, "Because he trusts the hypnotist."

Speaker shook his great head and turned away.

"Such trust in another is insane. I confess I do not understand hypnosis," said Nessus. "Do you, Louis?"

"Not entirely."

"I am relieved," said the puppeteer, and he looked for a moment into his own eyes, a pair of pythons inspecting each other. "I could not trust one who could understand nonsense."

"What have you found out about Ringworld plants?"

"They seem very like the life of Earth, as I told you.

However, some of the forms seem more specialized than one would expect."

"More evolved, you mean?"

"Perhaps. Again, perhaps a specialized form has more room to grow, even within its limited environment, here on the Ringworld. The important point is that the plants and insects are similar enough to attack us."

"And vice versa?"

"Oh, yes. A few forms are edible for me, a few others will fit your own belly. You will have to test them individually, first for poisons and then for taste. But any plant we find can safely be used by the kitchen on your 'cycle."

"We won't starve, then."

"This single advantage hardly compensates for the danger. If only our engineers had thought to pack a starseed lure aboard the *Liar!* This entire trek would have been unnecessary."

"A starseed lure?"

"A simple device, invented thousands of years ago. It causes the local sun to emit electromagnetic signals that attract starseeds. Had we such a device, we could lure a starseed to this star, then communicate our problem to any Outsider ship that followed it inward."

"But starseeds travel at a lot less than lightspeed. It might take years!"

"But think, Louis! However long we waited, we would not have had to leave the safety of the ship!"

"To you this is a full life?" Louis snorted. And he glanced at Speaker, fixed on Speaker, locked eyes with Speaker.

Speaker-To-Animals, curled on the ground some distance away, was staring back at him and grinning like an Alice-In-Wonderland Cheshire Cat. For a long moment they locked eyes; and then the kzin stood up with seeming leisure, sprang, and vanished into the alien bushes.

Louis turned back. Somehow he knew that something important had happened. But what? And why? He shrugged it away.

Straddling the contoured saddle of her 'cycle, Teela

seemed braced for acceleration . . . as if she were still flying. Louis remembered the few times he had been hypnotized by a therapist. It had felt a lot like play-acting. Cushioned in a rosy absence of responsibility, he had known that it was all a game he was playing with the hypnotist. He could break free at any time. But somehow one never did.

Teela's eyes cleared suddenly. She shook her head, turned and saw them. "Louis! How did we get down?"

"The usual way."

"Help me down." She put her arms out like a child on a wall. Louis put his hands on her waist and lifted her from the 'cycle. The touch of her was a thrill along his back and an opening warmth in his groin and solar plexus. He left his hands where they were.

"The last I remember, we were a mile in the air," Teela said.

"From now on, keep your eyes off the horizon."

"What did I do, fall asleep at the wheel?" She laughed and tossed her head, so that her hair became a great soft black cloud. "And you all panicked! I'm sorry, Louis. Where's Speaker?"

"Chasing a rabbit," said Louis. "Hey, why don't we get some exercise ourselves, now we've got the chance?"

"How about a walk in the woods?"

"Good idea." He met her eyes and saw that they had read each other's thoughts. He reached into his 'cycle's luggage bin and produced a blanket. "Ready."

"You amaze me," said Nessus. "No known sentient species copulates as often as you do. Go, then. Use caution where you sit. Remember that unfamiliar life-forms are about."

"Did you know," said Louis, "that *naked* once meant the same thing as *unprotected?*"

For it seemed to him that he was removing his safety with his clothes. The Ringworld had a functioning biosphere, ripe, no doubt, with bugs and bacteria and toothy things built to eat protoplasmic meat.

"No," said Teela. She stood naked on the blanket and

stretched her arms to the noon sun. "It feels good. Do you know that I've never seen you naked in daylight?"

"Likewise. I might add that you look tanj good that way. Here, let me show you something." He half-raised a hand to his hairless chest. "Tanjit—"

"I don't see anything."

"It's gone. That's the trouble with boosterspice. No memories. The scars disappear, and after a while . . ." He traced a line across his chest; but there was nothing under his fingertip.

"A Gummidgy reacher tore a strip off me from shoulder to navel, four inches wide and half an inch deep. His next pass would have split me in two. He decided to swallow what he had of me first. I must have been deadly poison to him, because he curled up in a shrieking ball and died.

"Now there's nothing. Not a mark on me anywhere."

"Poor Louis. But I don't have any marks either."

"But you're a statistical anomaly, and furthermore you're only twenty years old."

"Oh."

"Mmm. You are smooth."

"Any other missing memories?"

"I made a mistake with a mining beam once . . ." He guided her hand.

Presently Louis rolled onto his back, and Teela impaled herself as she straddled his hips. They looked at each other for a long, brilliant, unbearable moment before they began to move.

Seen through the glow of a building orgasm, a woman seems to blaze with angelic glory . . .

. . . Something the size of a rabbit shot out of the trees, scampered across Louis's chest and was gone into the undergrowth. An instant later, Speaker-To-Animals bounded into view. "Excuse me," the kzin called, and was gone, hot on the scent.

When they reconvened at the 'cycles, the fur around Speaker's mouth was stained red. "For the first time in my life," he proclaimed with quiet satisfaction, "I have hunted for my food, using no more weapons than my own teeth and claws."

But he followed Nessus's advice and took a broad-spectrum allergy pill.

"It is time we discussed the natives," said Nessus.

Teela looked startled. "Natives?"

Louis explained.

"But why did we run? How could they have hurt us? Were they really human?"

Louis answered the last question, because it had been bothering him. "I don't see how they could have been. What would human beings be doing this far from human space?"

"There is no possible doubt of that," Speaker interjected. "Trust your senses, Louis. We may find that their race differs from yours or Teela's. But they are human."

"What makes you so sure?"

"I smell them, Louis. The scent reached me when we turned off the sonic folds. Far away, thinly spread, a vast multitude of human beings. Trust my nose, Louis."

Louis accepted it. The kzinti nose was worn by a hunting carnivore. He suggested, "Parallel evolution?"

"Nonsense," said Nessus.

"Right." The human shape was convenient for a toolmaker, but no more so than other configurations. Minds came in all kinds of bodies.

"We are wasting time," said Speaker-To-Animals. "The problem is not how men arrived here. The problem is one of first contact. For us, every contact will be a first contact."

He was right, Louis realized. The 'cycles moved faster than any information-sending service the natives were likely to have. Unless they had semaphores . . .

Speaker continued, "We need to know something of the behavior of humans in the savage state. Louis? Teela?"

"I know a little anthropology," said Louis.

"Then when we make contact, you will speak for us. Let us hope that our autopilot makes an adequate translator. We will contact the first humans we find."

They were barely in the air, it seemed, when the forest gave way to a checkerboard of cultivated fields. Seconds later, Teela spotted the city.

It resembled some earthly cities of previous centuries. There were a great many buildings a few stories tall, packed shoulder to shoulder in a continuous mass. A few tall, slender towers rose above the mass, and these were joined together by winding groundcar ramps: definitely *not* a feature of earthly cities. Earth's cities of that era had tended to heliports instead.

"Perhaps our search ends here," Speaker suggested hopefully.

"Bet you it's empty," said Louis.

He was only guessing, but he was right. It became obvious as they flew over.

In its day the city must have been terrible in its beauty. One feature it had which would have been the envy of any city in known space. Many of the buildings had not rested on the ground at all, but had floated in the air, joined to the ground and to other buildings by ramps and elevator towers. Freed of gravity, freed of vertical and horizontal restrictions, these floating dream-castles had come in all shapes and a wide choice of sizes.

Now four flycycles flew over the wreckage. Every floating building had smashed lower buildings when it fell, so that all was shattered brick and glass and concrete, torn steel, twisted ramps and elevator towers still reaching into the air.

It made Louis wonder again about the natives. Human engineers didn't build air-castles; they were too safety-conscious.

"They must have fallen all at once," said Nessus. "I see no sign of attempted repairs. A power failure, no doubt. Speaker, would kzinti build so foolishly?"

"We do not love heights so well. Humans might, if they did not so love their lives."

"Boosterspice," Louis exclaimed. "That's the answer. They didn't have boosterspice."

"Yes, that might make them less safety-conscious. They

would have less of life to protect," the puppeteer speculated. "That seems ominous, does it not? If they think
less of their own lives, they will think less of ours."

"You're borrowing trouble."

"We will know soon enough. Speaker, do you see that
last building, the tall, cream-colored one with the broken
windows—"

They had passed over it while the puppeteer spoke.
Louis, who was taking his turn at flying the 'cycles, circled for another look.

"I was right. You see, Speaker? Smoke."

The building was an artistically twisted and sculpted
pillar some twenty stories tall. Its windows were rows of
black ovals. Most of the windows of the ground floor were
covered. The few that were open poured thin gray smoke
into the wind.

The tower stood ankle-deep among one- and two-story
homes. A row of those houses had been smashed flat by a
rolling cylinder which must have fallen from the sky.
But the rolling wreckage had disintegrated into concrete
rubble before it reached that single tower.

The back of the tower was the edge of the city. Beyond were only rectangles of cultivation. Humanoid figures were running in from the fields even as the flycycles
settled.

Buildings which had looked whole from high up were
obvious wrecks at rooftop level. Nothing was untouched.
The power failure and its accompanying disasters must
have occurred generations ago. Then had come vandalism,
rain, all the various corrosions caused by small life-forms,
oxidation of metals, and something more. Something that
in Earth's prehistoric past had left village mounds for
later archeologists to browse through.

The city-dwellers had not restored their city after the
power failure. Neither had they moved away. They had
lived on in the ruins.

And the garbage of their living had accumulated about
them.

Garbage. Empty boxes. Wind-borne dust. Inedible

parts of food, bones, and things comparable to carrot leaves and corn cobs. Broken tools. It built up, when people were too lazy or too hardworked to haul the rubbish away. It built up, and the parts softened and merged, and the pile settled under its own weight, and was compressed further by heavy feet, year by year, generation by generation.

The original entrance to the tower was already buried. Ground level had risen that far. As the flycycles settled on hard-packed dirt, ten feet above what had once been a parking area for large ground-bound vehicles, five humanoid natives strode in solemn dignity through a second-story window.

The window was a double bay window, easily large enough to accommodate such a procession. Its sill and lintel were decorated with thirty or forty human-looking skulls. Louis could see no obvious pattern to their arrangement.

The five walked toward the 'cycles. As they came near they hesitated, in visible doubt as to who was in charge. They, too, looked human, but not very. Clearly they belonged to no known race of man.

The five were all shorter than Louis Wu by six inches or more. Where it showed their skin was very light, almost ghost-white in contrast to Teela's merely Nordic pink or Louis's darker yellow-brown. They tended to short torsos and long legs. They walked with their arms identically folded; and their fingers were extraordinarily long and tapering, so that any of the five would have been a born surgeon in the days when men still performed surgery.

Their hair was more extraordinary than their hands. On all five dignitaries, it was the same shade of ash blond. They wore their hair and beards combed but uncut; and their beards covered their faces entirely, except for the eyes.

Needless to say, they all looked alike.

"They're so *hairy!*" Teela whispered.

"Stay on your vehicles," Speaker ordered in a low voice. "Wait until they reach us. Then dismount. I assume we are all wearing our communicator discs?"

Louis wore his inside his left wrist. The discs were linked to the autopilot aboard the *Liar*. They should work over such a distance, and the *Liar's* autopilot should be able to translate any new language.

But there was no way to test the tanj things except in action. And there were all those skulls . . .

Other natives were pouring into the former parking lot. Most of them halted at the sight of the confrontation-in-progress, so that the crowd formed a wide rough circle well outside the region of action. A normal crowd would have grumbled to itself in speculation and wagers and arguments. This crowd was unnaturally silent.

Perhaps the presence of an audience forced the dignitaries to decide. They chose to approach Louis Wu.

The five . . . they didn't really look alike. They differed in height. All were thin, but one was almost a skeleton, and one almost had muscles. Four wore shapeless, almost colorless brown robes, a fifth wore a robe of similar cut—cut from a similar blanket?—but in a faded pink pattern.

The one who spoke was the thinnest of them. A blue tattooed bird adorned the back of his hand.

Louis answered.

The tattooed one made a short speech. That was luck. The autopilot would need data before it could begin a translation.

Louis replied.

The tattooed man spoke again. His four companions maintained their dignified silence. So, incredibly, did their audience.

Presently the discs were filling in words and phrases . . .

He thought later that the silence should have tipped him off. It was their stance that fooled him. There was the wide ring of the crowd, and the four hairy men in robes, all standing in a row; and the man with the tattooed hand, talking.

"We call the mountain Fist-of-God." He was pointing directly starboard. "Why? Why not, if it please you, engineer?" He must have meant the big mountain, the one they had left behind with the ship. By now it was entirely concealed by haze and distance.

Louis listened and learned. The autopilot made a dandy translator. Gradually a picture built up, a picture of a farming village living in the ruins of what had once been a mighty city . . .

"True, Zignamuclickclick is no longer as great as it once was. Yet our dwellings are far superior to what we could make for ourselves. Where a roof is open to the sky, still the lower floor will remain dry during a short rainstorm. The buildings of the city are easy to keep warm. In time of war, they are easily defended, and difficult to burn down.

"So it is, engineer, that though we go in the morning to work our fields, at night we return to our dwellings along the edge of Zignamuclickclick. Why should we strain to make new homes when the old ones serve better?"

Two terrifying aliens and two almost-humans, unbearded and unnaturally tall; all four riding wingless metal birds, speaking gibberish from their mouths and sense from metal discs . . . small wonder if the natives had taken them for the Ringworld builders. Louis did nothing to correct the impression. An explanation of their origin would have taken days; and the team was here to learn, not to teach.

"This tower, engineer, is our seat of government. We rule more than a thousand people here. Could we raise a better palace than this tower? We have blocked off the upper stories so that the sections we use will retain heat. Once we defended the tower by dropping rubble from upper floors. I remember that our worst problem was the fear of high places . . .

"Yet we long for the return of the days of wonder, when our city held a thousand thousand people, and buildings floated in the air. We hope that you will choose to bring back those days. It is said that in the days of wonder, even this very world was bent to its present shape. Perhaps you will deign to say if it is true?"

"It's true enough," said Louis.

"And shall those days return?"

Louis made an answer he hoped was noncommittal. He sensed the other's disappointment, or guessed it.

Reading the hairy man's expression was not easy. Gestures are a kind of code; and the spokesman's gestures were not those of any terrestrial culture. Tightly-curled platinum hair hid his entire face, except for the eyes, which were brown and soft. But eyes hold little expression, contrary to public opinion.

His voice was almost a chant, almost a recital of poetry. The autopilot was translating Louis's words into a similar chant, though it spoke to Louis in a conversational tone. Louis could hear the other translator discs whistling softly in Puppeteer, snarling quietly in the Hero's Tongue.

Louis put questions . . .

"No, engineer, we are not a bloodthirsty people. We make war rarely. The skulls? They lie underfoot wherever one walks in Zignamuclickclick. They have been there since the fall of the city, it is said. We use them for decoration and for their symbolic significance." The spokesman solemnly raised his hand with its back to Louis, presenting the bird tattoo.

And everyone in sight shouted, "—!"

The word was not translated.

It was the first time anyone but the spokesman had said anything at all.

Louis had missed something, and he knew it. Unfortunately there wasn't time to worry about it.

"Show us a wonder," the spokesman was saying. "We doubt not your power. But you may not pass this way again. We would have a memory to pass to our children."

Louis considered. They'd already flown like birds; that trick would not impress twice. What about manna, from the kitchen slots? But even Earthborn humans varied in their tolerance of certain food. The difference between food and garbage was mostly cultural. Some ate locusts with honey, others broiled snails; one man's cheese was another's rotted milk. Best not chance it. What about the flashlight-laser?

As Louis reached into his 'cycle's cargo kit, the first

edge of a shadow square touched the rim of the sun. Darkness would make his demonstration all the more impressive.

With aperture wide and power low, he turned the light first on the spokesman, then on his four co-rulers, last on the faces of the crowd. If they were impressed, they hid it well. Hiding his disappointment, Louis aimed the implement high.

The figurine which was his target jutted from the tower's roof. It was like a modernized, surrealistic gargoyle. Louis's thumb moved, and the gargoyle glowed yellow-white. His index finger shifted, and the beam narrowed to a pencil of green light. The gargoyle sprouted a white-hot navel.

Louis waited for the applause.

"You fight with light," said the man with the tattooed hand. "Surely this is forbidden."

"—!" the crowd shouted, and was as suddenly silent.

"We did not know it," said Louis. "We apologize."

"Did not know it? How could you not know it? Did you not raise the Arch in sign of the Covenant with Man?"

"What arch is that?"

The hairy man's face was hidden, but his astonishment was evident. "The Arch over the world, O Builder!"

Louis understood then. He started to laugh.

The hairy man punched him unskillfully in the nose.

The blow was light, for the hairy man was slight and his hands were fragile. But it hurt.

Louis was not used to pain. Most people of his century had never felt pain more severe than that of a stubbed toe. Anaesthetics were too prevalent, medical help was too easily available. The pain of a skiier's broken leg usually lasted seconds, not minutes, and the memory was often suppressed as an intolerable trauma. Knowledge of the fighting disciplines, karate, judo, jujitsu, and boxing, had been illegal since long before Louis Wu was born. Louis Wu was a lousy warrior. He could face death, but not pain.

The blow hurt. Louis screamed and dropped his flash-light-laser.

The audience converged. Two hundred infuriated hairy men became a thousand demons; and things weren't nearly as funny as they had been a minute ago.

The reed-thin spokesman had wrapped both arms around Louis Wu, pinioning him with hysterical strength. Louis, equally hysterical, broke free with one frantic lunge. He was on his 'cycle, his hand was on the lift lever, when reason prevailed.

The other 'cycles were slaved to his. If he took off, they would take off, with or without their passengers.

Louis looked about him.

Teela Brown was already in the air. From overhead she watched the fight, her eyebrows puckered in concern. She had not thought of trying to help.

Speaker was in furious motion. He'd already felled half a dozen enemies. As Louis watched, the kzin swung his flashlight-laser and smashed a man's skull.

The hairy men milled about him in an indecisive circle.

Long-fingered hands were trying to pull Louis from his seat. They were winning, though Louis gripped the saddle with hands and knees. Belatedly he thought to switch on the sonic fold.

The natives shrieked as they were snatched away.

Someone was still on Louis's back. Louis pulled him away, let him drop, flipped the sonic fold off and then on again to eject him. He scanned the ex-parking lot for Nessus.

Nessus was trying to reach his 'cycle. The natives seemed to fear his alien shape. Only one blocked his way; but that one was armed with a metal rod from some old machine.

As Louis located them, the man swung the rod at the puppeteer's head.

Nessus snatched his head back. He spun on his fore-legs, putting his back to danger, but facing away from his flycycle.

The puppeteer's own flight reflex had killed him—unless Speaker or Louis could help him in time. Louis opened his mouth to shout, and the puppeteer completed his motion.

Louis closed his mouth.

The puppeteer turned to his 'cycle. Nobody tried to stop him. His hind hoof left bloody footprints across the hard-packed dirt.

Speaker's circle of admirers were still out of his reach. The kzin spat at their feet—not a kzinti gesture but a human one—turned and mounted his 'cycle. His flashlight-laser was gory up to the elbow of his left hand.

The native who had tried to stop Nessus lay where he had fallen. Blood pooled lavishly about him.

The others were in the air. Louis took off after them. From afar he saw what Speaker was doing, and he called, "Hold it! That's not necessary."

Speaker had drawn the modified digging tool. He said, "Does it have to be necessary?"

But he had stayed his hand. "Don't do it," Louis implored him. "It'd be murder. How can they hurt us now? Throw rocks at us?"

"They may use your flashlight-laser against us."

"They can't use it at all. There's a taboo."

"So said the spokesman. Do you believe him?"

"Yah."

Speaker put his weapon away. (Louis sighed in relief; he'd expected the kzin to level the city.) "How would such a taboo evolve? A war of energy weapons?"

"Or a bandit armed with the Ringworld's last laser cannon. Too bad there's nobody to ask."

"Your nose is bleeding."

Now that he came to think about it, Louis's nose stung painfully. He slaved his 'cycle to Speaker's and set about making medical repairs. Below, a churning, baffled lynch mob swarmed at the outskirts of Zignamuclickclick.

CHAPTER 13

Starseed Lure

"They should have been kneeling," Louis complained. "That's what fooled me. And the translation kept saying 'builder' when it should have been saying 'god'."

"God?"

"They've made gods of the Ringworld engineers. I should have noticed the silence. Tanjit, nobody but the priest was making a sound! They all acted like they were listening to some old litany. Except that I kept giving the wrong responses."

"A religion. How weird! But you shouldn't have laughed," Teela's intercom image said seriously. "Nobody laughs in church, not even tourists."

They flew beneath a fading sliver of noon sun. The Ringworld showed above itself in glowing blue stripes, brighter every minute.

"It seemed funny at the time," said Louis. "It's still funny. They've forgotten they're living on a ring. They think it's an arch."

A rushing sound penetrated the sonic fold. For a moment it was a hurricane, then it cut off sharply. They had crossed the speed of sound.

Zignamuclickclick dwindled behind them. The city would never have its vengeance on the demons. Probably it would never see them again.

"It *looks* like an arch," said Teela.

"Right. I shouldn't have laughed. We're lucky, though. We can leave our mistakes behind us," said Louis. "All

176

we have to do, any time, is get airborne. Nothing can catch us."

"Some mistakes we must carry with us," said Speaker-To-Animals.

"Funny you should say so." Louis scratched absently at his nose, which was as numb as a block of wood. It would be healed before the anaesthetic wore off.

He made up his mind. "Nessus?"

"Yes, Louis."

"I realized something, back there. You've been claiming that you're insane because you demonstrate courage. Right?"

"How tactful you are, Louis. Your delicacy of tongue—"

"Be serious. You and all the other puppeteers have been making the same wrong assumption. A puppeteer instinctively turns to run from danger. Right?"

"Yes, Louis."

"Wrong. A puppeteer instinctively turns *away* from danger. It's to free his hind leg for action. That hoof makes a deadly weapon, Nessus."

All in one motion, the puppeteer had spun on his forelegs and lashed out with his single hind leg. His heads were turned backward and spread wide, Louis remembered, to triangulate on his target. Nessus had accurately kicked a man's heart out through his splintered spine.

"I could not run," he said. "I would have been leaving my vehicle. That would have been dangerous."

"But you didn't stop to think about it," said Louis. "It was instinctive. You automatically turn your back on an enemy. Turn, and kick. A sane puppeteer turns to fight, not to run. You're not crazy."

"You are wrong, Louis. Most puppeteers run from danger."

"But—"

"The majority is always sane, Louis."

Herd animal! Louis gave it up. He lifted his eyes to watch the last sliver of sun disappear.

Some mistakes we must carry with us . . .

But Speaker must have been thinking of something else when he said that. Thinking of what?

At the zenith swarmed a ring of black rectangles. The one that hid the sun was framed in a pearly coronal glow. The blue Ringworld formed a paraboloid arch over it all, framed against a star-dotted sky.

It looked like something done with a Build-A-City set, by a child too young to know what he was doing.

Nessus had been steering when they left Zignamuclick-click. Later he had turned the fleet over to Speaker. They had flown all night. Now, overhead, a brighter glow along one edge of the central shadow square showed that dawn was near.

Sometime during these past hours, Louis had found a way to visualize the scale of the Ringworld.

It involved a Mercator projection of the planet Earth—a common, rectangular, classroom wall map—but with the equator drawn to one-to-one scale. One could relief-sculpt such a map, so that standing near the equator would be exactly like standing on the real Earth. But one could draw forty such maps, edge to edge, across the width of the Ringworld.

Such a map would be greater in area than the Earth. But one could map it into the Ringworld's topography, and look away for a moment, and never be able to find it again.

One could play cuter tricks than that, given the tools that shaped the Ringworld. Those matching salt oceans, one on each side on the ring, had each been larger in area than any world in human space. Continents, after all, were only large islands. One could map the Earth onto such an ocean and still have room left over at the borders.

"I shouldn't have laughed," Louis told himself. *It took me long enough to grasp the scale of this . . . artifact. Why should I expect the natives to be more sophisticated?*

Nessus had seen it earlier. Night before last, when they

had first seen the arch, Nessus had screamed and tried to hide.

"Oh, what the tanj . . ." It didn't matter. Not when all mistakes could be left behind at twelve hundred miles per hour.

Presently Speaker called and turned control of the fleet over to Louis. Louis flew while Speaker slept.

And dawn came on at seven hundred miles per second.

The line dividing day from night is called the *terminator*. On Earth the terminator is visible from the Moon; it is visible from orbit; but it cannot be seen from the Earth's surface.

But the straight lines dividing light from dark on the arch of the Ringworld were all terminators.

From spinward, the terminator line swept toward the flycycle fleet. From ground to sky it ran, from infinity-port to infinity-starboard. It came on like destiny made visible, a moving wall too big to go around.

It arrived. The corona brightened overhead, then blazed as the withdrawing shadow square exposed a rim of solar disc. Louis contemplated the night to his left, the day on his right, the terminator shadow receding across an endless plain. A strange dawn, staged for Louis Wu the tourist.

Far to starboard, beyond where the land turned to haze, the sharp outlines of a mountain peak materialized in the new daylight.

"Fist-of-God," said Louis Wu, tasting the rolling sound of it in his mouth. What a name for a mountain! But especially, what a name for the greatest mountain in the world!

Louis Wu the man ached. If his body didn't begin adjusting soon, his joints would freeze him in sitting position and he'd never move again. Furthermore, his food bricks were beginning to taste like—bricks. Moreover, his nose was still partly numb. And there *still* wasn't any coffee spigot.

But Louis Wu the tourist was being royally entertained.

Take the puppeteer flight reflex. Nobody had ever suspected that it might also be a fighting reflex. Nobody but Louis Wu.

Take the starseed lure. What a poetic thing to leave lying about! A simple device, invented thousands of years ago, Nessus had said. And no puppeteer had ever thought to mention it, until yesterday.

But puppeteers were so completely unpoetic.

Did the puppeteers know why Outsider ships followed starseeds? Did they gloat in the knowledge? Or had they learned that secret, then discarded it as irrelevant to the business of living forever?

Nessus was out of the intercom circuit. Asleep, probably. Louis signaled him, so that the puppeteer would see the light on his panel and call him when he woke.

Did he know?

The starseeds: mindless beings who swarmed in the galactic core. Their metabolism was the solar phoenix, their food was the thinly-spread hydrogen of interstellar space. Their motive power was a photon sail, enormous and highly reflective, controlled like a skydiver's parachute. A starseed's egg-laying flight commonly took it from the galactic axis out to the edge of intergalactic space, and then back, without the egg. The hatched starseed chick must find its own way home, riding the photon wind, to the warm, hydrogen-rich core.

Where the starseeds went, there went the Outsiders.

Why did Outsiders follow starseeds? Whimsical question, though poetic.

Maybe not so whimsical. Back around the middle of the first Man–Kzin war, a starseed had zigged instead of zagging. The Outsider ship following it had cruised past Procyon. Had paused long enough to sell We Made It a hyperdrive shunt.

The ship could as easily have wandered into kzinti instead of human space.

And hadn't the puppeteers been studying the kzinti about that time?

"Tanjit! That's what I get for letting my mind wander. Discipline, that's what I need."

But hadn't they? Sure they had. Nessus had said so. The puppeteers had been researching the kzinti, investigating whether they could be exterminated safely.

Then the Man–Kzin war had solved their problem. An Outsider ship had wandered into human space to sell We Made It a hyperdrive shunt, while the kzinti armada was sweeping inward from the opposite border. Once human warships had the hyperdrive shunt, the kzinti had ceased to be a threat to man and puppeteer alike.

"They wouldn't dare," Louis told himself. He was appalled.

"If Speaker ever—" But that possibility was even worse.

"An experiment in selective breeding," said Louis. "Selective there-ain't-no-justice breeding. But they *used* us. They used *us!*"

"Yes," said Speaker-To-Animals.

For an instant Louis was sure he had imagined it. Then he saw Speaker's transparent, miniature image at the top of his dashboard. He had left the intercom open.

"Tanj for torment! You were listening!"

"Not by choice, Louis. I neglected to switch off my intercom."

"Oh." Too late, Louis remembered Speaker grinning at him, supposedly out of hearing range, after Nessus had finished describing a starseed lure. Remembered that kzinti ears were made to serve a hunting carnivore. Remembered that the kzinti smile reflex is intended to free the teeth for battle.

"You mentioned selective breeding," said Speaker.

"I was just—" Louis floundered.

"The puppeteers pitted our species against each other in order to restrict kzinti expansion. They had a starseed lure, Louis. They used it to guide an Outsider ship into your space, to ensure a human victory. An experiment in selective breeding, you called it."

"Listen, that's a very chancy chain of assumptions. If you'll just calm down—"

"But we both followed that chain."

"Um."

"I was in doubt as to whether to broach the subject to Nessus, or whether to wait until we had accomplished our major objective, which is to leave the Ringworld. Now that you know the situation, I have no choice."

"But—" Louis closed his mouth. The siren would have drowned him out anyway. Speaker had signaled *emergency*.

The siren was a maniac mechanical scream, a subsonic and supersonic and jarringly painful sound. Nessus appeared above the dash, crying, "Yes? Yes?"

Speaker roared his answer. "You have meddled in a war in the enemy's favor! Your action is tantamount to a declaration of war against the Patriarchy!"

Teela had cut in in time to hear the last part. Louis caught her eye, shook his head. *Don't mix in.*

The puppeteer's heads reared like snakes to show his astonishment. His voice was without inflection, as usual. "What are you talking about?"

"The First War with Men. Starseed lures. The Outsider hyperdrive shunt."

A triangular head dipped out of sight. Louis watched a silver flycycle drop out of formation, and knew it was Nessus.

He was not terribly worried. The other two flycycles looked like silver midges, so far away were they, and so far apart. If the fight had taken place on the ground, someone could have been seriously hurt. Up here, what could happen? The puppeteer's flycycle had to be faster than Speaker's. Nessus would have seen to that. He would have made certain he could outrun a kzin when necessary.

Except that the puppeteer wasn't fleeing. He was looping around at Speaker's 'cycle.

"I do not wish to kill you," said Speaker-To-Animals.

"If you intend to attack from the air, you should remember that the range of your tasp may be less than the range of the Slaver digging beam. *SNARL!*"

The kzinti killing yell was blood-freezing. Louis's muscles locked in position, as with tetanus. He was only dimly aware of the silver dot that looped away from Speaker's 'cycle.

But he did notice Teela's look of open-mouthed admiration.

"I do not intend to kill you," Speaker-To-Animals said more calmly. "But I will have answers, Nessus. We know that your race can guide starseeds."

"Yes," said Nessus. His 'cycle was receding to port at improbable speed. The feral calm of the aliens was an illusion. It existed only because Louis Wu could not read expression in an alien face, and because the aliens could not put human expression into the Interworld language.

Nessus was fleeing for his life, but the kzin had not left his place in formation. He said, "I will have answers, Nessus."

"You have guessed correctly," said the puppeteer. "Our investigation of safe methods to exterminate the vicious, carnivorous kzinti showed that your species has a high potential, that you could conceivably be of use to us. We took steps to evolve you to the point where you could deal peaceably with races alien to you. Our methods were indirect, and very safe."

"Very. Nessus, I am not happy."

"Neither am I," said Louis Wu.

He had not missed the fact that both aliens were still speaking Interworld. They could have had privacy by using the Hero's Tongue. They had preferred to include the humans—and quite rightly, for it was Louis Wu's quarrel, too.

"You used us," he said. "You used us just as thoroughly as you used the kzinti."

"But to our detriment," Speaker objected.

"A number of *men* were killed in the Man–Kzin wars."

"Louis, get off his back!" Teela Brown entered the lists of battle. "Tanjit, if it hadn't been for the puppeteers, we'd all be kzinti slaves! They kept the kzinti from destroying civilization!"

Speaker smiled and said, "We had a civilization, too."

The puppeteer was a silent, ghostly image, a one-eyed python poised to strike. Presumably the other mouth was steering his 'cycle, which by now was a good distance away.

"The puppeteers used us," said Louis Wu. "They used us as a tool, a tool to evolve the kzinti."

"But it worked!" Teela insisted.

The sound was almost a snore, a low and ominous snarl. By now nobody could have mistaken Speaker's expression for a smile.

"It did work!" Teela flared. "You're a peaceful race now, Speaker. You can get along with——"

"Be silent, *man!*"

"With your equals," she finished generously. "You haven't attacked another species in——"

The kzin produced the modified Slaver digging tool and held it before the intercom so that Teela could see it. She stopped talking suddenly.

"It could have been us," said Louis.

He had their attention. "It could have been us," he repeated. "If the puppeteers had wanted to breed humans for some trait . . ." he stopped. "Oh," he said. "Teela. Sure."

The puppeteer did not react.

Teela shifted under Louis's stare. "What's the matter, Louis? Louis!"

"Sorry. Something just occurred to me . . . Nessus, speak to us. Speak to us of the Fertility Laws."

"Louis, have you gone *crazy?*"

"Uurrr," said Speaker-to-Animals. "I would have thought of that myself, given time. Nessus?"

"Yes," said Nessus.

The puppeteer's 'cycle was a silver mote, still dwindling to port. It was almost lost against a larger, vaguer bright point ahead, somewhat more distant from the fleet than any two points can be on Earth. The puppeteer's intercom image wore the unchanging, unreadable silly face produced by a flat triangular skull and loose, prehensile lips. He could not look dangerous, this one.

"You meddled with the Fertility Laws of Earth."

"Yes."

"Why?"

"We like humans. We trust humans. We have dealt profitably with humans. It is to our advantage to encourage humans, since they will certainly reach the Lesser Cloud before we do."

"Wonderful. You like us. So?"

"We sought to improve you genetically. But what should we improve? Not your intelligence. Intelligence is not your great strength. Nor is your sense of self-preservation, nor your durability, nor your fighting talents."

"So you decided to make us lucky," said Louis. And he began to laugh.

Teela got it then. Her eyes went round and horrified. She tried to say something, but it came out as a squeak.

"Of course," said Nessus. "Please stop laughing, Louis. The decision was sensible. Your species has been incredibly lucky. Your history reads like a series of hair-breath escapes, from intraspecies atomic war, from pollution of your planet with industrial wastes, from ecological upsets, from dangerously massive asteroids, from the vagaries of your mildly variable sun, and even from the Core explosion, which you discovered only by the merest accident. Louis, why are you still laughing?"

Louis was still laughing because he was looking at Teela. Teela was blushing furiously. Her eyes shifted as if seeking a place to hide. It is not pleasant to realize that one is part of a genetics experiment.

"And so we changed the Fertility Laws of Earth. It was surprisingly easy. Our withdrawal from known space caused a stock market crash. Economic manipulation ruined several members of the Fertility Board. We bribed some of these, blackmailed others with the threat of debtor's prison, then used corruption in the Fertility Board as publicity to force a change. It was a hideously expensive undertaking, but quite safe, and partially successful. We were able to introduce the Birthright Lotteries. We hoped to produce a strain of unusually lucky humans."

"Monster!" Teela shouted. "Monster!"

Speaker had sheathed his Slaver digging tool. He said, "Teela, you did not complain when you learned that the puppeteers had manipulated the heredity of my race. They sought to produce a docile kzin. To that end they bred us as a biologist breeds stheets, killing the defectives, keeping others. You gloated that this crime was to the benefit of your species. Now you complain. Why?"

Teela, weeping with rage, cut herself out of the intercom.

"A docile kzin," Speaker repeated. "You sought to produce a docile kzin, Nessus. If you think you have produced a docile kzin, come and rejoin us."

The puppeteer did not answer. Somewhere far ahead of the fleet, the silver point of his 'cycle had become too small to see.

"You do not wish to rejoin our fleet? But how can I protect you from this unknown land unless you rejoin the fleet? But I do not blame you. You do well to be wary," said the kzin. His claws were showing, needle-sharp and slightly curved. "Your attempt to produce a lucky human was also a failure."

"No," said Nessus via intercom. "We produced lucky humans. I could not contact them for this ill-fated expedition. They were too lucky."

"You have played god with both our species. Do not attempt to rejoin us."

"I will remain in intercom contact."

Speaker's image disappeared.

"Louis, Speaker has cut me off," said Nessus. "If I have something to tell him, I must pass it through you."

"Fine," said Louis, and cut him off. Almost instantly a tiny light burned where the puppeteer's ghost-head had been. The puppeteer wanted to talk.

Tanj upon him.

Later that day they crossed a sea the size of the Mediterranean. Louis dipped to investigate, and found that the other 'cycles followed him down. The fleet, then, was still under his guidance, despite the fact that nobody would speak to him.

The shoreline was a single city, and the city was a ruin. Aside from the docks, it did not differ in kind from Zignamuclickclick. Louis did not land. There was nothing to be learned here.

Afterward the land sloped gradually upward, always upward, until ears popped and pressure sensors dropped. The green land became brown scrub, then high desert tundra, then miles and miles of bare rock, then—

Along half a thousand miles of ridgeback mountain peak, the winds had scraped away scrub and soil and rock. Nothing was left but an exposed backbone of ring foundation material, translucent gray and hideous.

Sloppy upkeep! No Ringworld engineer would have permitted such a thing. The Ringworld civilization, then, must have begun to die long ago. The process would have started here, with bare spots poking through the façade in the places where nobody went . . .

Far ahead of the fleet, in the direction Nessus had gone, was an extensive shiny spot in the landscape. At a guess, it was thirty to fifty thousand miles away. A great shiny spot as big as Australia.

More exposed ring floor? Vast, shiny areas of ring foundation poking through once-fertile soil, soil that dies and dries and blows away when the river systems break down. The fall of Zignamuclickclick, the universal power failure, must have been the last stage of the breakdown.

How long had it taken? Ten thousand years?

Longer?

"Tanjit! I wish I could talk it over with someone. It might be important." Louis scowled at the landscape.

Time was different when the sun was always straight overhead. Morning and afternoon were identical. Decisions seemed less than permanent. Reality seemed less than real. It was, Louis thought, like the instant of time spent traveling between transfer booths.

That was it. They were between transfer booths, one at the *Liar,* one at the rim wall. They only dreamed that they flew above flat gray land in a triangle pattern of flycycles.

They flew to port through frozen time.

How long had it been since anyone had spoken to

anyone? It had been hours since Louis had signaled Teela that he wanted to talk to her. Not much later he had signaled Speaker. Lights had burned above their dashboards, ignored, as Louis ignored the light above his own.

"Enough of that," Louis said suddenly. He opened the intercom.

He caught an incredible burst of orchestral music before the puppeteer noticed him. Then— "We must see to it that the expedition is reunited without bloodshed," said Nessus. "Have you any suggestions, Louis?"

"Yes. It's not polite to start a conversation in the middle."

"I apologize, Louis. Thank you for returning my call. How have you been?"

"Lonely and irritated, and it's all your fault. Nobody wants to talk to me."

"Can I help?"

"Maybe. Did you have anything to do with changing the Fertility Laws?"

"I headed the project."

Louis snorted. "That's the wrong answer. May you be the first victim of retroactive birth control! Teela won't ever speak to me again."

"You should not have laughed at her."

"I know. You know what scares me the most about this whole thing? Not your there-ain't-no-justice arrogance," said Louis. "It's the fact that you can make decisions of that magnitude, then do something as downright *stupid* as, as—"

"Can Teela Brown hear us?"

"No, of course not. *Tanj* you, Nessus! Do you *know* what you've *done* to her?"

"If you knew her ego would be so wounded, why did you speak?"

Louis moaned. He had solved a thought-problem and immediately revealed the solution. It had not occurred to him, it would never have occurred to him, that the solution was better hidden. He didn't think that way.

The puppeteer asked, "Have you thought of a way to reunite the expedition?"

"Yes," said Louis, and he switched off.

Let the puppeteer sweat over that one.

The land sloped down and became green again.

They passed another sea, and a great triangular river delta. But the riverbed was dry, and so was the delta. Alterations in the wind currents must have dried up the source.

As Louis dipped low, it became clear that all of the haphazard, meandering channels that made up the delta had been carved permanently into the land. The Ringworld artists had not been content to let the river dig its own channels. And they had been right; the soil wasn't deep enough on the Ringworld. Artifice was necessary.

But the empty channels were ugly. Louis pursed his lips in disapproval, and flew on.

CHAPTER 14

Interlude, With Sunflowers

Not far ahead, there were mountains.

Louis had flown all night and well into the morning. He wasn't sure how long. The motionless noon sun was a psychological trap; it either compressed or stretched time, and Louis wasn't sure which.

Emotionally, Louis was on sabbatical. He had almost forgotten the other flycycles. Flying alone over unending, endlessly changing terrain was no different from ranging alone in a singleship beyond the known stars. Louis Wu was alone with the universe, and the universe was a plaything for Louis Wu. The most important question in the universe became: Is Louis Wu still satisfied with himself?

It came as a shock when a furry orange face formed above the dash.

"You must be tiring," said the kzin. "Do you wish me to fly?"

"I'd rather land. I'm getting cramped."

"Land, then. The controls are yours."

"I don't want to force my company on anyone." As he said it, Louis realized that he meant it. The sabbatical mood had been too easily recaptured.

"Do you feel that Teela would avoid you? You may be right, she has not called even me, though I share her shame."

"You're taking it too hard. No, wait, don't switch off."

"I wish to be alone, Louis. The leaf-eater has shamed me terribly."

"But it was so long ago! No, don't switch off; have

190

pity on a lonely old man. Have you been watching the landscape?"

"Yes."

"Did you notice the bare regions?"

"Yes. In places erosion has cut through bedrock to the indestructible ring floor. Something must have badly upset the wind patterns a very long time ago. Such erosion cannot happen overnight, even on the Ringworld."

"Right."

"Louis, how could a civilization of such size and power, fall?"

"I don't know. Let's face it: there's no way to guess, not for us. Even the puppeteers never reached the Ringworld's level of technology. How can we tell what might have knocked them back to the fist-ax level?"

"We must learn more about the natives," said Speaker-To-Animals. "Our evidence thus far indicates that they could not possibly move the ruined *Liar* anywhere. We must find those who can."

It was the opening Louis had hoped for. "I have some ideas on that score—an effective way to contact the natives as often as we like."

"Well?"

"I'd like to land before we talk it over."

"Land, then."

Mountains formed a high, blocky range across the path of the flycycle fleet. Their peaks and the passes between glowed with a pearly sheen Louis recognized. Winds roaring over and between the peaks had polished away the rock, exposing the framework of ring floor material.

Louis dropped the fleet toward gently rounded foothills. His target was the mouth of a silver stream that poured out of the mountains and disappeared into a forest, itself seemingly endless, that covered the foothills like green fur.

Teela called. "What are you doing?" she demanded.

"I'm landing. I'm tired of flying. But don't hang up. I'd like to apologize."

She switched off.

"Best I could hope for," Louis told himself without conviction. But she would be more willing to listen now that she knew an apology was coming.

"I got the idea from all our talk about 'playing god'," said Louis. Unfortunately he was talking only to Speaker. Teela had dismounted her 'cycle, thrown him one smoking glare and stalked off into the woods.

Speaker nodded his shaggy orange head. His ears twitched like small Chinese fans held in nervous fingers.

"We're reasonably safe on this world," Louis told him, "as long as we're in the air. There's no question but that we can get where we're going. We could probably reach the rim wall without ever landing, if it came to that; or we could land only where the ring foundation pokes through. No predatory life could survive on that stuff.

"But we can't learn much without landing. We want to get off this oversized toy, and to do that we're going to need native help. It still looks as though someone is going to have to haul the *Liar* across four hundred thousand miles of landscape."

"Get to the point, Louis. I need exercise."

"By the time we reach the rim wall we'll want to know a lot more about the Ringworlders than we do now."

"Unquestionably."

"Why not play god?"

Speaker hesitated. "You speak with literal precision?"

"Right. We're naturals for Ringworld engineers. We don't have the powers they had, but what we do have must look godlike enough to the natives. You can be the god—"

"Thank you."

"—Teela and I the acolytes. Nessus would make a good captive demon."

Speaker's claws came out. He said, "But Nessus is not with us, and will not be."

"That's the hitch. In—"

"This is not open to argument, Louis."

"Too bad. We need him to make this work."

"Then you must forget it."

Louis was still in doubt about those claws. Were they or were they not under voluntary control? In any case, they were still showing. Had he been speaking over intercom, Speaker would certainly have switched off by now.

Which was why Louis had insisted on landing.

"Look at the sheer intellectual beauty of it. You'd make a *great* god. From a human viewpoint you're impressive as all hell—though I suppose you'd have to take my word for that."

"Why would we need Nessus?"

"For the tasp, for reward and punishment. As a god, you tear a doubter to shreds and gobbets, then eat the gobbets. That's punishment. For reward, you use the puppeteer's tasp."

"Can we not do without the tasp?"

"But it's such a great way to reward the faithful! A blast of pure pleasure, straight to the brain. No side effects. No hangover. A tasp is supposed to be better than sex!"

"I do not like the ethics. Though the natives are only human, I would not like to addict them to a tasp. It would be more merciful to kill them," said Speaker. "In any case, the puppeteer's tasp works against kzinti, not human."

"I think you're wrong."

"Louis, we know that the tasp was designed for use against a kzinti brain structure. I felt it. In this you are right: it was a religious experience, a diabolical experience."

"But we don't know the tasp doesn't work on a human being. I think it does. I know Nessus. Either his tasp works on both of us, or he's carrying two tasps. *I* wouldn't be here unless he had a way to control humans."

"You speculate wildly."

"Shall we call him and ask him?"

"No."

"What's the harm in asking him?"

"There would be no purpose in it."

"I forgot. No curiosity," said Louis. Monkey curiosity was not powerful in most sentient species.

"Were you playing on my curiosity? I see. You tried to commit me to a course of action. Louis, the puppeteer may find his own way to the rim wall. Until then, he travels alone."

And before Louis could answer, the kzin turned and bounded into a thicket of elbow root. It ended the discussion as effectively as if he had switched off an intercom.

The world had caved in on Teela Brown. She sobbed miserably, wrackingly, in an orgy of self-pity.

She had found a wonderful place for her mourning.

Dark green was the motif. The vegetation was lush overhead, too thick to permit the direct passage of sunlight. But it thinned out near the ground, to make walking easy. It was a somber paradise for nature lovers.

Flat, vertical rock walls, kept constantly wet by a waterfall, surrounded a deep, clear pool. Teela was in the pool. The falling water nearly drowned out her sobbing, but the rock walls amplified the sound like a shower stall. It was as if Nature wept with her.

She had not noticed Louis Wu.

Stranded on an alien world, even Teela Brown would not have gone far without her first aid kit. It was a small, flat box on her belt, and it had a finder circuit built into it. Louis had followed its signal to Teela's clothes, which were piled on a natural granite tabletop at the pool's edge.

Dark green illumination, the roar of a waterfall, and the echoed sound of sobbing. Teela was almost under the falling water. She must be sitting on something, for her arms and shoulders were out of the pool. Her head was bent, and her dark hair streamed forward to cover her face.

There was no point in waiting for her to come to him. Louis took off his clothes, piled them beside Teela's. He frowned at the chill in the air, shrugged, and dove in.

He saw his mistake instantly.

On sabbatical, Louis did not commonly run across Earthlike worlds. Those he did land on were generally as civilized as Earth itself. Louis was not stupid. If it had occurred to him to wonder about the temperature of the water . . .

But it didn't.

The water was runoff water from snow-capped mountains. Louis tried to scream with the cold, but his head was already underwater. He did have sense enough not to inhale.

His head broke water. He splashed and gasped with the cold and the need for air.

Then he began to enjoy it.

He knew how to tread water; though he had learned in warmer waters than these! He stayed afloat, kicking rhythmically, feeling the currents from the plunging waterfall eddy over his skin.

Teela had seen him. She sat beneath the waterfall, waiting. He swam to her.

He would have had to scream into her face to tell her anything. Apologies and words of love would have been misplaced. But he could touch her.

She did not flinch away. But she bent her head, and her hair hid her again. Her rejection was almost telepathically intense.

Louis respected it.

He swam about, stretching muscles cramped by eighteen hours in a flycycle seat. The water felt wonderful. But at some point the numbness of the cold became an ache, and Louis decided he was courting pneumonia.

He touched Teela on the arm and pointed toward shore. This time she nodded and followed.

They lay beside the pool, shivering, wrapped in each other's arms, with the thermocontrolled coveralls open and spread around them like blankets. Gradually their chilled bodies soaked up the heat.

"I'm sorry I laughed," Louis said.

She nodded, accepting the fact of his apology, without forgiveness.

"It *was* funny, you know. The puppeteers, the cowards

of the universe, having the gall to breed humans and
kzinti like two strains of cattle! They must have known
what a chance they were taking." He knew he was talking
too much, but he had to explain, to justify himself. "And
then look what they did with it! Breeding for a reasonable
kzin, that wasn't a bad idea. I know a little about the
Man–Kzin wars; I know the kzinti used to be pretty fierce.
Speaker's ancestors would have blasted Zignamuclickclick down to the Ring floor. Speaker stopped.

"But breeding humans for luck—"

"You think they made a mistake, making me what I
am."

"Tanjit, do you think I'm trying to insult you? I'm
trying to say that it's a funny idea. For puppeteers to do
it is even funnier. So I laughed."

"Do you expect me to giggle?"

"That'd be going too far."

"All right."

She didn't hate him for laughing. She wanted comfort,
not revenge. There was comfort in the heat of the coveralls, and comfort in the heat of two bodies pressed together.

Louis began to stroke Teela's back. It made her relax.

"I'd like to get the expedition back together again," he
said presently. He felt her stiffen. "You don't like that
idea."

"No."

"Nessus?"

"I hate him. I hate him! He bred my ancestors like—
like beasts!" She relaxed minutely. "But Speaker would
blast him out of the sky if he tried to come back. So it's
all right."

"Suppose I could talk Speaker into letting Nessus rejoin us?"

"How could you do that?"

"Suppose I could?"

"But *why?*"

"Nessus still owns the *Long Shot*. The *Long Shot* is
the only way to get the human race to the Clouds of

Magellan in less than centuries. We lose the *Long Shot* if we leave the Ringworld without Nessus."

"How, how *crass,* Louis!"

"Look. You claimed that if the puppeteers hadn't done what they did to the kzinti, we'd all be kzinti slaves. True. But if the puppeteers hadn't interfered with the Fertility Laws, you wouldn't even have been born!"

She was rigid against him. Her mind showed in her face, and her face was like her eyes: tightly closed.

He kept trying. "What the puppeteers did, they did a long time ago. Can't you forgive and forget?"

"No!" She rolled away from him, out from under the heated coveralls and into the icy water. Louis hesitated, then followed her. A cold, wet shock . . . he surfaced . . . Teela was back at her place beneath the waterfall.

Smiling in invitation. How could her moods change so suddenly?

He swam to her.

"That's a charming way to tell a man to shut up!" he laughed. She couldn't possibly have heard him. He couldn't hear himself, with the water pounding down around them. But Teela laughed back, equally soundlessly, and reached for him.

"They were stupid arguments anyway!" he screamed.

The water was cold, cold. Teela was the only warmth. They knelt clasping each other, supported by rough, shallow underwater rock.

Love was a delicious blend of warm and cold. There was comfort in making love. It solved no problems: but one could run away from problems.

They walked back toward the 'cycles, shivering a little within their heated cocoons. Louis didn't speak. He had realized a thing about Teela Brown.

She had never learned how to reject. She could not say *no* and make it stick. She could not deliver reproofs of calculated intensity, humorous or jabbing or deadly vicious, as other women could. Teela Brown had not been hurt socially, not often enough to learn these things.

Louis could browbeat her until doomsday, and she would not know how to stop him. But she could hate him for it. And so he remained silent, for that reason and for another.

He didn't want to hurt her.

They walked in silence, holding hands, making love-play with their fingers.

"All right," she said suddenly. "If you can talk Speaker into it, you can bring Nessus back."

"Thanks," said Louis. He showed his surprise.

"It's only for the *Long Shot*," she said. "Besides, you can't do it."

There was time for a meal and for formal exercises: pushups and situps, and for informal exercises: tree climbing.

Presently Speaker returned to the 'cycles. His mouth was not bloody. At his 'cycle he dialed, not for an allergy pill, but for a wet brick-shaped slab of warm liver. *The mighty hunter returns,* Louis thought, keeping his mouth firmly shut.

The sky had been overcast when they landed. It was still overcast, a uniform leaden gray, as they took off. And Louis resumed his argument by intercom.

"But it was so long ago!"

"A point of honor is not affected by time, Louis, though of course you would not know that. Further, the consequences of the act are very much with us. Why did Nessus select a kzin to travel with him?"

"He told us that."

"Why did he select Teela Brown? The Hindmost must have instructed Nessus to learn if humans have inherited psychic luck. He was also to learn if kzinti have become docile. He chose me because as ambassador to a characteristically arrogant species, I am likely to demonstrate the docility his people seek."

"I'd thought of that too." Louis had carried the idea even further. Had Nessus been instructed to mention starseed lures, in order to gauge Speaker's reactions?

"It matters not. I say that I am not docile."

"Will you stop using that word? It warps your thinking!"

"Louis, why do you intercede for the puppeteer? Why do you wish his company?"

Good questions, Louis thought. Certainly the puppeteer deserved to sweat a little. And if what Louis suspected was true, Nessus was in no danger at all.

Was it only that Louis Wu liked aliens?

Or was it more general than that? A puppeteer was different. Difference was important. A man of Louis Wu's age would get bored with life itself, without variety. To Louis the company of aliens was a vital necessity.

The 'cycles rose, following the slope of the mountains.

"Viewpoints," said Louis Wu. "We're in a strange environment, stranger than any world of men or kzinti. We may need all the insights we can bring to bear, just to figure out what's going on."

Teela applauded without sound. *Nicely argued!* Louis winked back. A very human conversation; Speaker couldn't possibly read its meaning.

The kzin was saying, "I do not need a puppeteer to explain the world to me. My own eyes, nose, ears are sufficient."

"That's moot. But you do need the *Long Shot.* We all need the techniques that ship represents."

"For profit? An unworthy motive."

"Tanjit, that's not fair! The *Long Shot* is for the entire human race, and the kzinti too!"

"A quibble. Though the profit is not to you alone, still you sell your honor for profit."

"My honor is not in danger," Louis grated.

"I think it is," said Speaker. And he switched off.

"That's a handy little gadget, that switch," Teela observed, with malice. "I knew he'd do that."

"So did I. But, Lord Finagle! He's hard to convince."

Beyond the mountains was an endless expanse of fleecy cloud, graying out at the infinity-horizon. The flycycles seemed to float above white cloud, beneath a bright blue sky in which the Arch was an outline at the threshold of visibility.

The mountains fell behind. Louis felt a twinge of regret for the forest pool with the waterfall. They would never see it again.

A wake followed the 'cycles, a roiling wavefront where three sonic booms touched the cloud cover. Ahead, only one detail broke the infinity-horizon. Louis decided that it was either a mountain or a storm, very distant, very large. It was the size of a pinhead held at arm's length.

Speaker broke the silence. "A rift in the cloud cover, Louis. Ahead and to spinward."

"I see it."

"Do you see how the light shines through? Much light is being reflected from the landscape."

True, the edges of the cloud break glowed brightly. Hmmm . . . "Could we be flying over Ringworld foundation material? It would be the biggest break yet in the landscaping."

"I want to look more closely."

"Good," said Louis.

He watched the speck that was Speaker's flycycle curve frantically away to spinward. At Mach 2 Speaker would get no more than a glimpse of the ground . . .

There was a problem here. Which to watch? The silver fleck that was Speaker's flycycle, or the small orange cat-face above the dash? One was real, one was detailed. Both offered information, but of different kinds.

In principle, no answer was entirely satisfactory. In practice, Louis naturally watched both.

He saw that Speaker was over the rift . . .

The intercom echoed Speaker's yowl. The silver fleck had gone suddenly brighter; and Speaker's face was a glare of white light. His eyes were closed tight. His mouth was open, screaming.

The image dimmed. Speaker had crossed the rift. One arm was thrown across his face. The fur that covered him was smoking black char.

Beneath the diverging silver speck of Speaker's flycycle, a bright spot showed on the cloud cover . . . as if a spotlight followed Speaker from below.

"Speaker!" Teela called. "Can you see?"

Speaker heard and uncovered his face. The orange fur was unburned in a broad band across his eyes. Elsewhere the fur was ash-black. Speaker opened his eyes, closed them tight, opened them again. "I'm blind," he said.

"Yes, but can you *see?*"

In his worry over Speaker, Louis hardly noticed the strangeness of that question. But something in him noted her tone of voice: the anxiety, and beneath that, the suggestion that Speaker had given a wrong answer and should be given a second chance.

But there wasn't time. Louis called, "Speaker! Slave your 'cycle to mine. We've got to get to cover."

Speaker fumbled at the board. "Done. Louis, what kind of cover?" Pain thickened and distorted his voice.

"Back to the mountains."

"No. We would lose too much time. Louis, I know what attacked me. If I am right, then we are safe as long as we have cloud cover."

"Oh?"

"You will have to investigate."

"You need medical attention."

"I do indeed, but first you must find us a safe place to land. You must descend where the clouds are most dense . . ."

It was not dark, down here below the clouds. Some light came through, and enough of that was reflected toward Louis Wu. It *glared*.

The land was an undulating plain. It was not Ring floor material, but soil and vegetation.

Louis dropped lower, squinting against the glare.

. . . A single species of plant, evenly dispersed across the land, from here to the infinity-horizon. Each plant had a single blossom, and each blossom turned to follow Louis Wu as he dropped. A tremendous audience, silent and attentive.

He landed and dismounted beside one of the plants.

The plant stood a foot high on a knobbly green stalk. Its single blossom was as big as a large man's face. The back of that blossom was stringy, as if laced with veins or tendons; and the inner surface was a smooth concave mirror. From its center protruded a short stalk ending in a dark green bulb.

All the flowers in sight watched him. He was bathed in the glare. Louis knew they were trying to kill him, and he looked up somewhat uneasily; but the cloud cover held.

"You were right," he said, speaking into the intercom. "They're Slaver sunflowers. If the cloud cover hadn't come up, we'd have been dead the instant we rose over the mountains."

"Is there cover where we can hide from the sunflowers? A cave, for example?"

"I don't think so. The land's too flat. The sunflowers can't focus the light with any precision, but there's a lot of glare anyway."

Teela broke in. "For pity's sake, what's the matter with you two? Louis, we've got to land! Speaker's in pain!"

"Truly, I am in pain, Louis."

"Then I vote we risk it. Come down, you two. We'll just have to hope the clouds hold."

"Good!" Teela's intercom image went into action.

Louis spent a minute or so searching between the plants. It was as he had surmised. There was no alien survivor anywhere in the domain of the sunflowers. No smaller plant grew between the stalks. Nothing flew. Nothing burrowed beneath the ashy-looking soil. On the plants themselves there were no blights, fungus growths, disease spots. If disease struck one of their own, the sunflowers would destroy it.

The mirror-blossom was a terrible weapon. Its primary purpose was to focus sunlight on the green photosynthetic node at its center. But it could also focus to destroy a plant-eating animal or insect. The sunflowers burned all enemies. Everything that lives is the enemy of a photosynthesis-using plant; and everything that lived became fertilizer for the sunflowers.

"But how did they come *here?*" Louis wondered. For sunflowers could not coexist with less exotic plant life. Sunflowers were too powerful. Thus they could not be native to the Ringworlders' original planet.

The engineers must have scouted nearby stars for their useful or decorative plants. Perhaps they had even come as far as Silvereyes, in human space. And they must have decided that the sunflowers were decorative.

"But they would have fenced them in. Any idiot would have that much sense. Give them, say, a plot of ground with a high, broad ring of bare Ring flooring around it. That would keep them in.

"Only it didn't. Somehow a seed got across. No telling how far they've spread by now," said Louis to himself. And he shuddered. This must be the "bright spot" he and Nessus had noticed ahead of them. As far as the eye could see, no living thing challenged the sunflowers.

In time, if they were given time, the sunflowers would rule the Ringworld.

But that would take much time. The Ringworld was roomy. Roomy enough for anything.

CHAPTER 15

Dream-Castle

Louis, musing, was only half aware of two flycycles dropping beside his own. He was jerked from his reverie when Speaker barked, "Louis! You will take the Slaver disintegrator from my 'cycle and use it to dig us a hiding-hole. Teela, come and tend my injuries."

"A hiding-hole?"

"Yes. We must burrow like animals and wait for night-fall."

"Yah." Louis shook himself. Speaker should not have had to think of that, injured as he was. Obviously they could not risk a break in the clouds. All the sunflowers needed to murder them was a point-source of light. But at night—

Louis avoided looking at Speaker while he searched Speaker's 'cycle. One look had been enough. The kzin was burnt black across most of his body. Fluids leaked through the oily ash that had been fur. Flesh showed bright red in wide cracks. The smell of burnt hair was strong and terrible.

Louis found the disintegrator: a double-barreled shot-gun with a fluid-seeming handle. The weapon next to it made him grin sourly. If Speaker had suggested burning off the sunflowers with flashlight-lasers, Louis probably would have gone along with it, fuddled as he was.

He took the weapon and withdrew quickly, feeling queasy, ashamed of his weakness. He hurt with the pain of Speaker's burns. Teela, who knew nothing of pain, could help Speaker better than Louis could.

Louis aimed the gun thirty degrees downward. He was wearing the breathing-helmet from his pressure suit. As he was in no hurry, he flipped only one of the two triggers.

The pit formed fast. Louis couldn't see how fast, for the dust was all around him after the first instant. A minor hurricane blew at him from where the beam fell. Louis had to lean hard into the wind.

In the cone of the beam the electron became a neutral particle. Soil and rock, torn to atoms by the mutual repulsion of the nuclei, reached him as a fog of monatomic dust. Louis was glad of the breathing-helmet.

Presently he turned off the disintegrator. The pit looked big enough to fit the three of them and the flycycles too.

So quickly, he thought. And he wondered how fast the tool would dig with both beams on. *But then there would be a current flow,* he thought, borrowing Speaker's euphemism. At the moment he wasn't looking for that much excitement.

Teela and Speaker had dismounted. Speaker was now hairless over most of his body. A large orange patch still covered him where he sat, and a broad orange band crossed his eyes. Elsewhere his nude skin was veined redviolet, showing clusters of deep red cracks. Teela was spraying him with something that foamed white where it touched.

The stench of burnt hair and meat stayed Louis from coming too close. "It's done," he said.

The kzin looked up. "I can see again, Louis."

"Good!" He'd been worried.

"The puppeteer brought military medical supplies, vastly superior to kzinti civilian medicines. He should not have had access to military supplies." The kzin sounded angry. Perhaps he suspected bribery; and perhaps he was right.

"I'm going to call Nessus," Louis said. And he circled the pair. White foam now covered the kzin from head to foot. There was no smell at all.

"I know where you are," he told the puppeteer.

"Marvelous. Where am I, Louis?"

"You're behind us. You circled round behind us as soon as you were out of sight. Teela and Speaker don't know. They can't think like puppeteers."

"Do they expect a puppeteer to break trail for them?

"Perhaps it is best they continue to think so. What chance is there that they will permit me to rejoin them?"

"Not now. Maybe later. Let me tell you why I called . . ." And he told the puppeteer about the sunflower field. He was detailing the extent of Speaker's injuries when Nessus's flat face dropped below the level of the intercom camera.

Louis waited a few moments for the puppeteer to reappear. Then he switched off. He was sure that Nessus would not remain long in catatonic withdrawal. The puppeteer was too sanely careful of his own life.

Ten hours of daylight remained. The team waited it out in the disintegrator-dug trench.

Speaker slept through it. They walked him into the trench, then used a spray from the kzinti medkit to put him to sleep. The white stuff had congealed on him to the consistency of a foam rubber pillow.

"The world's only bouncy kzin," said Teela.

Louis tried to sleep. He dozed for a time. Once he half woke to bright daylight and to the sharp black shadow of the slope falling across him. He stirred and went back to sleep . . .

And woke later in a cold sweat. Shadows! If he had sat up to look, he'd have been burnt crisp!

But the clouds were back, safely blocking the vengeance of the sunflowers.

Finally one horizon dimmed. As the sky darkened, Louis set about waking the others.

They flew beneath the clouds. It was vital that they be able to see the sunflowers. If dawn approached while the fleet was still over sunflowers, they would have to hide out during the next day.

Occasionally Louis dipped his 'cycle for a closer look.

For an hour they flew . . . and then the sunflowers grew sparse. There was a region where sunflowers were scarce, half-grown seedlings growing among the blackened stumps of a recently burned forest. Grass actually seemed to compete with the sunflowers in this area.

Then there were no sunflowers at all.

And Louis could sleep at last.

Louis slept as if drugged. It was still night when he woke. He looked about him and found a glimmer of light ahead and to spinward.

Groggy as he was, he thought it would turn out to be a firefly caught in the sonic fold, or something equally silly. But it was still there after he rubbed his eyes.

He pushed the Call button for Speaker.

The light grew nearer and clearer. Against the darkness of the Ringworld night landscape it showed bright as a point of reflected sunlight.

Not a sunflower. Not at night.

It might be a house, Louis thought; but where would a native get his lighting? Then again, a house would have gone by like *that*. At flycycle cruising speed, you could cross the North American continent in two-and-a-half hours.

The light was drifting past them on the right, and still Speaker hadn't answered.

Louis cut his 'cycle out of formation. He was grinning in the dark. Behind him the fleet, now under Speaker's guidance (at Speaker's insistence), was only two 'cycles strong. Louis picked Speaker's from memory. He flew toward it.

Shock waves and sonic fold showed faintly outlined by cloud-dimmed Archlight, a network of straight lines converging to a point. Speaker's flycycle, and Speaker's ghost-gray silhouette, seemed caught in a Euclidian spiderweb.

Louis was perilously close when he turned his spotlight on and immediately off. In the dark he saw the ghost come suddenly alert. Louis guided his 'cycle carefully between the kzin and the point of light.

He blinked his spotlight again.

Speaker came on the intercom. "Yes, Louis, I see it now. A lighted something going past us."

"Then let's look it over."

"Very well." Speaker turned toward the light.

They circled it in the dark, like curious minnows nosing a sinking beer bottle. It was a ten-story castle floating a thousand feet high, and it was all lit up like the instrument board on some ancient rocket ship.

A single tremendous picture window, curved so that it formed both wall and ceiling, opened on a cavity the size of an opera house. Within, a labyrinth of dining tables surrounded a raised circle of floor. There was fifty feet of space above the tables, empty but for a free-form sculpture in stressed wire.

Always it came as a fresh surprise, the elbow room on the Ringworld. On Earth it was a felony to fly any vehicle without an autopilot. A falling car would be bound to kill someone, no matter where it fell. Here, thousands of miles of wilderness, buildings suspended over cities, and head room for a guest fifty feet tall.

There was a city beneath the castle. It showed no lights. Speaker skimmed over it like a swooping hawk, scanned it hastily in the blue Archlight. He came up to report that the city looked very like Zignamuclickclick.

"We can explore it after dawn," he said. "I think this stronghold is more important. It may have been untouched since the fall of civilization."

"It must have its own power source," Louis speculated. "I wonder why? None of the buildings in Zignamuclickclick did."

Teela sent her 'cycle skimming directly under the castle. In the intercom her eyes went big with wonder, and she cried, "Louis, Speaker! You've got to see this!"

They dropped after her without thought. Louis was moving up alongside her when he became suddenly, freezingly aware of the mass suspended over his head.

There were windows all over the underside; and the underside was all angles. There was no way to land the castle. Who had built it, and how, with no bottom to it? Concrete and metal, asymmetrically designed, and what the tanj was holding it up? Louis's stomach lurched, but he set his jaw and pulled up alongside Teela, underneath a floating mass equivalent to a medium-sized passenger starship.

Teela had found a wonder: a sunken swimming pool, bathtub-shaped and brightly lit. Its glass bottom and glass walls were open to the outer darkness, but for one wall which bordered on a bar, or a living room, or . . . it was hard to tell, looking through two thicknesses of transparency.

The pool was dry. In the bottom was a single great skeleton resembling that of a bandersnatch.

"They kept large pets," Louis speculated.

"Isn't that a Jinxian bandersnatch? My uncle was a hunter," said Teela. "He had his trophy room built inside a bandersnatch skeleton."

"There are bandersnatchi on a lot of worlds. They were Slaver food animals. I wouldn't be surprised to find them all through the galaxy. The question is, what made the Ringworlders bring them *here?*"

"Decoration," Teela said promptly.

"Are you kidding?" A bandersnatch looked like a cross between Moby Dick and a caterpillar tractor.

Still, Louis thought, why not? Why wouldn't the engineers have raided a dozen or a hundred stellar systems to populate their artificial world? By hypothesis, they had had ramscoop-fusion drives. By necessity, every living thing on the Ringworld had been brought from somewhere else. Sunflowers. Bandersnatchi. What else?

Forget it. Go straight for the rim wall; don't try to explore. Already they had come far enough to circle the Earth half a dozen times. Finagle's law, how much there was to find!

Strange life. (Harmless, so far.)

Sunflowers. (Speaker flaming in a glare of light, yowling into the intercom.)

Floating cities. (Which fell disastrously.)

Bandersnatchi. (Intelligent and dangerous. They would be the same here. Bandersnatchi did not mutate.)

And death? Death was always the same, everywhere.

They circled the castle again, looking for openings. Windows there were, all shapes, rectangles and octagons and bubbles and thick panes in the floor; but all were closed. They found a dock for flying vehicles, with a great door built like a drawbridge to act as a landing ramp; but, like a drawbridge, the door was up and closed. They found a couple of hundred feet of spiral escalator hanging like a bedspring from the lowermost tip of the castle. Its bottom ended in open air. Some force had twisted it away, leaving sheared beams and broken treads. Its top was a locked door.

"To Finagle with this! I'm going to ram a window," said Teela.

"Stop!" Louis commanded. He believed she would do it. "Speaker, use the disintegrator. Get us in."

In the light streaming from the great picture window, Speaker unslung the Slaver digging tool.

Louis knew about the disintegrator. Objects within its variable-width beam acquired, suddenly, a positive charge powerful enough to tear them apart. The puppeteers had added a second, parallel beam to suppress the charge on the proton. Louis had not used it to dig in the sunflower field, and he knew it would not be needed for this job.

He might have guessed that Speaker would use it anyway.

Two points a few inches apart on the great octagonal window acquired opposite charges, with a potential difference between.

The flash was blinding. Louis clenched his eyes over tears and pain. The crack of thunder was simultaneous, and deafening even through the sonic fold. In the stunned calm that followed, Louis felt gritty particles settled thickly over his neck and shoulders and the backs of his hands. He kept his eyes closed.

"You had to test it," he said.

"It works very well. It will serve us."

"Happy birthday. Don't point it at Daddy, because Daddy will be very angry."

"Do not be flippant, Louis."

His eyes had recovered. Louis found millions of tiny glass slivers all over him and the 'cycle. Flying glass! The sonic fold must have stopped the particles, then released them to drift down over every horizontal surface.

Teela was already floating into the ballroom-sized cavity. They followed . . .

Louis woke gradually, feeling wonderful. He was lying on his arm, on a soft surface. His arm was asleep.

He rolled over and opened his eyes.

He was in a bed, looking up at a high white ceiling. An obstruction under his ribs turned out to be Teela's foot.

Right. They had found the bed last night, a bed as big as a miniature golf course, in an enormous bedroom in what would have been the basement of a less unusual castle.

By then they had already found marvels.

The castle was a castle indeed, and not merely a posh hotel. A banquet hall with a picture window fifty feet tall was startling enough. But the tables circled a central, ring-shaped table on a raised dais. The ring surrounded a contoured, high-backed chair the size of a throne. Teela, experimenting, had found how to make the chair rise halfway to the ceiling, and how to activate a pickup to amplify the voice of the occupant into a thunder of command. The chair would turn; and when it turned, the sculpture above it turned too.

The sculpture was in stressed wire, very light, mostly empty space. It had seemed an abstraction until Teela started it turning. Then—it was obviously a portrait.

The sculpted head of an entirely hairless man.

Was he a native, from a community whose members shaved their faces and scalps? Or had he been a member of another race from far around the curve of the Ring?

They might never know. But the face was decidedly human: handsome, angular, the face of one used to command.

Louis looked up at the ceiling and remembered that face. Command had worn lines into that face, around the eyes and mouth, and the artist had somehow managed to include those lines into the wire framework.

This castle had been a seat of government. Everything pointed to it: the throne, the banquet hall, the unique windows, the floating castle itself with its independent power source. But for Louis Wu the clincher was that face.

Afterward they had wandered through the castle. They had found lavishly decorated, beautifully designed staircases everywhere. But they didn't move. There were no escalators, no elevators, no slidewalks, no dropshafts. Perhaps the stairs themselves had moved once.

So the party had wandered downward, because it was easier than climbing up. In the bottom of the castle they had found the bedroom.

Endless days of sleeping in flycycle seats, of making love wherever the fleet had happened to touch down, had made that bed irresistible to Teela and Louis Wu. They had left Speaker to continue his explorations alone.

By now there was no telling what he had found.

Louis raised himself on one elbow. The dead hand was coming back to life. He was careful not to jar it. *Never happens with sleeping plates,* he reflected, *but what the tanj . . . at least it's a bed . . .*

One glassy wall of the bedroom opened on a dry pool. Framed by glass walls and a glass floor, the white skeleton of a Frumious bandersnatch looked back at him with empty eyes set in a spoon-shaped skull.

The opposite wall, equally transparent, opened a thousand feet over the city

Louis rolled over three times and dropped off the edge of the bed. The floor was soft, covered with a fur rug whose texture and color disturbingly resembled a native's beard. Louis padded to the window and looked out.

(Something was interfering with his vision, like a minor

flicker in a tridee screen. Consciously he had not even noticed it. Nonetheless it was annoying.)

Beneath a white and featureless sky, the city was all the colors of gray. Most of the buildings were tall, but a bare handful were tall enough to dwarf the rest; taller, a few of them, than the bottom of this floating castle. There had been other floating buildings. Louis could see the scars, broad gaps in the cityscape where thousands of tons of masonry had smashed down.

But this one dream-castle had had its own independent power supply. And a bedroom big enough to fit any decent-sized orgy. With a tremendous window-wall from which a sultan might contemplate his domain, might see his subjects as the ants they were.

"This place must have been conducive to *hubris*," said Louis Wu.

Something caught his eye. Something fluttering outside the window.

Thread. A length of it had hung up on a cornice; but more of it was still drifting down from the sky. Coarse thread. He could see the two strands trailing from the cornice down over the city. It must have been falling for as long as he had been looking out the window. Interfering with his vision.

Not knowing its origin, Louis accepted it for what it was. Something pretty. He lay nude on his back on the hairy wall-to-wall rug, and he watched the thread drifting past his window. He felt safe and rested, perhaps for the first time since an X-ray laser had touched the *Liar*.

The thread drifted endlessly down, loop after loop of black line curving out of a gray-white sky. It was fine enough to flicker in and out of visibility. How to know the length of it? How to count the snowflakes in a blizzard?

Suddenly Louis recognized it.

"Welcome back," he said. But he was jolted.

Shadow square wire. It had followed them here.

Louis climbed five flights of stairs to find his breakfast. Naturally he didn't expect the kitchen to be operating.

He was looking for the banquet hall; but he found the kitchen instead.

It confirmed ideas he had had earlier. It takes servants to make an autocrat; and there had been servants here. The kitchen was tremendous. It must have required a score of chefs, with their own servants to carry the finished product out to the banquet hall, return the dirty dishes, clean up, run errands . . .

There were bins that had held fresh fruit and vegetables, and now held dust and fruit-pits and dried skins and mold. There was a cold room where carcasses had hung. It was empty and warm. There was a freezer, still working. Some of the food on the freezer shelves might have been edible; but Louis would not have risked it.

There were no cans.

The water spigots were dry.

Aside from the freezer, there was not a machine more complex than a door hinge. There were no temperature indicators or timers on the stoves. There was nothing equivalent to a toaster. There were threads hanging over the stove, with nodules of crud on them. Raw spices? No spice bottles?

Louis looked once around him before he left. Otherwise he might have missed the truth.

This room had not originally been a kitchen.

What, then? A storage room? A tridee room? Probably the latter. One wall was very blank, with a uniform paint job that looked younger than the rest; and there were scars on the floor where chairs and couches might have been removed.

All right, then. The room had been an entertainment room. Then, maybe the wall set had broken down, and nobody remembered how to fix it. Later the autokitchen had gone the same route.

So the big tridee room had been turned into a manually operated kitchen. Such kitchens must have been common by then, if nobody remembered how to fix an autokitchen. Raw foods had been brought up by flying truck.

And when the flying trucks broke down, one by one . . . ?

Louis left.

He found the banquet hall at last, and the only dependable source of food in the castle. There he breakfasted on a brick from the kitchen slot in his 'cycle.

He was finishing up when Speaker entered.

The kzin must have been starving. He went straight to his 'cycle, dialed three wet dark-red bricks, and gulped them down in nine swallows. Only then did he turn to look at Louis.

He was no longer ghost-white. Sometime during the night, the foam had finished healing him and had sloughed away. His skin showed glossy and pink and healthy, if pink was the color of healthy kzinti skin, with a few ridges of grey scar tissue and an extensive network of violet veins.

"Come with me," the kzin commanded. "I have found a map room."

CHAPTER 16

The Map Room

The map room was at the very top of the castle, as befitted its importance. Louis was blowing hard from the climb. He had had a time keeping up. The kzin did not run, but he walked faster than a man could walk.

Louis reached the landing as Speaker pushed through a double door ahead of him.

Through that gap Louis saw a horizontal band of jet black, eight inches broad and three feet off the ground. He looked beyond it, looked for a similar strip of baby blue checked with midnight blue rectangles; and he found it.

Jackpot.

Louis stood in the doorway, taking in details. The miniature Ringworld was almost as large as the room, which was circular and perhaps a hundred and twenty feet across. At the hub of the circular map was a rectangular screen, heavily mounted, facing away from the doorway but built to turn.

High on the walls were ten turning globes. They varied in size, and they turned at different rates; but each was the characteristic color, rich blue with swirled white frosting, of an Earthlike world. There was a conic-section map below each globe.

"I spent the night here, working," said Speaker. He was standing behind the screen. "I have many things to show you. Come here."

Louis almost ducked under the Ring. A thought stopped him. The hawk-featured man who ruled the ban-

216

quet hall would never have stooped so, not even to
enter this holy of holies. Louis walked at the Ring, and
through it, and found it was a holo projection.

He took up a stance behind the kzin.

Control panels surrounded the screen. All the knobs
were large and massive, made of silver; and each was
carved to represent the head of some animal. The boards
were contoured in swirls and curves. *Prettified,* Louis
thought. *Decadent?*

The screen was alight, but unmagnified. Looking into
it was like looking down on the Ringworld from the vicinity of the shadow squares. Louis felt a touch of *déjà vu.*

"I had it focused earlier," said the kzin. "If I remem-
ber rightly . . ." He touched a knob, and the view ex-
panded so fast that Louis's hand clutched for a throttle.
"I want to show you the rim wall. Rrrr, a bit off . . ."
He touched another fierce-visaged knob, and the view slid.
They were looking over the edge of the Ringworld.

Somewhere were telescopes to give them this view.
Where? Mounted on the shadow squares?

They were looking down on thousand-mile-high mountains. Still the view expanded as Speaker found ever-finer
controls. Louis marveled at how abruptly the mountains,
appearing very natural but for their size, were cut by the
knife-edged shadow of space.

Then he saw what ran along the peaks of the mountains.

Though it was only a line of silver dots, he knew what
it would be. "A linear accelerator."

"Yes," said Speaker. "Without transfer booths, it is the
only feasible way to travel Ringworld distances. It must
have been the major transport system."

"But it's a thousand miles high. Elevators?"

"I found elevator shafts all along the rim wall. There,
for instance." By now the silver thread was a line of tiny
loops, widely spaced, each hidden from the land below by
a mountain peak. A tube so slender as to be barely visible
led from one of the loops, down the slope of a mountain,
into a layer of clouds at the bottom of the Ringworld atmosphere.

Speaker said, "The electromagnetic loops cluster thickly around the elevator shafts. Elsewhere they are up to a million miles apart. I surmise that they are not needed except for starting and stopping and guidance. A car could be accelerated to free fall, coast around the rim at a relative 770 miles per second, to be stopped near an elevator tube by another cluster of loops."

"It'd take up to ten days to get a man where he wants to go. Not counting accelerations."

"Trivial. It takes you sixty days to reach Silvereyes, the human world farthest from Earth. You would need four times that long to cross known space from edge to edge."

True. And the living area on the Ringworld was greater than that of all known space. *They built for room when they built this thing.* Louis asked, "Did you see any sign of activity? Is anyone still using the linear accelerator?"

"The question is meaningless. Let me show you." The view converged, slid sidewise, expanded slowly. It was night. Dark clouds diverged over dark land, and then . . .

"City lights. Well." Louis swallowed. It had come too suddenly. "So it's not all dead. We can get help."

"I do not think so. This may be difficult to find . . . ah."

"Finagle's black mind!"

The castle, obviously their own castle, floated serenely above a field of light. Windows, neon, streams of floating light motes which must be vehicles . . . oddly shaped floating buildings . . . lovely.

"Tapes. Tanjit! We're watching old tapes. I thought they must be live transmissions." For one glorious moment it had seemed that their search was over. Lighted, bustling cities, pinpointed on a map for them . . . but these pictures must be ages old, civilizations old.

"I thought so also, for many hours last night. I did not suspect the truth until I failed to find the thousands of miles of meteor crater slashed by the *Liar's* landing."

Louis, speechless, thwacked the kzin on his nude pink-and-lavender shoulder. It was as high as he could reach.

The kzin ignored the liberty. "After I had located the castle, things proceeded quickly. Observe." He caused the view to slide rapidly to port. The dark land blurred, lost all detail. Then they were over black ocean.

The camera seemed to back up . . .

"You see? A bay of one of the major salt oceans falls across our path to the rim wall. The ocean itself is several times as large as any on Kzin or Earth. The bay is as large as our largest ocean."

"More delay! Can't we go over it?"

"Perhaps we can. But we face greater delay than that." The kzin reached for a knob.

"Hold it. I want a closer look at those groups of islands."

"Why, Louis? That we might stop for provisions?"

"No . . . Do you see how they tend to form clusters, with wide stretches of deep water between? Take that grouping there." Louis's forefinger circled images on the screen. "Now look up at that map."

"I do not understand."

"And *that* grouping in what you called a bay, and *that* map behind you. The continents in the conic projections are a little distorted . . . See it now? Ten worlds, ten clusters of islands. They aren't one-to-one scale; but I'll bet that island is as big as Australia, and the original continent doesn't look any bigger than Eurasia on the globe."

"What a macabre jest. Louis, does this represent a typically human sense of humor?"

"No, no, no. Sentiment! Unless—"

"Yes?"

"I hadn't thought of that. The first generation—they had to throw away their own worlds, but they wanted to keep something of what they were losing. Three generations later it would be funny. It's always that way."

When the kzin was sure Louis had finished, he asked somewhat diffidently, "Do you humans feel that you understand kzinti?"

Louis smiled and shook his head.

"Good," said the kzin, and changed the subject. "I spent some time last night examining the nearest spaceport."

They stood at the hub of the miniature Ringworld, looking through a rectangular window into the past.

The past they saw was one of magnificent achievement. Speaker had focused the screen on the spaceport, a wide projecting ledge on the spaceward side of the rim wall. They watched as an enormous blunt-ended cylinder, alight with a thousand windows, was landed in electromagnetic cradling fields. The fields glowed in pastel shades, probably so that the operators could manipulate them visually.

"The tape is looped," said Speaker. "I watched it for some time last night. The passengers seem to walk directly into the rim wall, as if a kind of osmosis process were being used."

"Yah." Louis was badly depressed. The spaceport ledge was far to spinward of them—a distance to dwarf the distance they had already traveled.

"I watched a ship take off. They did not use the linear accelerator. They use it only for landings, to match the velocity of the ship to that of the spaceport. For takeoffs they simply tumble the ship off into space.

"It was as the leaf-eater guessed, Louis. Remember the trap door arrangement? The Ringworld spins easily fast enough for a ramscoop field to operate. Louis, are you listening?"

Louis shook himself. "Sorry. All I can think about is that this adds about seven hundred thousand miles to our trip."

"It may be possible to use the main transport system, the small linear accelerator at the top of the rim wall."

"Not a chance. It's probably wrecked. Civilization tends to spread, if there's a transport system to spread it. And even if we can get it working, we aren't moving toward an elevator shaft."

"That is true," said the kzin. "I looked for one."

In the rectangular screen, the ship was down. Floating trucks ran a jointed tube to the ship's main lock. Passengers spilled into the tube.

"Shall we change our goal?"

"We can't. The spaceport is still our best chance."

"Is it?"

"Yes, tanjit! Big as it is, the Ringworld is a colony world. Civilization always centers around the spaceport on a colony world."

"Because craft come from the home world, carrying news of technological innovations. We surmise that the Ringworlders have abandoned their home world."

"But the ships can still come in," Louis said doggedly. "From the abandoned worlds! From centuries ago! Ramships are subject to relativity, to time dilation."

"You hope to find old spacemen trying to teach the old skills to savages who have forgotten them. And you may be right," said Speaker. "But I weary of this structure, and the spaceport is very far. What else can I show you on the map screen?"

Suddenly Louis asked, "How far have we come since we left the *Liar?*"

"I told you I could not find our impact crater. Your guess is as accurate as mine. But I know how far we must go. From the castle to the rim is approximately two hundred thousand miles."

"A long way . . . But you must have found the mountain."

"No."

"The big one. Fist-of-God. We crashed practically on its slope."

"No."

"I don't like that. Speaker, is there any way we could have gotten off course? You should have found Fist-of-God just by backtracking starboard from the castle."

"But I did not," Speaker said with finality. "Do you wish to see anything more? For example, there are blank areas. Probably they are due only to worn tape, but I wondered if they might not conceal places on the Ringworld whose nature is secret."

"But we'd have to go there ourselves to find out."

Speaker suddenly turned to face the double doors, his ears spread like fans. Silently he dropped to all fours, and leapt.

Louis blinked. What could have caused that? And then he heard it . . .

Considering its age, the castle machinery had been remarkably silent. Now there came a low-pitched hum from
outside the double doors.

Speaker was out of sight. Louis drew his flashlight-laser
and followed cautiously.

He found the kzin at the head of the stairs. He put the
weapon away; and together they watched Teela ride up.

"They only go up," Teela told them. "Not down. The
one between the sixth and seventh floors won't go at all."

Louis asked the obvious question. "How do you make
them move?"

"You just grip the banister and push forward. That way
it won't go unless you're hanging on. Safer. I only found
out by accident."

"You would. I climbed ten flights of stairs this morning.
How many did you climb before you found out?"

"None. I was going up for breakfast, and I tripped on
the first step and grabbed for the banister."

"Right. It figures."

Teela looked hurt. "It's not my fault if you—"

"Sorry. Did you get your breakfast?"

"No. I've been watching people move around below us.
Did you know there's a public square just under the building?"

Speaker's ears opened wide. "Is there? And it is not
deserted?"

"No. They've been filing in from all directions, all morning. By now there must be hundreds of them." She smiled
like dawn breaking. "And they're singing."

There were wide spots along all the corridors of the
castle. Each such alcove was furnished with rugs and
couches and tables, apparently so that any group of stroll-
ers could take a meal whenever he fancied, wherever he
might be. In one such dining-nook, near the "basement
level" of the castle, was a long window bent at right angles
to form half a wall, half a floor.

Louis was panting a little from having descended ten
flights of stairs. He found himself fascinated by the dining
table. Its top seemed—sculpted; but the contours were

shaped and placed to suggest soup plates, salad or butter or dinner plates, or coasters for the bottom of a mug. Decades or centuries of use had stained the hard white material.

"You wouldn't use plates," Louis speculated. "You'd dish the food into the depressions, and hose the table off afterward."

It seemed unsanitary, but——? "They wouldn't bring flies or mosquitoes or wolves. Why should they bring bacteria?

"Colonic bacteria," he answered himself. "For digestion. And if one bacterium mutated, turned vicious——" By then there would be no immunity to anything. Was that how the Ringworld civilization had died? Any civilization requires a minimum number to maintain it.

Teela and Speaker were paying him no attention. They knelt in the bend of the window, looking down. Louis went to join them.

"They're still at it," said Teela. And they were. Louis guessed that a thousand people were looking up at him. They were not chanting now.

"They *can't* know we're here," he said.

Speaker suggested, "Perhaps they worship the building."

"Even so, they can't do this every day. We're too far from the edge of town. They couldn't reach the fields."

"Perhaps we happened by on a special day, the holy day."

Teela said, "Maybe something happened last night. Something special, like us, if someone spotted us after all. Or like *that*." She pointed.

"I wondered about that," said Speaker. "How long has it been falling?"

"Since I woke up, at least. It's like a rain, or a new kind of snow. Wire from the shadow squares, mile after mile of it. Why do you suppose it fell here?"

Louis thought of six million miles of distance between each shadow square . . . of an entire six-million-mile strand torn loose by its impact with the *Liar* . . . falling with the *Liar* toward the Ringworld landscape, on nearly the same course. It was hardly surprising that they had come across part of that enormous strand.

He was not in a long-winded mood. "Coincidence," he said.

"Anyway, it's draped all over us, and it's been falling since last night, probably. The natives must have worshipped the castle already, because it floats."

"Consider," the kzin said slowly. "If Ringworld engineers were to appear today, floating down from this floating castle, it would be taken as more appropriate than surprising. Louis, shall we try the God Gambit?"

Louis turned to answer—and couldn't. He could only try to keep a straight face. He might have made it, but Speaker was explaining to Teela:

"It was Louis's suggestion that we might succeed better with the natives by posing as Ringworld engineers. You and Louis were to be acolytes. Nessus was to be a captive demon; but we can hope to do without him. I was to be more god than engineer, a kind of war god—"

Then Teela started to laugh, and Louis broke up.

Eight feet tall, inhumanly broad across the shoulders and hips, the kzin was too big and too toothy to be other than fearsome, even when burnt bald. His ratlike tail had always been his least impressive feature. Now his skin was the same color: baby pink crisscrossed with lavender capillaries. Without the fur to bulk out his head, his ears became ungainly pink parasols. Orange fur made a domino mask across his eyes, and he seemed to have grown his own fluffy orange pillow to sit on.

The danger of laughing at a kzin only made it funnier. Doubled over, with his arms around his middle, laughing silently now because he could not inhale, Louis backed toward what he hoped was a chair.

An inhumanly large hand closed on his shoulder and lifted him high. Still convulsed with mirth, Louis faced the kzin at eye level. He heard, "Truly, Louis, you must explain this behavior."

Louis made an enormous effort. "A k-k-kind of war god," he said, and was off again. Teela was making hiccupping sounds.

The kzin set him down and waited for the fit to pass.

"You simply aren't impressive enough to play god," Louis said some minutes later. "Not until the hair grows back."

"But if I tore some humans to pieces with my hands, perhaps they would respect me then."

"They'd respect you from a distance, and from hiding. That wouldn't do us any good. No, we'll just have to wait for the hair. Even then, we ought to have Nessus's tasp."

"The puppeteer is unavailable."

"But—"

"I say he is unavailable. How shall we contact the natives?"

"You'll have to stay here. See what you can learn from the map room. Teela and I," said Louis, and suddenly remembered. "Teela, you haven't seen the map room."

"What's it like?"

"You stay here and get Speaker to show you. I'll go down alone. You two can monitor me by communicator disc, and come for me if there's trouble. Speaker, I want your flashlight-laser."

The kzin grumbled, but he did relinquish the flashlight-laser. It still left him with the modified Slaver disintegrator.

From a thousand feet over their heads, he heard their reverent silence become a murmur of astonishment; and he knew that they had seen him, a bright speck separating from the castle window. He sank toward them.

The murmur did not die. It was suppressed. He could hear the difference.

Then the singing began.

"It drags," Teela had said, and, "They don't keep in step," and, "It all sounds flat." Louis's imagination had gone on from there. As a result the singing took him by surprise. It was much better than he had expected.

He guessed they were singing a twelve-tone scale. The "octave" scale of most of the human worlds was also a twelve-tone scale, but with differences. Small wonder it had sounded flat to Teela.

Yes, it dragged. It was church music, slow and solemn and repetitive, without harmony But it had grandeur.

The square was immense. A thousand people were a
vast throng after the weeks of loneliness; but the square
could have held ten times that number. Loudspeakers
could have kept them singing in step, but there were no
loudspeakers. A lone man waved his arms from a pedestal
in the center of the square. But they would not look at
him. They were all looking up at Louis Wu.

For all that, the music was beautiful.

Teela could not hear that beauty. The music of her
experience had come from recordings and tridee sets, always by way of a microphone system. Such music could be
amplified, rectified, the voices multiplied or augmented,
the bad takes thrown away. Teela Brown had never heard
live music.

Louis Wu had. He slowed his 'cycle to give his nerve-
ends time to adapt to the rhythms of it. He remembered
the great public sings on the cliffs above Crashlanding
City, throngs which had boasted twice this number, sings
which had sounded different for that and another reason;
for Louis Wu had been singing too. Now, as he let the
music vibrate in him, his ears began to adjust to the
slightly sharp or flat notes, to the blurring of voices, to
the repetition, to the slow majesty of the hymn.

He caught himself as he was about to join in the singing. *That's not a good idea,* he thought, and let his 'cycle
settle toward the square.

The pedestal in the center of the square had once held
a statue. Louis identified the humanlike footprints, each
four feet long, that marked where the statue had stood.
Now the pedestal housed a kind of triangular altar, and a
man stood with his back to the altar waving his arms as
the people sang.

Flash of pink above gray robe . . . Louis assumed that
the man was wearing a headpiece, perhaps of pink silk.

He chose to land on the pedestal itself. He was just
touching down when the conductor turned to face him. As
a result he almost wrecked the 'cycle.

It was pink scalp Louis had seen. Unique in this crowd
of heads like golden flowers, faces of blond hair with eyes

peeping through, this man's face was as naked as Louis Wu's own.

With a straight-armed gesture, palms down, the man held the last note of the singing . . . held it for seconds . . . then cut it. A fragment of a second later the tail of it drifted in from the edges of the square. The—priest?—faced Louis Wu in a sudden silence.

He was as tall as Louis Wu, tall for a native. The skin of his face and scalp were so pale as to be nearly translucent, like a We Made It albino. He must have shaved many hours ago with a razor that was not sharp enough, and now the stubble was emerging, adding its touch of gray everywhere but for the two circles around his eyes.

He spoke with a note of reproof, or so it seemed. The translator disc instantly said, "So you have come at last."

"We didn't know we were expected," Louis said truthfully. He was not confident enough to try a God Gambit based on himself. In a long lifetime he had learned that telling a consistent set of lies could get hellishly complicated.

"You grow hair on your head," said the priest. "One presumes that your blood is less than pure, O Engineer."

So that was it! The race of the Engineers must have been totally bald; so that this priest must imitate them by using a blunt razor on his tender skin. Or . . . had the Engineers used depil cream or something just as easy, for no reason more pressing than fashion? The priest looked very like the wire-portrait in the banquet hall.

"My blood is of no concern to you," Louis said, shelving the problem. "We are on our way to the rim of the world. What can you tell us about our route?"

The priest was transparently puzzled. "You ask information from me? You, an Engineer?"

"I'm not an Engineer." Louis held his hand ready to activate the sonic fold.

But the priest only looked more bewildered. "Then why are you half-hairless? How do you fly? Have you stolen secrets from Heaven? What do you want here? Have you come to steal my congregation?"

The last question seemed the important one. "We're on our way to the rim. All we need here is information."

"Surely your answers are in Heaven."

"Don't be flippant with me," Louis said evenly.

"But you came directly from Heaven! I saw you!"

"Oh, the *castle!* We've gone through the castle, but it didn't tell us much. For instance, were the Engineers really hairless?"

"I have sometimes thought that they only shave, as I do. Yet your own chin seems naturally hairless."

"I depilate." Louis looked about him, at the sea of reverent golden flower-faces. "What do they believe? They don't seem to share your doubts."

"They see us talking as equals, in the language of the Engineers. I would have this continue, if it please you." Now the priest's manner seemed conspiratorial rather than hostile.

"Would that improve your standing with them? I suppose it would," said Louis. The priest really had feared to lose his congregation—as any priest might, if his god came to life and tried to take over. "Can't they understand us?"

"Perhaps one word in ten."

At this point Louis had cause to regret the efficiency of his translator disc. He could not tell if the priest was speaking the language of Zignamuclickclick. Knowing that, knowing how far the two languages had diverged since the breakdown in communications, he might have been able to date the fall of civilization.

"What was this castle called Heaven?" he asked. "Do you know?"

"The legends speak of Zrillir," said the priest, "and of how he ruled all the lands under Heaven. On this pedestal stood Zrillir's statue, which was life-sized. The lands supplied Heaven with delicacies which I could name if you like, as we learn their names by rote; but in these days they do not grow. Shall I—?"

"No thanks. What happened?"

A singsong quality had crept into the man's voice. He must have heard this tale many times, and told it many times . . .

"Heaven was made when the Engineers made the world and the Arch. He who rules Heaven rules the land from edge to edge. So Zrillir ruled, for many lifetimes, throwing sunfire from Heaven when he was displeased. Then it was suspected that Zrillir could no longer throw sunfire.

"The people no longer obeyed him. They did not send food. They pulled down the statue. When Zrillir's angels dropped rocks from the heights, the people dodged and laughed.

"There came a day when the people tried to take Heaven by way of the rising stairway. But Zrillir caused the stairway to fall. Then his angels left Heaven in flying cars.

"Later it was regretted that we had lost Zrillir. The sky was always overcast; crops grew stunted. We have prayed for Zrillir's return—"

"How accurate is all this, do you think?"

"I would have denied it all until this morning, when you came flying down from Heaven. You make me terribly uneasy, O Engineer. Perhaps Zrillir does indeed intend to return, and sends his bastard ahead to clear the way of false priests."

"I could shave my scalp. Would that help?"

"No. Never mind; ask your questions."

"What can you tell me about the fall of Ringworld civilization?"

The priest looked still more uneasy. "Is civilization about to fall?"

Louis sighed and—for the first time—turned to consider the altar.

The altar occupied the center of the pedestal on which they stood. It was of dark wood. Its flat rectangular surface had been carved into a relief map, with hills and rivers and a single lake, and two upward-turning edges. The other pair of edges, the short edges, were the bases of a golden paraboloid arch.

The gold of that arch was tarnished. But from the curve of its apex a small golden ball hung by a thread; and *that* gold was highly polished.

"Is civilization in danger? So much has happened. The

sunwire, your own coming—is it sunwire? Is the sun falling on us?"

"I strongly doubt it. You mean the wire that's been falling all morning?"

"Yes. In our religious training we were taught that the sun hangs from the Arch by a very strong thread. This thread is strong. We know," said the priest. "A girl tried to pick it up and undo a tangle, and it cut through her fingers."

Louis nodded. "Nothing's falling," he said. Privately he thought: *Not even the shadow squares. Even if you cut all the wires, the squares wouldn't hit the Ringworld.* The Engineers would have given them an orbital aphelion inside the Ring.

He asked, without much hope, "What do you know about the transport system at the rim?" And in that instant he knew something was wrong. He'd caught something, some evidence of disaster; but what?

The priest said, "Would you mind repeating that?"

Louis did.

The priest answered, "Your thing that talks said something else the first time. Something about a restricted—something."

"Funny," said Louis. And this time he heard it. The translator spoke in a different tone of voice, and it spoke at length.

" 'You are using a restricted wavelength in violation—' I do not remember the rest," said the priest. "We had best end this interview. You have reawakened something ancient, something evil—" The priest stopped to listen, for Louis's translator was speaking again in the priest's language. " '—in violation of edict twelve, interfering with maintenance.' Can your powers hold back—"

Whatever else the priest said was not translated.

For the disc suddenly turned red hot in Louis's hand. He instantly threw it as hard as he could. It was white hot and brightly glowing when it hit the pavement—without hurting anyone, as far as he could see. Then the pain backlashed him and he was half-blinded by tears.

He was able to see the priest nod to him, very formal and regal.

He nodded back, his face equally expressionless. He had never dismounted his 'cycle; now he touched the control and rose toward Heaven.

When his face could not be seen he let it snarl with the pain, and he used a word he had heard once on Wunderland, from a man who had dropped a piece of Steuben crystal a thousand years old.

CHAPTER 17

The Eye of The Storm

The 'cycles were moving to port when they left Heaven, beneath the steel-gray lid that in these regions served as a sky. It had saved their lives above the sunflower fields. By now it was merely depressing.

Louis touched three points on the dash to lock into his present altitude. He had to watch what he was doing, because there was very little feeling in his right hand under the medicines and the spray-skin and the single white blister on each fingertip. He regarded his hand now, thinking how much worse it might have been . . .

Speaker appeared above the dash. "Louis, do we not wish to rise above the clouds?"

"We might miss something. We can't see the ground from up there."

"We have our maps."

"Would they show us another sunflower field?"

"You are right," Speaker said instantly. He clicked off.

Speaker and Teela, waiting in Heaven's map room while Louis braced a shaven priest far below, had spent the time well. They had sketched contour maps of their route to the rim wall, and had also sketched in the cities that showed as bright yellow patches in the magnifying screen.

Then something had taken exception to their use of a reserved frequency. Reserved by whom, for what purpose, how long ago? Why had it not objected until now? Louis suspected an abandoned machine, like the meteor guard that had shot down the *Liar*. Perhaps this one worked only intermittently, in spasms.

And Speaker's translator disc had turned red hot and stuck to his palm. It would be days before he could use his hand again, even with the miracle kzinti "military" medicines. The muscles would have to regenerate.

The maps would make a difference. Resurging civilization would almost certainly show first in the great metropoli. The fleet could cross those sites, watching for lights or rising smoke.

Nessus's call button burned on the dash, as it might have burned for a score of hours. Louis answered it.

He saw the puppeteer's straggly brown mane and glove-soft back rising and slowly falling with his breath. For a moment he wondered if the puppeteer were back in catatonic withdrawal. Then the puppeteer lifted a triangular head and sang, "Welcome, Louis! What news?"

"We found a floating building," said Louis. "With a map room." He told the puppeteer of the castle called Heaven, the map room, the screen, the maps and globes, the priest and his tales and his model of the universe. He had been answering questions for some time when he thought of one of his own.

"Hey. Is your translator disc working?"

"No, Louis. A short time ago the instrument turned white hot before me, frightening me badly. Had I dared, I would have gone catatonic; but I knew too little."

"Well, the others are gone too. Teela's burned its case and left a scar on her 'cycle. Speaker and I both got our hands burned. You know something? We're going to have to learn the Ringworld language."

"Yes."

"I wish the old man had remembered something about the fall of the old Ring society. I had an idea . . ." And he told the puppeteer his theory of a mutating colonic bacterium.

"That is possible," said Nessus. "Once they lost the secret of transmutation, they would never recover."

"Oh? Why not?"

"Look about you, Louis. What do you see?"

Louis did. He saw a lightning-storm developing ahead; he saw hills, valleys, a distant city, twin mountain peaks tipped with the dirty translucency of raw Ring flooring . . .

"Land anywhere on the Ringworld, and dig. What do you find?"

"Dirt," said Louis. "So?"

"And then?"

"More dirt. Bedrock. Ring floor material," said Louis. And as he said these words the landscape seemed to alter. Storm clouds, mountains, the city to spinward and the city dwindling behind, the edge of brilliance far away on the infinity-horizon, that might be a sea or a sunflower invasion . . . now the landscape showed as the shell it was. The difference between an honest planet and *this* was the difference between a human face and an empty rubber mask.

"Dig on any world," the puppeteer was saying, "and eventually you will find some kind of metal ore. Here, you will find forty feet of soil, and then the Ring foundation. That material cannot be worked. If it could be pierced, the miner would strike vacuum—a harsh reward for his labor.

"Give the Ring a civilization capable of building the Ring, and it must necessarily have cheap transmutation. Let them lose the technology of transmutation—no matter how—and what would be left? Surely they would not stockpile raw metals. There are no ores. The metal of the Ring would be all in machines and in tools and in rust. Even interplanetary capability would not help them, for there is nothing to be mined anywhere around this star. Civilization would fall, and never rise."

Softly Louis asked, "When did you figure this out?"

"Some time ago. It did not seem important to our survival."

"So you just didn't mention it. Right," said Louis. The hours he'd spent worrying that problem! And it all seemed so vividly obvious now. What a trap, what a terrible trap for thinking beings.

Louis looked ahead of him (and was marginally aware that Nessus's image was gone). The storm was nearer now, and it was wide. Doubtless the sonic folds could handle it, but still . . .

Better to fly over it. Louis pulled on a handle, and the

flycycles rose toward the world's gray lid, toward the clouds that had covered them since they reached the tower called Heaven.

Louis's mind ran in idle . . .

Learning a new language would take time. Learning a new language every time they set down, would be impossible. The question was becoming crucial. How long had the Ring natives been barbarian? How long since they had all spoken the same language? How far had the local languages diverged from the original?

The universe blurred, then went entirely gray. They were in the clouds. Tendrils of mist streamed around the bubble of Louis's sonic fold. Then the 'cycles broke through into the sunlight.

From the Ringworld's indefinite horizon, a vast blue eye looked at Louis Wu across a flat infinity of cloud.

If God's head had been the size of the Earth's Moon, that eye would have been about the right size.

It took Louis a moment to grasp what he was seeing. For another moment his brain flatly refused to believe it. Then the whole picture tried to fade like a badly illuminated holo.

Through the humming in his ears he heard/felt someone screaming.

Am I dead? he wondered.

And, *Is that Nessus screaming?* But he'd cut that circuit.

It was Teela. Teela, who had never been afraid of anything in her life. Teela covered her face with her hands, hiding from that vast blue stare.

The eye lay dead ahead, dead to port. It seemed to be drawing them toward itself.

Am I dead? Is the Creator come to judge me? Which Creator?

It was finally time for Louis Wu to decide which Creator he believed in, if any.

The eye was blue and white, with a white eyebrow and a dark pupil. White of cloud, blue of distance. As if it were part of the sky itself.

"Louis!" Teela screamed. "Do something!"

It isn't happening, Louis told himself. His throat was a column of solid ice. His mind ran about in his skull like something trapped. *It's a big universe, but some things really are impossible.*

"Louis!"

Louis found his voice. "Speaker. Hey, Speaker. What do you see?"

The kzin took his time answering. His voice was curiously flat. "I see a great human eye ahead of us."

"Human?"

"Yes. Do you see it too?"

The word Louis would never have used made all the difference. *Human.* A *human* eye. If the eye were a supernatural manifestation, then a kzin should see a kzinti eye, or nothing at all.

"Then it's natural," Louis told himself. "It has to be."

Teela looked at him hopefully.

But how was it drawing them toward itself?

"Oh," said Louis Wu. He moved the steering handle hard right. The 'cycles curved away to spinward.

"This is not our route," Speaker said instantly. "Louis, bring us back. Or put the fleet under my command."

"You aren't thinking of going *through* that thing, are you?"

"It is too large to go around."

"Speaker, it's no bigger than Plato crater. We can circle it in an hour. Why take chances?"

"If you are afraid, drop out of formation, Louis. Circle the eye and meet me on the other side. Teela, you may do the same. I will go through."

"Why?" Louis's voice sounded ragged even to him. "Do you think that—accidental cloud formation is a challenge to your manhood?"

"My what? Louis, my ability to procreate is not at issue. My courage is."

"Why?"

The 'cycles fell across the sky at cruising velocity, twelve hundred miles per hour.

"Why is your courage at issue? You owe me an answer. You're risking our lives."

"No. You may go around the Eye."

"And how do we find you afterward?"

The kzin considered. "I concede the point. Have you heard of the Kdapt-Preacher heresy?"

"No."

"In the dark days that followed the Fourth Truce with Man, Mad Kdapt-Preacher headed a new religion. He was executed by the Patriarch himself in single combat, since he bore a partial name, but his heretical religion survives in secret to this day. Kdapt-Preacher believed that God the Creator made man in his own image."

"Man? But—Kdapt-Preacher was a kzin?"

"Yes. You kept *winning*, Louis. For three centuries and four wars you had been winning. Kdapt's disciples wore masks of human skin when they prayed. They hoped to confuse the Creator long enough to win a war."

"And when you saw that eye peering over the horizon at us—"

"Yes."

"Oh, boy."

"I put it to you, Louis, that my own theory is more likely than yours. An accidental cloud formation! Really, Louis!"

Louis's brain was working again. "Strike *accidental*. Maybe the Ring engineers set up the Eye formation for their own amusement, or as a pointer to something."

"To what?"

"Who knows? Something big. An amusement park, a major church. The headquarters of the Optometrists' Union. With the techniques they had, and the *room*, it might be anything!"

"A prison for Peeping Toms," said Teela, suddenly getting into the spirit of the thing. "A university for private detectives! A test pattern on a giant tridee set! I was as scared as you were, Speaker." Teela sounded normal again. "I thought it was—I don't know what I thought. But I'm with you. We'll go through together."

"Very well, Teela."

"If he blinks, we'll both be killed."

" 'The majority is always sane,' " Louis quoted. "I'm going to call Nessus."

"Finagle, yes! He must have gone through it already, or around it!"

Louis laughed harder than he ordinarily would have. He had been very frightened. "You don't think Nessus is breaking trail for us, do you?"

"Huh?"

"He's a puppeteer. He circled around behind us, then he probably slaved his 'cycle to Speaker's. That way Speaker can't catch him, and any danger he's likely to meet, we'll meet first."

Speaker said, "You have a remarkable ability to think like a coward, Louis."

"Don't knock it. We're on an alien world. We need alien insights."

"Very well, call him since you and he seem to think so much alike. I intend to face the Eye, and learn what lies behind it, or within it."

Louis called Nessus.

In the intercom image, only the puppeteer's back was visible. His mane stirred slowly with his breathing.

"Nessus," Louis called. Then, louder, "Nessus!"

The puppeteer twitched. A triangular head rose in enquiry.

"I was afraid I'd have to use the siren."

"Is there an emergency?" Both heads came up, quiveringly alert.

Louis was finding it impossible to return the vast blue stare ahead of him. His eyes kept sliding away. He said, "A kind of emergency. My crazy teammates are about to wreck themselves. I don't think we can afford to lose them."

"Explain, please."

"Look ahead of you and tell me if you can see a cloud formation in the shape of a human eye."

"I see it," said the puppeteer.

"Any idea what's causing it?"

"Obviously it is a storm of some kind. You will already have reasoned that there will be no spiral hurricane formations on the Ringworld."

"Oh?" Louis hadn't even wondered about that.

"The spiral form of a hurricane derives from coriolis force, from the difference in the velocities of two air masses at different latitudes. A planet is a rotating spheroid. If two masses of air move toward each other to fill a partial vacuum, one moving north and the other south, their residual velocities will carry them past each other. Thus a whirlpool of air is formed."

"I *know* what causes hurricanes."

"Then you must realize that on the Ringworld, all contiguous masses of air have virtually the same velocity. There will be no whirlpool effect."

Louis looked ahead of him toward the eye-shaped storm. "But what kind of a storm *would* you get? None at all, I'd think. You wouldn't get any circulation of air at all."

"Untrue, Louis. Hot air would rise, cold air would sink. But these effects could not produce such a storm as that ahead of us."

"Too right."

"What is Speaker threatening to do?"

"Fly through the center of that Finagle-sired thing, with Teela loyally following after him."

The puppeteer whistled a tone as pure and beautiful as ruby laser light. "That seems dangerous. The sonic folds would protect them against the ravages of any ordinary storm. But this looks to be no ordinary storm . . ."

"I was thinking that it might be artificial."

"Yes . . . The Ringworlders would have set up their own Ring-girdling circulation system. But that system would have stopped working when the Ring power supply failed. I don't see . . . ah. I have it, Louis."

"What is it?"

"We must postulate an air-sink, a region where air disappears near the middle of the storm. All the rest follows.

"Consider. The air sink creates a partial vacuum. Air masses flow in from spinward and antispinward—"

"And port and starboard."

"These we can ignore," the puppeteer said crisply. "But air moving in from spinward will become fractionally lighter than the surrounding air. It will rise. Air moving in from the opposite direction, from antispinward, will become fractionally heavier—"

Louis was groping with an improperly visualized picture. "Why?"

"From antispinward it comes, Louis. Its rotational velocity is increased fractionally with respect to the Ring. Centrifugal force causes it to sink slightly.

"It forms the lower eyelid of the eye. The air from spinward, rising, forms the upper eyelid. There is a whirlpool effect, surely, but the axis of the whirlpool is horizontal, where on a planet it would be vertical."

"But it's such a minor effect!"

"But it is the only effect, Louis. There is nothing to interfere with its action, or to stop it. It might go on for millenia, building to what you see now."

"Maybe. Maybe." The eye seemed less frightening now. As the puppeteer had said, it must be some kind of storm. It was all the colors of a storm, of black clouds and upper sunlit white clouds and the dark "eye" of the storm acting as the iris of the Eye.

"The problem is the air sink, of course. Why does air disappear near the center of the storm?"

"Maybe a pump is still working in there."

"I doubt that, Louis. If that were so, the air disturbances in this vicinity would be planned."

"Well?"

"Have you noticed the places where the ring foundation material pokes through the soil and the bedrock? Surely such erosion must be unplanned. Have you noticed how such places appeared more frequently as we neared this place? The Eye storm must have upset weather patterns for tens of thousands of miles around, over an area greater than your world or mine."

This time it was Louis who whistled. "Tanj for torment! But then—oh, now I see. There must be a meteor puncture in the center of the Eye storm."

"Yes. You see the importance of this. The ring floor can be penetrated."

"But not by anything we're armed with."

"True. Still, we must know if the puncture is there."

Already Louis's superstitious panic seemed a remembered dream. The puppeteer's analytical calm was contagious and steadying. Louis Wu looked fearlessly into the eye and said, "We'll have to go in and look. You think it'll be safe, flying through the iris?"

"It should be no more than clear, still air in a partial vacuum."

"Okay. I'll relay the good news. We'll *all* fly through the eye storm."

The sky was darkening as they approached the iris. Was night falling overhead? Impossible to tell. The thickening, blackening clouds made darkness enough.

The eye was at least a hundred miles long from corner to corner, and something like forty miles tall. Its outline seemed to blur as they approached. Layers and streamers became visible. The true shape of the eye began to show: a tunnel of churning winds, reasonably uniform, whose cross-section was a picture of a human eye.

But it still looked like an eye as they hurtled toward the iris.

It was like falling into the eye of God. The visual effect was horrifying, terrifying, almost comically overdone. Louis was ready to laugh or scream. Or back out. It would only take one observer to find out whether there was a hole in the Ringworld floor. Louis could go around . . .

They were in.

They flew down a black corridor lit by lightning. Lightning flashed almost continuously, ahead and behind and on all sides. For a uniform distance around them the air was clear. Beyond the iris region, opaque black clouds swirled around them, moving at greater than hurricane velocities.

"The leaf-eater was right," Speaker roared. "It is nothing but a storm."

"Funny thing. He was the only one of the four of us who didn't panic when he saw that eye. I guess puppeteers aren't superstitious," screamed Louis Wu.

Teela called, "I see something ahead of us!"

It was a dip in the floor of the tunnel. Louis grinned with tension and rested his hands lightly on the controls. There might be a tanj of a downdraft over that dip.

He was less wary now, less tense, than he had been when they entered the Eye. What could happen where even a puppeteer found safety?

Clouds and lightning whirled around them as they neared the dip.

They braked and hovered over the dip, their flycycle motors fighting the downdraft. Through the muffling action of the sonic folds, the storm screamed in their ears.

It was like looking into a funnel. Obviously there was air disappearing down there; but was it being pumped away at high speed, or was it being spewed at the stars through the black bottom of the Ringworld? They couldn't actually see much . . .

Louis did not notice when Teela dropped her 'cycle. She was too far away, the flickering light was too strange, and he was looking down. He saw a tiny speck dwindling into the funnel, but he thought nothing of it.

Then, thinned by the howl of the storm, he heard Teela's scream.

Teela's face was clear in the intercom image. She was looking down, and she was terrified.

"What is it?" he bellowed.

He could barely hear her answer. ". . . It's got me!"

He looked down.

The funnel was clear between its whirling conical sides. It was oddly and steadily lit, not by lightning per se, but by cathode-ray effects caused by current differences in a nearly complete vacuum. There was a speck of . . . something down there, something that might conceivably have been a flycycle, if anyone were stupid enough to dive a flycycle into a maelstrom merely to get a closer look at a puncture hole into outer space.

Louis felt sick. There was nothing to be done, nothing at all. He wrenched his eyes away—

Only to see Teela's eyes above the dashboard. She was looking down into something dreadful—

And blood was running from her nose.

He saw the terror drain out of her face, to leave a white corpselike calm. She was about to faint. Anoxia? The sonic fold would hold air against vacuum, but it had to be set first.

Half-conscious, she looked up at Louis Wu. *Do something,* she begged. *Do something.*

Her head fell forward against the dash.

Louis's teeth were in his lower lip. He could taste the blood. He looked down into the funnel of streaming neon-lit cloud, and it was sickeningly like the whirlpool over a bathtub drain. He found the tiny speck that must be Teela's cycle—

—and saw it lunge straight forward and into the sloping, whirling wall of the funnel.

Seconds later he saw the vapor trail appear ahead of him, far down the eye of the horizontal hurricane. A thread of white, sharply pointed. Somehow it never occurred to him to doubt that it was Teela's 'cycle.

"What happened?" Speaker called.

Louis shook his head, declining to answer. He felt numb. Reason was short-circuited; his thoughts traced a circle, round and round.

Teela's intercom image was face down, showing mostly hair. She was unconscious, in an uncontrolled flycycle moving far faster than twice sonic speed. Somebody really ought to do something about that . . .

"But she was about to die, Louis. Could Nessus have activated a control we don't know about?"

"No. I'd rather believe that than . . . no."

"I think that must be what happened," said Speaker.

"You *saw* what happened! She fainted, her head hit the control board, and her 'cycle shot out of that *drain* like hell wouldn't have it! She punched the right controls with her forehead!"

"Nonsense."

"Yah." Louis wanted to sleep, to stop thinking . . .

"Consider the probabilities, Louis!" The kzin got it then, and he left his mouth open while he thought about it. His verdict was, "No. Impossible."

"Yah."

"She would not have been chosen to join us. If her luck were even partially dependable, Nessus would never have found her. She would have stayed on Earth."

Lightning sparkled, illuminating the long, long tunnel of churning storm cloud. A straight, narrow line pointed dead ahead: the vapor trail from Teela's flycycle. But the 'cycle itself was beyond visibility.

"Louis, we would never have crashed on the Ringworld!"

"I'm still wondering about that."

"Perhaps you had better wonder how to save her life."

Louis nodded. With no real sense of urgency, he pushed the call button for Nessus—a thing Speaker could not do.

The puppeteer answered instantly, as if he had been waiting for the signal. Louis was surprised to see that Speaker remained on the line. Rapidly he outlined what had happened.

"It appears that we were both wrong about Teela," said Nessus.

"Yah."

"She is moving under emergency power. Her forehead would not be enough to activate the proper controls. First she must manipulate the override slot. It is difficult to see how she could do that by accident."

"Where is it?" And when the puppeteer had shown him, Louis said, "She might have stuck her finger in it, just out of curiosity."

"Really?"

Speaker interrupted Louis's answer. "But what can we *do?*"

"When she wakes up, have her signal me," Nessus said

crisply. "I can show her how to go back on normal thrust, and how to find us afterward."

"Meanwhile, we can do nothing?"

"That is correct. There is the danger that elements may burn out in the propulsion system. However, her vehicle will avoid obstacles; she will not crash. She is receding from us at 'prox Mach four. The worst danger she faces is anoxia, which can lead to brain damage. I suspect she is safe from that."

"Why? Anoxia is dangerous."

"She is too lucky," said Nessus.

CHAPTER 18

The Perils of Teela Brown

It was black night when they emerged from the iris of the eye storm. There were no stars; but faint blue Archlight reached through an occasional break in the cloud cover.

"I have reconsidered," Speaker said. "Nessus, you may rejoin us if you will."

"I will," said the puppeteer.

"We need your alien insights. You have demonstrated great ingenuity. You must understand that I will not forget the crime your species has committed against mine."

"I would not wish to tamper with your memory, Speaker."

Louis Wu hardly noticed this triumph of practicality over honor, intelligence over xenophobia. Where the cloud bank met the infinity-horizon, he searched for the mark of Teela's vapor trail. But it had entirely disappeared.

Teela was still unconscious. Her intercom image stirred restlessly, and Louis shouted, "Teela!" But she did not answer.

"We were wrong about her," said Nessus. "But I cannot understand why. Why should we have crashed, if her luck is so powerful?"

"Exactly what I have been telling Louis!"

"But," said the puppeteer, "if her luck has no power, how could she have activated the emergency thruster? I believe I was right from the first. Teela Brown has psychic luck."

"Then why was she picked in the first place? Why did the *Liar* crash? Answer me!"

"Stop it," said Louis.

They ignored him. Nessus was saying, "Her luck is clearly undependable."

"If her luck had failed her just once, she would be dead."

"Were she dead or damaged, I would not have selected her. We must allow for coincidence," said Nessus. "You must remember, Speaker, that the laws of probability do provide for coincidence."

"But they do not provide for magic. I cannot believe in breeding for luck."

"You'll have to," said Louis.

This time they heard him. He continued, "I should have known much earlier. Not because she kept missing disasters. It was the little things, things in her personality. She's lucky, Speaker. Believe it."

"Louis, how can you credit this nonsense?"

"She's never been hurt. Never."

"How can you know?"

"I know. She knew all about pleasure, nothing about pain. Remember when the sunflowers blasted you? She asked you if you could see. 'I'm blinded,' you said. She said, 'Yes, but can you *see?*' She didn't believe you.

"Then, oh, right after the crash. She tried to walk barefoot up a lava slope that was just short of melting hot."

"She is not very intelligent, Louis."

"She *is* intelligent, tanjit! She's just never been hurt! When she burned her feet, she charged straight down the slope onto a surface a dozen times more slippery than ice —and she never fell down!

"But you don't need details," said Louis. "All you've got to do is watch her walk. Clumsy. Every second, it looks like she's going to fall over. But she doesn't. She doesn't knock things over with her elbows. She doesn't spill things or drop things. She never did. She never learned not to, don't you see? So she's not graceful."

"This would not be apparent to nonhumans," Speaker

said dubiously. "I must take your word for it, Louis. Still
—how can I believe in psychic luck?"

"I do. I have to."

"If her luck were dependable," said Nessus, "she would
never have tried to walk on recently molten rock. Yet the
luck of Teela Brown does protect us sporadically. Reassuring, is it not? You three would be dead had not clouds
shielded you when you crossed the sunflower field."

"Yah," said Louis; but he remembered that the clouds
had parted long enough to sear the skin of Speaker-To-
Animals. He remembered the stairs of Heaven which had
carried Teela Brown nine flights upward, while Louis Wu
had had to walk. He felt the bandages on his hand, and
remembered Speaker's hand charred to the bone, while
Teela's translator burned in its saddle case. "Her luck
seems to protect her somewhat better than it protects us,"
he said.

"And why not? But you seem upset, Louis."

"Maybe I am . . ." Her friends would long since have
stopped telling her their troubles. Teela didn't understand
troubles. Describing pain to Teela Brown would be like
trying to describe color to a blind man.

Whiplash of the heart? Teela had never been thwarted
in love. The man she wanted came to her, and stayed
until she had almost tired of him, then volunteered to go.

Sporadic or not, Teela's odd power made her . . . a
little different from human, perhaps. A woman, surely, but
with different strengths and talents, and blind spots, too . . .
And this was a woman Louis had loved. It was very odd.

"She loved me too," Louis mused. "Strange. I'm not
her type. And if she hadn't loved me, then—"

"What? Louis, are you speaking to me?"

"No, Nessus, I'm speaking to me . . ." Was that her
real reason for joining Louis Wu and his Motley Crew?
Then the mystery was compounded. Luck made Teela
fall in love with an unsuitable man, motivating her to join
an expedition both uncomfortable and disastrous, so that
she had several times brushed close to violent death. It
didn't make sense.

Teela's intercom image looked up. Blank eyes and

empty face . . . puzzled . . . filling suddenly with stark terror. Her eyes, wide and white, looking down. Teela's lovely oval face was ugly with insanity.

"Easy," said Louis. "Take it easy. Relax. You're all right now."

"But—" A falsetto squeak was Teela's voice.

"We're out of it. It's way behind us. Look behind you. Tanj you, look behind you!"

She turned. For a long moment Louis saw only soft dark hair. When she turned back, she had better control of herself.

"Nessus," said Louis, "tell her."

The puppeteer said, "You have been moving at Mach four for more than half an hour. To bring your flycycle back to normal speed, insert your index finger in the slot marked with a green rim—"

Though still frightened, Teela was capable of following orders.

"Now you must rejoin us. My signal indicates that your course has followed a curve. You are to port and spinward of us. As you have no indicator, I will have to guide you to us by ear. For the present, turn directly to antispinward."

"Which way is that?"

"Turn left until you are aimed at one base of the Arch."

"I can't see the Arch. I'll have to go above the clouds." She seemed almost composed now.

Tanj, but she'd been frightened! Louis couldn't remember ever seeing anyone that frightened. Certainly he'd never seen Teela that frightened.

Had he ever seen Teela frightened?

Louis turned to look over his shoulder. The land was dark beneath the clouds; but the eye storm, a vast distance behind them, glowed blue in the Archlight. It watched them go with total concentration, and no sign of regret.

Louis was deep in his own thoughts when a voice spoke his name. "Yah," he said.

"Aren't you mad?"

"Mad?" He thought about it. It occurred to him, briefly, that by normal standards she had done an incredibly stupid thing, diving her 'cycle like that. And so he probed for anger as he would have probed for an old toothache. And he found nothing.

Normal standards didn't fit Teela Brown.

The tooth was dead.

"I guess not. What did you see down there, anyway?"

"I could have been killed," Teela said with mounting anger. "Don't shake your head at *me*, Louis Wu! I could have been *killed!* Don't you *care?*"

"Don't you?"

She jerked back as if he'd slapped her. Then—he saw her hand move, and she was gone.

She was back a moment later. "There was a hole," she cried furiously, "And mist at the bottom. Well?"

"How big?"

"How should I know?" And she was gone again.

Right. How could she have guessed scale, in that flickering neon light?

She risks her own life, Louis thought, *then blames me for not getting angry. An attention-getting device? How long has she been doing it?*

Anyone else would die young, with a habit like that!

"But not her," said Louis Wu. "Not . . ."

Am I afraid of Teela Brown?

"Or have I finally flipped?" It had happened to others his age. A man as old as Louis Wu must have seen impossible things happen again and again. For such a man, the line between fantasy and reality sometimes blurred. He might become ultra conservative, rejecting the impossible even after it had become fact . . . like Kragen Perel, who would not believe in the thruster drive because it violated the second law of motion. Or he might believe anything . . . like Zero Hale, who kept buying fake Slaver relics.

Either way lay ruin and madness.

"No!" *When Teela Brown escapes certain death by banging her head on a flycycle dashboard, that's more than coincidence!*

But why did the Liar *crash?*

A silver fleck edged between Louis and the smaller silver fleck to spinward. "Welcome back," said Louis.

"Thank you," said Nessus. He must have used emergency thrust to catch up so fast. Speaker had issued his invitation only ten minutes ago.

Two triangular heads, small and transparent, considered Louis from above the dash. "I feel safe now. When Teela joins us in half an hour, I will feel safer still."

"Why?"

"The luck of Teela Brown shields us, Louis."

"I don't think so," said Louis Wu.

Speaker, silent, watched them both in the intercom. Only Teela was out of the circuit.

"Your arrogance bothers me," said Louis Wu. "Breeding for a lucky human was arrogant as the Devil. You've heard of the Devil?"

"I have read of the Devil, in books."

"Snob. But your stupidity is worse than your arrogance. You blithely assume that what's good for Teela Brown is good for you. Why should it be?"

Nessus sputtered. Then, "Surely this is natural. If we are both enclosed by the same spacecraft hull, a rupture is bad luck for both of us."

"Sure. But suppose you're passing a place where Teela wants to go, and suppose you don't want to land. A drive failure just then would be lucky for Teela, but not for you."

"What nonsense, Louis! Why would Teela Brown want to go to the Ringworld? She never knew it existed until I told her so!"

"But she's lucky. If she needed to come here without knowing it, she'd come here anyway. Then her luck wouldn't be sporadic, would it, Nessus? It would have been working all the time. Lucky that you found her. Lucky that you didn't find anyone else who qualified. All those bad phone connections, remember?"

"But—"

"Lucky that we crashed. Remember how you and Speaker argued over who was in charge of the expedition? Well, now you know."

"But *why*?"

"I don't *know*." Louis raked his fingernails across his scalp in utter frustration. His straight black hair had grown out to the length of a crew cut, excluding the queue.

"Does the question upset you, Louis? It upsets me. What could be here on the Ringworld to attract Teela Brown? This place is, is *unsafe*. Strange storms and badly programmed machinery and sunflower fields and unpredictable natives all threaten our lives."

"Hah!" Louis barked. "Right. That's part of it, at least. Danger doesn't exist for Teela Brown, don't you see? Any assessment we make of the Ringworld has to take that into account."

The puppeteer opened and closed his mouths several times in rapid succession.

"Does make things difficult, doesn't it?" Louis chortled. For Louis Wu, solving problems was a pleasure in itself. "But it's half the answer. If you assume—"

The puppeteer screamed.

Louis was shocked. He had not expected the puppeteer to take it so badly. The puppeteer wailed in two tones, then, without apparent haste, he tucked his heads under himself. Louis saw only the straggly mane that covered his brain case.

And Teela was on the intercom.

"You've been talking about me," she said without heat. (She was unable to hold a grudge, Louis realized. Did that make the ability to hold a grudge a survival factor?) "I tried to follow what you were saying, but I couldn't. What happened to Nessus?"

"My big mouth. I scared him. Now how are we going to find you?"

"Can't you tell where I am?"

"Nessus has the only locator. Probably for the same reason he saw to it that we didn't know how to operate the emergency thrust."

"I wondered about that," said Teela.

"He wanted to be sure he could run away from an angry kzin. Never mind that. How much did you understand?"

"Not much. You kept asking each other why I wanted

to come here. Louis, I didn't. I came with *you,* because I love you."

Louis nodded. Sure, if Teela needed to come to the Ringworld, she had had to have a motive to ride with Louis Wu. It was hardly flattering.

She loved him for the sake of her own luck. Once he had thought she loved him for himself.

"I'm passing over a city," Teela said suddenly. "I can see some lights. Not many. There must have been a big, durable power source. Speaker could probably find it on his map."

"Is it worth looking at?"

"I told you, there are *lights.* Maybe——" The sound went off without a click, without a warning.

Louis considered the empty space above his dashboard. Then he called, "Nessus."

There was no response.

Louis activated the siren.

Nessus came out of it like a family of snakes in a burning zoo. Under other circumstances it would have been funny: the two necks frantically untangling, posing like two question marks above the dashboard; then Nessus barking, "Louis! What is it?"

Speaker had answered the call instantly. Apparently sitting at attention, he waited for instructions and enlightenment.

"Something's happened to Teela."

"Good," said Nessus. And the heads withdrew.

Grimly, Louis flicked the siren off, waited a moment, flipped it on again. Nessus reacted as before. This time Louis spoke first.

"If we don't find out what happened to Teela, I'll kill you," he said.

"I have the tasp," said Nessus. "We designed it to work equally well on kzinti and human. You have seen its effect on Speaker."

"Do you think it would stop me from killing you?"

"Yes, Louis, I do."

"What," Louis asked carefully, "will you bet?"

The puppeteer considered. "To rescue Teela can hardly

be as dangerous as to take that gamble. I had forgotten that she is your mate." He glanced down. "She no longer registers on my locator. I cannot tell where she is."

"Does that mean her 'cycle's been damaged?"

"Yes, extensively. The sender was near one thruster unit of her flycycle. Perhaps she ran afoul of another working machine, kin to the one which burned our communicator discs."

"Um. But you know where she was when she dropped out of the conversation."

"Ten degrees to spinward of port. I do not know the distance, but we can estimate this from the speed tolerances of her flycycle."

They flew ten degrees to port of spinward, a slanting line across Speaker's hand-drawn map. For two hours there had been no lights; and Louis had begun to wonder if they were lost.

Thirty-five hundred miles from the rolling hurricane that was the Eye storm, the line across Speaker's map ended at a seaport. Beyond the seaport was a bay the size of the Atlantic Ocean. Teela couldn't have flown further than that. The seaport would be their last chance . . .

Suddenly, beyond the crest of a deceptively gradual slope of hill, there were lights.

"Pull up," Louis whispered fiercely, not knowing why he whispered. But Speaker had already stopped them in midair.

They hovered, studying the lights and the terrain.

The terrain: city. City everywhere. Below, shadowy in the blue Archlight, were houses like beehives with rounded windows, separated by curved sidewalks too narrow to be called streets. Ahead: more of the same, and then taller buildings further on, until all was skyscrapers and floaters.

"They built differently," Louis whispered. "The architecture—it's not like Zignamuclickclick. Different styles . . ."

"Skyscrapers," said Speaker. "With so much room on the Ringworld, why build so tall?"

"To prove they can do it. No, that's asinine," said Louis.

"There'd be no point, if they could build something like the Ringworld itself."

"Perhaps the tall buildings came later, during the decline of civilization."

The lights: blazing white tiers of windows, a dozen isolated towers blazing from crown to base. They were clustered in what Louis already thought of as the Civic Center because all six of the floating buildings were there.

One thing more: a small suburban patch to spinward of the Civic Center glowed dim orange-white.

On the second floor of one of the beehive houses, the three sat in a triangle around Speaker's map.

Speaker had insisted that they bring the flycycles inside with them. "Security." Their light came from the headlamps of Speaker's own 'cycle, reflected and softened by a curved wall. A table, oddly sculpted to form plates and coaster depressions, had toppled and smashed to dust when Louis brushed against it. Dust was an inch thick on the floor. The paint on the curved wall had crumbled and settled in a soft ridge of sky-blue dust along the baseboard.

Louis felt the age of the city settling on him.

"When the map room tapes were made, this was one of the largest of Ringworld cities," Speaker said. His crescent claw moved across the map. "The original city was a planned city, a semicircle with its flat side along the sea. The tower called Heaven must have been built much later, when the city had already spread wings far along the coast."

"Pity you didn't draw a map of it," said Louis. For all that showed on Speaker's map was a shaded semicircle.

Speaker picked up the map and folded it. "Such an abandoned metropolis must hold many secrets. We must be wary here. If civilization can rise at all in this land—on this structure—then it must be where clues point the way to vanished technology."

"What of vanished metals?" Nessus objected. "A fallen civilization could not rise again on the Ringworld. There are no metals to mine, no fossil fuels. Tools would be restricted to wood and bone."

"We saw lights."

"The pattern seemed random—a result of many self-contained power sources failing one by one. But you may be right," said Nessus. "If toolbuilding has resumed in this place, we must contact the toolbuilders. But on our own terms."

"We may already have been located by our intercom emissions."

"No, Speaker. Our intercom emissions are closed beams."

Louis, half listening, thought: *She could be hurt. She could be lying somewhere, unable to move, waiting for us.*

And he couldn't make himself believe it.

It seemed that Teela had run afoul of some old Ringworld machine: perhaps a sophisticated automatic weapon, if the Ringworlders had such things. Conceivably it had zapped only her intercom and locator-sender, leaving the motive systems intact. But it seemed improbable.

Then why couldn't he work up a sense of urgency? Louis Wu, cool as a computer while his woman faced unknown peril.

His woman . . . yes, but something more, and something different.

How stupid of Nessus, to assume that a bred-for-luck human would think like the humans he was used to! Would a lucky puppeteer think like, say, the sane puppeteer Chiron?

Maybe fear was in a puppeteer's genes.

But in a human beings fear had to be learned.

Nessus was saying, "We must assume a momentary failure of Teela's sporadic luck. Under that assumption, Teela is not injured."

"What?" Louis was jolted. The puppeteer seemed to have paralleled his own thinking.

"A failure of her flycycle would probably leave her dead. If she were not killed instantly, then she must have been rescued as soon as her luck resumed its power."

"That's ridiculous. You can't expect a psychic power to follow *rules* like that!"

"The logic is impeccable, Louis. My point is that Teela

does not need rescue immediately. If alive, she can wait. We can wait for morning to spy out the land."

"Then what? How do we find her?"

"She is in safe hands, if her luck held. We search for those hands. If there are no hands, we will know that tomorrow, and we can hope she will signal us. There are various ways she can do that."

Speaker broke in. "But they all use light."

"And if they do?"

"They do. I have considered this. It is possible that her headlamps still function. If so, she will have left them on. You claim she is intelligent, Louis."

"She is."

"And she has no regard for security. She would not care *what* found her, so long as *we* found her. If her headlamps are dead, she might use her flashlight-laser to signal anything that moves—or to start a signal fire."

"What you're saying is that we can't find her in daylight. And you're right," Louis admitted.

Nessus said, "First we must explore the city by daylight. If we find citizens, well and good. Otherwise we may search for Teela tomorrow night."

"You'd leave her lying somewhere for thirty hours? You cold-blooded— Tanjit, that patch of light we saw could be her! Not street lamps, but burning buildings!"

Speaker stood up. "True. We must investigate."

"I am Hindmost to this fleet. I say that Teela's value does not match the risk of a night flight over an alien city."

Speaker-To-Animals had mouted his flycycle. "We are in territory which may be hostile. Thereby I command. We will go to seek Teela Brown, a member of our company."

The kzin lifted off, eased his flycycle through a great oval window. Beyond the window were fragments of a porch, then the suburbs of an unnamed city.

The other flycycles were on the ground floor. Louis descended the stairwell hurriedly but with care, as part of the stairs had collapsed, and the escalator machinery had long since turned to rust.

Nessus looked down at him over the rim of the stairwell.
"I stay here, Louis. I consider this mutiny."

Louis did not answer. His flycycle rose, edged through
the oval doorway, and angled up into the night.

The night was cool. Archlight painted the city in navy
blue shadows. Louis found the gleam of Speaker's 'cycle
and followed it toward the glowing section of suburb, to
spinward of the brilliantly lighted Civic Center.

It was all city, hundreds of square miles of city. There
weren't even parks. With all the room on the Ringworld,
why build so *close?* Even on Earth, men valued their
elbow room.

But Earth had transfer booths. That must be it: the
Ringworlders had valued travel time more than elbow
room.

"We stay low," said Speaker via intercom. "If the lights
of the suburbs are mere street lighting, we return to Nessus. We must not risk the possibility that Teela was shot
down."

"Right," said Louis. But he thought: listen to him, worrying about security in the face of a purely hypothetical
enemy. A kzin, sanely reckless, looked cautious as a puppeteer next to Teela Brown.

Where was she now? Well, or hurt, or dead?

They had been searching for civilized Ringworlders
since before the *Liar* crashed. Had they finally found
them? That chance was probably what had kept Nessus
from deserting Teela entirely. Louis's threat meant nothing, as Nessus must be well aware.

If they had found civilized Ringworlders as enemies,
well, that was hardly unexpected . . .

His 'cycle was drifting to the left. Louis corrected.

"Louis." Speaker-To-Animals seemed to be wrestling
something. "There seems to be interference—" Then, urgently, with the practiced whip of command in his voice,
"Louis. Turn back. Now."

The kzin's command voice seemed to speak directly to
Louis's hindbrain. Louis turned immediately.

His flycycle, however, went straight.

Louis threw all his weight on the steering bar. No good. The 'cycle continued moving toward the lights of the Civic Center.

"Something's got us!" Louis shouted; and with that the terror had him. They were puppets! Huge and dark and sentient, the Puppet Master twitched their arms and legs and moved them about to an unseen script. And Louis Wu knew the Puppet Master's name.

The luck of Teela Brown.

CHAPTER 19

In The Trap

Speaker, being more practical, flipped the emergency siren.

The multiple frequency scream went on and on. Louis wondered if the puppeteer would answer at all. The boy who cried Wolf . . . ? But Nessus was crying, "Yes? Yes?" with the volume too loud. Of course, he'd had to get downstairs first.

"We are under attack," Speaker told him. "Some agency is flying our vehicles by remote control. Have you suggestions?"

You couldn't tell what Nessus was thinking. His lips, twice too many, loose and broad and knobbed to serve as fingers, moved continually but without meaning. Would the puppeteer be able to help? or would he panic?

"Turn your intercoms about to give me a view of your path. Are either of you hurt?"

"No, but we are stuck," said Louis. "We can't jump. We're too high, moving too fast. We're headed straight for the Civic Center."

"For what?"

"The cluster of lighted buildings. Remember?"

"Yes." The puppeteer seemed to consider. "A bandit signal must be overriding the signals from your instruments. Speaker, I want readings from your dashboard."

Speaker read off, while he and Louis drew ever closer to the lights of the central city. At one point Louis interrupted. "We're passing that patch of suburbia with the street lights."

260

"Are they indeed street lights?"

"Yes and no. All the oval doors of the houses glow bright orange. It's peculiar. I think it's honest street lighting, but the power's been dimmed and cooled by time."

"I concur," said Speaker-To-Animals.

"I hate to nag, but we're getting closer. I think we're headed for the big building in the middle."

"I see it. The double cone with lights only in the top half."

"That's the one."

"Louis, let us try to interfere with the bandit signal. Slave your 'cycle to mine."

Louis activated the slave circuit.

His 'cycle slammed hard up against him, as if he'd been booted in the butt by a giant foot. An instant later the power cut off entirely.

Crash balloons exploded before and behind him. They were shaped balloons, and they interlocked around him like a pair of clasped hands. Louis could not so much as move his hands or turn his head.

He was falling.

"I'm falling," he reported. His hand, pressed against the dashboard by the balloons, still touched the slave circuit. Louis waited another moment, still hoping the slave circuit would take hold. But the beehive houses were coming too close. Louis shifted back to manual.

Nothing happened. He was still falling.

With a calm that was sheer braggadocio, Louis said, "Speaker, don't try the slave circuit. It doesn't work." And because they could see his face, he waited with his face immobile and his eyes open. Waited for the Ringworld to slap him dead.

Deceleration came suddenly, pushing hard upward on the 'cycle. The 'cycle turned over, leaving Louis Wu head down under five gees of pull.

He fainted.

When he came to, he was still head down, held by the pressure of the crash balloons. His head was pounding. He saw a hazy crazy vision of the Puppet Master cursing and

trying to get his strings untangled, while the puppet Louis
Wu dangled head down over the stage.

The floating building was short and wide and ornate.
Its lower half was an inverted cone. As the flycycles approached it, a horizontal slit slid open and swallowed them.

They were passing into the dark interior when Speaker's
flycycle, which had been edging closer to Louis's, quietly
turned over. Balloons exploded around Speaker before he
could fall. Louis scowled in sour satisfaction. He had been
miserable long enough to appreciate the company.

Nessus was saying, "Your inverted attitude implies that
you are being supported by fields electromagnetic in nature. Such fields would support metal but not protoplasm,
with the result . . ."

Louis wriggled against his confinement; but not too
hard. He would fall if he wriggled free of the balloons. Behind him the door slid shut, just faster than Louis's eyes
could adjust to the dark. He saw nothing of the interior.
He couldn't guess how far down the floor might be.

He heard Nessus saying, "Can you reach it with your
hand?"

And Speaker, "Yes, if I can push between the . . .
Yowrr! You were right. The casing is hot."

"Then your motor has been burnt out. Your flycycles
are inert, dead."

"Fortunate that my saddle is shielded from the heat."

"We can hardly be surprised if the Ringworlders were
adept at harnessing electromagnetic forces. So many other
tools were denied them: hyperdrive, thrusters, induced
gravity . . ."

Louis had been straining to see something, anything.
He could turn his head, slowly, his cheek scraping against
the balloon surface; but there was no light anywhere.

Moving his arms against the pressure, he felt across the
dashboard until he thought he had found the headlight
switch. Why he expected it to work, he could not have
said.

The beams went out tight and white, and bounced dimly back from a distant curved wall.

A dozen vehicles hung about him, all at the same level. There were packages no larger than a racing jet backpack, and others as large as flying cars. There was even a kind of flying truck with a transparent hull.

Within the maze of floating junk, a flycycle held Speaker-To-Animals upside down. The kzin's bald head and hairy orange mask protruded below the shaped crash balloons; and one clawed hand had been pushed forcefully out to touch the side of the 'cycle.

"Good," said Nessus. "Light. I was about to suggest that. Do you both understand the implication? Every electrical and electromagnetic circuit in your vehicle has been burnt out, provided it was working when you were attacked. Speaker's vehicle, and presumably yours, Louis, was attacked again as you entered the building."

"Which is pretty clearly a prison," Louis forced out. His head felt like a water balloon being filled too full, and he had trouble speaking. But he couldn't let the others do all the work, even if the work was only speculating on alien technology while hanging head down.

"And if it's a prison," he went on, "then why isn't there a third zap gun in here with us? In case we should happen to have working weapons. Which we do."

"There unquestionably is one," said Nessus. "Your headlamps prove that the third zap gun is *not* working. The zap guns are clearly automatic; otherwise someone would be guarding you. It should be safe for Speaker to use the Slaver digging tool."

"That's good news," Louis said. "Except that I've been looking around—"

He and Speaker were floating upside down in an airborne Sargasso Sea. Of three archaic flying jet packs, one was still occupied. The skeleton was small but human. Not a trace of skin remained on the white bones. The clothing must have been good, for shreds of it still survived: brightly colored rags, including a tattered yellow cloak that hung straight down from the point of the flyer's jaw.

The other packs were empty. But the bones had to be somewhere . . . Louis forced his head back, back . . .

The basement of the police building was a wide, dim,

conical pit. Around the wall were concentric rings of cells. The doors were trap doors above the cells. There were radial stairways leading down to the pit at the apex. In and around the pit were the bones Louis was searching for, shining dimly back at him from far below.

He couldn't wonder that one man in a ruined flying pack had been afraid to turn himself loose. But others, trapped here in cars and backpacks, had preferred the long fall to death by thirst.

Louis said, "I don't see what Speaker is supposed to use the Slaver disintegrator *on*."

"I have been thinking about that very seriously."

"If he blows a hole in the wall, it doesn't help us. Likewise the ceiling, which he can't reach anyway. If he hits the generator for the field holding us here, we fall ninety feet to the floor. But if he doesn't, we'll be here until we starve, or until we give up and turn ourselves loose. Then we fall ninety feet to the floor."

"Yes."

"That's all? Just *yes?*"

"I need more data. Will one of you please describe what you see around you? I see only part of a curved wall."

They took turns describing the conical cell block, what they could see of it in the dim, point-source light. Speaker turned on his own lights, and that helped.

But when Louis ran out of things to say, he was still trapped, upside down, without food or water, hanging above a lethal drop.

Louis felt a bubbling scream somewhere in him, buried deep and well under control, but rising. Soon it would be near the surface . . .

And he wondered if Nessus would leave them.

That was bad. It was a question with an obvious answer. There was every reason why the puppeteer should leave, and no reason why he should not.

Unless he still hoped to find civilized natives here.

"The floating vehicles and the age of the skeletons both indicate that there is nobody tending the machinery of the cell block," Speaker speculated. "The fields that trapped us must have collected a few vehicles after the city was deserted; but then there were no more vehicles on the Ringworld. So the machines still work, because nothing has strained their powers in so long a time."

"That may be so," said Nessus. "But someone is monitoring our conversation."

Louis felt his ears prick up. He *saw* Speaker's fan out.

"It must have required excellent technique to tap a closed beam. One wonders if the eavesdropper has a translator."

"What can you tell about him?"

"Only his direction. The source of the interference is your own present whereabouts. Perhaps the eavesdropper is above you."

Reflexively Louis tried to look up. Not a prayer. He was head down, with two crash balloons and the flycycle between him and the ceiling.

"We've found the Ringworld civilization," he said aloud.

"Perhaps. I think a civilized being could have repaired the third zap gun, as you called it. But the main thing . . . let me think."

And the puppeteer went off into Beethoven, or the Beatles, or *something* classical-sounding. For all Louis could tell he was making it up as he went along.

And when he said *Let me think,* he meant it. The whistling went on and on. Louis was getting thirsty. And hungry. And his head was pounding.

He had given up hope, several separate times, when the puppeteer came on again. "I would have preferred to use the Slaver disintegrator, but it is not to be. Louis, you will have to do it; you are primate-descended, better than Speaker at climbing. You will secure the—"

"Climbing?"

"When I finish you may ask questions, Louis. Secure the flashlight-laser from wherever you put it. Use the beam to puncture the balloon in front of you. You will have to snatch at its fabric as you fall. Use it to climb over the flycycle until you are balanced on top. Then—"

"You're out of your mind."

"Let me finish, Louis. The purpose of all this activity is to destroy the zap gun, as you called it. Probably there are two zap guns. One is over the door you entered by, or under it. The other may be anywhere. Your only clue may be that it looks like the first zap gun."

"Sure, and it may not. Never mind that. How do you expect me to grab at the fabric of an exploding balloon fast enough to— No. I can't."

"Louis. How can I reach you if a weapon waits to burn out my machinery?"

"I don't know."

"Do you expect Speaker to do the climbing?"

"Can't cats climb?"

Speaker said, "My ancestors were plains cats, Louis. My burnt hand is healing slowly. I cannot climb. In any case, the leaf-eater's proposition is insane. Surely you see that he is merely looking for an excuse to desert us."

Louis saw. Perhaps he let the fear show.

"I will not leave you yet," Nessus said. "I will wait. Perhaps you will conceive a better plan. Perhaps the eavesdropper will show himself. I will wait."

Louis Wu, wedged upside down and motionless between two shaped balloons, naturally found it difficult to measure time. Nothing changed. Nothing moved. He could hear Nessus whistling in the distance; but nothing else seemed to be happening.

Eventually Louis started counting his own heartbeats. Seventy-two to the minute, he figured.

Precisely ten minutes later he was heard to say, "Seventy-*two*. *One*. What *am* I doing?"

"Were you speaking to me, Louis?"

"Tanjit! Speaker, I can't take this. I'd rather die now than go crazy first." He began forcing his arms down.

"I command, Louis, under combat conditions. I order you to remain calm, and wait."

"Sorry." Louis forced his arms *down*, relax, jerk *down*, relax. There it was: his belt. His hand was too far forward. He forced his elbow back, relax, jerk *back* . . .

"What the puppeteer suggests is suicide, Louis."

"Maybe." He had it: the flashlight-laser. Two more jerks freed it from his belt and pointed it forward; he would burn into the dashboard but would not burn himself.

He fired.

The balloon collapsed slowly. As it did, the one at his back pushed him forward into the dashboard. Under the lighter pressure, it was easy to push the flashlight-laser into his belt and to clutch two handfuls of wrinkling, collapsing fabric.

He was also sliding out of his seat. Faster, faster—he gripped with manic force, and when he turned over, falling, his hands did not slip on the fabric. He hung by his hands beneath his flycycle, with a ninety foot drop below and—

"Speaker!"

"Here I am, Louis. I have secured my own weapon. Shall I pop the other balloon for you?"

"Yes!" It was right across his path, blocking him entirely.

The balloon did not collapse. One side of it puffed dust for two seconds, then disappeared in a great puff of air. Speaker had zapped it with one beam of the disintegrator.

"Finagle knows how you can aim that thing," Louis wheezed. He began to climb.

It was easy going while the fabric held out. Translate: Despite the hours he'd spent with blood flowing to his brain, Louis managed not to let go. But the fabric ended in the vicinity of the foot throttle; and the 'cycle had rolled half over with his weight, so that he still hung from underneath.

He pulled himself close against the 'cycle, braced himself with his knees. He began to rock.

Speaker-To-Animals was making curious sounds.

The 'cycle rocked back and forth, further with each swing. Louis assumed, because he had to, that most of the metal was in the belly of the 'cycle. Otherwise the 'cycle would roll, and wherever he placed himself Louis would be underneath, and therefore Nessus would not have made the suggestion.

The 'cycle rolled far. Louis, nauseated, fought the urge to vomit. If his breathing passages got clogged now, it was all over.

The 'cycle rolled back, and over, and was precisely upside down. Louis lunged across the underside and snatched at the other end of the collapsed balloon. And had it.

The 'cycle continued its roll. Louis was flattened chest-down across the belly of the machine. He waited, clinging.

The inert hulk paused, hesitated, rolled back. His vestibular canals spun, and Louis lost—what? Yesterday's late lunch? He lost it explosively, in great agonizing heaves, across the metal and across his sleeve; but he didn't shift his position more than an inch.

The flycycle continued to heave like the sea. But Louis was anchored. Presently he dared to look up.

A woman was watching him.

She seemed to be entirely bald. Her face reminded Louis of the wire-sculpture in the banquet hall of the Heaven tower. The features, and the expression. She was as calm as a goddess or a dead woman. And he wanted to blush, or hide, or disappear.

Instead he said, "Speaker, we're being watched. Relay to Nessus."

"A minute, Louis. I am discomposed. I made the mistake of watching you climb."

"Okay. She's— I thought she was bald, but she isn't. There's a fringe of hair-bearing scalp that crosses over her ears and meets at the base of her skull. She wears the hair long, more than shoulder length." He did not say that her hair was rich and dark, falling past one shoulder as she bent slightly forward to watch Louis Wu; nor that her skull was finely and delicately shaped, nor that her eyes seemed to spear him like a martini olive. "I think she's an Engineer; she either belongs to the same race or follows the same customs. Have you got that?"

"Yes. How can you climb so? It seemed that you defied gravity. What *are* you, Louis?"

Clutching himself to his dead flycycle, Louis laughed. It seemed to take all his strength. "You're a Kdaptist," he said. "Admit it."

"I was raised so, but the teachings did not take."

"Sure they didn't. Have you got Nessus?"

"Yes. I used the siren."

"Relay this. She's about twenty feet from me. She's watching me like a snake. I don't mean she's intensely interested in me; I mean she's not interested in anything else at all. She blinks, but she never looks away.

"She's sitting in a kind of booth. There used to be glass or something in three of the walls, but that's gone, leaving not much more than some stairs and a platform. She's sitting with her legs over the edge. It must have been a way of watching the prisoners.

"She's dressed in . . . well, I can't say I go for the style. Knee-length and elbow-length overalls, ballooning out—" But aliens wouldn't be interested in that. "The fabric is artificial, obviously, and either it's new or it's self-cleaning and very durable. She—" Louis interrupted himself, because the girl had said something.

He waited. She repeated it, whatever it was; a short sentence.

Then she stood gracefully and went up the stairs.

"She's gone," said Louis. "Probably lost interest."

"Perhaps she went back to her listening devices."

"Probably right." If there was an eavesdropper in the building, Occam's Razor said it was her.

"Nessus asks you to focus your flashlight-laser to low and wide, and to be seen using it for lighting when next the woman appears. I am not to show the Slaver weapon. The woman could probably kill us both by turning off a switch. She must not see us with weapons."

"Then how can we get rid of the zap guns?"

A moment before Speaker relayed the answer. "We do not. Nessus says that he will try something else. He is coming here."

Louis let his head sag against the metal. The relief he felt was so great that he didn't even question it, until Speaker said, "He will only have us all in the same trap. Louis, how can I dissuade him?"

"Tell him so. No, don't even do that. If he didn't know it was safe he'd stay away."

"How can it be safe?"

"I don't know. Let me rest." The puppeteer must know what he was doing. He could trust Nessus's cowardice. Louis rubbed his cheek against the smooth, cool metal.

He dozed.

He was never less than marginally aware of where he was. If his 'cycle stirred or shifted he came wide-eyed out of sleep, clutching metal in his knees and fabric in his fists. His sleep was a running nightmare.

When light flashed through his eyelids he came awake immediately.

Daylight poured through the horizontal slit that had served them as a doorway. Within that glare Nessus's flycycle was a black silhouette. The flycycle was upside down, and so was the puppeteer, held by seat webbing rather than crash balloons.

The slit closed behind him.

"Welcome," said Speaker, slurring the words. "Can you turn me upright?"

"Not yet. Has the girl reappeared?"

"No."

"She will. Humans are curious, Speaker. She cannot have seen members of our species before."

"What of it? I want to be right side up," Speaker moaned.

The puppeteer did something to his dashboard. A miracle happened: his flycycle turned over.

Louis said one word. "How?"

"I turned everything off after I knew that the bandit signal had my controls. If the lifting field had not caught me, I could have turned on my motors before I struck pavement. Now," the puppeteer said briskly, "the next step should be easy. When the girl appears, act friendly.

Louis, you may attempt to have sex with her if you think you might succeed. Speaker, Louis is to be our master; we are to be his servitors. The woman may be xenophobic; it would lull her to believe that a human being commands these aliens."

Louis actually laughed. Somehow the nightmarish half-sleep had rested him. "I doubt she'll be feeling friendly, let alone seductive. You didn't see her. She's as cold as the black caves of Pluto, at least where I'm concerned, and I can't really blame her." She had watched him lose his lunch across his sleeve—generally an unromantic sight.

The puppeteer said, "She will be feeling happy whenever she looks at us. She will cease to feel happy when she tries to leave us. If she brings one of us closer to her, her joy will increase—"

"Tanjit, *yes!*" cried Louis.

"You see? Good. In addition, I have been practicing the Ringworld language. I believe my pronunciation is correct, and my grammar. If I only knew what more of the words meant . . ."

Speaker had stopped complaining long ago. Inverted above a lethal drop, with burns all over him and one hand charred to the bone, he had raged at Louis and Nessus for being unable to help him. But he had been quiet for hours now.

In the dim quiet, Louis dozed.

In his sleep he heard bells, and woke.

She tinkled as she came down the steps. There were bells on her mocassins. Her garment was different too, a top-shaped, high-necked dress fitted with half a dozen big bulging pockets. Her long black hair fell forward over one shoulder.

The serene dignity in her face had not changed.

She sat down with her feet over the edge of the platform, and she watched Louis Wu. She did not shift position; neither did Louis. For several minutes they held each other's eyes.

Then she reached into one of the big pockets and produced something fist-sized and orange. She tossed it toward Louis, aiming it so that it would go past him, a few inches beyond his reach.

He recognized it as it went by him. A knobby, juicy fruit he had found on a bush two days ago. He had dropped several into the intake hopper of his kitchen, without tasting them.

The fruit splattered red across the roof of a cell. Suddenly Louis's mouth was trying to water, and he was taken with a raging thirst.

She tossed him another. It came closer this time. He could have touched it if he had tried, but he would also have overturned the 'cycle. And she knew it.

Her third shot tapped his shoulder. He clung to his two fistfuls of balloon and thought black thoughts.

Then Nessus's flycycle drifted into view.

And she smiled.

The puppeteer had been floating behind the truck-sized derelict. Upside down again, he drifted obliquely toward the viewing platform as if wafted there by a stray induced current, and, as he passed Louis, he asked, "Can you seduce her?"

Louis snarled. Then, realizing that the puppeteer really wasn't mocking him, he said, "I think she thinks I'm an animal. Forget it."

"Then we need different tactics."

Louis rubbed his forehead against the cool metal. He had seldom felt so miserable. "You're in charge," he said. "She won't buy me as an equal, but she might buy you. She won't see you as competition; you're too alien."

The puppeteer had drifted past him. Now he said something in what sounded to Louis like the language of the shaven choir-leading priest: the holy language of the Engineers.

The girl did not respond. But . . . she wasn't smiling exactly, but the corners of her mouth did seem to turn up slightly, and there was more animation in her eyes.

Nessus must be using low power. Very low power.

He spoke again, and this time she answered. Her voice was cool and musical, and if she sounded imperious to Louis Wu, he was predisposed to hear that quality.

The puppeteer's voice became identical to the girl's. What developed then was a language lesson.

To Louis Wu, uneasily balanced above a lethal drop, it was bound to be dull. He picked up a word here and there. At one point she tossed Nessus one of the fist-sized orange fruits, and they established that it was a *thrumb*. And Nessus kept it.

Suddenly she stood up and left.

Louis said, "Well?"

"She must have become bored," said Nessus. "She gave no warning."

"I'm dying of thirst. Could I have that *thrumb*?"

"Thrumb is the color of the peel, Louis." He edged his 'cycle alongside Louis and handed him the fruit.

Louis was only just desperate enough to free one hand. That meant he had to bite through the thick peel and tear it away with his teeth. At some point he reached real fruit and bit into it. It was the best thing he had tasted in two hundred years.

When he had quite finished the fruit, he asked, "Is she coming back?"

"We may hope so. I used the tasp at low power that it might affect her below the conscious level. She will miss it. The lure will become stronger every time she sees me. Louis, should we not make her fall in love with you?"

"Forget it. She thinks I'm a native, a savage. Which brings up the question: what is *she?"*

"I could not say. She did not try to hide it, but it did not come across, either. I do not know enough language. Not yet."

CHAPTER 20

Meat

Nessus had landed to explore the dimness below. Cut off from the intercom, Louis tried to watch what the puppeteer was doing. Eventually he gave that up.

Much later, he heard footsteps. No bells this time.

He cupped his hands and shouted downward. "Nessus!"

The sound bounced off the walls and focused itself horrendously in the apex of the cone. The puppeteer jumped to his feet, swarmed aboard his 'cycle and took off. Cast off, more likely. No doubt he had left the motor going to hold the 'cycle down against the trapping field. Now he simply cut the motor.

He was back among the hovering metal when the footsteps stopped somewhere above them.

"What the tanj is she *doing*?" Louis whispered.

"Patience. You could not expect her to be conditioned by one exposure to a tasp at low power."

"Try to get it into your thick, brainless heads. *I can not keep my balance indefinitely!*"

"You must. How can I help?"

"Water," said Louis, with a tongue like two yards of flannel rolled up.

"Are you thirsty? But how can I get water to you? If you turn your head you may lose your balance."

"I know. Forget it." Louis shuddered. Strange, that Louis Wu the spacer should be so afraid of heights. "How's Speaker?"

"I fear for him, Louis. He has been unconscious for uncomfortably long."

274

"Tanj, tanj—".

Footsteps.

She must have a mania for changing clothes, Louis thought. What she wore now was all overlapping pleats in orange and green. Like previous garments, it showed nothing at all of her shape.

She knelt at the edge of the observation platform, coolly watching them. Louis clutched his metal raft and waited for developments.

He saw her soften. Her eyes went dreamy; the corners of her small mouth turned up.

Nessus spoke.

She seemed to consider. She said something that might have been an answer.

Then she left them.

"Well?"

"We shall see."

"I get so *sick* of waiting."

Suddenly the puppeteer's flycycle was floating upward. Up and forward. It bumped against the edge of the observation platform like a rowboat making dock.

Nessus stepped daintily ashore.

The girl came to greet him. What she held in her left hand *had* to be a weapon. But with her other hand she touched the puppeteer's head, hesitated, then ran her fingernails down his secondary spine.

Nessus made a sound of delight.

She turned and walked upstairs. Not once did she glance back. She seemed to assume that Nessus would follow like a dog; and he did.

Good, thought Louis. *Be subservient. Make her trust you.*

But when the oddly matched sounds of their footsteps faded away, the cell block became a tremendous tomb.

Speaker was thirty feet away across the Sargasso Sea of metal. Four padded black fingers and a puff of orange face showed around the green crash balloons. Louis had no way of getting near. The kzin might be dead already.

Among the white bones below were at least a dozen

skulls. Bones, and age, and rusted metal, and silence. Louis Wu clung to his 'cycle and waited for his strength to give out.

He was dozing, not many minutes later, when something changed. His balance shifted—

Louis's life depended on his balance. The momentary disorientation sent him into rigid panic. He looked wildly about him, moving only his eyes.

The metal vehicles were all around him, motionless. But *something* was moving . . .

A distant car bumped, screeched like tearing metal, and went up.

Huh?

No. It had grounded against the upper ring of cells. The whole Sargasso was sinking uniformly through space.

One by one, noisily, the cars and flying packs docked and were left behind.

Louis's 'cycle smacked jarringly into concrete, turned half around in the turbulence of electromagnetic forces, and toppled. Louis let go and rolled clear.

Immediately he was trying to get to his feet. But he couldn't get his balance; he couldn't stay upright. His hands were claws, contorted with pain, useless. He lay panting on his side, thinking that it must already be too late. Speaker's flycycle must have landed on Speaker.

Speaker's flycycle, easily recognizable, lay on its side two tiers up. Speaker was there—and he wasn't under the 'cycle. He must have been under it before the 'cycle fell on its side; but even then the balloons would have protected him to some extent.

Louis reached him by crawling.

The kzin was alive and breathing, but unconscious. The weight of the flycycle had not broken his neck, possibly because he didn't really have a neck. Louis clawed the flashlight-laser from his belt, used its green needle beam to free Speaker from his balloons.

Now what?

Louis remembered that he was dying of thirst.

His head seemed to have stopped spinning. He stood,

wobbly-legged, to look for the only functional water source he knew.

The cell block was all concentric circular ledges, each ledge the roof of a ring of cell blocks. Speaker had grounded on the fourth ring from the center.

Louis found one 'cycle with tattered crash-balloon fabric draped across it. There was another, one tier down and across the central pit, equipped with a human-style saddle. The third—

Nessus's 'cycle had grounded a tier below Speaker's.

Louis went down to it. His feet jarred him as they hit the steps. His muscles were too tired to absorb the shock.

He shook his head at the sight of the dashboard. Nobody would be stealing Nessus's flycycle! The controls were incredibly cryptic. But he did identify the water spout.

The water was warm, tasteless as distilled water, and utterly delicious.

When Louis had quenched his thirst, he tried a brick from the kitchen slot. It tasted very strange. Louis decided not to eat it yet. There might be additives deadly to human metabolism. Nessus would know.

He carried water to Speaker in his shoe, the first container he thought of. He dribbled it into the kzin's mouth, and the kzin swallowed it in his sleep, and smiled. Louis went back for another load, and ran out of stamina before he could reach the puppeteer's flycycle.

So he curled up on the flat construction plastic and closed his eyes.

Safe. He was safe.

He should have been asleep instantly, the way he felt. But something nagged at him. Abused muscles, cramps in hands and thighs, the fear of falling that would not let him go even now . . . and something more . . .

He sat up. "No justice," he mumbled.

Speaker?

The kzin was sleeping curled around himself, with his ears tight to his head and his Slaver weapon hugged tight to his belly so that only the double snout showed. His breathing was regular, but very fast. Was that good?

Nessus would know. Meanwhile, let him sleep.

"No justice," Louis repeated under his breath.

He was alone and lonely, without the advantage of being on sabbatical. He was responsible for the well-being of others. His own life and health depended on how well Nessus gulled the crazy, half-bald woman who was keeping them prisoner. Small wonder if he couldn't sleep.

Still . . .

His eyes found it and locked. His own flycycle.

His own flycycle with the broken crash balloons trailing, and Nessus's flycycle here beside him, and Speaker's flycycle beside Speaker, and the flycycle with the human-shape saddle and no crash balloons. Four flycycles.

Frantic for water, he'd missed the implications the first time round. Now . . . Teela's flycycle. It must have been behind one of the bigger vehicles. And no crash balloons. No crash balloons.

She must have fallen off when the 'cycle turned over. Or been torn away when the sonic fold failed at Mach 2.

What was it Nessus had said? *Her luck is clearly undependable.* And Speaker: *If her luck had failed her just once, she would be dead.*

She was dead. She must be.

I came with you, *because I love you.*

"Bad luck," said Louis Wu. "Bad luck you met me." He curled up on the concrete and slept.

Much later, he woke with a jolt to find Speaker-To-Animals looking down into his face. The lurid orange fur mask made his eyes doubly prominent, and there was a *wistful* look . . . Speaker asked, "Can you eat the leaf-eater's food?"

"I'm afraid to try," said Louis. The vast, echoing cavity of his belly suddenly made all his other problems trivial, except one.

"I think that of the three of us, I alone have no food supply," said the kzin.

That *wistful* look . . . the hair stood up on Louis's neck. In a steady voice, he said, "You know you have a food supply. The question is, will you use it?"

"Certainly not, Louis. If honor requires me to starve within reach of meat, then I will starve."

"Good." Louis turned over and pretended to go back to sleep.

And when he woke up, some hours later, he knew that he *had* been asleep. His hindbrain, he decided, must trust Speaker's word completely. If the kzin said he would starve, he would starve.

His bladder was full, and there was a stink in his nostrils, and his muscles ached obtrusively. The pit solved one problem, and the puppeteer's flycycle supplied water to wash the muck off his sleeve. Then Louis limped down a flight of steps to reach his own flycycle and first-aid kit.

But the kit was not a simple box of medicines; it mixed dosages on command, and made its own diagnoses. A complex machine; and the zap guns had burnt it out.

The light was fading.

Cells with trap doors over them, and small transparent panes around the trap doors. Louis dropped to his belly to look into a cell. Bed, peculiar-looking toilet, and—daylight coming through a picture window.

"Speaker!" Louis called.

They used the disintegrator to break in. The picture window was big and rectangular, a strange luxury for a prison cell. The glass was gone but for a few sharp crystal teeth around the edges.

Windows to taunt the prisoner, to show him freedom?

The window faced to port. It was half-daylight; the shadow of the terminator was coming in from spinward like a black curtain. Ahead was the harbor: cubes that must be warehouses, rotting docks, cranes of elegantly simplistic design, and one tremendous ground-effect ship in drydock. All rust-red skeletons.

To left and right stretched mile after mile of twisting shore. A stretch of beach, then a line of docks, then a stretch of beach . . . The scheme must have been built into the shore itself, a stretch of shallow beach like Waikiki, then deep water meeting steep shore perfect for a harbor, then more shallow beach.

Beyond, the ocean. It seemed to go on forever, until
it faded in the infinity-horizon. Try to look across the Atlantic . . .

Dusk came on like a curtain, right to left. The sur-
viving lights of the Civic Center brightened, while city
and dock and ocean merged in darkness. To antispinward the golden light of day still glowed.

And Speaker had copped the cell's oval bed.

Louis smiled. He looked so peaceful, the kzin warrior.
Sleeping away his injuries, was he? The burns must have
weakened him. Or was he trying to sleep away his growing hunger?

Louis left him there.

In the near-darkness of the prison he found Nessus's
'cycle. His hunger was such that he choked down a food
brick intended for a puppeteer gullet, ignoring the peculiar taste. The gloom had begun to bother him, so he
turned on the headlamps on the puppeteer's flycycle, then
hunted down the other flycycles and turned them on too.
By the time he finished the place was pretty bright, and
all the shadows were intricate and strange.

What was taking Nessus so *long*?

There wasn't much entertainment in the ancient floating prison. You could spend just so much time sleeping,
and Louis had used his quota. You could spend just so
much time wondering what the tanj the puppeteer was
doing up there, before you began to wonder if he was
selling you out.

After all, Nessus wasn't just an alien. He was a Pierson's puppeteer, with a record a mile long for manipulat-
ing humans to his own ends. If he could reach an understanding with a (presumed) Ringworld Engineer, he might
abandon Louis and Speaker right now, no hesitation. A
puppeteer might have no reason not to.

And there were two good reasons why he should.

Speaker-To-Animals would almost certainly make some
last-ditch attempt to take the *Long Shot* from Louis Wu,
to reserve the second quantum hyperdrive for kzinti alone.
A puppeteer could get hurt in the resulting battle. Safer

to leave Speaker *now*—and to leave Louis Wu, because he probably wouldn't stand for such a betrayal.

Besides, they knew too much. With Teela dead, only Speaker and Louis knew about the puppeteer experiments in guided evolution. The starseed lure, the Fertility Laws—if Nessus had been ordered to divulge such information, to gauge his crewmates' reactions, probably he had also been ordered to abandon them sometime during the trip.

These were not even new thoughts. Louis had been alert for some such action ever since Nessus had admitted to guiding an Outsider ship to Procyon via starseed lure. His paranoia was justified in a way. But there wasn't a tanj thing he could *do* about it.

To save his mind, Louis broke into another cell. He cut across suspected locks with his flashlight-laser turned to high and narrow, and on the fourth try the door came up.

A terrible stench came up too. Louis held his breath, stuck his head and his flashlight-laser in long enough to find out why. Someone had died in there, after the ventilation had quit. The corpse was hunched up against the picture window with a heavy pitcher in his hand. The pitcher was broken. The window was intact.

The cell next door proved to be empty. Louis took possession.

He had crossed the pit to get a cell with a starboard view. He could see the rolling hurricane directly before him. Its size was respectable, considering that they had left it twenty-five hundred miles behind. A big, brooding blue eye.

To spinward was a tall, narrow floating building as big as a passenger starship. Briefly Louis daydreamed that it was a starship, hidden here in superb misdirection, and that all they had to do to get off the Ringworld was . . .

It was thin entertainment.

Louis schooled himself to memorize the pattern of the city. It might be important. This was the first place they had found with any sign of a still-active civilization.

He was taking a break, maybe an hour later. He was sitting on the dirty oval bunk, staring back at the Eye, and . . . beyond the Eye, well to the side, was a tiny vivid gray-brown triangle.

"Mph," Louis said softly. The triangle was only just big enough to be visible as such. It was set squarely in the gray-white chaos of the infinity-horizon. Which meant that it was still day there . . . although he was looking almost directly to starboard . . .

Louis went for his binoculars.

The binoculars made every detail as clear and sharp as the craters of the Moon. An irregular triangle, red-brown near the base, bright as dirty snow near the apex . . . Fist-of-God. Vastly larger than they had thought. To be visible this far away, most of the mountain must project above the atmosphere.

The flycycle fleet had flown around a hundred and fifty thousand miles since the crash. Fist-of-God had to be at least a thousand miles high.

Louis whistled. Again he raised the binoculars.

Sitting there in the near-darkness, Louis gradually became aware of noises overhead.

He stuck his head up out of the cell.

Speaker-To-Animals roared, "Welcome, Louis!" He waved at him with the raw, red, half-eaten carcass of something approximately goat-sized. He took a bite the size of a Chateaubriand steak, immediately took another, and another. His teeth were for tearing, not for chewing.

He reached out to pick up a bloody-ended hind leg with the hoof and skin still on. "We saved some for you, Louis! It has been hours dead, but no matter. We should hurry. The leaf-eater prefers not to watch us eat. He is sampling the view from my cell."

"Wait'll he sees mine," said Louis. "We were wrong about Fist-of-God, Speaker. It's at least a thousand miles high. The peak isn't snow-covered, it—"

"Louis! Eat!"

Louis found his mouth watering. "There has to be some way to cook that thing . . ."

There was. He got Speaker to tear the skin off for him, then wedged the hoof of the beast into a broken stair, stood back and roasted the meat with the flashlight-laser turned to high intensity, wide aperture.

"The meat is not fresh," Speaker said dubiously, "but cremation is not the answer."

"How's Nessus? Is he a prisoner, or is he in control?"

"In partial control, I think. Look up."

The spacer-girl was a tiny doll-figure on the observation platform, her feet trailing in space, her face and scalp showing white as she looked down.

"You see? She will not let him out of her sight."

Louis decided the meat was ready. As he ate, he was aware that Speaker watched him without patience, watched as Louis Wu slowly masticated each small bite. But to Louis it seemed that he ate like a ravening beast. He was *hungry*.

For the puppeteer's sake they pushed the bones through the broken window, to fall on the city. They reconvened around the puppeteer's flycycle.

"She is partially conditioned," said Nessus. He was having trouble with his breathing . . . or with the smells of raw and burnt animal. "I have learned a good deal from her."

"Did you learn why she mousetrapped us?"

"Yes, and more. We have been lucky. She is a spacer, a ramship crewman."

"Jackpot!" said Louis Wu.

CHAPTER 21

The Girl From Beyond The Edge

Her name was Halrloprillalar Hotrufan. She had been riding the ramship . . . *Pioneer,* Nessus called it after slight hesitation . . . for two hundred years.

The *Pioneer* ran a twenty-four-year cycle that covered four suns and their systems: five oxygen-atmosphere worlds and the Ringworld. The "year" used was a traditional measurement which had nothing to do with the Ringworld. It may have matched the solar orbit for one of the abandoned worlds.

Two of the *Pioneer's* five worlds had been thick with humanity before the Ringworld was built. Now they were abandoned like the others, covered with random vegetation and the debris of crumbling cities.

Halrloprillalar had run the cycle eight times. She knew that on these worlds grew plants or animals which had not adapted to the Ringworld because of the lack of a winter-summer cycle. Some plants were spices. Some animals were meat. Otherwise—Halrloprillalar neither knew nor cared.

Her job had nothing to do with cargos.

"Nor was she concerned with propulsion or life support. I was unable to learn just what she did," said Nessus. "The *Pioneer* carried a crew of thirty-six. Doubtless some were superfluous. Certainly she could have done nothing complex nor crucial to the well-being of ship or crew. She is not very intelligent, Louis."

"Did you think to ask about the ratio of sexes aboard ship? How many of the thirty-six were women?"

"She told me that. Three."

"You might as well forget about her profession."

Two hundred years of travel, security, adventure. Then at the end of Halrloprillalar's eighth run, the Ringworld refused to answer the *Pioneer's* call.

The electromagnetic cannon didn't work.

As far as telescopes could determine, there was no sign of activity at *any* spaceport.

The five worlds of the *Pioneer's* circuit were not equipped with electromagnetic cannons for braking. Therefore the *Pioneer* carried braking fuel, condensed en route from interstellar hydrogen. The ship could land . . . but where?

Not on the Ringworld. The meteor defenses would blow them apart.

They had not received permission to land on the spaceport ledge. And something was *wrong* there.

Back to one of the abandoned home worlds? In effect they would be starting a new colony world, with thirty-three men and three women.

"They were hidebound prisoners of routine, ill-equipped to make such a decision. They panicked," said Nessus. "They mutinied. The *Pioneer's* pilot managed to lock himself in the control room long enough to land the *Pioneer* on the spaceport ledge. They murdered him for it, for risking the ship and their lives, says Halrloprillalar. I wonder if they did not in truth murder him for breaking tradition, for landing by rocket and without formal permission."

Louis felt eyes on him. He looked up.

The spacer-girl was still watching them. And Nessus was looking back at her with one head, the left.

So *that* one held the tasp. And *that* was why Nessus had been looking steadily upward. She wouldn't let Nessus out of her sight, and he dared not let her off the tasp's lovely hook.

"After the killing of the pilot, they left the ship," said Nessus. "Then it was that they learned how badly the pilot had hurt them. The *cziltang brone* was inert, broken.

They were stranded on the wrong side of a wall a thousand miles high.

"I do not know the equivalent of *cziltang brone* in Interworld or the Hero's Tongue. I can only tell you what it does. What it does is crucial to us all."

"Go ahead," said Louis Wu.

The Ringworld engineers had designed fail-safe. In many ways it seemed that they had anticipated the fall of civilization, had planned for it, as if cycles of culture and barbarism were man's natural lot. The complex structure that was the Ringworld would not fail for lack of tending. The descendants of the Engineers might forget how to tend airlocks and electromagnetic cannon, how to move worlds and build flying cars; civilization might end, but the Ringworld would not.

The meteor defenses, for instance, were so utterly fail-safe that Halrloprillalar—

"Call her Prill," Louis suggested.

—that Prill and her crew never considered that they might not be working.

But what of the spaceport? How fail-safe would it be, if some idiot left both doors of the airlock open?

There weren't any airlocks! Instead, there was the *cziltang brone*. This machine projected a field which caused the structure of the Ringworld floor, and hence of the rim wall, to become permeable to matter. There was some resistance. While the *cziltang brone* was going—

"Osmosis generator," Louis suggested.

"Perhaps. I suspect that *brone* is a modifier, possibly obscene."

—air would leak through, but slowly, while the osmosis generator was going. Men could push through in pressure suits, moving as against a steady wind. Machines and large masses could be drawn through by tractors.

"What of pressurized breathing-air?" Speaker asked.

But they made that outside, with the transmutors!

Yes, there was cheap transmutation on the Ringworld. It was cheap only in great quantity, and there were other limits. The machine itself was gigantic. It would make just one element into just one other element. The spaceport's two transmutors would turn lead into nitrogen and oxygen; lead was easy to store and easy to move through the rim wall.

The osmosis generators were a fail-safe device. When and airlock fails, a veritable hurricane of breathing-air can be lost. But if the *cziltang brone* broke down, the worst that could happen would be that the airlock would be closed to space—and incidentally to returning spacemen.

"Also to us," said Speaker.

Louis said, "Not so fast. It sounds like the osmosis generator is just what we need to get home. We wouldn't have to move the *Liar* at all. Just point the *cziltang brone*—" He pronounced it as if it started with a sneeze— "at the Ring floor under the *Liar*. The *Liar* would sink through the Ring floor like quicksand. Down, and out the other side."

"To be trapped in the foamed plastic meteor buffer," the kzin retorted. Then, "Correction. The Slaver weapon might serve us there."

"Quite so. Unfortunately," said Nessus, "there is no *cziltang brone* available to us."

"She's *here*. She got through somehow!"

"Yes . . ."

The magnetohydrodynamicists virtually had to learn a new profession before they could begin to rebuild the *cziltang brone*. It took them several years. The machine had failed in action: it was partly twisted and partly melted. They had to make new parts; recalibrate; use elements they *knew* would fail, but maybe they'd hold long enough . . .

There was an accident during that time. An osmosis beam, modified by bad calibration, went through the *Pioneer*. Two crewmen died waist-deep in a metal floor, and seventeen others suffered permanent brain damage in addition to other injuries when certain permeable membranes became too permeable.

But they got through, the remaining sixteen. They took the idiots with them. They also took the *cziltang brone*, in case the new Ringworld turned out to be inhospitable.

They found savagery, nothing but savagery.

Years later, some of them tried to go back.

The *cziltang brone* failed in action, trapping four of them in the rim wall. And that was that. By then they knew that there would be no new parts available anywhere on the Ringworld.

"I don't understand how barbarism could come so *fast*," said Louis. "You said the *Pioneer* ran a twenty-four year cycle?"

"Twenty-four years in ship's time, Louis."

"Oh. That does make a difference."

"Yes. To a ship traveling at one Ringworld gravity of thrust, stars tend to be three to six years apart. The actual distances were large. Prill speaks of an abandoned region two hundred light years closer to the mean galactic plane, where three suns clustered within ten light years of each other."

"Two hundred light years . . . near human space, do you think?"

"Perhaps in human space. Oxygen-atmosphere planets do not in general tend to cluster as closely as they do in the vicinity of Sol. Halrloprillalar speaks of long-term terraforming techniques applied to these worlds, many centuries before the building of the Ringworld. These techniques took too long. They were abandoned halfway by the impatient humans."

"That would explain a lot. Except . . . no, never mind."

"Primates, Louis? There is evidence enough that your species evolved on Earth. But Earth might have been a convenient base for a terraforming project aimed at worlds in nearby systems. The engineers might have brought pets and servants."

"Like apes and monkeys and Neanderthals . . . ?" Louis made a chopping gesture. "It's just speculation. It's not something we need to know."

"Granted." The puppeteer munched a vegetable brick while he talked. "The loop followed by the *Pioneer* was more than three hundred light years long. There was time for extensive change during a voyage, though such change was rare. Prill's society was a stable one."

"Why was she so sure that the whole Ringworld had gone barbarian? How much exploring did they do?"

"Very little, but enough. Prill was right. There will be no repairs for the *cziltang brone*. The entire Ringworld must be barbarous by now."

"How?"

"Prill tried to explain to me what happened here, as one of her crew explained it to her. He had oversimplified, of course. It may be that the process started years before the *Pioneer* departed on its last circuit . . ."

There had been ten inhabited worlds. When the Ringworld was finished, all of these had been abandoned, left to go their way without the benefit of man.

Consider such a world:

The land is covered with cities in all stages of development. Perhaps slums were made obsolete, but somewhere there are still slums, if only preserved for history. Across the land one can find all the by-products of living: used containers, broken machines, damaged books or film tapes or scrolls, anything that cannot be reused or reprocessed at a profit, and many things which could be. The seas have been used as garbage dumps for a hundred thousand years. Somewhere in that time, they were dumping useless radioactive end products of fission.

How strange is it if the sea life evolves to fit the new conditions?

How strange, if new life evolves capable of living on the garbage?

"That happened on Earth once," said Louis Wu. "A yeast that could eat polyethyline. It was eating the plastic bags off the supermarket shelves. It's dead now. We had to give up polyethyline."

Consider *ten* such worlds.

Bacteria evolved to eat zinc compounds, plastics, paints, wiring insulation, fresh rubbish, and rubbish thou-

sands of years obsolete. It would not have mattered but
for the ramships.

The ramships came routinely to the old worlds, seeking forms of life that had been forgotten or that had not
adapted to the Ringworld. They brought back other
things: souvenirs, objets d'art which had been forgotten
or merely postponed. Many museums were still being
transferred, one incredibly valuable piece at a time.

One of the ramships brought back a mold capable of
breaking down the structure of a room-temperature superconductor much used in sophisticated machinery.

The mold worked slowly. It was young and primitive
and, in the beginning, easily killed. Variations may have
been brought to the Ringworld several times by several
ships, until one variation finally took hold.

Because it did work slowly, it did not ruin the ramship
until long after the ramship had landed. It did not destroy the spaceport's *cziltang brone* until crewmen and
spaceport workmen had carried it inside. It did not get
into the power beam receivers until the shuttles that
traveled through the electromagnetic cannon on the rim
wall had carried it everywhere on the Ringworld.

"Power beam receivers?"

"Power is generated on the shadow squares by thermoelectricity, then beamed to the Ringworld. Presumably
the beam, too, is fail-safe. We did not detect it coming in.
It must have shut itself down when the receivers failed."

"Surely," said Speaker, "one could make a different
superconductor. We know of two basic molecular structures, each with many variations for different temperature
ranges."

"There are at least four basic structures," Nessus corrected him. "You are quite right, the Ringworld should
have survived the Fall of the Cities. A younger, more
vigorous society would have. But consider the difficulties
they faced.

"Much of their leadership was dead, killed in falling
buildings when the power failed.

"Without power they could do little experimenting to
find other superconductors. Stored power was generally

confiscated for the personal use of men with political power, or was used to run enclaves of civilization in the hope that someone else was doing something about the emergency. The fusion drives of the ramships were unavailable, as the *cziltang brones* used superconductors. Men who might have accomplished something could not meet; the computer that ran the electromagnetic cannon was dead, and the cannon itself had no power."

Louis said, "For want of a nail, the kingdom fell."

"I know the story. It is not strictly applicable," said Nessus. "Something could have been done. There was power to condense liquid helium. With the power beams off, the repair of a power receiver would have been useless; but a *cziltang brone* could have been adapted to a metal superconductor cooled by liquid helium. A *cziltang brone* would have given access to spaceports. Ships might have flown to the shadow squares, reopened the power beams so that other liquid-helium-cooled superconductors could be adapted to the power beam receivers.

"But all this would have required stored power. The power was used to light street lamps, or to support the remaining floating buildings, or to cook meals and freeze foods! And so the Ringworld fell."

"And so did we," said Louis Wu.

"Yes. We were lucky to run across Halrloprillalar. She has saved us a needless journey. There is no longer any need to continue toward the rim wall."

Louis's head throbbed once, hard. He was going to have a headache.

"Lucky," said Speaker-To-Animals. "Indeed. If this is luck, why am I not joyful? We have lost our goal, our last meager hope of escape. Our vehicles are ruined. One of our party is missing in this maze of city."

"Dead," said Louis. When they looked at him without comprehension, he pointed into the dusk. Teela's flycycle was obvious enough, marked by one of four sets of headlamps.

He said, "We'll have to make our own luck from now on."

"Yes. You will remember, Louis, that Teela's luck is

sporadic. It had to be. Else she would not have been aboard the *Liar*. Else we would not have crashed." The puppeteer paused, then added, "My sympathies, Louis."

"She will be missed," Speaker rumbled.

Louis nodded. It seemed he should be feeling more. But the incident in the Eye storm had somehow altered his feelings for Teela. She had seemed, for that time, less human than Speaker or Nessus. She was myth. The aliens were real.

"We must find a new goal," said Speaker-To-Animals. "We need a way to take the *Liar* back to space. I confess I have no ideas at all."

"I do," Louis said.

Speaker seemed startled. "Already?"

"I want to think about it some more. I'm not sure it's even sane, let alone workable. In any case, we're going to need a vehicle. Let's think about that."

"A sled, perhaps. We can use the remaining flycycle to tow it. A big sled, perhaps the wall of a building."

"We can better that. I am convinced that I can persuade Halrloprillalar to guide me through the machinery that lifts this building. We may find that the building itself can become our vehicle."

"Try that," said Louis.

"And you?"

"Give me time."

The core of the building was all machinery. Some was lifting machinery; some ran the air conditioning and the water condensers and the water taps; and one insulated section was part of the electromagnetic trap generators. Nessus worked. Louis and Prill stood by, awkwardly ignoring one another.

Speaker was still in prison. Prill had refused to let him up.

"She is afraid of you," Nessus had said. "We could press the point, no doubt. We could put you aboard one of the flycycles. If I refused to board until you were on the platform, she would have to lift you."

"She might lift me halfway to the ceiling, then drop me. No."

But she had taken Louis.

He studied her while pretending to ignore her. Her mouth was narrow, virtually lipless. Her nose was small and straight and narrow. She had no eyebrows.

Small wonder if she seemed to have no expression. Her face seemed little more than markings on a wigmaker's dummy.

After two hours of work, Nessus pulled his heads out of an access panel. "I cannot give us motive power. The lift fields will do no more than lift us. But I have freed a correcting mechanism designed to keep us over one spot. The building is now at the mercy of the winds."

Louis grinned. "Or a tow. Tie a line to your flycycle and pull the building behind you."

"There is no need. The flycycle uses a reactionless thruster. We can keep it within the building."

"You thought of it first, hmm? But that thruster's awfully powerful. If the 'cycle tore itself loose in here—"

"Yesss—" The puppeteer turned to Prill and spoke slowly and at length in the language of the Ringworld gods. Presently he said to Louis, "There is a supply of electrosetting plastic. We can embed the flycycle in plastic, leaving only the controls exposed."

"Isn't that a little drastic?"

"Louis, if the flycycle tore itself loose, I could be *hurt*."

"Well . . . maybe. Can you land the building when you need to?"

"Yes, I have altitude control."

"Then we don't need a scout vehicle. Okay, we'll do it."

Louis was resting, not sleeping. He lay on his back on the big oval bed. His eyes were open, staring through the bubble window in the ceiling.

A glow of solar corona showed over the edge of the shadow square. Dawn was not far off; but still the Arch was blue and bright in a black sky.

"I must be out of my mind," said Louis Wu.

And, "What *else* can we do?"

The bedroom had probably been part of the governor's suite. Now it was a control room. He and Nessus had mounted the flycycle in the walk-in closet, poured plastic over and around it, then—with Prill's help—run a current through the plastic. The closet had been just the right size.

The bed smelled of age. It crinkled when he moved.

"Fist-of-God," Louis Wu said into the dark. "I saw it. A thousand miles high. It doesn't make *sense* they'd build a mountain that high, not when . . ." he let it trail off.

And suddenly sat bolt upright in bed, shouting, "Shadow square wire!"

A shadow entered the bedroom.

Louis froze. The entrance was dark. Yet, by its fluid motion and by the distribution of subtle shadings of curvature, a naked woman was walking toward him.

Hallucination? The ghost of Teela Brown? She had reached him before he could decide. Totally self-confident, she sat beside him on the bed. She reached out and touched his face and ran her fingertips down his cheek.

She was nearly bald. Though her hair was dark and long and full-bodied, so that it bobbed as she walked, it was only an inch-wide fringe growing from the base of her skull. In the dark the features of her face virtually disappeared. But her body was lovely. He was seeing the shape of her for the first time. She was slim, muscled with wire like a professional dancer. Her breasts were high and heavy.

If her face had matched her figure . . .

"Go away," Louis said, not roughly. He took her wrist, interrupted what her fingertips were doing to his face. It had felt like a barber's facial massage, infinitely relaxing. He stood up, pulled her gently to her feet, took her by the shoulders. If he simply turned her around and patted her on the rump—?

She ran her fingertips along the side of his neck. Now she was using both hands. She touched him on the chest, and *here,* and *there,* and suddenly Louis Wu was blind with lust. His hands closed like clamps on her shoulders.

She dropped her hands. She waited without trying to help as he peeled out of his falling jumper. But as he exposed more skin, she stroked him *here,* and *there,* not always where nerves clustered. Each time it was as if she had touched him in the pleasure center of his brain.

He was on fire. If she pushed him away now, he would use force; he must have her—

—But some cool part of him knew that she could chill him as quickly as she had aroused him. He felt like a young satyr, yet he dimly sensed that he was also a puppet.

For the moment he couldn't have cared less.

And still Prill's face showed no expression.

She took him to the verge of orgasm, then held him there, held him there . . . so that when the moment came it was like being struck by lightning. But the lightning went on and on, a flaming discharge of ecstacy.

When it ended he was barely aware that she was leaving. She must know how thoroughly she had used him up. He was asleep before she reached the door.

And he woke thinking: *Why did she do that?*

Too tanj analytical, he answered himself. *She's lonely. She must have been here a long time. She's mastered a skill, and she hasn't had a chance to practice that skill . . .*

Skill. She must know more anatomy than most professors. A doctorate in Prostitution? There was more to the oldest profession than met the eye. Louis Wu could recognize expertise in any field. This woman had it.

Touch these nerves in the correct order, and the subject will react thus-and-so. The right knowledge can turn a man into a puppet . . .

. . . puppet to Teela's luck . . .

He almost had it then. He came close enough that the answer, when it finally came, was no surprise.

Nessus and Halrloprillalar came backward out of the freezer room. They were followed by the dressed carcass of a flightless bird bigger than a man, Nessus had used a cloth for padding, so that his mouth need not touch the dead meat of the ankle.

Louis took the puppeteer's burden. He and Prill pulled in tandem. He found that he needed both hands, as did she. He answered her nod of greeting and asked, "How old is she?"

Nessus did not show surprise at the question. "I do not know."

"She came to my room last night." That would not do; it would mean nothing to an alien. "You know that the thing we do to reproduce, we also do for recreation?"

"I knew that."

"We did that. She's good at it. She's so good at it that she must have had about a thousand years of practice," said Louis Wu.

"It is not impossible. Prill's civilization had a compound superior to boosterspice in its ability to sustain life. Today the compound is worth whatever the owner cares to ask. One charge is equivalent to some fifty years of youth."

"Do you happen to know how many charges she's taken?"

"No, Louis. But I know that she walked here."

They had reached the stairway leading down to the conical cell block. The bird trailed behind them, bouncing.

"Walked here from where?"

"From the rim wall."

"Two hundred thousand miles?"

"Nearly that."

"Tell me all of it. What happened to them after they reached the right side of the rim wall?"

"I will ask. I do not know it all." And the puppeteer began to question Prill. In bits and pieces the story emerged:

They were taken for gods by the first group of savages they met, and by everyone thereafter, with one general exception.

Godhood solved one problem neatly. The crewmen whose brains had been damaged by backlash from the half-repaired *cziltang brone* were left to the care of various villages. As resident gods they would be well treated; and as idiots they would be relatively harmless as gods.

The remainder of the *Pioneer's* crew split up. Nine, including Prill, went to antispinward. Prill's home city was in that direction. Both groups planned to travel along the rim wall, looking for civilization. Both parties swore to send help if they found any.

They were taken for gods by all but the other gods. The Fall of the Cities had left a few survivors. Some were mad. All took the life-extending compound if they could get it. All were looking for enclaves of civilization. None had thought to build his own.

As the *Pioneer's* crew moved to antispinward, other survivors joined them. They became a respectable pantheon.

In every city they found the shattered towers. These towers had been set floating after the settling of the Ringworld, but thousands of years before the perfection of the youth drug. The youth drug had made later generations cautious. For the most part those who could afford it simply stayed away from the floaters, unless they were elected officials. Then they would install safety devices, or power generators.

A few of the floaters still floated. But most had smashed down into the centers of cities, all in the same instant, when the last power receiver flared and died.

Once the traveling pantheon found a partially recivilized city, inhabited only on the outskirts. The God Gambit would not serve them here. They traded a fortune in the youth drug for a working, self-powered bus.

It did not happen again until much later. By then they had come too far. The spirit had gone out of them, and the bus had broken down. In a half-smashed city, among other survivors of the Fall of the Cities, most of the pantheon simply stopped moving.

But Prill had a map. The city of her birth was directly to starboard. She persuaded a man to join her, and they started walking.

They traded on their godhoods. Eventually they tired of one another, and Prill went on alone. Where her godhood was not enough, she traded small quantities of the youth drug, if she had to. Otherwise—

"There was another way in which she could maintain power over people. She has tried to explain it to me, but I do not understand."

"I think I do," said Louis. "She could get away with it, too. She's got her own equivalent of a tasp."

She must have been quite mad by the time she reached her home city. She took up residence in the grounded police station. She spent hundreds of hours learning how to work the machinery. One of the first things she accomplished was to get it airborne; for the self-powered tower had been landed as a safety precaution after the Fall of the Cities. Subsequently she must have come close enough to dropping the tower and killing herself.

"There was a system for trapping drivers who broke the traffic laws," Nessus finished. "She turned it on. She hopes to capture someone like herself, a survivor from the Fall of the Cities. She reasons that if he is flying a car, he must be civilized."

"Then why does she want him trapped and helpless in that sea of rusted metal?"

"Just in case, Louis. It is a mark of her returning sanity."

Louis frowned into the cell block below. They had lowered the bird's carcass on a ruined metal car, and Speaker had taken possession. "We can lighten this building," said Louis. "We can cut the weight almost in half."

"How?"

"Cut away the basement. But we'll have to get Speaker out of there. Can you persuade Prill?"

"I can try."

CHAPTER 22

Seeker

Halrloprillalar was terrified of Speaker, and Nessus was leery of letting her out of the influence of the tasp. Nessus claimed to be jumping the tasp on her every time she saw Speaker, so that eventually she would welcome the sight of him. Meanwhile they both shunned the kzin's company.

So it was that Prill and Nessus waited elsewhere while Louis and Speaker lay flat on the floor of the observation platform looking down into the gloom of the cell block.

"Go ahead," said Louis.

The kzin fired both beams.

Thunder boomed and echoed within the cell block. A brilliant point the color of lightning appeared high on the wall, just beneath the ceiling. It moved slowly clockwise, leaving a redly glowing trail.

"Cut chunks," Louis directed. "If that mass lets go all at once, we'll be shaken loose like fleas on a shaven dog."

Speaker obligingly changed the angle of his cutting.

Still, the building lurched when the first chunk of cable and construction plastic fell away. Louis hugged the floor. Through the gap he saw sunlight, and city, and people.

He did not have a view straight down until half a dozen masses had been cut loose.

He saw an altar of wood, and a model of silvery metal whose shape was a flat rectangle surmounted by a parabolic arch. It was there for an instant, before a mass of cell block structure struck next to it and splashed fragments in all directions. Then it was sawdust and crumpled tinsel. But the people had fled long since.

"People!" he complained to Nessus. "In the heart of an empty city, miles from the fields! That's an all-day round trip. What were they doing there?"

"They worship the goddess Halrloprillalar. They are Prill's food source."

"Ah. Offerings."

"Of course. What difference does it make, Louis?"

"They might have been hit."

"Perhaps some of them were."

"And I thought I saw Teela down there. Just for an instant."

"Nonsense, Louis. Shall we test our motive power?"

The puppeteer's flycycle was buried in a gelatinous mound of translucent plastic. Nessus stood alongside the exposed control panel. The bay window gave them an imposing view of the city: the docks, the flat-sided towers of the Civic Center, the spreading jungle that had probably been a park. All several thousand feet below.

Louis struck an attitude: parade rest. *An inspiration to his crew, the heroic commander stands astride the bridge. The damaged rocket motors may explode at the first touch of thrust; but it must be tried. The kzinti battleships must be stopped before they reach Earth!*

"It'll never work," said Louis Wu.

"Why not, Louis? The stresses should not exceed—"

"A flying castle, for Finagle's sake! I only just realized how insane the whole thing is. We must have been out of our minds! Tootling home in the upper half of a skyscraper—" The building shifted then, and Louis staggered. Nessus had started the thruster.

The city drifted past the bay window, gathering speed. Acceleration eased off. It had never been higher than a foot per second squared. Top speed seemed to be about one hundred miles per hour, and the castle was rock steady.

"We centered the flycycle correctly," said Nessus. "The

floor is level, as you will note, and the structure shows no tendency to rotate."

"It's still silly."

"Nothing that works is silly. And now, where shall we go?"

Louis was silent.

"Where shall we go, Louis? Speaker and I have no plans. What direction, Louis?"

"Starboard."

"Very well. Directly starboard?"

"Right. We've got to get past the Eye storm. Then turn forty-five degrees or so to antispinward."

"Do you seek the city of the tower called Heaven?"

"Yes. Can you find it?"

"That should be no problem, Louis. Three hours flying time brought us here; we should be back at the tower in thirty hours. And then?"

"Depends."

The picture was so vivid. It was pure deduction and imagination, yet—so vivid. Louis Wu tended to daydream in color.

So vivid. But was it real?

It was frightening, how suddenly his confidence in the flying tower had leaked away. Yet the tower was flying. It didn't need Louis Wu to make it go.

"The leaf-eater seems content to follow your lead," said Speaker.

The flycycle hummed quietly to itself a few feet away. Landscape flowed past the bay window. The Eye storm was off to the side, its gray gaze large and daunting.

"The leaf-eater's out of his mind," said Louis. "I take it you've got better sense."

"Not at all. If you have a goal, I am content to follow you. But if it may involve fighting, I should know something about it."

"Um."

"I should know something about it regardless, in order to decide whether it will involve fighting."

"Well put."

Speaker waited.

"We're going after the shadow square wire," said Louis. "Remember the wire we ran into after the meteor defenses wrecked us? Later it started falling over the city of the floating tower, loop after loop, endlessly. There should be at least tens of thousands of miles of it, more than we could possibly need for what I've got in mind."

"What do you have in mind, Louis?"

"Getting hold of the shadow square wire. Odds are the natives will just give it to us, if Prill asks politely, and if Nessus uses the tasp."

"And after that?"

"After that, we'll find out just how crazy I am."

The tower moved to starboard like a steamship of the sky. Starships were never so roomy. As for ships of the air, there was nothing comparable in known space. Six decks to climb around in! Luxury!

There were luxuries missing. The food supply aboard the flyscraper consisted of frozen meat, perishable fruit, and the kitchen of Nessus's flycycle. Food for puppeteers lacked nourishment for humans, according to Nessus. Thus Louis's breakfast and lunch were meat broiled by a flashlight-laser, and knobbly red fruit.

And there was no water.

And no coffee.

Prill was persuaded to find some bottles of an alcoholic beverage. They held a belated christening ceremony in the bridge room, with Speaker courteously backed into a far corner and Prill hovering warily near the door. Nobody would accept Louis's suggestion of the name *Improbable;* and so there were four christenings, in order, in four different languages.

The beverage was . . . well, sour. Speaker couldn't take it, and Nessus didn't try. But Prill consumed one bottle, sealed the others, and put them carefully away.

The christening became a language lesson. Louis learned a few of the rudiments of the Ringworld Engineers' speech. He found that Speaker was learning much faster than he was. It figured. Speaker and Nessus had both been trained to deal with human languages, modes of thinking, limitations in speech and hearing. This was only more of the same.

They broke for dinner. Again Nessus ate alone, using his flycycle kitchen, while Louis and Prill ate broiled meat and Speaker ate raw, elsewhere.

Afterward the language lesson went on. Louis hated it. The others were so far ahead of him that he felt like a cretin.

"But Louis, we *must* learn the language. Our rate of travel is low, and we must forage for our food. Frequently we will need to deal with natives."

"I know. I never liked languages."

Darkness fell. Even this far from the Eye storm, cloud cover was complete, and the night was like the inside of a dragon's mouth. Louis called a halt to the lesson. He was tired and irritable and vastly unsure of himself. The others left him to his rest.

They would be passing the Eye storm in about ten hours.

He was floating at the edge of a restless sleep when Prill came back. He felt hands stroking him lasciviously, and he reached out.

She backed out of reach. She spoke in her own language, but simplified it into a pidgin for Louis's understanding.

"You are leader?"

Bleary-eyed, Louis considered. "Yes," he said, because the actual situation was too complex.

"Make the two-headed one give me his machine."

"What?" Louis fumbled for words. "His which?"

"His machine that make me happy. I want it. You take it from him."

Louis laughed, for he thought he understood her.

"You want me? You take it," Prill said angrily.

The puppeteer had something she wanted. She had no lever to use on him, for he was not a man. Louis Wu was the only man around. Her power would bend him to her will. It had always worked before; for was she not a goddess?

Perhaps Louis's hair had misled her. She may have assumed that he was one of the hairy lower class, by his bare face perhaps half Engineer, but no more. Then he must have been born after the Fall of the Cities. No youth drug. He must be in the first flush of youth.

"You were quite right," Louis said in his own tongue. Prill's fists clenched in anger, for his mockery was clear. "A thirty-year-old man would be putty in your hands. But I'm older than that." And he laughed again.

"The machine. Where does he keep it?" In the darkness she leaned toward him, all lovely suggestive shadow. Her scalp gleamed softly; her black hair spilled over her shoulder. The breath caught in Louis's throat.

He found the words to say, "Glue against his bone, under skin. One head."

Prill made a sound like a growl. She must have understood; the gadget was surgically implanted. She turned and left.

Louis thought briefly of following her. He wanted her more than he was willing to admit. But she would own him if he let her, and her motives did not jibe with Louis Wu's.

The whistle of the wind rose gradually. Louis's sleep became shallow . . . and merged into an erotic dream.

His eyes opened.

Prill knelt facing him, straddling him like a succubus. Her fingers moved lightly over the skin of his chest and belly. Her hips moved rhythmically, and Louis moved in response. She was playing him like a musical instrument.

"When I finish I will own you," she crooned. The pleasure showed in her voice, but it was not the pleasure of a woman taking pleasure from a man. It was the thrill of wielding power.

Her touch was a joy as thick as syrup. She knew a terribly ancient secret: that every woman is born with a tasp, and that its power is without limit if she can learn to use it. She would use it and withhold it, use it and withhold it, until Louis begged for the right to serve her . . .

Something changed in her. Her face could not show it; but he heard the crooning sound of her pleasure, and he felt the change in her motion. She moved, and they came together, and the *slam!* that rolled across them then seemed entirely subjective.

She lay beside him all that night. Occasionally they woke and made love, and went back to sleep. If Prill felt disappointment at these times, she did not show it, or Louis did not see it. He knew only that she was no longer playing him like an instrument. They were playing a duet.

Something had happened to Prill. He suspected what it was.

The morning dawned gray and stormy. Wind howled around the ancient building. Rain lashed the bay window of the bridge, and stormed through broken windows higher up. The *Improbable* was very close to the Eye storm.

Louis dressed and left the bridge.

He saw Nessus in the hallway. "You!" he shouted.

The puppeteer shied. "Yes, Louis?"

"What did you do to Prill last night?"

"Show proper gratitude, Louis. She was trying to control you, to condition you into subservience. I heard."

"You used the tasp on her!"

"I gave her three seconds at half-power while you were engaged in reproductive activity. Now it is she who is conditioned."

"You monster! You egotistical monster!"

"Come no closer, Louis."

"Prill is a human woman with free will!"

"What of your own free will?"

"It was in no danger! She can't control me!"

"Is there something else bothering you? Louis, you

are not the first human couple I have watched in reproductive activity. We felt that we must know all about
your species. Come no closer, Louis."

"You hadn't the *right!*" Certainly Louis never intended
harm to the puppeteer. He clenched his fists in rage, but
he did not intend to use them. In rage he stepped forward—

Then Louis was in ecstasy.

In the heart of the purest joy he had ever known,
Louis knew that Nessus was using the tasp on him. Without allowing himself to realize the consequences, Louis
kicked out and up.

He used all the strength he could divert from his en-
joyment of the tasp. It was not great, but he used it, and
he kicked the puppeteer in the larynx, beneath the left
jaw.

The consequences were hideous. Nessus said, "Glup!"
and stumbled back, and turned off the tasp.

And turned off the tasp!

The weight of all the sorrow that men are heir to,
came down on the shoulders of Louis Wu. Louis turned
his back on the puppeteer and walked away. He wanted
to weep; but more than that, he wanted the puppeteer
not to see his face.

He wandered at random, seeing only his own inner
blackness. It was only coincidence that brought him to
the stairwell.

He had known full well what he was doing to Prill.
Balanced over a drop of ninety feet, he had been eager
enough to see Nessus use the tasp on Prill. He had seen
wireheads; he knew what it did to them.

Conditioned! Like an experimental pet! And she knew!
Last night had been her last valiant attempt to break
loose from the power of the tasp.

Now Louis had felt what she was fighting.

"I shouldn't have done it," said Louis Wu. "I take it
back." Even in black despair, that was funny. You can't
take back such a choice.

It was coincidence that he went down the stairwell instead of up. Or his hindbrain may have remembered a *slam!* that his forebrain had hardly noticed.

The wind roared around him, hurling rain from every direction, as he reached the platform. It took some of his attention outside himself. He was losing the grief that came with the loss of the tasp.

Once Louis Wu had sworn to live forever.

Now, much later, he knew that obligations went with such a decision.

"Got to cure her," he said. "How? No physical withdrawal symptoms . . . but that won't help her if she decides to walk out of a broken window. How do I cure myself?" For some minor part of him still cried for the tasp, and would never stop.

The addiction was nothing more than a below-threshold memory. Strand her somewhere with her supply of youth drug, and the memory would fade . . .

"Tanj. We need her." She knew too much about the engine room of the *Improbable*. She couldn't be spared.

He'd just have to get Nessus to stop using the tasp. Watch her for awhile. She'd be awfully depressed at first . . .

Abruptly Louis's mind registered what his eyes had been seeing for some time.

The car was twenty feet below the observation platform. A cleanly-designed maroon dart with narrow slits for windows, it hovered without power in the roaring wind, caught in an electromagnetic trap nobody had remembered to turn off.

Louis looked once, hard, to be sure that there was a face behind the windscreen. Then he ran upstairs shouting for Prill.

He didn't know the words. But he took her by the elbow and pulled her downstairs and showed her. She nodded and went back up to use the police trap adjustments.

The maroon dart moved tight up against the edge of the platform. The first occupant crawled out, using both hands to hang on, for the wind was howling like a fiend.

It was Teela Brown. Louis felt little surprise.

And the second occupant was so blatantly type-cast that he burst out laughing. Teela looked surprised and hurt.

They were passing the Eye storm. The wind roared up through the stairwell that led to the observation platform. It whistled throught the corridors of the first floor, and howled through broken windows higher up. The halls ran with rain.

Teela and her escort and the crew of the *Improbable* sat about Louis's bedroom, the bridge. Teela's brawny escort talked gravely with Prill in one corner; though Prill kept a wary eye on Speaker-To-Animals and another on the bay window. But the others surrounded Teela as she told her tale.

The police device had blown most of the machinery in Teela's flycycle. The locator, the intercom, the sonic fold, and the kitchen all burned out at once.

Teela was still alive because the sonic fold had had a built-in standing-wave characteristic. She had felt the sudden wind and had hit the retrofield immediately, before the Mach 2 wind could tear her head off. In seconds she had dropped below the municipal upper speed limit. The trap field had been about to blow her drive; it refrained. The wind was tolerable by the time it broke through the stabilizing effect of the sonic fold.

But Teela was nothing like stable. She had brushed death too closely in the Eye storm. This second attack had followed too quickly. She guided the flycycle down, searching in the dark for a place to land.

There was a tiled mall surrounded by shops. It had lights: oval doors that glowed bright orange. The 'cycle landed hard, but by then she didn't care. She was down.

She was dismounting when the vehicle rose again. The motion threw her head over heels. She rose to her hands and knees, shaking her head. When she looked up the flycycle was a dwindling dumbbell shape.

Teela began to cry.

"You must have broken a parking law," said Louis.

"I didn't *care* why it happened. I felt—" She didn't have the words, but she tried anyway. "I wanted to tell someone I was lost. But there wasn't anyone. So I sat down on one of the stone benches and cried.

"I cried for hours. I was afraid to move away, because I knew you'd be coming for me. Then—*he* came." Teela nodded at her escort. "He was surprised to find me there. He asked me something—I couldn't understand. But he tried to comfort me. I was glad he was there, even if he couldn't do anything."

Louis nodded. Teela would trust anybody. She would inevitably seek help or comfort from the first stranger to come along. And she would be perfectly safe in doing so.

Her escort was unusual.

He was a hero. You could tell. You didn't need to see him fighting dragons. You need only see the muscles, the height, the black metal sword. The strong features, uncannily like the wire-sculpture face in the castle called Heaven. The courteous way he talked to Prill, apparently without realizing that she was of the opposite sex. Because she was another man's woman?

He was clean-shaven. No, that was improbable. More likely he was half Engineer. His hair was long and ash blond and not too clean, and the hairline shaped a noble brow. Around his waist was a kind of kirtle, the skin of some animal.

"He fed me," Teela said. "He took care of me. Four men tried to jump us yesterday, and he fought them off with just his sword! And he's learned a lot of Interworld in just a couple of days."

"Has he?"

"He's had a lot of practice with languages."

"This was the most unkindest cut of all."

"What?"

"Never mind. Go on."

"He's old, Louis. He got a massive dose of something like boosterspice, long ago. He says he took it from an evil magician. He's so old that his grandparents remembered the Fall of the Cities.

"Do you know what he's doing?" Her smile became impish. "He's on a kind of quest. Long ago he took an oath that he would walk to the base of the Arch. He's doing that. He's been doing it for hundreds of years."

"The base of the Arch?"

Teela nodded. She was smiling very prettily, and she obviously appreciated the joke, but in her eyes there was something more.

Louis had seen love in Teela's eyes, but never tenderness.

"You're proud of him for it! You little idiot, don't you know there isn't any Arch?"

"I know that, Louis."

"Then why don't you tell him?"

"If you tell him, I'll hate you. He's spent too much of his life doing this. And he does good. He knows a few simple skills, and he carries them around the Ringworld as he travels to spinward."

"How much information can he carry? He can't be too intelligent."

"No, he's not." From the way she said it, it didn't matter. "But if I travel with him I can teach a great many people a great deal."

"I knew that was coming," said Louis. But it still hurt. Did she know that it hurt? She wouldn't look at him. "We'd been in the mall a day or so before I realized that you'd follow my flycycle, not me. He'd told me about Hal—Hal—about the goddess and the floating tower that trapped cars. So we went there.

"We stayed near the altar, waiting to spot your flycycles. Then the building started to fall apart. Afterward, Seeker—"

"Seeker?"

"He calls himself that. When someone asks him why, he can explain that he's on his way to the base of the Arch, and tell them about his adventures on the way . . . you see?"

"Yah."

"He started trying the motors in all the old cars. He said that the drivers used to turn off their motors when they were caught by the traffic police field, so that their motors wouldn't be burned out."

Louis and Speaker and Nessus looked at each other. Half those floating cars may have been still active!

"We found a car that worked," said Teela. "We were chasing you, but we must have missed you in the dark. But luckily the traffic police field caught us for speeding."

"Luckily. I think I heard the sonic boom last night, but I'm not sure," said Louis.

Seeker had stopped talking. He rested comfortably against the wall of the governor's bedroom, gazing at Speaker-To-Animals with a half-smile. Speaker held his eye. Louis had the impression that they were each wondering what it would be like to fight the other.

But Prill looked out the bay window, and on her face was dread. When the wind's howl became a shriek, she shuddered.

Perhaps she had seen formations like the Eye storm. Small asteroid punctures, quickly repaired, always occurring somewhere else; but always photographed for the newstapes or their Ringworld equivalent. Always a thing of fear, the Eye storm. Breathing-air roaring away into interstellar space. A hurricane on its side, with a drain at its bottom as final as the drain in a bathtub, if you should happen to be caught in its suction.

The wind howled momentarily louder. Teela's brows puckered with concern. "I hope the building's massive enough," she said.

Louis was astonished. *How she's changed!* But the Eye storm had threatened her directly, the last time through . . .

"I need your help," she said. "I want Seeker, you know."

"Yah."

"He wants me, too, but he's got a weird sense of honor. I tried to tell him about you, Louis, when I had to get

him to the floating building. He got very uncomfortable
and stopped sleeping with me. He thinks you own me,
Louis."

"Slavery?"

"Slavery for women, I think. You'll tell him you don't
own me, won't you?"

Louis felt pain in his throat. "It might save explana-
tions if I just sold you to him. If that's what you want."

"You're right. And it is. I want to travel around the
Ringworld with him. I love him, Louis."

"Sure you do. You were made for each other," said
Louis Wu. "It was fated that you should meet. The hundred billion couples who have felt exactly that way about
each other—"

She was looking at him very doubtfully. "You're not
being . . . sarcastic, are you, Louis?"

"A month ago you didn't know sarcasm from a glass
transistor. No, the weird thing is, I'm not being sarcastic.
The hundred billion couples don't matter, because they
weren't part of a there-ain't-no-justice puppeteer's planned
breeding experiment."

Suddenly he had everybody's complete attention. Even
Seeker stared at him to find out what everyone was looking at.

But Louis had eyes only for Teela Brown.

"We crashed on the Ringworld," he said gently, "because the Ringworld is your ideal environment. You
needed to learn things you couldn't learn on Earth, or
anywhere in known space, apparently. Maybe there were
other reasons—a better boosterspice, for instance, and
more room to breathe—but the major reason you're here
is to learn."

"To learn what?"

"Pain, apparently. Fear. Loss. You're a different woman
since you came here. Before, you were a kind of . . .
abstraction. Have you ever stubbed your toe?"

"What a funny word. I don't think so."

"Have you ever burned your foot?"

She glared at him. She remembered.

"The *Liar* crashed to bring you here. We traveled a

couple of hundred thousand miles to bring you to Seeker. Your flycycle carried you precisely over him, and ran into the traffic police field at just that point, because Seeker is the man you were born to love."

Teela smiled at this, but Louis did not smile back. He said, "Your luck required that you have time to get to know him. Therefore Speaker-To-Animals and I hung head down—"

"Louis!"

"—over ninety feet of empty space for something like twenty hours. But there's worse."

The kzin rumbled, "It depends on your viewpoint."

Louis ignored him. "Teela, you fell in love with me because it gave you a motive to join the expedition to the Ringworld. You no longer love me because you don't need to. You're *here*. And I loved you for the same reason, because the luck of Teela Brown used me as a puppet—

"But the real puppet is you. You'll dance to the strings of your own luck for the rest of your life. Finagle knows if you've got free will. You'll have trouble enough using it."

Teela was very pale, and her shoulders were very straight and rigid. If she wasn't crying, it was by an obvious exercise of self-control. She had not had that self-control before.

As for Seeker, he knelt watching the two of them, and he ran his thumb along the edge of the black iron sword. He could hardly be unaware that Teela was being made unhappy. He must still think she belonged to Louis Wu.

And Louis turned to the puppeteer. He was not surprised that Nessus had curled into a ball, tucked his heads into his belly, and withdrawn from the universe.

Louis took the puppeteer by the ankle of his hind leg. He found that he could roll the puppeteer onto his back with little trouble. Nessus weighed not much more than Louis Wu.

And he didn't like it. The ankle trembled in Louis's hand.

"You caused all this," said Louis Wu, "with your mon-

strous egotism. That egotism bothers me almost as much
as the monstrous mistake you made. How you could be
so powerful, and so determined, and so stupid, is beyond
me. Do you realize yet, that everything that's happened
to us here has been a side effect of Teela's luck?"

The ball that was Nessus contracted tighter. Seeker
watched in fascination.

"Then you can go home to the puppeteer worlds and
tell them that mucking with human breeding habits is a
chancy business. Tell them that enough Teela Browns
could make a hash of all the laws of probability. Even
basic physics is nothing more than probability at the atomic level. Tell them the universe is too complicated a toy
for a sensibly cautious being to play with.

"Tell them that after I get you home," said Louis Wu.
"But meanwhile, roll out of there, *now*. I need the shadow
square wire, and you've got to find it for me. We're almost
past the Eye storm. Come out of there, Nessus—"

The puppeteer unrolled and stood up. "You shame me,
Louis," he began.

"You dare say that here?"

The puppeteer was silent. Presently he turned to the
bay window and looked out at the storm.

CHAPTER 23

The God Gambit

For the natives who worshipped Heaven, there were now
two towers in the sky.

As before, the square of the altar swarmed with faces
like golden dandelions. "We came on another holy day,"
said Louis. He tried to find the shaven choir leader, but
couldn't.

Nessus was looking wistfully across at the tower called
Heaven. The bridge room of the *Improbable* was level
with the castle's map room. "Once I had not the opportunity to explore this place. Now I cannot reach it,"
the puppeteer mourned.

Speaker suggested, "We can break in with the disintegrator tool and lower you by rope or ladder."

"Again this chance must slip by me."

"It is not as dangerous as many things you have done
here."

"But when I took risks here, I sought knowledge. Now
I have as much knowledge of the Ringworld as my world
needs. If I risk my life now it will be to return home with
that knowledge. Louis, there is your shadow square wire."

Louis nodded soberly.

Across the spinward section of the city lay a cloud of
black smoke. By the way it hugged itself tight against the
cityscape, it must have been both dense and heavy. One
windowed obelisque near the center poked through the
mass. The rest was smothered.

It had to be shadow square wire. But there was so
much of it!

"But how can we transport *that?*"

Louis could only say, "I can't imagine. Let's go down for a closer look."

They settled their broken police building to spinward of the place of the altar.

Nessus did not turn off the lifting motors. He barely touched down. What had been an observation platform above prison cells became the *Improbable's* landing ramp. The mass of the building would have crushed it.

"We're going to have to find a way to handle the stuff," said Louis. "A glove made of the same kind of thread might do it. Or we could wind it on a spool made of Ringworld foundation material."

"We have neither. We must talk to the natives," said Speaker. "They may have old legends, old tools, old holy relics. More, they have had three days to learn how to deal with the wire."

"Then I must come with you." The puppeteer's reluctance was evident in his sudden fit of shivering. "Speaker, your command of the language is inadequate. We must leave Halrloprillalar to lift the building if there is need. Unless—Louis, could Teela's native lover be persuaded to bargain for us?"

It itched Louis to hear Seeker referred to in such terms. He said, "Even Teela won't call him a genius. I wouldn't trust him to do our bargaining."

"Nor would I. Louis, do we really need the shadow square wire?"

"I don't *know*. If I'm not spinning drug dreams, then we need it. Otherwise—"

"Never mind, Louis. I will go."

"You don't *have* to trust my judgment—"

"I will go." The puppeteer was shivering again. The oddest thing about Nessus's voice was that it could be so clear, so precise, yet never show a trace of emotion. "I know that we need the wire. What coincidence caused the wire to fall so neatly across our path? All coincidence leads back to Teela Brown. If we did not need the wire, it would not be here."

Louis relaxed. Not because the statement made sense, for it did not. But it reinforced Louis's own tenuous conclusions. And so Louis hugged that comfort to his bosom and did not tell the puppeteer what nonsense he was talking.

They filed down the landing ramp and out from under the shadow of the *Improbable*. Louis carried a flashlight-laser. Speaker-To-Animals carried the Slaver weapon. His muscles moved like fluid as he walked; they showed prominently through his half-inch of new orange fur. Nessus went apparently unarmed. He preferred the tasp, and the hindmost position.

Seeker walked to the side, carrying his black iron sword at the ready. His big, heavily calloused feet were bare, and so was the rest of him but for the yellow skin he wore for a loincloth. His muscles rippled like the kzin's.

Teela walked unarmed.

These two would have been waiting aboard the *Improbable* but for the bargaining that had taken place that morning. It was Nessus' fault. Louis had used the puppeteer as his interpreter when he offered to sell Teela Brown to the swordsman Seeker.

Seeker had nodded gravely, and had offered one capsule of the Ringworld youth drug, worth about fifty years of life.

"I'll take it," Louis had said. It was a handsome offer, although Louis had no intention of putting the stuff in his mouth. Certainly the drug had never been tested on anyone who, like Louis Wu, had been taking boosterspice for some one hundred and seventy years.

As Nessus afterward explained in the Interworld tongue, "I didn't want to insult him, Louis, or to imply that you held Teela cheaply. I raised his price. He now owns Teela, and you have the capsule to analyze when and if we return to Earth. In addition, Seeker will act as our bodyguard against any possible enemy, until we have possession of the shadow square wire."

"He's going to protect us all with his four-foot kitchen knife?"

"It was only to flatter him, Louis."

Teela had insisted on coming with him, of course. He was her man, and he was going into danger. Now Louis wondered if the puppeteer had counted on that. Teela was Nessus' own carefully bred good luck charm . . .

The sky would always be overcast this close to the Eye storm. In the gray-white noon light they filed toward a vertical black cloud tens of stories high.

"Don't touch it," Louis called, remembering what the priest had told him on his last visit to this city. A girl had lost some fingers trying to pick up the shadow square wire.

Close up, it still loooked like black smoke. You could look through it into the ruined city, to see the windowed beehive-bungalows of suburbia and a few flat glass towers that would have been department stores if this were a world of human space. They were there within the cloud, as if a fire were raging in there somewhere.

You could see the black thread, if your eye was within an inch of it; but then your eye would water and the thread would disappear. The thread was that close to being invisibly thin. It was much too much like Sinclair monofilament; and Sinclair monofilament was *dangerous*.

"Try the Slaver gun," said Louis. "See if you can cut it, Speaker."

A string of sparkling lights appeared within the cloud. Probably it was blasphemy. *You fight with light?* But the natives must have planned to destroy the strangers much earlier. When the Christmas lights appeared within the cloud of black thread, maniac shrieks answered from all directions. Men robed in particolored blankets poured from the buildings around, screaming and waving . . . swords and clubs?

The poor leucos, thought Louis. He flicked his flash-light-laser beam to high and narrow.

Light-swords, laser weapons, had been used on all the worlds. Louis's training was a century old, and the war he had trained for hadn't happened after all. But the rules were too simple to forget.

The slower the swing, the deeper the cut.

But Louis swung his beam in wide quick swipes. Men stumbled back, their arms wrapped around their abdomens, their golden fur faces betraying nothing. *With many enemies, swing fast. Cut half an inch deep, cut many of them. Slow them down!*

Louis felt pity. The fanatics had only swords and clubs. They hadn't a chance . . .

But one smashed a sword across Speaker's weapon arm, hard enough to cut. Speaker dropped the Slaver weapon. Another man snatched it and threw it. He was dead in the instant, for Speaker swiped at him with his good hand and clawed the spine out of him. A third man caught the weapon, turned, and ran. He didn't try to use it. He just ran with it. Louis couldn't hit him with the laser; they were trying to kill *him*.

Always swing across the torso.

Louis had killed nobody as yet. Now, while the enemy seemed to hesitate, Louis took a moment to kill the two men nearest him. *Don't let the enemy close.*

How were the others doing?

Speaker-To-Animals was killing with his hands, his good hand a claw for ripping, his bandaged one a weighted club. Somehow he could dodge a sword point while reaching for the man behind it. He was surrounded, but the natives would not press him. He was alien orange death, eight feet tall, with pointed teeth.

Seeker stood at bay with his black iron sword. Three men were down before him, and others stood back, and the sword dripped. Seeker was a dangerous, skillful swordsman. The natives *knew* about swords. Teela stood behind him, safe for the moment in the ring of fighting, looking worried, like a good heroine.

Nessus was running for the *Improbable*, one head held low and forward, one high. Low to see around corners, high for the long view.

Louis was unharmed, picking off enemies as they showed themselves, helping others when he could. The flashlight-laser moved easily in his hand, a wand of killing green light.

Never aim at a mirror. Reflecting armor could be a nasty shock to a laser artist. Here they'd apparently forgotten that trick.

A man dressed in a green blanket charged at Louis Wu, screaming, waving a heavy hammer, doing his best to look dangerous. A golden dandelion with eyes . . . Louis slashed green laser light across him, *and the man kept coming*.

Louis, terrified, stood fast and held the beam centered. The man was swinging at Louis's head when a spot on his robe charred, darkened, then flashed green flame. He fell skidding, drilled through the heart.

Clothing the color of your light-sword can be as bad as reflecting armor. Finagle grant that there be no more of those! Louis touched green light to the back of a man's neck . . .

A native blocked Nessus' flight path. He must have had courage to attack so weird a monster. Louis couldn't get a clear shot, but the man died anyway, for Nessus spun and kicked and finished the turn and ran on. Then—

Louis saw it happen. The puppeteer charged into an intersection, one head held high, one low. The high head was suddenly loose and rolling, bouncing. Nessus stopped, turned, then stood still.

His neck ended in a flat stump, and the stump was pumping blood as red as Louis' own.

Nessus wailed, a high, mournful sound.

The natives had trapped him with shadow square wire.

Louis was two hundred years old. He had lost friends before this. He continued to fight, his light-sword following his eyes almost by reflex. *Poor Nessus. But it could be* me *next* . . .

The natives had fallen back. Their losses must have been terrifying from their own viewpoint.

Teela stared at the dying puppeteer, her eyes very big, her knuckles pressed against her teeth. Speaker and Seeker were edging back toward the *Improbable*—

Wait a minute. He's got a spare!

Louis ran at the puppeteer. As he passed Speaker, the kzin snatched the flashlight-laser from him. Louis ducked to avoid the wire trap, stayed low, and used a shoulder block to knock Nessus on his side. It had seemed that the puppeteer was about to start panic running.

Louis pinned the puppeteer and fumbled for a belt.

He wasn't wearing a belt.

But he *had* to have a belt!

And Teela handed him her scarf!

Louis snatched it, looped it, dropped it over the puppeteer's severed neck. Nessus had been staring in horror at the stump, at the blood pumping from the single carotid artery. Now he raised his eye to Louis's face; and the eye closed, and he fainted.

Louis pulled the knot tight. Teela's scarf constricted and closed the single artery, two major veins, the larynx, the gullet, everything.

You tied a tourniquet around his neck, *doctor?* But the blood had stopped.

Louis bent and lifted the puppeteer in a fireman's carry, turned, and ran into the shadow of the broken police building. Seeker ran ahead of him, covering him, his black sword's point tracing little circles as he sought an enemy. Armed natives watched but did not challenge them.

Teela followed Louis. Speaker-To-Animals came last, his flashlight-laser stabbing green lines where men might be hiding. At the ramp the kzin stopped, waited until Teela was safely up the ramp, then—Louis glimpsed him moving away.

But why did he do that?

No time to find out. Louis went up the stairs. The puppeteer became incredibly heavy before Louis reached the bridge. He dropped Nessus beside the buried flycycle, reached for the first aid kit, rubbed the diagnostic patch onto the puppeteer's neck below the tourniquet. The puppeteer's first aid kit was still attached to the 'cycle by an umbilicus, and Louis rightly surmised that it was more complex than his own.

Presently the kitchen controls changed settings all by themselves. A few seconds later, a line snaked out of the dashboard and touched the puppeteer's neck, hunted over the skin, found a spot and sank in.

Louis shuddered. But—intravenous feeding. Nessus must be still alive.

The *Improbable* was aloft, though he had not felt the takeoff. Speaker was sitting on the bottom step above the landing ramp, looking down at the Heaven tower. He was cradling something carefully in both hands.

He asked, "Is the puppeteer dead?"

"No. He's lost a lot of blood." Louis sank down beside the kzin. He was bone-weary and terribly depressed. "Do puppeteers go into shock?"

"How would I know that? Shock itself is an odd mechanism. We needed centuries of study to know why you humans died so easily under torture." The kzin was clearly concentrating on something else. But he asked, "Was it the luck of Teela Brown?"

"I think so," said Louis.

"Why? How can the puppeteer's injury help Teela?"

"You'd have to see her through my eyes," said Louis. "She was very one-sided when I first met her. Like, well . . ."

The phrase he'd used sparked a memory, and he said, "There was a girl in a story. The hero was middle-aged and very cynical, and he went looking for her because of the myth about her.

"And when he found her he still wasn't sure that the myth was true. Not until she turned her back. Then he saw that from behind she was empty: she was the mask of a girl, a flexible mask for the whole front of a girl instead of just for a face. She couldn't be *hurt*, Speaker. That was what this man wanted. The women in his life kept getting *hurt*, and he kept thinking it was him, and finally he couldn't stand it any more."

"I understand none of this, Louis."

"Teela was like the mask of a girl when she came here. She'd never been hurt. Her personality wasn't human."

"Why is that bad?"

"Because she was designed human, before Nessus made her something else. Tanj him! Do you see what he did?

He created god in his own image, his own idealized image, and he got Teela Brown.

"She's just what any puppeteer would give his soul to be. She can't be injured. She can't even be uncomfortable, unless it's for her own benefit.

"That's why she came here. The Ringworld is a lucky place for her to be, because it gives her the range of experience to become fully human. I doubt the Birthright Lotteries produced many like her. They'd have had the same luck. They'd have been aboard the *Liar*, except that Teela was luckier than any of them.

"Still . . . there must be scores of Teela Browns left on Earth! The future is going to look somewhat peculiar when they start to learn their power. The rest of us will have to learn to get out of the way quick."

Speaker asked, "What of the leaf-eater's head?"

"She can't sympathize with someone else's pain," said Louis. "Maybe she needed to see a good friend hurt. Teela's luck wouldn't care what that cost Nessus.

"Do you know where I got the tourniquet? Teela saw what I needed and found something that would serve. It's probably the first time in her life she's functioned right in an emergency."

"Why would she need to do so? Her luck should protect her from emergencies."

"She's never known that she *can* function in an emergency. She's never had that much reason for self-confidence. It's never been true before, either."

"Truly, I do not understand."

"Finding your limits is a part of growing up. Teela couldn't grow up, couldn't become an adult, without facing some kind of physical emergency."

"It must be a very human thing," said Speaker.

Louis interpreted the comment as an admission of total confusion. He did not attempt to answer.

The kzin added, "I wondered if we should have parked the *Improbable* higher than the tower the natives call Heaven. They may have considered it blasphemy. But such considerations seem futile, while the luck of Teela Brown governs events."

Louis still hadn't seen what the kzin was holding so protectively. "Did you go back for the head? If you did, you wasted your time. We can't possibly freeze it cold enough, soon enough."

"No, Louis." Speaker produced a fist-sized thing the shape of a child's top. "Do not touch it. You might lose fingers."

"Fingers? *Oh.*" The pointed end of the teardrop-shaped thing tapered into a spike; and the point of the spike became the black thread that linked the shadow squares.

"I knew that the natives could manipulate the thread," said Speaker. "They must have done so, to string the trap that caught Nessus. I went back to see how they had done it.

"They had found one of the endpoints. I surmise that the other end is simple wire; that the wire broke in the middle when we rammed it with the *Liar,* but that this end tore loose from a socket on one of the shadow squares. We were lucky to get even one end."

"Too right. We can trail it behind us. The wire shouldn't get hung up on anything we can't cut through."

"Where do we go from here, Louis?"

"Starboard. Back to the *Liar.*"

"Of course, Louis. We must return Nessus to the *Liar's* medical facilities. And then?"

"We'll see."

He left Speaker guarding the teardrop-shaped handle, while he went up for what was left of the electrosetting plastic. They used a double handful of the stuff to stick the handle to a wall—and then there wasn't any way to run a current. The Slaver weapon could have served, but it had been lost. It was a frustrating emergency. until Louis found that the battery in his lighter would run enough current through the plastic to set it.

That left the wire end of the teardrop exposed and pointing to port.

"I remember the bridge room as facing starboard," said Speaker. "If not, we must do it over. The wire must trail behind us."

"It might work," said Louis. He wasn't at all sure . . . but they certainly couldn't carry the wire. They would simply have to trail it behind them. It probably wouldn't get hung up on anything it couldn't cut through.

They found Teela and Seeker in the engine room with Prill, who was working the lifting motors.

"We're going in different directions," Teela said bluntly. "This woman says she can edge us up against the floating castle. We should be able to walk through a window straight across into the banquet hall."

"Then what? You'll be marooned, unless you can get control of the castle's lifting motors."

"Seeker says he has some knowledge of magic. I'm sure he'll work it out."

Louis would not try to talk her out of it. He was afraid to thwart Teela Brown, as he would not have tried to stop a charging bandersnatch with his bare hands. He said, "If you have any trouble figuring out the controls, just start pulling and pushing things at random."

"I'll remember," she smiled. Then, more soberly, "Take good care of Nessus."

When Seeker and Teela debarked from the *Improbable* twenty minutes later, it was with no more goodbye than that. Louis had thought of things to say, but had not said them. What could he tell her of her own power? She would have to learn by trial and error, while the luck itself kept her alive.

Over the next few hours the puppeteer's body cooled and became as dead. The lights on the first aid kit remained active, if incomprehensible. Presumably the puppeteer was in some form of suspended animation.

As the *Improbable* moved away to starboard the shadow square thread trailed behind, alternately taut and slack. Ancient buildings toppled in the city, cut through scores of times by tangled thread. But the knob stayed put in its bed of electrosetting plastic.

The city of the floating castle could not drop below

the horizon. In the next few days it became tiny, then vague, then invisible.

Prill sat by Nessus's side, unable to help him, unwilling to leave him. Visibly, she suffered.

"We've got to do something for her," said Louis. "She's hooked on the tasp, and now it's gone and she's got to go it cold turkey. If she doesn't kill herself, she's likely to kill Nessus or me!"

"Louis, you surely don't want advice from *me*."

"No. No, I guess not."

To help a suffering human being, one plays good listener. Louis tried it; but he didn't have the language for it, and Prill didn't want to talk. He gritted his teeth when he was alone; but when he was with Prill he kept trying.

She was always before his eyes. His conscience might have healed if he could have stayed away from her, but she would not leave the bridge.

Gradually he was learning the language, and gradually Prill was beginning to talk. He tried to tell her about Teela, and Nessus, and playing god—

"I did think I was a god," she said. "I did. Why did I think so? I did not build the Ring. The Ring is much older than I."

Prill was learning too. She talked a pidgin, a simplified vocabulary of her obsolete language: two tenses, virtually no modifiers, exaggerated pronunciation.

"They told you so," said Louis.

"But I *knew*."

"Everyone *wants* to be god." Wants the power without the responsibility; but Louis didn't know those words.

"Then he came. Two Heads. He had machine?"

"He had tasp machine."

"Tasp," she said carefully. "I had to guess that. Tasp made him god. He lost tasp, not god any more. Is Two Heads dead?"

It was hard to tell. "He would think it stupid to be dead," said Louis.

"Stupid to get head cut off," said Prill. A joke. She'd tried to make a joke.

Prill began to take an interest in other things: sex and language lessons and the Ringworld landscape. They ran across a sprinkling of sunflowers. Prill had never seen one. Dodging the plants' frantic attempts to ray them down, they dug up a foot-high bloom and replanted it on the roof of the building. Afterward they turned hard to spinward to avoid denser sunflower concentrations.

When they ran out of food, Prill lost interest in the puppeteer. Louis pronounced her cured.

Speaker and Prill tried the God Gambit in the next native village. Louis waited apprehensively above them, hoping Speaker could carry it off, wanting to shave his head and join them. But his value as an acolyte was nil. After days of practice, he still had little facility with the language.

They came back with offerings. Food.

As days became weeks, they did it again and again. They were good at it. Speaker's fur grew longer, so that once again he was an orange fur panther, "a kind of war god." On Louis's advice he kept his ears folded flat to his head.

Being a god affected Speaker oddly. One night he spoke of it.

"It does not disturb me to play a god," he said. "It disturbs me to play a god badly."

"What do you mean?"

"They ask us questions, Louis. The women ask questions of Prill, and these she answers; and generally I can understand neither the problem nor the solution. The men should question Prill too, for Prill is human and I am not. But they question me. Me! Why must they ask an alien for help in running their affairs?"

"You're a male. A god is a kind of symbol," said Louis, "even when he's real. You're a male symbol."

"Ridiculous. I do not even have external genitalia, as I assume you do."

"You're big and impressive and dangerous-looking. That automatically makes you a virility symbol. I don't think you could lose that aspect without losing your godhood entirely."

"What we need is a sound pickup, so that you can answer odd and embarrassing questions for me."

Prill surprised them. The *Improbable* had been a police station. In one of the storerooms Prill found a police multiple intercom set with batteries that charged off the building's power supply. When they finished, two of the six sets were working again.

"You're smarter than I guessed," Louis told Prill that night. He hesitated then; but he didn't know enough of the language to be tactful. "Smarter than a ship's whore ought to be."

Prill laughed. "You foolish child! You have told me yourself that your ships move very quickly next to ours."

"They do," said Louis. "They move faster than light."

"I think you improve the tale," she laughed. "Our theory says that this cannot be."

"Maybe we use different theories."

She seemed taken aback. Louis had learned to read her involuntary muscle movements rather than her virtually blank face. But she said, "Boredom can be dangerous when a ship takes years to cross between worlds. The ways to amuse must be many and all different. To be a ship's whore needs knowledge of medicine of mind and body, plus love of many men, plus a rare ability to converse. We must know something of the working of the ship, so that we will not cause accidents. We must be healthy. By rule of guild we must learn to play a musical instrument."

Louis gaped. Prill laughed musically, and touched him *here* and *there* . . .

The intercom system worked beautifully, despite the fact that the ear plugs were designed for human rather than kzinti ears. Louis developed an ability to think on his feet, operating as the man behind the war god. When he made mistakes, he could tell himself that the *Improbable* was still faster than the maximum rate of travel of news on the Ringworld. Every contact was a first contact.

Months passed.

The land was slowly rising, slowly becoming barren.

Fist-of-God was visible by daylight, and growing larger every day. The routine had settled into Louis's thinking. It took him some time to realize what was happening.

It was broad daylight when he went to Prill. "There's something you should know," he said. "Do you know about induced current?" And he explained what he meant.

Then, "Very small electrical currents can be applied to a brain, to produce pleasure or pain directly." He explained that.

And finally, "This is how a tasp works."

That had taken about twenty minutes. Prill said, "I knew that he had a machine. Why describe it now?"

"We're leaving civilization. We won't find many more villages, or even food sources, until we reach our spacecraft. I wanted you to know about the tasp before you decided anything."

"Decided what?"

"Shall we let you off at the next village? Or would you like to ride with us to the *Liar,* then take the *Improbable?* We can give you food there too."

"There is room for me aboard the *Liar,*" she said with assurance.

"Sure, but—"

"I am sick of savages. I want to go to civilization."

"You might have trouble learning our ways. For one thing, they grow hair like mine." Louis's hair had grown out long and thick. He had cut the queue. "You'll need a wig."

Prill made a face. "I can adjust." She laughed suddenly. "Would you ride home alone, without me? The big orange one cannot substitute for a woman."

"That's the one argument that always works."

"I can help your world, Louis. Your people know little about sex."

Which statement Louis prudently let slide.

CHAPTER 24

Fist-of-God

The land grew dry and the air grew thin. Fist-of-God seemed to flee before them. The fruit was gone, and the meat supply was dwindling. This was the barren upward slope that culminated in Fist-of-God itself, a desert Louis had once estimated was larger than the Earth.

Wind whistled around the edges and corners of the *Improbable*. By now they were almost directly to spinward of the great mountain. The Arch glowed blue and sharp-edged, the stars were hard, vivid points.

Speaker looked upward through the big bay window. "Louis, can you locate the galactic core from here?"

"What for? We know where we are."

"Do it anyway."

Louis had tentatively identified some stars, had guessed at certain distorted constellations, in the months he had spent beneath this sky. "There, I think. Behind the Arch."

"Just so. The galactic core lies in the plane of the Ringworld."

"I said that."

"Remember that the Ringworld foundation material will stop neutrinos, Louis. Presumably it will stop other sub-atomic particles." The kzin was plainly getting at something.

". . . That's right. The Ringworld is immune to the Core explosion! When did you figure this out?"

"Just now. I had placed the Core some time ago."

"You'd get some scattering. Heavy radiation around the rim walls."

"But the luck of Teela Brown would place her away from the rim walls when the wave front arrives."

"Twenty thousand years . . ." Louis was appalled. "Finagle's bright smile! How can anyone think in such terms?"

"Sickness and death are always bad luck, Louis. By our assumptions, Teela Brown should live forever."

"But . . . right. *She's* not thinking in those terms. It's her luck, hovering over us all like a puppet master . . ."

Nessus had been a corpse at room temperature for two months now. He did not decay. The lights on his first aid kit remained alight, and even changed on occasion. It was his only sign of life.

Louis was gazing at the puppeteer, minutes later, when two thoughts rubbed together. "Puppeteer," he said softly.

"Louis?"

"I just wondered if the puppeteers didn't get their name by playing god with the species around them. They've treated humans and kzinti like puppets; there's no denying that."

"But Teela's luck made a puppet of Nessus."

"We've all been playing god at various levels." Louis nodded at Prill, who was catching perhaps every third word. "Prill and you and me. How did it feel, Speaker? Were you a good god or a bad one?"

"I cannot know. The species was not my own, though I have studied humans extensively. I stopped a war, you will remember. I pointed out to each side that it must lose. That had been three weeks ago."

"Yah. My idea."

"Of course."

"Now you'll have to play god again. To kzinti," said Louis.

"I do not understand."

"Nessus and the other puppeteers have been playing planned breeding games on humans and kzinti. They deliberately brought about a situation in which natural selection would favor a peaceable kzin. Right?"

"Yes."

"What would happen if the Patriarchy learned of this?"

"War," said the kzin. "A heavily provisioned fleet would attack the puppeteer worlds after a two-year flight. Perhaps humanity would join us. Surely the puppeteers have insulted you as badly."

"Surely they have. And then?"

"Then the leaf-eaters would exterminate my species down to the last kitten. Louis, I do not intend to tell anybody anything concerning starseed lures and puppeteer breeding plans. Can I persuade you to keep silence?"

"Right."

"Is this what you meant by playing god to my species?"

"That, and one more thing," said Louis. "The *Long Shot*. Do you still want to steal it?"

"Perhaps," said the kzin.

"You can't do it," said Louis. "But let's assume you could. Then what?"

"Then the Patriarchy would have the second quantum hyperdrive."

"And?"

Prill seemed to be aware that something crucial was happening. She watched them as if ready to stop a fight.

"Soon we would have warships capable of crossing a light year in one-and-one-quarter minutes. We would dominate known space, enslave every species within our reach."

"And then?"

"Then it ends. This is precisely our ambition, Louis."

"No. You'd keep conquering. With a drive that good, you'd move outward in all directions, spreading thin, taking every world you found. You'd conquer more than you could hold . . . and in all that expanded space you'd find something *really* dangerous. The puppeteer fleet. Another Ringworld, but at the height of its power. Another Slaver race just starting its expansion. Bandersnatchi with hands, grogs with feet, kdatlyno with guns."

"Scare images."

"You've seen the Ringworld. You've seen the puppeteer worlds. There must be more, in the space you could reach with the puppeteer hyperdrive."

The kzin was silent.

"Take your time," said Louis. "Think it through. You can't take the *Long Shot* anyway. You'd kill us all if you tried it."

The next day the *Improbable* crossed a long, straight meteoric furrow. They turned to antispinward, directly toward Fist-of-God.

Fist-of-God Mountain had grown large without coming near. Bigger than any asteroid, roughly conical, she had the look of a snow-capped mountain swollen to nightmare size. The nightmare continued, for Fist-of-God continued to swell.

"I don't understand," said Prill. She was puzzled and upset. "This formation is not known to me. Why was it built? At the rim there are mountains as high, as decorative, and more useful, for they hold back the air."

"That's what I thought," Louis Wu said. And he would say no more.

That day they saw a small glass bottle resting at the end of the meteoric gouge they had been following.

The *Liar* was as they had left it: on its back on a frictionless surface. Mentally Louis postponed the celebration. They were not home yet.

In the end Prill had to hover the *Improbable* so that Louis could cross from the landing ramp. He found controls that would open both doors of the airlock at the same time. But air murmured out around them all the time they were transferring Nessus' body. They could not reduce the cabin pressure without Nessus, and Nessus was, to all appearances, dead.

But they got him into the autodoc anyway. It was a puppeteer-shaped coffin, form-fitted to Nessus himself, and bulky. Puppeteer surgeons and mechanics must have intended that it should handle any conceivable circumstance. But had they thought of decapitation?

They had. There were two heads in there, and two more with necks attached, and enough organs and body parts to make several complete puppeteers. Grown from Nessus himself, probably; the faces on the heads looked familiar.

Prill came aboard, and landed on her head. Rarely had

Louis seen anyone so startled. He had never thought to tell her about induced gravity. Her face showed nothing as she stood up, but her posture— She was awed to silence.

In that ghostly silence of homecoming, Louis Wu suddenly screamed like a banshee.

"Coffeeee!" he yelled. And, "Hot water!" He charged into the stateroom he had shared with Teela Brown. A moment later he put his head out and screamed, "Prill!"

Prill went.

She hated coffee. She thought Louis must be insane to swallow the bitter stuff, and she told him so.

The shower was a long lost, badly missed luxury, once Louis explained the controls.

She went wild over the sleeping plates.

Speaker was celebrating the homecoming in his own fashion. Louis didn't know everything about the kzin's stateroom. He did know that the kzin was eating his head off.

"Meat!" Speaker exulted. "I was not happy eating long-dead meat."

"That stuff you're eating now is reconstituted."

"Yes, but it tastes freshly killed!"

That night Prill retired to a couch in the lounge. She appreciated the sleeping field, but not for sleeping. But Louis Wu slept in free fall for the first time in three months.

He slept ten hours, and woke feeling like a tiger. A half-disc of sun flamed beneath his feet.

Back aboard the *Improbable,* he used the flashlight-laser to free the knobbed end of the shadow square. When he finished, it still had some fused electrosetting plastic attached.

He did not try to carry it to the *Liar.* The black thread was far too dangerous, the Ring floor far too slippery. Louis moved on all fours on the frictionless surface, and he pulled the knob behind him.

He found Speaker silently watching from the airlock. Louis entered the airlock via Prill's stepladder, pushed past the kzin and went aft. Speaker continued to watch.

The farthest point aft in the wreck of the *Liar* was a channel the size of a man's thigh. It had passed wiring to machinery in the *Liar's* wing, when the *Liar* had had a wing. Now it was sealed by a metal hatch. Louis opened the hatch, tossed the knobbed end of the wire through and outside.

He moved forward. At intervals he checked the position of the wire by using it to slice a Jinxian sausage dialed from the *Liar's* kitchen. Then he marked the spot with bright yellow paint. When he finished, the path of the virtually invisible thread was marked in a line of yellow splotches running through the *Liar*.

When the wire drew taut, it would certainly cut through some internal partitions of the ship. The yellow paint allowed Louis to gauge the path it would take, and to assure himself that the wire would not damage any part of the life-support system. But the paint had another purpose. It would warn them all to keep away from the wire, lest they lose fingers or worse.

Louis left the airlock, waited for Speaker to follow him out. Then he closed the outer door.

At this point Speaker asked, "Is this why we came?"

"Tell you in a minute," said Louis. He walked aft along the General Products hull, picked up the knob in both hands, and tugged gently. The wire held.

He put his back into it. He pulled with all his strength. The wire did not budge. The airlock door held it fast.

"There's just no way to give it a stronger test. I wasn't sure the airlock door would be a close enough fit. I wasn't sure the wire wouldn't abrade a General Products hull. I'm still not sure. But yes, this is why we came."

"What shall we do next?"

"We open the airlock door." He did it. "We let the thread slide freely through the *Liar* while we carry the handle back to the *Improbable* and cement it in place." And they did that.

The thread that had linked the shadow squares trailed invisibly away to starboard. It had been dragged for thousands of miles behind the *Improbable*, because there was no way to get it aboard the flying building. Perhaps it trailed all the way back to the tangle of thread in the City Beneath Heaven; a tangle like a cloud of smoke, that might have held millions of miles of the stuff.

Now it entered the *Liar's* double airlock, circled through the *Liar's* fuselage, out the wiring channel, and back to a blob of electrosetting plastic on the underside of the flying building.

"So far so good," said Louis. "Now I'll need Prill. No, tanj it! I forgot. Prill doesn't have a pressure suit."

"A pressure suit?"

"We're taking the *Improbable* up Fist-of-God Mountain. The building isn't airtight. We'll need pressure suits, and Prill doesn't have one. We'll have to leave her here."

"Up Fist-of-God Mountain," Speaker repeated. "Louis, one flycycle has not the power to drag the *Liar* up that slope. You propose to burden the motor with the additional mass of a floating building."

"No, no, no. I don't want to drag the *Liar*. All I want to do is pull the shadow square wire behind us. It should slide freely through the *Liar,* unless I give Prill the word to close the airlock door."

Speaker thought about it. "That should work, Louis. If the puppeteer's flycycle has not the power we need, we can cut away chunks of the building to make it lighter. But why? What do you expect to find at the top?"

"I could tell you in one word; and then you'd laugh in my face. Speaker, if I'm wrong, I swear you'll never know," said Louis Wu.

And he thought: *I'll have to tell Prill what to do. And plug the* Liar's *wiring channel with plastic. It won't stop the thread from sliding, but it should make the* Liar *nearly airtight.*

The *Improbable* was not a spaceship. Her lifting power was electromagnetic, thrusting against the Ring foundation itself. And the Ring floor sloped up toward Fist-of-God; for Fist-of-God was hollow. Naturally the *Improbable* tended to tilt, to slide back down against the push of the puppeteer's flycycle.

To that problem, Speaker had already found the answer.

They were living in pressure suits before the journey had properly begun. Louis sucked pap through a tube, and thought yearningly of steak broiled with a flashlight-laser. Speaker sucked reconstituted blood, and thought his own thoughts.

They certainly didn't need the kitchen. They cut that part of the building loose, and improved the tilt of the building to boot.

They cut away air conditioning and police equipment. The generators that had ruined their flycycles went only after they had been positively identified as separate from the lifting motors. Walls went. Some walls were needed for their shade; for heating became a problem in the direct sunlight.

Day by day they neared the crater at the top of Fist-of-God, a crater that would have swallowed most asteroids. The lip of the crater looked like no impact crater Louis had ever seen. Shards like obsidian spearheads formed a jagged ring. Spearheads the size of mountains themselves. There was a gap between two such peaks . . . they could enter there . . .

"I take it," said Speaker, "that you wish to enter the crater itself."

"That's right."

"Then it is good that you noticed the pass. The slope above is too steep for our drive. We should reach the pass very soon."

Speaker was steering the *Improbable* by modifying the flycycle thrust. That had been necessary since they cut away the stabilizing mechanism in a final attempt to reduce the building's weight. Louis had grown used to the bizarre appearance of the kzin: the five transparent concentric balloons of his pressure suit, the fishbowl helmet with its maze of tongue controls half hiding the kzin's face, the tremendous backpack.

"Calling Prill," Louis said into the intercom. "Calling Halrloprillalar. Are you there, Prill?"

"I am."

"Stay there. We'll be through in twenty minutes."

"Good. You've been long enough at it."

The Arch seemed to blaze above them. A thousand miles above the Ringworld, they could see how the Arch merged into the rim walls and the flat landscape. Like the first man in space, a thousand years ago, looking down on an Earth that, by Jahweh and his mighty hammer, really was round.

"We couldn't have known," said Louis Wu, not loudly. But Speaker looked up from his work.

Louis didn't notice the kzin's odd look. "It would have saved us so much trouble. We could have turned back after we found the shadow square wire. Tanj, we could have dragged the *Liar* straight up Fist-of-God Mountain behind our flycycles! But then Teela wouldn't have met Seeker."

"The luck of Teela Brown again?"

"Sure." Louis shook himself. "Have I been talking to myself?"

"I have been listening."

"We should have known," said Louis. The gap between the sharp peaks was very near. He felt the urge to babble. "The Engineers would never have built a mountain this high *here*. They've got *over a billion miles* of thousand-mile-high mountains, if you count both rim walls."

"But Fist-of-God is real, Louis."

"No, no, no. It's just a shell. Look down; what do you see?"

"Ringworld foundation material."

"We thought it was dirty ice when we first saw it. Dirty ice, in hard vacuum! But forget that aspect. Remember the night you explored a giant map of the Ringworld? You couldn't find Fist-of-God. Why not?"

The kzin didn't answer.

"It wasn't there, that's why not. It wasn't there when the map was made. Prill, are you there?"

"I am here. Why would I leave you?"

"Good. Close the airlock doors. Repeat, close the airlock doors *now*. Don't cut yourself on the thread."

"My people invented this thread, Louis." Prill's voice was garbled with static. She was off for a minute, then: "Both doors are closed."

The *Improbable* was passing between the standing shards of mountain. Tense as Louis was, he would have been still more tense; but subconsciously he was expecting a kind of canyon or pass between those peaks.

"Louis, just what *do* you expect to find in Fist-of-God crater?"

"Stars," said Louis Wu.

The kzin was tense too. "Do not mock me! In all honor—"

—And they were through. There wasn't any pass. There was only a broken eggshell of Ringworld foundation material, stretched by terrific stresses to a few feet of thickness; and beyond that, the crater in Fist-of-God Mountain.

They were falling. And the crater was full of stars.

Louis Wu had an excellent imagination. In his mind's eye the event was perfectly clear.

He saw the system of the Ringworld, sterile, tidily clean, empty of ramships, empty but for a G2 star and a daisy chain of shadow squares and the Ringworld.

He saw a foreign body passing near, too near. He watched its hyperbolic fall from interstellar space, and he saw its path interrupted—by the underside of the Ringworld.

In his vision the foreign body was about the size of the Earth's Moon.

It must have been ionized plasma in the first seconds. A meteorite can be cooled by ablation, by the boiling away of its own skin. But here the vaporized gas could not expand; it had forced its way into a deforming pocket of the Ringworld floor. The landscape had deformed upward, its carefully planned ecology and rainfall patterns shot to hell over a region greater than the surface of the Earth. All that desert . . . and Fist-of-God itself, raised a full thousand miles upward before the incredibly tough Ring floor ripped to let the fireball through.

Fist-of-God? Tanj, yes! Watching from a Ringworld prison cell, Louis Wu had seen it clear in his mind's eye. It must have been visible clear to both rims: a ball of hell-fire the size of the Earth's Moon ripping up through the floor of the Ringworld like a strong man's fist through a cardboard box.

The natives could be thankful that the Ring floor had deformed as much as it did. The hole was easily big enough to let all the air out of the Ringworld; but it was a thousand miles too high . . .

The crater was full of stars.

And there wasn't any gravity; there wasn't anything for the lifting motors to push against. Louis hadn't really thought this far ahead.

"Grab something," he bellowed, "and hang on! If you fall through the bay window, there'll be no rescue."

"Naturally not," said Speaker. He was wrapped around a naked metal beam. Louis had found another.

"Was I right? Stars!"

"Yes, Louis, but how did you know?"

There was gravity, a steady, heavy pull on the *Improbable*. The skeleton of a building turned on its side, and the bay window was up.

"It's holding," Louis said fiercely. He wriggled to get right side up on the beam. "It better! I hope Prill strapped down; she'll have a bouncy ride. Up the side of Fist-of-God Mountain, riding at the end of ten thousand miles of shadow square wire. Up and over the lip, then—"

They looked up at the underside of the Ringworld. An infinity of sculptured surface. In the middle, a tremendous conical meteor puncture, shiny at the bottom. As the *Improbable* swung like a plumb bob beneath the Ringworld, the sun flashed suddenly in the bottom of the crater.

"—Out and down. Then we'll be tied to the *Liar*, and the *Liar* will be on its way to clear space at 770 miles per second. Plenty of time for the wire to pull us together; but if that doesn't work, we've got the thruster motor in Nessus's flycycle.

"How did I know? I've been *telling* you that. Didn't I mention the landscape?"

"No."

"That was the clincher. All the peaks of foundation material showing through the rock, and the fall of civilization only fifteen hundred years old! It was because those two asteroid punctures had fouled up the wind patterns. Do you realize that most of the traveling we did was between those two punctures?"

"Very indirect reasoning, Louis."

"It worked."

"Yes. And so I will live to see another sunset," the kzin said softly.

Louis felt an electric thrill. "You too?"

"Yes, I watch sunsets on occasion. Let us speak of the *Long Shot.*"

". . . What did you say?"

"If I could steal the *Long Shot* from you, my kind would dominate known space until a stronger species impinged on our expanding sphere. We would forget all we have learned so painfully, regarding cooperation with alien species."

"True," Louis said into the dark. The pull from the stolen shadow square wire was steady now. The *Liar* must be well on its way up Fist-of-God's ten degree slope.

"We might not get that far, while the luck of many Teela Browns protects Earth. Yet honor would compel me to make the attempt," said Speaker-To-Animals. "How could I lead my species away from the honorable path of war? The kzinti gods would revile me."

"I warned you about playing god. It hurts."

"Fortunately the difficulty does not arise. You have said that I would destroy the *Long Shot* if I tried to take it. The risk is too great. We will need the puppeteer hyperdrive to escape the wave front from the Core explosion."

"True enough," said Louis. The kzin would back into the nearest gravity well if he tried to take the *Long Shot* into hyperdrive. Knowing that, Louis asked, "But suppose I were lying?"

"I could not hope to outwit a being of your intelligence."

Sunfire flashed again in Fist-of-God crater.

"Think how short a way we came," said Louis. One hundred and fifty thousand miles in five days, the same distance back in two months. A seventh of the short way across the Ringworld. And Teela and Seeker think they're going the long way round."

"Fools."

"We never saw the rim wall. They will. I wonder what else we missed? If the Ringworld ramships got as far as Earth, they may have picked up some blue whales and sperm whales, before we made them extinct. We never got out onto the ocean.

"The people they'll meet. There's no end to the ways a culture can go. And the *room* . . . the Ringworld's so *big* . . ."

"We can't go back, Louis."

"No, of course not."

"Not until we can deliver our secret to our respective worlds. And acquire an intact ship."

The End

About the Author

Larry Niven is one of today's leading science-fiction authors, recognized particularly for his mercurial scientific imagination as exercised in his "Tales of Known Space," short fiction published in several collections, and the prize-winning novel, *Ringworld*. His other recent books include the mainstream bestseller, *Lucifer's Hammer*, written with Jerry Pournelle.